HOW
TO
LIVE
FOREVER

BARRY BURNETT

The Fool Press
How To Live Forever

Chapters 1-10 originally appeared as 'Vol. 1' in Smashwords,
February 2011
A modestly different eBook edition was first published in April 2011

The Fool Press ISBN 978-0-9796043-1-1

The Fool Press
Hermosa Beach, California
thefoolpress@gmail.com

Printed in the United States of America

Dear Reader:

This is a work of fiction. The Boulder depicted is a blended Boulder of the two-odd decades I've lived here, an impression no more accurate than any dream. Names, characters, places and incidents are either products of this author's imagination or used fictitiously – especially the characters, whose resemblance to anyone, living or dead, is entirely accidental. Hopefully, the advice they spout is sound, if sometimes contradictory, and should be weighed against one's own experience, as any reader or patient must always do.

ALSO BY BARRY BURNETT

Resonance

Thrilling Romance

The Mortalist

Dr. Lucky and Other Stories

For these and more, please visit
howtoliveforever.com

HOW TO LIVE FOREVER

Where There's Smoke, There's Ire

- or -

Intrapustular Fidelopenia

HEAD IN HANDS, elbows on knees, David Black looked out between his fingers. Beyond them lay a warm evening in late spring – new leaves and new flowers, the sun behind the mountains, an infinitely deep blue sky. High within it, a single band of cloud glowed with a copper-colored radiance that traveled down between the low brick buildings, the telephone wires and the still-dark streetlights to burnish the concrete at his feet.

A good day, he thought, to die.

"Oh, come on..." said the executioner.

David squinted sideways, over his thumb. "Did I say that aloud?"

"Sit up, will you?" Ozvaldo Garcia, MBA, CPA – and, for one year and counting, AA – brushed pastry crumbs from a drum-tight suit vest and sighed. Then added, as the gleam from his titanium laptop's screen bounced off his gold Rolex, "It's only money."

David appreciated the sentiment, sort of. About as much as the venue Oz had picked to deal the fatal blow.

His oldest friend – and now business consultant – had snagged a prime sidewalk table at the Triad, Boulder's oldest, calmest Buddhist coffeehouse. It was the unofficial spiritual epicenter of a town that guarded itself against any kind of carnage, be it physical, emotional, or financial. Inside and out, the place was dense with self-medicated students, mutually therapeutic sets of midlife women, and philo-sophically if reluctantly aging men. Together, they generated a sort of metaphysical chitchat, a murmur set to the distant bonging of recorded temple bells and punctuated by the hiss of the espresso machine inside the open bank of windows just behind them. In other words, it was not the kind of place a thirty-two-year-old doctor would choose to lose it. No matter what, or who, he'd just lost.

David unfolded broad shoulders, raked his dark hair into a modicum of respectability, and rolled up the sleeves of his shirt, the fine faded denim softened by another long day at his office. Fear battled hope, a hopeless hope that fought on for a final few seconds before he throttled it and said, "Okay, I'm ready."

"You sure? Really, really sure?"

"Oz..."

Oz cast a brief and supplicating glance up to that glowing cloud and swung his laptop around. The screen displayed a month-by-month spreadsheet, the dwindling earnings in black, the definitely not-dwindling losses in red.

"A solo family practice..." Oz began, full cheeks sagging in economic sorrow. "A thing of the past, and this is why." He tapped a well-manicured finger on the screen. "No one to split the rent, no underpaid staff to hound the insurance companies, plus the breaks you give, the free care... You might be keeping your patients alive, but the practice is beyond resuscitation. Time to let it go, David: it's dead."

David's eyes dropped from the hemorrhaging columns to the exsanguinating sums below them, following Oz's finger to the biggest saddest spurter, the *über*total of his totaled medical career, on the far right.

"First Sheyoni," David said softly, "now this." Sheyoni who'd told him she was tired of being married, at a small round table just inside. Had she brought him here for the same reason, to be surrounded by the subdued and muffling crowd? Probably – like Oz, Sheyoni knew what was best for him. Or said she did, and he believed her. A clean break: no kids, no pain, no tears allowed.

"You let her have the house," Oz said. "A lot of guys wouldn't have done that." A level look. "A lot of guys might have noticed it was their only asset."

Perfect, David thought. Generous and stupid. But of course he'd signed it over; it was the right thing to do. As Sheyoni had pointed out, she had given their marriage a full four years – now she needed to fly free, needed it in her most genuine, core, neglected-but-finally-flowering self. Then she'd clasped his hands and reassured him, with that special kindness Oz somehow missed, that their persistently reduced lifestyle had nothing, absolutely nothing to do with her decision.

He gripped the sides of the razor-thin laptop in his large hands and, as the keyboard flexed and popped and Oz began to look a little nervous, stared at the numbers, hard. What had he done with her gift of years? Heedlessly buried himself in taking care of patients – patients who were, when it all came down to dust, only strangers. Heedlessly trusted that if he simply did the right thing, his and Sheyoni's life would work out fine. Heedlessly, completely, utterly, failed.

Oz might act like his practice was just another tanking business, but it was all he had left. Since Sheyoni's announcement it had come to stand for everything – his life, his hopes, his otherwise broken dreams. They said you couldn't feel the axman's blade when it hit your neck, but this *hurt*.

THREE MILES TO THE SOUTH, where the highway from Denver crests a grassy rise and the wide valley that corrals Boulder is first visible, Junie Blanche spotted a reflective green sign for a lookout point. Still not quite one-hundred-percent ready to commit to her new home, she pulled her venerable Pontiac convertible into the exit lane and stepped on its stuttering brakes, barely stopping before the front tires rolled over the far edge of the parking strip. Unwinding her fingers from the steering wheel she'd gripped for the last fifteen hundred miles, Junie ran them through the cocoa channels between the tiny pigtails that bobbed around her head, then cranked the tattered top open and considered the lake of lights below her.

A new start, she thought, and as new starts go, *completely* new starts, this landscape easily fit the bill. The cliffs that rose toward the broken spine of the Divide, the indigo sky that framed one side-lit copper band of cloud – all of it as beautiful as the glossy brochure the University of Colorado had sent her. As beautiful as she'd expected, but also unexpectedly unsettling.

Junie found herself longing for the pancake landscape, flat and urban, she'd spent the better part of an academic year scraping

Mississippi River mud from – a landscape she'd abandoned the instant she received the University's offer of a graduate placement and a functioning, mud-free lab. A ruthless choice, her mother said, a comment Junie's watching younger siblings did not have to echo. But her mom had made plenty of ruthless choices – evicting a faithless husband and whipping five too-smart but too-poor children through New Orleans's struggling public schools – and Junie's family was now safe and dry, folded in the embrace of countless cousins in the city's Seventh Ward. And as her professor had known when he sent out his pleas to save a favorite student, Tulane's former molecular biology lab wasn't going to rise up from those saturated ashes soon.

Colorado's offer had been one of those post-Katrina gestures that really could change a life, at least for this impoverished near-PhD. A lifeline, and maybe a lifeline she'd been reaching for all along, a chance to fly free into an unfamiliar world. She'd read the letter, looked at the brochure's deceptively welcoming peaks, packed her bags and hardly looked back. Or wanted to, until this minute. Now, all she could do was put her chin on the steering wheel and watch the strange Western scene blur and blend, the first bright stars above and the mercury-vapor lights sparking on below, all softening to something as soft-edged as a Delta memory, distorted by the melting pools – Could those be tears, the first since her faithless father walked the walk? – that swelled and threatened to overflow each latticework of lashes before she could bring herself to wipe those tears – Yes, tears – away.

AFTER DAVID'S BOUT of self-loathing had subsided, he registered the rainbow-hued distortions from his iron grip on Oz's computer screen and gingerly eased it closed.

"Maybe..." he began, "Someone *else* could make it work."

"Someone else?" Oz's eyebrows went up.

"Another doctor," David said, ignoring that skeptical look. "Someone with different... priorities. Someone who could, you know, bend things here and there."

"*Bend* things?" The eyebrows went up further, heading towards Oz's almost convincing comb-over.

"Sure," David tried. He'd thought bending things was Oz's specialty. "I mean, the patients are great—"

"When they pay their bills—"

"And the inventory," David tried again. "The vaccine stock, for instance. That could be worth, well, thousands, right? If I found the right doctor, someone with some business sense—"

"The kind you've never listened to?"

David stopped and glared. "*Anyway...*"

"Yes?" A beatific smile lit Oz's face.

He took an even breath. "Well, I thought I could sell it, and..."

David hadn't been completely blind; he *had* a back-up plan, or kind of. Face burning, he took a folded printout – a listing for a small but ocean-going sailboat – from his pocket. An errant gust rattled the spindly sidewalk tree in front of them, and David felt a sudden chill. Oz plucked the paper from his fingers and read the details below the photo, then shook his head and pointed to the numbers on the screen.

"Even a crummy one?" David asked. "I could stay close to shore."

Oz shook his head again. "Remember what you said last week, when you weren't telling me how everything would turn out fine? How in the worst case, however unlikely, your patients had to have a two-month warning? I'd like to make it easier on you, but things didn't work out fine, the worse case wasn't unlikely, and it'll take every penny from those vaccines – which I've already figured in, by the way – to buy that time."

David looked down to the espresso that sat cold and forlorn in front of him. So much for a clean getaway. Raising the tiny cup to dry lips, he drained it, but the bitterness brought no relief.

"I never expected more than a living wage," he said, "but everybody, Sheyoni more than anyone, acted like we could have anything. Even you, telling me I'd gotten a license to steal."

"You *did* get one."

"It's not all about money, Oz."

Oz snapped the computer shut and drummed his fingers on the top. "Really."

David didn't like it, but Oz was right. "It's almost funny... a doctor who isn't worth a secondhand sailboat."

"A family doctor," Oz said. "A doctor who spends too much time with patients."

"I didn't hear you complain."

Oz shrugged. "Too busy squealing from that rectal. But I would have, if you'd showed me your books sooner. You're inefficient; you can't help yourself, whether your patients pay or not. And that – plus those exams, big guy – is why we love you."

"Some people think a good doc should be broke, or nearly," Oz added. "Not only you family practice types, but all of them." He scratched reflectively at his beard, a close-trimmed carpet above a starched collar. "If healing's a religion – the white coats, the secret Latin words and all of it – maybe you're *supposed* to offer it up." Oz pulled a cigarette from the open pack in his monogrammed shirt pocket, then paused, catching David's look.

"What I'm *supposed* to do," David said, "is convince you not to do that."

"See? Like I was saying: you can't help helping." Twisting onto one buttock, Oz rummaged for his lighter.

"I wouldn't be doing my job if I didn't, as your friend or as your doctor. Health starts with stopping those." David was warming to the task, to any task that would take his mind off his disasters, recent or impending. "The cholesterol meds, the blood pressure, those extra fifty pounds? None of it comes close."

"I can skip it all? Great!"

"No, of course not: life is short, too short... make it longer any way you can. Cigarettes kill more than half of smokers; smoking outweighs everything."

"Excuse me," Oz said, cradling the heavy gold lighter in his palm. "Didn't you say that about the drinking?"

"That was then – this is you killing yourself now." He'd found Oz lying at the bottom of his wine cellar steps, drooling sweet nothings into the empty mouth of a Mouton-Rothschild '45. David had cleaned him up and pointed him towards rehab, but maybe he should have hammered Oz on every one of his bad habits. He could have pushed Oz harder, but no, that wasn't his style. Oz had him nailed: he was a helper, filling other people's needs, and look where that had gotten him... broke and divorced. On the other hand, between David's light touch and Oz's chagrin at siphoning the cornerstone of his investment-grade wine portfolio, Oz *had* quit drinking. Not only that, but he'd yet to light that cigarette, and almost looked like he was ready to listen.

And so, as a thoroughly sober Oz glanced at his watch but gave up center stage with an unusual degree of equanimity, David kept on delivering the message. Doing the right thing, the helping thing, pushing along the information, not too hard but lots of it. Starting with everybody's greatest mortal risk, heart disease, which most people didn't realize was more than doubled by smoking, not to mention...

JUNIE'S EYES HAD DRIED and the night had grown darker – those far peaks etched with a fine gold line that made them even sharper – by the time another vehicle crunched to a stop on the gravel beside her. The rumbling engine died, leaving a ticking silence, the rare car rushing along the unseen highway, and a rusted red pickup, huge and flecked with mud, that was almost as low-rent and sketchy as her ride. Without moving her head, she counted two unshaven males. They were white, of course, white and gaping at the same falling night and complex topography spread out in front of their parking space.

Then the nearest slowly turned, with a lopsided grin, and leered down at her. Worse, that looming leer was completely unimpeded, with nothing more than her convertible's raised windows and the rapidly cooling night air to separate her bare mahogany shoulders from whatever they did to strangers, strangers of *color*, in this vertiginous Western place.

Carefully, but casually, Junie put the car in reverse, and managing to only spin her nearly treadless wheels a little, slumped down so as not to present too clear a target during her anxious exit.
Wayne and Jeremiah turned to watch her go, watched the fishtail swerve before she hit the on-ramp's pavement and the sudden acceleration after. As Wayne's hand clasped Jeremiah's, rough warm palm to rough warm palm, both sympathized with that rapidly receding driver, feeling the same bright eagerness to get on with their new lives – to love in a Western city that accepted all lovers, or so

they'd heard, and even had cool black people who drove interesting cars.

Oz LISTENED as David waded on to the perils of emphysema, doing his best to look like he was paying attention. The oxygen, the drowning phlegm... Whatever. Oz would quit the instant he was ready, something he'd been sure of since his first sweet pre-teen inhalation two decades ago – so sure that it was beneath his dignity to try. But he knew David was finding solace in the meddling that was medical care, and that David needed solace now.

For another moment, perhaps two. Then he had to bring him back on point. Because Oz had big plans for David, and this evening's event, or something very much like it, had been headed David's way for decades, ever since Oz's boyhood pal decided that doing the Right Thing would be his guiding light. Not the Smart Thing; not the thing you really wanted to do but were only *calling* the Right Thing; but the single course of action that would both satisfy all ethical criteria and please absolutely everyone, alive or dead – an impossible presumption that David, nonetheless, had often managed to pull off.

Throughout their shared adolescence, Oz had tried to demonstrate that David's approach might be too simple, that bad could be good and often truly excellent. But all his attempts, from the school-lunch Ponzi schemes to the after-hours liberation of a certain church's sacramental wine, hadn't make a mark. Behind David's beneficence, defeating Oz's efforts, lay the pernicious moral influence of David's parents.

Oz had known them well; in fact he'd loved them, if only for living next door. Their kindly presence – a white-haired Unitarian pastor married to a junior college professor – had proved a useful counterpoint to his own father, who'd been unfortunately inclined to limber up his belt for anything less than an A-minus. While David's A's came easy, and his choices easier: always the Right Thing. Too easily, Oz thought. Maybe David had needed Oz's father as much as Oz had needed David's.

Then, as Oz labored and David floated through college, that vague humanitarian dad had died – an early stroke from his nonjudgmental Lord, a classic Western sun-filled funeral, and

David's mother collecting cash donations for their church's African orphanage where she planned to teach English, soon. Oz's gruff *paterfamilias* had taken David aside, telling him he needed to be practical, now more than ever, practical despite the tears. After David made it into medical school, Oz's father thought David had heard him, but Oz knew David hadn't. Medicine, primary care, an absurdly small and self-sacrificing practice: his friend might have been working hard but he was still cruising on moral autopilot. The Right Thing, no questions asked.

And now, finally, a chance for his friend to grow up. David's fall from his unthinking, impractical grace had taken this particular alignment of ill-favored stars: Sheyoni finally serving a purpose by softening him up, and then, right on cue, a set of wickedly bad spreadsheet numbers.

Could, Oz asked himself, he have pulled this evening's financial punch? He'd been disgustingly soft-headed enough to try, but even with the mitigating influence of this meeting's venue (civilized, if a mite too Boulderesque), the surprisingly well-crafted coffee (an oxymoronic decaf espresso for David vs. a triple-hit caramel-vanilla latte for yours truly), and his careful selection of two organic (but all butter) scones, the boy was going down hard.

DAVID WAS HEADED for a triumphant rollout of truly horrible lung cancer factoids when Oz, whose eyelids seemed to be inexplicably losing a fight with gravity, flicked the tooled molybdenum wheel of his lighter, dragged in the gold-blue tip of flame, and said, "Stop, already – I've heard the lecture. Maybe I don't *want* to live forever."

"But I want you to."

"Why?" Oz asked, exhaling a cloud of smoke. "So you can keep torturing me?

"Um... yes," David answered. For every dirtball Oz had tossed over the fence between their backyards, and especially for talking David into stealing the Unitarians' Judeo-Christian kosher wine, a pseudo-sin that still brought a wincing cringe. "Definitely yes."

"Cute." Oz polished off David's scone, then looked up. "What about your other patients? Do you want them all to live forever?"

"Sure I do. As forever as they can." David's knee was jostled by one of the pedestrians streaming by on the sidewalk.

"Do you tell them that? That forever is what you're aiming for?" A certain calculating light was illuminating Oz's features, a light David had long since learned to be wary of.

"Of course not." He tucked his offending legs closer in. "It would sound... it wouldn't be right."

"Why not?" Oz leaned forward. "More hope than they can stand? Think they can't handle it?"

David studied him. "Is this to take my mind off your smoking?" Oz's personal campfire, the pale white column twisting upwards, lost between the streetlight and the now-dark sky. David almost wanted one himself.

"Just answer the question."

"Then no, I don't think they can't... I mean, I think they *can* handle it," David said. "Hope's a good thing; most studies of the dying show that. Believing in your future might make you live longer – long enough to see that future. Unless it's false hope, which is, well, *false*."

"Never mind that. You never know for sure, do you?"

"Yeah... I guess."

"That's it – guesswork. Doing the best you can. That and what you said, the power of belief. Positive belief – like positive thinking. That's good, right there. And if *you* believe... Can you let yourself believe, David?"

"Believe in what?" David asked, cautiously.

"Believe in *their* belief, the chance to be well, to try to live forever. Help them believe it, keep them believing in it – which, like you said, keeps them ticking."

"Wait a second." David sat up straight. "I didn't say that, not exactly."

Oz's eyes moved to the perforated metal tabletop, crowded with empty cups and plates and David's printout. "Most of all..." he began, as one immaculate cuff eased towards the color-saturated paper, "...you should believe in... *this!*" Oz thrust the image out, a white bow breaking azure waves.

David pushed back, tilting his chair. "Would you stop? The boat was just an idea, a bad idea. What I really want... what I really want is..." The front legs of his chair wavered above the concrete.

"The boat, David. You showed me the boat – *you* came up with it. Something you want, which is good. Something fun, something for *you*."

"What about the numbers?" David said, chair slamming down. "The ones that never lie."

"You already said it, about my drinking: 'That was then.' This is now; we're moving on to the future, the very near future."

"I could never earn—"

"Never say never, David. Leave that to your business manager."

"I don't have a—"

"Your *new* business manager." Oz spread his arms, the printout dangling from one hand, while the other – the hand so nonchalantly holding the cigarette – hovered dangerously close to the frizzy gray ponytail of the eternohippie at the adjacent table.

"No," David said. "No, no, *no*. Even if I could support myself, I can't pay for you. I only asked you to look at the books." The owner of the ponytail waved the smoke away with a dismissive flap of an age-spotted hand, another weary vote in the struggle between the various camps who claimed the outdoor tables, between the nicotine-addicted, the self-styled *boulevardiers,* and those who only wished to sit beneath the dome of sky.

"Relax," Oz said, holding the pose. "I'll work for a percentage." He peered at David's open collar; David tried to close it over the orange prayer string Sheyoni liked him to wear, but too late. Oz cocked an eyebrow. "You're already an alterna-guy; make it an alterna-clinic. An alterna-*longevity*-clinic."

Tiny yellow sparks began to climb the gray hairs beside the cigarette's burning tip as Oz, oblivious, added, "Build it up – *really* build it up, and—"

David grabbed Oz's wrist, hauled it back, and the mini-flames self-extinguished. "You know I'm into all of that, from Ayurveda to the Zone. But another clinic, here in Boulder?"

"They're no competition – patients trust you. You care enough to lose money; a doctor with a difference."

Oz tugged to free his arm but David didn't notice. He was strong for no good reason, just built that way, tall and strong. And frowning, as he thought, What if I did?

"*David...*" Oz crooned, still pulling, "Let *go...*" At the next table, the ponytail's companion was informing the aging hipster of his hair's near-death experience. Oz tugged again, harder, saying, "Come on, David – if you don't want to change, you don't have to."

Could I change? David wondered. Be more than a helper, always doing what was needed, and actually do what I want? He looked down, focused on Oz's cigarette, and thought: Why not? Then snatched it from between two pudgy fingers and – for once without a thought to who saw him – inhaled deeply.

Oz looked surprised, but no more than the ponytail, who'd turned to find David sucking on the smoking gun.

David's eyes grew wide as he registered who it was – a patient, Don Gilmore. At which point the smoke hit, or maybe the last traces of that burning hair, and he doubled over coughing.

OZ, RUBBING HIS WRIST, took in the situation and leapt to damage control, explaining how David was... grief-stricken – That was it! – grief-stricken and out of control, his wife having just been diagnosed – Oh, this was good – with the worst of rare diseases. Keeping his voice down, he leaned back toward the singed victim, confidential. "Intra-something," he said, then hesitated. Did Sheyoni deserve it? Actually, Oz decided, she did.

"...Intra*pustular*..." he elaborated, and with another flash of inspiration, "...Intrapustular *Fidelopenia*." An instant neologism that rather neatly wrapped it up, and David was thankfully coughing too loud to overhear.

Oz's inspiration was a series of rumors that had been only rumors, at least until a coarse aside from a business client, a prominent local guru-slash-Lothario who'd boasted of privately instructing Sheyoni in his special high-contact partner-meditation technique – Kuntolingua, Oz seemed to recall, or something even ruder. In any case, Oz had made an executive decision to hold off on telling David, and now that Sheyoni had made her move, it looked like he wouldn't have to.

Fidelity, then, melded to *penia*, another rude-sounding term that actually meant, if Oz remembered his prep school Latin, 'extreme deficiency of.'

He went on to add the disgusting but entertaining details necessary to flesh out any mortal illness – suppurating fistulas, that sort of thing – and finished with a searching, commiserating stare. As expected, the ponytail's outrage had been replaced by the simple desire to believe. It was a quality that, since Oz had first talked anyone into anything – Had it been David? Sneaking into church that night? – he'd grown deeply fond of in others. After the last polish, Oz lowered his head in silence, feeling particularly proud.

MEANWHILE, the pedestrians kept streaming – one of them being Sheyoni, naturally, in radiant health as always. David saw her coming and hunched down further, peeking through the upstream tables at knee-level. She wore bright white running shoes fresh from their recycled-fiber box, a filmy nylon trekking shirt that had never seen a trek, and stretch biking shorts that hadn't cycled a bike, stationary or not. Those shining Lycra-compressed curves, the sculptured columns of her legs... even now, he couldn't tear his fool eyes off her.

Luckily, she turned to cross Pearl Street, missing him completely.

BUT SHEYONI HADN'T; she couldn't miss him in a crowd, even bent away and avoiding her. Part her guilt, she knew, part his pure physical presence, and part a fondness, residual but undeniable, for the big idiot. Why hadn't it worked? After all, they were both beautiful enough, the kind of healthy New Age couple that everyone envied, turning their heads to follow her – and him, of course, her thirty-something doctor-cum-accessory.

She pretended not to see David, which was completely painless and got her out of another difficult conversation with her soon-to-be ex-husband. Sheyoni found that pretending nearly always worked, though her last spiritual advisor, a mature and amazingly virile yogi who'd instructed her in the deepest possible Kundalini energy release, had told her it was emotionally corrosive, and she always trusted her advisors. In fact, she had vowed on the spot – kneeling naked on the hand-woven rug inside his candlelit *shtupa* – that she would never pretend anything again, with the possible exception of orgasms that didn't specifically involve him. And she *would* stop pretending, Sheyoni decided, as she tossed her white-blond mane to screen out the last turning glimpse of David. Genuine, absolute honesty, starting... tomorrow.

The street was empty, blocked off for tomorrow's art fair, vendors setting up their carts and tents. Between them stood a pair of shaggy permanent campers, down from the mountains for a day of variable musicianship and begging, who'd just spotted an apparently abandoned aluminum keg that sat on the yellow line bisecting the open asphalt.

Sheyoni hesitated on the curb, planning her way around them. She felt a certain heat behind her, a faint pressure gathering just above her root charka – her favorite chakra, the source of sexual energy at the base of her spine. It had to be David, watching her. It was a warmth not all that different from the campers' attention, two foreign but predictable stares that were a constant part of the world that swirled around her.

David, those two campers, even her talented ex-guru... *men.* They didn't know how hard it was – none of them, her mother always said, knew the work it took to keep them happy. All they wanted was what she offered them, never looking deeper, never looking for the deep true self that had to be down there somewhere. Or was it? Beneath the beauty, beneath the poise, beneath the work – *was* there something deep and true and down there, something deeper than the reverberating brass bell her former Kundaliner had bonged so thoroughly and well? Sheyoni frowned as she stood in the open street, a frown that could not be seen by David, and was furthermore unnoticed by the campers as they perused points south and souther.

Perfectly balanced, perfectly frozen in mid-stride on the balls of two perfect feet, the pristine white rubber tread of each shoe barely caressing the grit of the cement sidewalk and stone curb beneath, Sheyoni felt the cool evening air between her fingers, the heat of David's glance and the heat of the rest of the swirling world and decided that, for the moment, the answer to that deep down question did not matter, no more than pretending or promises or whatever it had taken to get her to this radiantly poised but about-to-move-forward moment. And then she did move forward, stepping off the curb and onto the asphalt, pretending David wasn't staring and those two crude gentlemen weren't either, picking up speed and breezing straight between them, their backpedaling forms signaling the vendor who was setting up a vegan soymeat corn-dog stand to collect his undefended keg of organic brew. Sheyoni didn't notice; she was headed away from her old life and towards her new one, a life in which the brand new *non*-man friend who ran the Womyn's Bookstore around the corner was waiting.

DAVID WATCHED her cross the street, let go a final wheeze and ground the cigarette stub into the concrete between his feet, saving Oz and all the passive victims near and far.

Who, he asked himself, was he kidding? He'd never been a smoker, or a sailor or anything more adventurous than a kid who wanted to do the right thing, something rarely adventurous at all.

He peeked up at Don Gilmore, to find him gazing back with a goopy sympathy he knew he'd have to deal with later. David tried an innocent smile, and Don seemed to buy it. Patients, David thought. The truth was, he liked helping them, liked knowing their lives and making a difference, liked it because he liked them. The way Sheyoni said she still liked him – *liked* him – and probably a lot more.

He'd had it with boats and fantasies; of course he couldn't change his life – that was for people like Sheyoni, or Oz with all his plans. Change, of course, was happily including him in its proceedings, but for now he managed to forget that, forget her and his practice and the bills he couldn't pay, by concentrating on one more small right thing, in this case pinching up the cooling ashes and dutifully smudging the rest away, erasing the evidence of his transgression with a natural latex sole. While somewhere in the Magic 8-Ball depths of David's really rather blocky head, a certain question still shimmered, in letters so faint and submerged that he was currently unaware of them – but a question that could still be read, by any fictionally interested visitor who might descend into that murky realm of cognition and possibility:

What if I *did*?

2

SHEYONI'S REVENGE

- or -

Semiholistic Continuosis

EARLY THE NEXT MORNING, a warm Saturday sun shone over the low hills and low roofs of the neighborhood due east of the hospital, blinding David as he walked up to the depression-era duplex that housed his office. Passing into shadow, he stumbled on the wheelchair ramp he'd hammered together for his patients, managing to recover, amazingly unsplintered, by the time he swung the front door open. Its brass bell brightly announced his entrance, and the office's only employee – other than himself – looked up with an equally bright smile.

After the nanosecond pause it took Sheyoni to process who she was smiling at, the bright smile froze, as did the flawless face around it. Following a longer and noticeably darker interval, she asked, in a painfully even voice, "Why did he say he's sorry?"

That look, he thought. The same as when they closed up yesterday, grilling him to make sure he'd mailed the final papers.

"Who?" David asked, voice dangerously close to cracking. The concept of the friendly divorce was seeming less viable every... well, every nanosecond.

"Don Gilmore – while I was doing his vitals. In room one."

Gilmore. Here. And whatever story Oz had spun while David coughed and choked. "I... um..."

"You told him."

"No – I wouldn't. I promised. Closest friends only, right? You called Aspen and told Sharon. So I got to tell Oz."

"Oz. Fantastic. Maybe *he* told him."

Sometimes, David decided, it's best to shrug and move on down the hallway. Even if the glare that follows you chars two small holes in the back of your second-favorite denim shirt.

SHEYONI SQUINTED after him, then went about her business – at first still wondering, but soon planning the freedoms of her new life: a new job, new friends, a studio for the art project that, she was confident, would bubble up into her receptive consciousness soon. This morning's schedule was almost as empty as the waiting room; she rolled her chair back from the Formica counter, slipped out of her hand stitched green felt vegan flats, lay her hands in her lap and closed her eyes. Emptiness was exactly what she was after, and – no matter what a snarky blowhard like Oz might think – emptiness was not easy to achieve.

There... Waiting... Waiting... Nope. Nothing, but she knew something would come in time. She let her lashes slowly part and gazed, untroubled, at the random collection of patient charts scattered across the work area. It would come, just as the impulse to file those charts would arrive at its own sweet speed. A project that would be... rewarding. Something... creative. And more than that: something... *moldable*. After all, she'd always planned to be a sculptor. Her small but capable hands flexed, fingers digging into air. Like clay... like the clay she would have learned to master, if her art professor – all those private evening tutorials! – hadn't had something else in mind. Like clay, but warmer: like flesh, and this time it wasn't going to be hers.

Hers... Nancy, her new friend at the Womyn's Bookstore, was also a masseuse. Flesh, like clay. Sheyoni's hands grew even warmer. She pursed her lips, now entirely thawed, closed her eyes again and, this time, opened every sensory pathway to her brain, from her deliciously unsheathed toes, ascending to the root chakra that her previous guru (or perhaps the one before) had liked to call her Magic Zone, to climb up every perfectly-aligned vertebrae of her spine. And then back down once more, pausing here and there to feel for the slightest tingle. Nothing, again. As expected, really: Nancy, and the rest of her and Nancy's half of the human genome, wasn't Sheyoni's thing at all. Anyway, *she* was going to be the sculptor now.

And it was going to be a *human* art project, definitely. She pursed her lips, generously allowing the extra few seconds of deep thought that a project this significant deserved. A type of project, she realized, that wasn't entirely new. She'd molded herself into this job, for instance, dressed up and lived her art every day. And tried to mold David, but David was David, stubborn with ideals that sounded good but turned out dreary – just look at this place! That lumpy couch was ancient when they'd bought it, and while none of David's patients had actually gotten stuck in the corduroy depths of the brokeback recliner, plenty had come close. Ditto the rest of the former living room, the shag carpeting that smelled like spilled formula, and especially the plywood reception desk, which *she* certainly wasn't going to repaint, not before she escaped this sad beige hole.

A few more months, she'd promised him, a few more months in exchange for the house. While she waited for that new project to materialize. Someone like David, only more... rewarding.

Oh, well. Perhaps a distraction – perhaps Sharon, a quick call to dish the dirt on Aspen. Where there was lots to dig, beneath the last melting patch of snow, beneath the last emerging lawn of that mountain town's late spring. And with the dirt, came secrets, connections, even introductions. Perhaps, if Sharon had already taken care of Sharon, she'd gone on to dig up a warm, moldable, *rewarding* male project for Sheyoni as well. With a smile that was measurably less bright but this time natural, she slipped her perfect feet back into her luscious vegan shoes and tapped out Sharon's number.

DAVID STOOD in his office-consultation room, door securely closed. Hearing only silence, and then the muffled conversation of a phone call – Sheyoni, back at work. If not forgiven, he was at least temporarily forgotten. And still had five minutes on his ticking wall clock, five minutes before Don's slot on the schedule, five minutes before he had to brace Sheyoni and the outer-office world again. Over on his crowded desk, a email icon flashed on the screen of a scratched white plastic iBook, but he chose to pay no attention, preferring to ruminate instead.

A holistic clinic... unbelievable.

Not only that the idea had come from Oz, whose health obsessions began and ended with the health-care marketplace (where holistic medicine's slice came out to a nice, round Ozzy-ish hundred billion dollars), but that he, David, had allowed it to raise his pulse.

What if I *did*, indeed.

Though it actually was interesting – just not what he was trained to do. Like administer antibiotics for pneumonia and insulin for diabetes and all the other professionally-approved, agreed-upon, standard medical treatments, the ones that patients needed to struggle though their standard, deserved, agreed-upon four-score-and-maybe-even-ten. His job might not be too creative – after all, a doctor couldn't pick which drug to give on a whim – but it was, perhaps more than any other occupation, the right thing to do. And even if he was sort of interested (in fact, a whole lot interested) in all that not-agreed-upon and not-exactly-necessary and unfortunately-unproven holistic stuff, he'd always regarded his interest as more a hobby. Not something that patients, who didn't really *need* it, should be asked to pay for.

The icon was still flashing. With a sigh, David clicked the cursor and watched a single message slowly download. It was, surprise, from Oz, who had attached that final spreadsheet. Assuming a decent price for the vaccines and absolutely no new expenses, David could have the months his patients needed to find new doctors. Two months, Oz wrote, and that was it.

Great.

He printed it out, stared again at that red-ink row of losses, and stood for a moment with his forehead pressed against the cool painted plaster of the duplex's former bedroom. The med-school loans, the rent, his patients who'd lost their insurance and their jobs...

He'd already started weekend hours. Today, for instance, but there had only been a couple of filled spaces on the otherwise unmarred schedule in front of Sheyoni. Short of dressing up like a generic doctor – his long white coat from med school and a stethoscope around his neck – and waving a sign out on the curb, there wasn't much else he could do.

Oz might have been off base about the holistic thing, but he was never wrong with numbers. Two months, and then David would grant his practice what it *really* needed. The same as we all needed at the end: a death with quiet dignity, the ultimate Right Thing.

Cracking the door, he peeked down the carpeted hallway. Sheyoni was still chatting comfortably with a patient on the phone – she had that personal touch with them, as though each was a close, close friend. She'd really tried, he had to give her that. She'd turned herself into the perfect partner in his practice – an equal partner, working beside him, the perfect receptionist and perfect nurse, the last of which she had no training for but seemed to like the sound of. He should have told her that was nuts, that she didn't need to fake it, that she'd been an artist and could be one again. He should, in fact, have pushed her out of his little medical world, pushed her onto her own path. But he knew that wouldn't have worked, that she would have had to push herself. And now, unfortunately, she had. The thought of losing her... the weight of grief began to fill his heart again, grief and loss and failure.

Enough. The coast was clear. Hugging the wall down to the open door of exam room one, he grabbed Don's chart and slipped quietly in.

DON HAD BEEN MUSING about Sheyoni, too, musing as he bent forward over the vinyl-cushioned edge of the exam table, reached toward his dangling left foot and drew up a baggy, soft-knit, earth-toned pant leg. The scene outside the coffeehouse had been strange, more than strange: his own doctor, smoking – tobacco! – and probably intoxicated, so distressed and distracted he'd accidentally burnt a divot in Don's prize ponytail. But Don could understand – Sheyoni Black had *Intrapustular Fidelopenia*!

Wow.

The name itself sent a chill down his spine, further shrinking the neglected chakras that even a successful New-Age businessman like himself couldn't really attend to. The literal meaning of her diagnosis might be professionally opaque, but it was fully double-barreled, each Latinate syllable so threatening, so impressive, so deeply intriguing to a concerned and sensitive soul like himself. Even worse – as his doctor's colleague had kindly explained – her hidden disease would inevitably progress to *eruptive* IFP, the pustules first erupting through the surface of the delicate dermatologic regions that were most shielded from the sun, and then, in a fatal but mercifully brief course, absolutely everywhere.

And she looked so *vibrant*. So very, very, very *alive*.

Still clutching the bunched fabric in his fingers, he crossed his exposed leg over his other knee and looked down at the sagging muscles and sharp-edged shin of a fifty-nine-year-old calf. His doctor was a mess, but if it were him, would he be doing any better? Don liked to think so, though he knew his three ex-spouses – whose indisputable health was only surpassed by their vindictiveness – would not have agreed. And maybe they would have been correct. Any illness was frightening, and the older he got, the scarier each one became.

Deep in thought, Don examined every bump and wrinkle on his fragile dermis. To think that right now – right now! – the same pustules could be down there, growing...

DAVID PAUSED just inside the exam room door. Whatever imaginary illness Don Gilmore was obsessing over now, he was clearly too absorbed to have heard David enter. Which was fine, in fact a whole lot better than fielding questions about last night. He watched Don until his relief turned to boredom, then quietly cleared his throat; Don almost helicoptered off the table, whirling to face him and as he tried to whip a knit pant leg down.

David hardly blinked, just smiled benignly and pretended to review the chart. His hypochondriacal patient was way too tightly wound – the founder of a hemp clothing company that had grown way too big, and long given to wearing only his product, trying to look way relaxed when he way wasn't. All while worrying about his health until he was too worried to do anything to improve it – like work on his blood pressure, a problem that was both the best evidence of Don's approach to life (hypertension in every meaning of the word) and the thing most likely to end it.

Deciding that the best tactic was to completely ignore last evening, David held up the chart so Don could read it, and pointed to the blood pressure reading Sheyoni had penciled in.

"The top number's lower," Don offered.

"It's definitely down, and that's good. Less pressure surge, less blowouts. But the bottom number's higher, and that's the rest between the beats, when your arteries are supposed to take it easy. If they can't, they just get tighter, narrower, stiffer."

Don looked unhappy, and David glanced at the note from the previous visit. "There's still the diuretic."

His patient shook his head. "I said it last time – all drugs are poisons."

"And you're right... sort of. Most meds work by messing something up – in this case, how well your kidneys hold on to salt. But that's so something else, in fact almost everything else, can work better."

"The body is a perfect mechanism," Don pronounced, tugging his pant leg further down to completely hide a mottled calf.

"Okay," David said, trying not to remember the formaldehyde-reeking cadavers of med school, splayed wide beneath gloved hands. Then he *did* remember every blessedly healthy body, every sports physical and well child check, he'd examined since. "No argument there. But only... only in its native state."

"Native. Exactly. As in, natural – *perfectly* natural."

"The thing is," David said, exasperation creeping in, "there's a totally *unnatural* amount of salt in our diet. If you took a diuretic, it would force – I know how that sounds, but I'm just being honest – your kidneys to wash the salt out. You want to call that a poison? Fine. But it's a poison to counteract a poisonous world, a poison to keep your arteries happy."

Don sat, unpersuaded. At least he hadn't mentioned last night... yet. With that small blessing, David moved on to the exam – listened to Don's lungs and heart and looked in the back of his eyes, focusing his ophthalmoscope down to the ruby threads of blood flowing through the nearly-transparent arteries traversing each retina, happy to see no hypertensive damage... yet.

Don had seemed extra-nervous about the skin of his left calf, so David checked it extra-closely. And it was fine, just the usual age changes, though he probably shouldn't have muttered that most of the spots were 'senile keratoses', a diagnosis that was accurate but unpleasant, popping Don's eyes until he talked him down.

After that, he put his tools away and, fighting the slogging sense that he'd never overcome Don's medical inertia, began to go over everything they'd covered last visit.

First, as always, was exercise, and Don said he'd started running again – six miles a week! Unfortunately, because he needed to travel (hemp being very big all over), he'd had to compress the whole week's miles to one mini-marathon morning. Don told him how he'd run as fast as in his track-star twenties – but only for the first half-mile, and then his knees hurt so much he had to quit. But the swelling was down and he was going to try again... when he got back from his next trip or, he promised, as soon after that as humanly possible.

Right, David thought, and segued to diet, namely salt avoidance. The less Don took in, the less he'd have to flush out with a diuretic. Don said he was totally on top of that. On top of it, that was, at home – he was a committed, a totally committed vegetarian, and on the road it was all salty cheese and hotel salad dressing, and even a vegetarian had to eat.

Which left meditation, and while Don said he really, really appreciated David's recommendation that he try it, a friend said if he didn't perform the proper, straight-backed Buddhist posture for at least an hour twice daily, plus breath preparation and a nice stretch afterwards, he'd be wasting the time he didn't have enough of anyway.

David sat on the stool beside the exam room's tiny desk. He considered banging his head on the hardrock maple top but knew that really wasn't professional, not banging his, or banging Don's. Instead, he drummed his fingers on the chart and kept his expression blank. Getting someone to change, to really change, was so much tougher than prescribing a new pill. Just talking – teaching, even persuading – was rarely enough for that kind of heavy lifting. More was needed... something more intensive, maybe. He wasn't sure; something... *more.*

But David, as usual, had given it a shot, throwing together all the lifestyle changes he could think of, in the hope that they would add up to an intervention large enough to drop his patient's pressure. And they could, if Don would only do them... plus make him feel at least half as relaxed as his clothing looked.

THE UNIVERSITY had been remarkably generous, putting Junie up –
for a single night – in a century-old red-brick pile of a 'downtown'
hotel. But she'd been awake since dawn, when she'd cinched a
complimentary but too-short bathrobe around her waist and, after
carefully surveying for any other mammalian presence, snuck
around the lobby's creaking oak balcony for the unmanned and
steaming coffee service across the way. Once there, she'd stood in
caffeinating bliss beneath the Tiffany glass ceiling, her spidery fingers
wrapped around the searing cup; dark brown steaming in white
porcelain, dark brown legs sticking out of snow-white terrycloth.
Until a distant, polite cough destroyed the moment, setting her
searching right and left and finally down – to meet the night clerk's
eyes, deep in his cubby on the main level. Junie scuttled back, face
burning, quick through the oak door as she pulled it shut behind her.

Since then she'd been working on her thesis, sitting at an ancient
table that smelled of wax and dust, her computer screen glowing
against a field of green-and-pink William Morris wallpaper. Waiting
for the town to wake up around her, and surprised, but not really,
when it didn't. When her room grew warm with the sun, she opened
the huge double-hung windows that faced the street, admitting actual
birdsongs but not one lingering jazztown echo of late-night-to-early-
morning music, or any other kind of sound that wasn't unnaturally
natural.

At nine, she gave up and stood at a screened window, spotting
two idle college-student bellboys, a strangely un-idling line of yellow
plug-in hybrid taxis, and a couple, kids in tow, heading purposefully
towards some sort of gathering human action a few blocks down the
street. Junie jumped into her clothes and soon learned from the
room clerk – a shift-replacement, thank the Lord – about the nearby
pedestrian mall that every visitor had to experience at least once.

HAVING GIVEN UP on changing Don, at least today, David was letting
him wind down.

"I appreciate your trying," Don said. "And I'll keep trying, too,
keep coming in... every week I'm in town, anyway." One hand was on
his ponytail, absently calming himself, smoothing it down. "So we

can talk about what I'm eating, and my running – there's got to be a way to make that work – and of course the meditation thing, which you're right, I really need to do, and I don't care how much time my friend says it takes. I mean, I know you, and I trust you..." Don's fingers wandered over a cigarette-sized depression in the hank of grey hair; a shadow of doubt crossed his face but quickly cleared. "...and I'm sure I could pull it together, with your help."

Help and continuity, the ongoing human part of medicine, David thought. The part he was going to hate to walk away from. The thing that patients and doctors, at least primary care doctors, wanted: care that was safe, familiar, informed, trusted. Comfort for the journey, through life and illness to... well. Anyway, comfort and a guide.

"Though I know," Don was saying, "how hard a time this has got to be for you."

David was about to blurt out that Don didn't know the half of it, when a familiar voice came through the open door, asking sweetly, "I'm sorry... 'How hard a time'?"

Don turned a nice purplish hue, gaining the color rapidly draining from David's face. Sheyoni swiveled from one to the other, then stepped to her standard position close beside the patient, a position that David had always thought a little *too* close.

Don exhaled, slowly, then turned to put a hand on her shoulder. "You don't have to pretend, Sheyoni."

What? David watched Sheyoni, who didn't shrug Don's hand off – may even, in fact, have been considering the future value of hemp clothing on the world market.

"Remember," Don added, "no matter how much pain there is, how much suffering, you'll always have..."

She followed his eyes to David. "Him?"

Don nodded. "Your own doctor. No matter where your... I might as well say it: no matter where your... disease... takes you."

Holy crap, David thought, as Sheyoni's expression froze over for the second time that morning.

"You know, your—"

"Don!" David barked, and Don turned to him, confused. "It's... private."

Sheyoni stood there, processing. "Thank you *so* much," she said finally, taking Don's hand from her shoulder and lowering it to his hemp-covered thigh, where she let her own hand linger, before adding, "We'll just be a moment – I need to tear my doctor, my very special doctor, away."

With a brittle smile, she backed from the room. David followed, closing the door behind him as he tracked her down the hallway, at the end of which she spun and hissed, "My *disease*?"

"I... I..." It was the best he could do.

His left arm cradled Don's chart, with Oz's spreadsheet on top and facing her. Spying it, she ripped both from his grasp – the once and future artist was no slouch when it came to recognizing the color red. "This is it?" She ran her eyes up and down the columns, tracking the negatives enough to get the trend. "Half of *nothing*?"

"Um..." Again, less than brilliant, but at least the waiting room was empty.

"That's it – that is the absolute end." Sheyoni slammed the chart on the reception counter, grabbed her jacket, tore the spreadsheet in half, and let the pieces flutter to the ground. "Go crazy," she added, "You can have it all." With a grim look and no trace of tears she grabbed her purse and stomped across the room.

David took a step after her, then stopped – she was gone. He watched the screen door slowly ratchet closed, her figure hazy and then sharp when she came around the front bay window, marching down the cement walkway to her car. When she reached the broken sidewalk, she turned and stood square with hands on hips, taking one last look. Bare blue sky behind her, a breeze that blew a few white-gold strands across her face, a sudden swelling in his heart. Could she see him? No, but he could see she wasn't trying. Sheyoni was studying the building – the life they'd built, or tried to build, together. On her face, a look that said, not good enough. Not good enough at all.

The balloon in his chest deflated, leaving his heart small and dry and beating for no reason whatsoever.

Sheyoni walked across the faded grass to her Prius, slammed the tinny door, and – with less drama than she probably desired but a finality that could not be denied – floored the accelerator and electrically purred away. Behind the space she had occupied, over the low office buildings and the parking lots and the sun-washed hospital, towered the Flatirons, those rust-gray walls of stone that tell the Great Plains that the buck stops here, that its long flat rolling miles have come to an end.

FROM OZ'S PERSPECTIVE, standing next to the intricate arc-welded railing of a stainless-steel deck above town, the Great Plains looked to be doing just fine. The sun was pleasantly warm where it penetrated his comb-over, and a summer breeze, sweet with green and growing things and the taste of melting snow, gently ruffled his fresh-from-the-box short sleeve shirt.

He didn't usually dress down like this on a working Saturday. His clients expected the businesslike attire of an up-and-coming ethnic striver, suited up and armored to defend the bottom line. But these clients, who'd produced the shirt in question, had first pressured him to try it on and then insisted on making it a gift. The brightly patterned fabric was cut for the affluent post-boomer of a certain increasing dimension, a pigeonhole round enough to fit his sleek sea-lion shape. Not only the sizeology department, which was obvious, but matching their new clothing company's target yuppie market as well. Young Urban Professional, and he *was* young (well, thirty-something) and urban (well, Boulder was getting there) and a professional to the marrow of his well-padded bones.

In business, supposedly, where your people came from didn't count. But it always did, of course, and he wasn't against putting their errant preconceptions to good use. And why not? He might have grown up across a backyard fence from David, a birthright member of Denver's solid middle class, but his hero and his model was a *true* striver – the stern and only occasionally belt-wielding father who, forty years ago, had slipped across the border with a newly-printed diploma from the Universidad de Guanajuato and fought his way up to a bank vice-presidency.

This pair thought they had his *café-con-leche* aspirations figured out, and Oz liked that – it had been useful and, he was sure, would continue to be. The prototype shirt he was wearing had been hand-stitched by the former investment banker, a post-success pilgrim from a distant metropolis, working alongside his recovered-lawyer wife in the *über*moderne glass-and-steel studio behind him. Incredibly, the supple fabric was woven from bamboo fiber, an eco-friendly process that would either make them a ton more money or entertainingly redistribute their investment. Entertaining for Oz, at least, as his contract made sure he was covered either way. The latter was a detail that the eager couple, who were bred to power and couldn't conceive of failing, thought too trivial to protest.

The shirt's patterns were already winging towards a sweatshop far, far away – a modern production facility, they were quick to inform him, that was also a primary school. Oz imaged those children laboring in the constant healthy drizzle that sustained their bamboo forest, being read the Western canons that they would slowly grow to hate as their water supply ran rainbow with bitter but vitamin-rich biodegradable dyes. On the other hand, the material only cost pennies per unit, supposedly looked great with hemp, and in a pinch you could burn it for kindling.

DAVID SAT on the empty waiting-room floor, back against the wall in more ways than one, legs splayed out on the musty carpet. The square yard or so between the battered chairs and the counter seemed larger from this perspective, a vast fuzz-balled plateau beneath motes of dust that moved randomly, slowly, in the lazy morning sun. The scent of Sheyoni's perfume lingered, a hint of lilac-tinged patchouli that he couldn't let himself get into. He held the two pieces of paper together, stared at the evil columns, and slowly shook his head.

Sheyoni, gone.

A snorkeling wet sniff, a broken exhalation, a flood of memories:

Sheyoni, always there for their patients... or at least picking up her cell at home if she wasn't too busy with her demanding twice-daily self-care regime.

Sheyoni, telling him how tired he looked... with a small sad expression that nearly made her look less than fresh and rested herself.

Sheyoni, sharing the work of the practice... except for her spiritual retreats, her private sessions (cheaper than therapy, she'd said), and that trip to India she'd so plainly deserved.

Sheyoni, happy at the wheel of the same Prius her friends had, a sight easily worth that second mortgage.

All while he worked and worked, neglecting her. His own pride and narcissism had gotten him into this fix – his own vain need to be help people, to do the stupidly right thing, to have his oh-so-selfish selflessness acknowledged. Could he live without his daily dose of 'Thank you, Dr. David'? He guessed he'd find out.

Like Oz said, like Sheyoni said, it was over.

And then a thought, a petty thought, but one that wheedled in Oz's voice, a fiscal conscience he had begun, like it or not, to absorb – with Sheyoni gone, he'd have to pay someone to help out in front, which would cost thousands more than Oz had figured in that spreadsheet.

Because his patients, no matter what the cost, still had to have those two months. Like the only other patient of the morning, who should be here by now. David craned his head around to the short hallway and saw her chart already hanging in the Plexiglas rack on the closed door of the other exam room. At least she wouldn't wander in and find him sitting here, flopped against the wall like an oversized rag doll.

Maybe he could make up the difference by selling his personal stuff, the little he'd walked away with from the breakup. His banjo, for example, that Sheyoni strangely hadn't argued for. Plus whatever he could get for his old Civic, a tiny rusting thing he could just fold into. Then he could drag his feet with his landlord, false promises followed by a midnight exit. Heaping on a bit more shame, but he was getting used to it.

And after that? After those few months, after he was more than broke, after everything was gone? There's be *some* kind of job in Denver, enough to cover her divorce lawyer's fees and eventually pay back the landlord. Perhaps an opening in one of the bigger hospitals, tweaking meds on other doctors' patients while they slept. Or hourly work at the clinic in the county jail: shame-wise, that crew would have nothing on him.

Down to zero. The thought was disorienting, vertiginous… but also something else. A strange resonance, a reverberation from last night – a feeling he could almost, but not quite, identify.

Distant stirrings came from both exam rooms, and David got up with a barely suppressed groan. His second patient of the morning – that chart hanging on the door – would have to wait a minute while he finished up with Don. Then he'd take care of whatever she required, then give himself a break and put a sign on the front door: Closed early, Sheyoni had to leave, page me if you need me.

AFTER JUNIE POCKETED the room clerk's written directions (totally unnecessary, as there certainly wasn't anything happening anywhere else), she found her way to Pearl Street and an art fair's early-morning crowd.

The 'art', mostly crafts and clothing and nature photography, was nearly identical to the FreshArt fair at home, the same traveling merchants salted with a few booths of local stuff. The New Orleans local stuff had been more your dark and funky juju, but here it ran toward aura energy paintings and a display of plasticized chunks of toxic intestinal effluvia flushed out by a high colonicist, which was plenty juju, too.

On the plus side, there was the simple ease of the environment – the human scale of the pedestrian mall, the old storefront buildings, the bricks beneath her feet and the squared-off planting areas packed with pale-green leaning stems and crimson blossoms, more orderly and European than Way-Out-West had any right to be. And every square meter of it less spiritually demanding, less freighted with years and memory, than her shadow-haunted home town.

The crowd, gradually thickening, had moved slowly down the street, oohing and ahhing over the pedestrian exhibits, happy to be pedestrians mixing with their pedestrian counterparts – even happy to be mixing with her, the sole soul raisin in their sugar cookie, as she bumped around and between them in the fragrant cool-warm morning, carried along by the pervasively pleasant herd, a concoction of some mid-American fantasy of the fifties combined with an imagined ideal future, all whipped into a very, very casually dressed new bourgeois gentility. And so she'd bumped and floated and felt, somehow, accepted, felt an absence of the usual urban tension, felt dropped into a world that had strangely let its guard down.

That said, it was still plain softserve vanilla, safe and non-ironic and existing in complete and willful ignorance of the suffering of her people or any others. But the stunning thing, the truly stunning thing was that she *liked* it.

Man. While there was plenty more to see – or socio-microscopically observe – Junie needed a break from all this early morning culture-shock. Luckily, her stomach, feeling a bit concave, reminded her of the all-inclusive reservation's free 'brunch', which was probably sweet rolls and corn flakes but what the heck.

DAVID RETURNED to the exam room and Don's painfully understanding gaze. "No matter how tough it is," Don said, "it's got to be harder on her."

David wondered what he'd heard – muffled voices, probably, carrying emotion and nothing more.

"You're losing her," his patient added, "but she's losing a whole world. She might look well… incredibly well… but she can't be feeling—"

"Don – she's feeling fine."

"In remission? That's… that's *wonderful*. A chance to treasure every moment she's got left."

"I mean, she's not—"

"I know… your friend told me all about it; you don't have to say another word."

Okay, David thought, and gave up.

"But I was thinking…"

"About?" A wooden chair creaked on the other side of the wall. His second patient was growing restive; he really should be heading in there.

"Well…" Don hesitated, then, seeming to have come to a decision, asked, "Can you recommend a decent workout guy? And a dietician, and maybe someone I could meet with, learn how to get on top of stress? I've got to get serious, and this way I won't bother you. I'll just check back in a few months – I know you'll be busy."

David stared at him. Busy? Not around here. Unless…

That feeling again… an odd and opening sensation, a tingling that spread out through his limbs. Not exactly vertiginous this time, not precisely reeling – more a sense of *possibility*, something that made absolutely no sense at all.

Unless...

Unless he hired everyone Don was talking about, unless he did just what Oz had said the night before. If you're going down, why not go down big? For all he knew, Oz had already cooked up some safe Oz-protecting scheme for getting a loan. Even if it didn't protect David – in their long history, he was always the one to get caught – he couldn't get more broke than he already was.

Now that the numbers had soaked in, now that Sheyoni was totally and completely gone, now that he was going down to zero anyway – now that all those things had happened, taking the risk, any risk, was transformed into a no-lose proposition. The end of things, making room for a beginning. It probably wouldn't work any better than the rest of the life that lay in ruins around him, but why not?

What, in fact, if I *did*?

Of course! That was the feeling – that was it, exactly.

It would certainly buy his patients the months they needed. The right thing... and maybe something even righter. Take Don, for instance. He *sounded* married to his plan, but the anxious clothier wasn't likely to pull it off on his own. He'd probably drop those healthy, time-consuming things the instant the next big hemp order rolled in. But if Don had to keep coming to the same office to learn how to meditate, to exercise, to eat healthy on or off the road – and if, at the end of every visit, he had to sign up for the next visit or session or workout – he just might stick with it, after all. Don could be the core, Don and patients like him.

Patients that might even be able to pay their bills... David realized he kind of liked his rusty Civic. And the banjo, too.

Starting slow, then gaining confidence, he told his hemp-covered patient how – What a coincidence! – he'd actually been thinking of broadening his practice, hiring all the stress counselors and exercise therapists and dieticians Don was talking about. That way, Don could get everything he needed and still stay focused, here. And to no one's surprise but David's, Don liked it.

Which was a good start, new-life-wise, as his other patient, the last Sheyoni-scheduled patient of his old life, had wandered out, puzzled by the empty office, by the time he followed Don down the hallway to the silent front room.

3

Where the Money Is

- or -

Ambulatory Mortiphobia

"YOUR PLAN SOUNDS STRANGELY FAMILIAR," Oz said, and put his lips to the white plastic lid on a full-fat quadruple-shot latte. As he strolled, he bent forward carefully, making sure that none escaped to stain (or melt, for all he knew) his brand new bamboo shirt. The long flat blocks of Pearl Street stretched in front of him, already filled to overflowing for yet another Boulder-boosting art-fair weekend.

His few words brought David's many to a halt, a good thing. Oz didn't want to extinguish all those brilliant new ideas, but some recognition of his own contribution would be nice. He glanced over at his childhood friend, who now gnawed a corner of his lower lip, unsure how to respond. Like Oz's clients, David clung desperately to the belief that he followed his own true path, unaffected by even the most benign outside influence. Oh, let him struggle – it was his call that hauled me to this Saturday morning circus, after all.

In the meantime, Oz scanned the human obstacle course ahead. Not exactly Fifth Avenue at Christmas, but close. Unlike December in Manhattan, shorts seemed to be the style *du jour*, from the lean stretch-clad couples ramming a flotilla of yard-wide vitro-twin strollers through the masses, to pale specimens aspiring to his shape (a shape he was wise enough not to expose in so desperate a fashion), fish-belly thighs flapping as they herded older, and unfortunately less-restrained, progeny away from tilty art-fair tent poles and listing shelves of hand-blown glassware.

Judging from the collective complexion, these early birds had flown in from the spanking white suburbs to the east. The more cosmopolitan mix from Denver should just be getting out of bed; their late-lunch arrival would add a little color, Oz decided, after which his mind happily veered – with his customary absence of both economic prejudice and liberal sensibility – to the thought of thousands of tiny hands, brown as his or browner, that would soon be shredding and softening and weaving bamboo, laboring for his clients and ultimately for him.

"You're absolutely right," David said, finally. "It was your idea, and a great one. Just took me a day to wrap my head around it."

"That and Sheyoni cutting the cord." Oz's third-world financial vision faded as he concentrated on simultaneously keeping David in the real world, balancing his coffee, and anticipating the next lateral fake of one particular twin-stroller pilot, as hard-eyed as her observant passengers, who had mistakenly identified him as the soft spot in the scrum opposing their rightful forward progress.

David paused beside a shop window full of carbon-fiber white-water surfboards and tartan fleece bikinis. "Sheyoni," he said softly. "Part of me hoped we could still…"

Reluctantly conceding an opening to the pushy stroller mom, Oz stepped over and waited David out.

"But when she went out that door, well, that was it. It really did feel like… the end."

Oz nodded, a sympathetic look on his face, though inwardly as delighted with Sheyoni's hopefully final exit as for any other good thing to come his way.

"I guess she knew she had to, I don't know… cut the cord?"

"Whatever you say." Even if, Oz thought, I just said it.

"To help me make a new start," David added, moving back into the flow. "Not that she dreamed I'd have this new plan, I mean, that we'd go with our – I mean, um, *your* idea."

"Never mind that," Oz said, following. "But you were telling me, before… Did she really say those words? 'You can have it all'?"

"Sure. Though I don't see what—"

"Excellent." As usual, his pocket recorder was on; Oz made a mental note to have David sign the transcript later.

"It *is* excellent – she'd know this new step would be good for me; she'd be, you know, happy. A new kind of practice, a new beginning, a chance to work with colleagues."

"Colleagues… as in, other doctors?" Oz ran the numbers, quick as ever, in his head. "That's going to cost."

"I meant rolfers, nutritionists, that sort of thing."

"Oh, *alternative* colleagues." They circled wide around a street performer – rainbow clothes, albino dreadlocks, juggling two velveteen kittens and a bright yellow toy chainsaw in a high, crowd-gasping arc. The plush kittens emitted a plaintive bleat every time the juggler caught one, a counterpoint to the chainsaw's battery-powered rasp.

"Absolutely," replied David.

Oz was reassured, salary-wise, and kept himself from any further impolitic comments about holistic providers, as almost every local in the crowd either was one, in training to become one, or donating a substantial fraction of his or her income directly to one. Though he hardly had to worry, as the humanity around him offered a kind of privacy in motion, his and David's fellow travelers constantly changing as each was drawn, magpie-like, from this hand knit Rasta bag to that laser-cut sunset to that one-of-a-kind carved bristlecone-pine toilet seat.

"I'm assuming you'll be the boss," Oz said instead, as they pierced a line of happy bovine strangers.

"Of course – somebody has to be. But we'll all have the same patients – sharing the responsibility, sharing the load. Hard science and soft touch, medical care and alternative care, a human mix that works. This could be wonderful, Oz. I'll even be able to take care of my old patients."

"Your old *nonpaying* patients."

"There aren't all that many," David said. "And there's the loan we'll get, a big new office. With some sort of yoga and meditation place upstairs, massage rooms, counseling – as much space as needed."

"Every square foot of which we, speaking as your business manager, will have to pay for."

David frowned. "What about how great it was going to do, how we could build it up?" He slipped around a retired couple selling didgeridoos, walked up the sandstone path between two towering rocks – a huge boulder sheared in half and planted in the middle of the mall as a kind of sculpture – and turned to face him.

IT WASN'T THAT DAVID didn't trust Oz, or that he wanted to confront him in this solid, stone-framed place – just the dim awareness, behind the moment and the crowds and the excitement of this fresh start on this fresh Spring day, that his future was yet in flux, his spirit still maimed and limping, and that his enthusiasm, a new and fragile thing, was dependent on Oz's reassurance to stay in play.

"We can build it up," Oz was saying. "But only if we're smart. And careful. Careful enough to *stay* in business. When it comes to billing, frankly, we need to be... ruthless."

We, David thought. And ruthless. And Oz, consulting his gold Rolex. As David noticed these things, his enthusiasm began to dwindle fast.

As, across the narrow space, Oz added, "Or..."

David, having plenty of experience with his friend's 'Or's...', was afraid of this. "Or... what?"

"You bring in another income stream. The one we talked about last night."

The didgeridoos' buzzing drones seemed louder, filling David's ears as they echoed off the polished surfaces of the bisected rock.

"Like you said last night – like I just said – alternative care." Actually, David wasn't entirely sure that was what Oz had meant. "Health and hope, hope especially, hope that they can..." He was beginning to remember.

Oz nodded. "That they can live forever."

"I can't promise that." David stared at the backs of the didgeridoo merchants' white-haired heads, but they didn't get any quieter.

"Who said anything about promises? Last night got me thinking, too... Just take a look, a good close look, at this," Oz balanced his briefcase in front of him, extracted a medical magazine, and handed it to David.

The journal had fallen open to the title page: *Longevity Now!* – a notion that, frankly, seemed internally inconsistent – above a fine-lined list of contents.

"A *close* look?" David was trained to be methodical in his approach to everything medical, though he could be as befuddled as any doctor when it came to parsing the near-impenetrable exactitudes of research articles. This particular publication might contain more than a few, but a least he could try.

Oz turned slightly ashen, as though he may have made a grave mistake. Then consulted his watch once more as he crossed his arms, resigned.

TWO BUSY BLOCKS EAST and a silent sidewalk to the north, Junie pushed back from the table and laced her hands around a belly that had morphed from concave to gently rounded, blaming it on a few thousand calories of organic pancakes, pure maple syrup, a small portion of a hog that, she had been unnecessarily informed, had lived a happy and pesticide-free life before giving it up serenely, plus the rest of a just-squeezed and just-picked and now just-eaten brunch. She stood with a quiet groan (a groan far less morose, although she couldn't know it, than David's earlier that morning) and left the old hotel's white-linen restaurant. Not bad, she thought, and not one bit cheap either. But the room clerk, who'd turned out to be a moon-lighting grad student, had said the University was covering it along with her night's stay, so all was right with the world.

He'd also told her there was a decent bookstore – large and independent – a few blocks down the mall. Junie retraced her way to the brick-paved blocks and, now metabolically content, eased back into the human tide.

OZ LEANED AGAINST a polished granite face, idly surveying the masses on the move. Like most of those who felt transformed, by dint of pure persistence, into Boulder natives, he'd navigated a few too many Pearl Street fairs. His observation post was protected, if echoing with the pseudo-Bushman racket from those geriatric tie-dyed maniacs. The digiderooers meant well, of course, as did their potential customers, who'd left behind their workday conflicts for this peaceable weekend arts-and-crafts reverie. Looking deep into his fiscal heart, Oz discovered that he felt nothing less than kindness toward their rambling, benignly yearning, and especially sales-tax-generating bliss.

David, as he'd feared, was taking forever, pouring over every article as though it might hold some essential secret of the medical universe. Oz sighed and coughed and even belched, but David was too absorbed to notice. Then Oz spotted Sheyoni through the hanging wind chimes in a nearby booth, examining a potter's wares.

She seemed puzzled by a small glazed sculpture that was about as rude as a *non*-phallic ceramic could get, two parting mounds lined with petal-like lips that were obvious to even an anatomically-challenged layman like himself. Close beside her stood a solid figure in flowing jewel-tones – the manager of the woman's bookstore that occupied the ground floor space under his office. She looked fondly on as Sheyoni held the piece up, peering at the pink-rose ceramic from one angle and then another. After the light finally dawned, the woman placed her fingertips lightly on Sheyoni's shoulder, who looked up with a shy, nervous smile.

Maybe, Oz thought, he'd been wrong about Sheyoni – and why she was leaving David – all along.

JUNIE WANDERED INTO and then rapidly out of a series of 'ism' bookstores, from mysticism to feminism to leftism to a peculiar blend of mystico-femino-leftism. It was nice to know that each clot of true believers had a shrine of their choice, but she hadn't found anything close to the kind of every-ism temple of knowledge she was looking for. Frustrated, she stepped up onto the raised brick curb surrounding nine square yards of close-packed tulips, and peered back down the block, searching for the brass doors and book-filled plate-glass windows the hotel clerk had described.

The crowd wasn't as monochromatic as she'd thought. Lots of Asians, or Asian kids at least, glossy-haired girls darting away from weather-beaten blond parents. Or that Hispanic gentleman between those slabs of rock, a real *maqereau* daddy, bright loose shirt draped over his sleek curves, standing next to some tall white guy, all elbows and dark hair buried in a magazine.

THE DENVER CROWD, Oz noted, seemed to be arriving. Like that sweetheart in the sundress, black as his own dark heart, long limbs and full lips, random tiny pigtails bouncing like a crown of thorns around her. She stood poised and balanced on one leg at the edge of a flower planting, head above the crowds. Work it, girl – be that style, work it for advantage. Same as he did, really, stand out and work the contrast.

Working the contrast. It wasn't just Liberal Guilt – that label was too easy to attach, too predictable for a man of his neoconservative leanings, and he liked to think he was anything but predictable. It was the kind of handle that reduces everything to politics, and he'd lived here long enough to learn that the sting and power of ethnicity depended on a vast pale expanse of pure boredom, the boredom of an affluence that, having successfully isolated and protected itself, reaches out of its own closed world for something more. Hey, I'm a philosopher, Oz thought, amused, then realized that his ethnic sort-of-sister was staring directly at him.

SHIT CRAP PISS – that guy in the shirt had nailed her with his eyes. Like he knew her, not her name but *knew* her, saw her, knew how she didn't fit. All these mobile happy sleepers, baking in the noontime sun, and he was *awake*. And now, connected by that gaze, she was as well.

That knowing look, brown to black, like they were in this together. Like black was what she was about – true enough but not: she was more than that, a lot more, though the too-white crowd seemed suddenly to be pressing in around her. And there he stood, peeling back the layers from fifty yards away.

Junie made herself look beyond him, as though it was an accident – and it was, wasn't it? – that their eyes had met. She lowered her hovering foot to the planter's brick-wide edge, but still she lost her balance, had to recover with a step down to the crowd, to be jostled by the bodies in random motion around her. Forget the bookstore, forget that pleasant drift, forget his look, a look that couldn't possibly know her. It might be the locals' Saturday, an eddy in their lives, but she had to get moving with her own life. Swimming against the human current, she headed back to her hotel, her packed bags, and the printed map to her designated student-slum dwelling.

Maque Daddy, she was sure, could take care of himself.

DAVID TURNED THE LAST PAGE of a medical journal that was in many ways identical to the unsolicited freebies that filled his mailbox every day. Oz, he noted, was up on his toes, apparently searching for someone in the crowd. As David watched, Oz dropped to his heels, shrugged, and looked over, impatient.

David was about to hand the magazine back when he noticed the cover. Most journals featured a photo of some nasty-looking slice of diseased tissue, or a close-up of a suffering patient. But this one starred a woman who was beautiful and fit, almost scary fit, looking directly at the camera. She wasn't suffering at all. Her hair was silver gray, as gray as Don's but gleaming, and everything else about her was, well, perfect. *Young* and perfect. After Sheyoni, he was wary of beauty, but this weird age-crossing thing was... memorable.

"Whoa," David said, without thinking.

"I'll say."

He looked up at Oz and blushed. "Not, um, her."

"Of course not." Oz didn't actually roll his eyes, but close.

"I was *referring* to the articles," David said, quickly reopening the journal, hiding that vision in silver from view. And he *had* been referring to them, sort of. While the articles looked like research – a few columns and tables, the standard statistical analysis, all the trappings of disinterested objectivity – it was research that was sketchy and brief, cursory research, research that just wants to get all that distasteful scientific business done with before moving on to praise. Worse, every study looked at a strange new chemical or supplement, all named with weird neologisms, like biostimvastol and longevidine, names that almost but didn't quite make sense. "They seem kind of, um, shoddy."

"Tough. Look again."

Oz was pointing to the ads. There was a bright glossy one opposite the first page of every study, and always for the studied product. It was almost – *almost* – as if the manufacturers had already known the studies' findings would be positive, long before the publication date. Even less professionally, the ads actually listed the products' prices, which were... yikes. And David thought the drugs *he* prescribed, the antibiotics and statins and every other non-generic, were expensive.

"That's what caught me," Oz said, seeing the look on David's face. "And yes, that's wholesale. You won't believe what a clinic can turn around and sell them for."

"Sell them? I can't do that – I hate this stuff."

"What? Supplements?"

"These? Yes. The thing is, the ads make them sound like prescription drugs. They do everything but say they are."

"It's called marketing, I think."

"Oh. Marketing. My favorite thing. And the way the ads work with the studies? It's like the research was only marketing, too."

"Isn't it always?" Oz asked, genuinely puzzled.

"No. And before you start, I know, big pharm companies aren't saints. But a decent journal – a journal not obviously owned by them – at least *tries* to filter out the self-interest."

"That's sweet," Oz said. "How often do they succeed?"

"Ha." David paused, then held up the journal, still folded to keep the cover safely hidden. "It's more than just the marketing. With supplements, you expect a kind of trade-off. Maybe they haven't been proven effective, but they're natural, benign, so what's the harm? The uncertainty is balanced by the safety, everybody's happy and the FDA looks the other way. But every one of these studies seems to be working hard to turn them into real drugs: boosting the doses, tweaking the formulations, giving them by injection, even intravenous infusions."

Oz looked at him, blankly.

"They're taking all these innocent, organic, herbal things," David tried again, "chemically pumping them up and giving them in ways that break through the body's thin defenses."

Oz shrugged. "It's not like people are dying."

"I guess. Not that I've heard of, yet. But when you encourage doctors to mess around like this, use their authority to legitimize invented therapies..." He put a hand to his forehead. "This was a mistake. I shouldn't... I can't..."

"You have no idea what you can or can't do," Oz said. "No one does, until they do it. What you have to ask yourself is, Do I want that sailboat?"

"Would you stop with the sailboat?"

"Okay, fine – then ask: Do I want to take care of my patients?

Because if they need you, need all that time and all those services, then this is how *you'll* need to pay for it."

He knew Oz was right, or probably, and re-examined the glossy publication in his hand – searching his conscience, trying to convince himself.

The cover was exposed, but if David didn't look directly at that silver siren, he was fine. Until he noticed something else: the date. The issue had been mailed six months ago. The didgeridoos went silent – everything went silent – as David asked, "Oz?"

"Yes?" Oz's eyebrows arched as he looked at the mailing label under David's finger.

"When did you get this?"

"Oh, that. Actually... I've been doing a little research of my own."

"*Before* we talked last night."

"David. Be realistic. How many times have I been in your office? I used to wonder if you could pull it off, but it's been going down for at least this long." He tapped the date. "It should have been obvious, even to you."

"While you did your – what did you call it? 'Research'? – waiting for me to tank."

"Waiting for you to come around. You think patients need hope? You need hope too, pal."

"*Pal*?" David stood tall and Oz backed up against the stone. "You... snake. No... spider. Whatever. Waiting to pounce. Waiting until I came crying. What kind of friend are you?"

David turned, about to storm off, but Oz said, "Stop," and David did. The sound of the didgeridoos had returned; beyond David, the bricks were uninhabited, a short pathway bleached in yellow sunlight before it met the shadows of the milling crowd. Oz reached out, carefully, turned the magazine over in David's hands, and pointed to the back cover.

David glanced down and saw an announcement of the yearly meeting of the Anti-Senescence Society – no acronym needed or wanted there. It was scheduled, actually, to start in just over a week. "Wonderful," he said. "Las Vegas. The moral center of the universe."

"Get off your pedestal, will you? Las Vegas is about money, and money is what you need." Oz reached into his briefcase, removed a sheath of printouts and fanned them in one hand: confirmations for David's plane reservation, the conference, the hotel and the car. "This is the kind of friend I am, or try to be. I just ordered and paid for them at my office, on the way here."

"Oh – excuse me. A controlling friend. A friend who jerks me around."

"If you say so, but also one that loves you. Maybe even more than making money, which I know we can do. So go and be happy. My investment; my treat."

David took the wad of papers, grasped them in the middle, hands together, knuckles white, and almost ripped it lengthwise. Then hesitated. The trip was a foolish, pointless expense… but an expense that Oz *deserved* to pay. Had deserved it, in fact, ever since the sacramental wine-drinking, dirtball thrower moved in next door at eight.

A vacation I can't afford in a city I hate, David thought. The perfect cap to my old life.

Slipping the papers into his back pocket, he held out his open palm. "What about meals?"

Oz frowned and fished though his wallet for a credit card. "No gambling, right?"

David smiled his most evil smile – which was actually almost evil, because he didn't use it often – and said, "We'll see." Before Oz could change his mind, he popped the card from his oldest friend's chubby fingers and walked into the teeming, woodwork-buying crowds.

ON ANOTHER SUNBAKED STREET, its asphalt bleached of everything but dust and rippled waves of heat, a dull progression of southern Californian office buildings ended at the lip of a bone-dry irrigation ditch. Deep inside the last one, down an air-conditioned and florescent–lit corridor, a door stood emblazoned with a rectangular black plastic sign, the incised white letters of which spelled out, simply, Sales. Behind it, a striking silver-haired woman leant against a wall-map of the nation and watched her boss. His tie was loose, his ebony skull gleamed, the heels of his mirror-polished shoes were propped on the desk – *her* desk – and he was aiming the sharp steel point of a feathered dart directly at her. Make that a few degrees to her right.

With a whip of the wrist – Paula didn't flinch, had long since trained herself not to – his hand was empty and the dart vibrated bare inches from an exceedingly well-shaped deltoid.

Arms still crossed, she glanced down, noted the now-perforated state, and said, "Denver?"

"Look again, baby. My aim is true."

"Right." The tip had nailed a small yellow circle, just above the more substantial dot – Over a million! Gosh! – of Colorado's cowtown capital. "That's not much of a city," she said.

"Doesn't have to be."

"Why? Is the money there?"

"Oh, yeah." He smiled and stretched back, way back, pushing up with his arms until his weightlifter's body formed a solid arc of muscle, a human bridge balanced between the top of her desk and her rolling office chair. She prayed for a minor miracle but, sadly, he stayed both horizontal and three feet off the linoleum.

"Remember," he added, "when my folks sold their bungalow? The historic one that would to buy a McMansion anywhere else?"

She remembered, but only because his vanity demanded she retain that sort of idiotic detail. "Didn't they end up in Arizona?"

Returning his pressed chinos to her seat, he clasped his hands, cracked his knuckles, and pointed at the dart. "Yes, Paula. Eventually. But that's where they started looking – Boulder. All they found was million-dollar condos, bid up by the Angelinos who got there first."

She looked over her shoulder at the map again. "Money is good... but we need customers. We need a population."

"It's only a start, a foothold. A foothold with a rep."

"No, no, no." She shook her head. She might be HorTech's chief representative, but she hadn't signed on for the great unlaundered West. "Absolutely not. I'll fly out once a month, but I refuse to—"

"I meant a *reputation*. You know: health, fitness. What we're all about. And that's the place to be about it."

"To plant our flag? I don't know... maybe."

"Trust me, will you?"

Trust him? Paula didn't think so. But if she knew one thing about the good Dr. Biggs, it was this: he was always right.

4

No-Sexercise

- or -

Cerebral Isolatum

A SMALL PLANK-SIDED CABIN, held together by one hundred years of paint, containing Junie, looking out a four-pane window. The view was of a grassy hill that ascended to a dark green band of conifers and then the soaring cliffs of the Flatirons. She leaned forward and craned her neck to take the latter in, peering beneath the top edge of the peeling wooden frame. Three pairs of climbers, high on the rock… couples, it looked like, the male of each in the lead. Like tandem bicycling, or any outdoor sport, the guys pushing to the front. Junie shook her head and went back to her calculations.

The problem with molecular pharmacology is that it takes a lot of time. A whole lot. Especially when you're about to formally present two years of work to a faculty that must be wondering if their transcontinental gesture to a flooded-out lab rat from New Orleans, now that the tidal surge of headlines was receding, had been all that smart.

You'd think a Sunday would provide a good quiet stretch of empty hours – theoretically, the day of rest. But no, not in *her* new hometown. If it wasn't raining, and she was pretty sure it was never raining, it seemed like everybody was supposed to be out there having fun. Or doing an excellent imitation, to justify the equipment that must have cost half a trust fund. She looked up through the window again, hoping for a heavy-bellied cloud, big and gray and coming up behind sheer sandstone. But it wasn't going to happen. You could count on rain where she was from, at least a damp soaking heat that made it impossible to do anything but sweat. That's what she'd be doing – sweating and calculating back at Tulane, if those basement labs weren't filled with fermenting Katrina funk. Instead, she was dry and cranky and working on her presentation here.

The soft popping sounds of tennis came through the uninsulated wooden walls, that and the complex start-and-stop of the orchestra practicing in the barnlike auditorium, and the music of children playing, and the murmur and clatter of the Sunday-brunchers filling the porch of the nearby Dining Hall. Chautauqua: a tiny community of rental cottages jammed between the mountains and the tilted edge of town. A nice, quiet environment, the grad student housing office said, which may have been true for the academic year but ignored the hoards of Texans (Houstonians, from the sound of them) fleeing their own sweltering clime for a long, activity-filled summer. She shouldn't complain – people were just having fun. All good and good for you. But, man...

DAVID SAT in the dim confines of his apartment. The last few days, in fact every day since Sheyoni had served him with the papers, had been a roller coaster with precious little coasting. He couldn't afford to think about her again, but now he had to, at least think about replacing her at work. He could keep the schedule light for this week, let the telephone ring and see patients on his own, but he needed a body in the office before he headed off on Oz's Las Vegas goose chase. Oz had already swung a buffer loan for basic operating expenses... maybe he could hire a guy this time, someone who wouldn't remind him of Sheyoni in any way, shape, or form. A classified would take too much time, so he went to the web and entered the job description in the local List instead.

That done, he found himself staring out the single window at the Boulder Creek Path. There really wasn't anything else to look at, just the standard soul-crushing divorced bachelor scheme of beige carpet, bare walls, and all the bent and tilting Levalor blinds anyone could possibly want. And, of course, the furnishings: a painfully new twin mattress, a few folding chairs left by the last tenant, and the aforementioned banjo, lying spiritless and unplayed in the corner. At least the banjo felt like home, that and the small maple table by the window, taken from what used to be his – no, *their* – bedroom.

A studio apartment next to Boulder Creek had seemed a great

idea, but now he had to watch everyone else do what he should be doing. Like that woman running by. An attractive woman, he noted, distantly. But too young, an undergrad, and he wasn't going to get into *that*. It didn't matter – his beaten spirit was beyond lust, post-lust, not even a trace of a memory of an ache of lust. Maybe he was lucky: the Buddhists in town said peace only came when you escaped desire. As a physician, though, he was aware of only one physiologic state in which all desire was completely absent, and that too-deep rest was also absent a pulse, or a temperature greater than the room the body was, by that time, quietly decomposing in. David sighed a long, defeated sigh and got up to put on his running shoes.

Minutes later, he was moving through the warming spring air, finding a pattern and starting to push himself, starting to clear the cloud that had been following him around. He passed the girl – nope, still nothing – and continued over and under the myriad pedestrian bridges and underpasses he'd been happy to pay taxes for, heading towards downtown and the dirt paths beyond.

A fully-spandexed bicyclist bellowed "On your left!" and David winced and ducked right, then soon recovered and found his rhythm again. What a dick, but a dick in tune with history: the Creek Path was originally called the Bike Path, before countless similar internecine conflicts between bikers and walkers and runners and a score of other exercise pigeon-holers forced the change to its current, less territorial title of Creek Path. Whether the new name helped was much in question, but either way, the city had used its expensive network of whatever-paths to make exercise an omnipresent social obligation. To a doctor, that was a very good thing. Personally, it was sometimes hard to bear – like in his apartment, ten minutes ago – but that meant the obligation part was working so what the heck.

Because just about everybody needed it, if not for the spirit then for the flesh alone. Study after study showed the benefits: decreased heart disease, more muscle mass to see you through your eighties, less colds and even less cancer. The last couple might be due to a general firing up of the immune system, reminding the body that it was alive and had to keep on fighting. There was, of course, a downside – pitiful exercise-addicted anorexics, righteous Body Nazis like that passing penis on two wheels, and tragic fools chasing college girls, which was a bit too close to home.

But the obesity epidemic sweeping the rest of the country had not taken hold in Boulder, so the body politic, at least the medical body politic, was doing all right.

A positive thought – the first of the day. While he was pretty sure his mood would tumble when he returned to his bleak beige hovel, for the moment that faint optimism powered him up Sixth to a running path above Chautauqua, and then, with a last grasp at joy, around and down the closed park road by the cottages beneath.

JUNIE'S LAPTOP played a sweet jazz chord and she swam up from the depths of computer-modeled mutagenesis. In particular, the difficulties of describing her knotty work in a few lines of simple, elegant, and, most of all, digitally projectable prose for the dog-and-pony show tomorrow. Thelonious's minor seventh was still fading as she read the details of the halftime spot her little job-bot program had turned up. She definitely needed one: the university might cover tuition and rent, but the rest was on her. Plus, she knew she had to periodically haul herself from the micro world to the macro one, from teasing molecules apart to getting out where molecules walked around in interesting combinations.

It was exactly what she'd been looking for: mornings only, an honest hourly rate, and in medical care. She needed more clinical experience if she was going to be designing drugs, and this was a family practice office. Okay, they obviously wanted some kind of glorified receptionist, but she could descend from the exalted if impoverished heights of academia and mix with the heathens. A chance to see things from the other side, across the gulf that separated budding research pharmacologists from the hands-on docs who wrote prescriptions. It would also put her on the other side of the even wider divide (one she was all too familiar with) that yawned between those prescribers and the army of drug-company reps pitching every month's new-and-improved product. During the years between undergrad and grad school, she'd barged into countless primary care clinics doing just that. Pure sales – ingratiating, manipulative, and, for those and more private reasons, a time she didn't like to dwell on. She'd learned the price of selling half-truths; it had paid the bills but did not make her proud.

The smaller practices she'd serviced had fallen into either of two camps. In Louisiana, primary care used to mean denture-chewing GP's, gleefully collecting free pens, dinner coupons, and other petty bribes. Then there was the growing population of residency-trained Young Idealists, who barred their doors against commercial and/or corrupting influences. And this doc? She did a quick online search: a recent grad, a decent med school, and no complaints about economic cheesiness or, for that matter, overall sleaziness that anyone had bothered to zing into the blogosphere. Good – she'd just as soon gloss over that 'commercial corruptor' phase on her resume. Junie picked up her cell, left a brief message, and returned to her labors.

She was interrupted by the sight of a large running male with a goofy smile plastered on his face, galumphing full-tilt down the narrow park road between the slope and her cabin, gravel grinding beneath his feet. Large as in tall, and not too gangly, or too dressed for the sport. Not like some of the locals, who must have a closet full of costumes for everything, from backcountry Frisbee to downhill team speed-skipping. Still, she was trying to work here. And look at him: disgustingly happy, totally self-absorbed, like every other guy in this town, and entirely the wrong color. As he panted by her open window, she could almost smell the sweat, his body pumping, moving, reminding her, reminding her of…

No, no, no, not that – she'd sworn off all entanglements since New Orleans's last tangled train wreck, the absolute *finis* of a series of preening, oiled boyfriends who invariably proved more complicated than smart. She had promised herself an uncomplicated twelve months to complete her research, get her degree, and scoot home to her sunken city by the sea.

Twelve months? Man. Or, more precisely, not.

Junie shook herself, hard. That passing heat and sweat must be reminding her of… *exercise.* That was it, had to be it. And she needed a break, something to get her moving. There'd been a flyer stapled to the telephone pole outside. She turned in her seat, craning to see it through her front window, and was stopped by her reflection in the glass. The boys said she was beautiful, and the doctors – the *clients*, her boss had stressed – had obviously thought so to. But she was beyond that, beyond makeup and combed-straight hair and the unbuttoned top of a 'professional' white shirt, the suggestion of something lacy beneath. Her life was real now, real facts and real drugs and, with any luck, real cures. In the meantime, she'd look the way she wanted to, the way she was born to, and screw what the boys thought, the boys or anyone.

Her full lips, red enough for her, flattened as she focused on the weathered pole beyond the window, near the street. The flyer wrapped around it was readable, if barely, from where she sat – Sunday Yoga: Low Asanas at High Noon. In the Community House, a few blocks on the photocopied Chautauqua map. It was already almost eleven; she'd go when she finished. Yoga… doing that Boulder thing. It might be funny, and it *was* exercise, even if it didn't totally fire the adrenaline up.

Which, despite all the yoga ads, looked like kind of a problem around here. People went at fitness like their real goal was to beat themselves to a pulp, and all they needed was to do something, anything, most every day. A nice New Orleans walk, for instance, a saunter in that heat. If you wanted to be compulsive about it – and she was, sort of – walk the same distance your supposedly-ideal self would have run. But take it slower, easier; lots of gain with hardly any pain. Her physiology professor had nattered on and on about that pulse-rate stuff, but she'd looked it up and it was meaningless. Unless your real agenda was competition, training up to breeze by all the Lycra-suited wonders she'd seen chug down the street. A nice thought – those clowns could use a wailing – but then she'd be one of them and anyway it wasn't for her. Time counted as much as effort, and fun and pleasure counted most of all. Otherwise, why would any fool keep doing it?

But first she had to finish her presentation, and so she did, power-pointing graphs and pixilating mock-molecules and trying to keep the whole thing simple enough to read from the back row. Before any time at all passed, she had to save and close the file – it still wasn't *perfect* – and change into her faithful nylon gym shorts. As she was going for the cottage's keys, the computer played Thelonious's sweet hanging seventh again. An email: incredibly, a response to her message. Could she interview at nine tomorrow? Her long lean fingers hovered over the keyboard: if she went on the way to her presentation, it'd help to take her mind off it, not one bit a bad thing. She emailed back, snagged her keys and left.

THE FOLLOWING MORNING, Junie walked into a cute enough office, a little beat up by her new hometown's standards but with enough lived-in furniture and lived-on carpet to remind her of her real hometown. The empty waiting room was dwarfed by the doc that met her, who was also cute enough, with gray-green eyes, a broad javelin-thrower's build, a dark shock of hair that framed a pale flat face. Even if he looked like that idiot pounding down the gravel road by her cottage, yesterday. She squinted: he *was* that idiot pounding down the trail. The one who'd got her thinking about the yoga class, where every other woman had a perfect yoga outfit and the secret competition to be the stretchiest almost killed her. None of which was this guy's fault – in fact, as they traded a few semi-awkward pleasantries, Junie was not only impressed with the lack of I'm-the-doc ranking, but also got the distinct sense that hidden behind his earnest manner lay a living, breathing human she could work with.

DAVID saw her squint and turned to check the reception counter behind him. When Sheyoni walked out, she'd left the charts for the last few week's patients splayed in her secret random order, a horizontal landslide over every working surface that he could not bring himself to put away. "We're, um, in transition."

"To…?"

"I'm still figuring that out." He moved between the worst of the mess and his interviewee.

"Ah."

"Which means you'll be doing everything, but not much of it," David said, very much interested in changing the subject before it veered into the real mess of his life, something he certainly didn't want to go into with a part-time stranger. "Only mornings, if that works for you – answering the phone, checking in scheduled patients, that sort of thing." He'd work alone in the afternoon, seeing urgent care walk-ins who'd be too grateful for the convenience to notice the lack of staffing.

"Between your biology and computer background," he added, paging through the resume she'd handed him, "it should all fall into place."

David paid no attention to the resume gap before grad school – he was delighted to get anyone presentable so soon. The tiny braids were interesting, he thought, as were her wide, almost hyperthyroid eyes. He considered mentioning a thyroid test, but no, she didn't have a tremor. Besides, that was a classic doctor move, turning anything unusual into a medical problem. Those poppy eyes, for instance, might be thought some rare type of beauty, if not his type.

The best thing was the full-coverage suit she wore. Sort of... professional. Was it for this interview, or did she always dress that way? The fabric was dark, the skirt long; white shirt buttoned to the neck, white sleeves down to cocoa wrists; totally, absolutely non-seductive. While she definitely wasn't a guy, she otherwise seemed as far from Sheyoni as possible. Plus smart. Not that Sheyoni wasn't smart, but this Junie had something... a certain alertness... maybe she was even smarter than him. Actually, he liked that.

"So," he said, still trying to make conversation, "New Orleans. Wow." She looked at him expectantly, and he slid into his name thing, which he knew was lame but often worked with patients, a way in to their background and their family. "Blan-*shay*," he tried. The way she'd said it sounded sort of European, though he'd never been good with languages, other than the Latin forced on him at school. Given New Orleans, he ventured, "Is that French? Does Blan-shay mean something?"

She didn't reply, but was squinting again, and he heard himself slip into the sort-of-Western accent that afflicted him when he was nervous. "We, ah, don't hear that much around these parts." Now her eyes were positively slits – God, when would he learn? Like Oz always said, he should never, ever try to make a joke. And with a job interview!

UNBELIEVABLE, Junie thought. He's screwing with me. "Blanche? Funny you should ask... it means *white*." She blinked her big round eyes, her family's eyes, said to be a gift from the same googly-eyed slave trader who'd blessed them with the name. "And yours, Dr. Black? What's 'Black' French for?"

"B-Black?" The doctor took half a step back.

"Can't handle it?" Of course he couldn't – he couldn't handle the backtalk, and he couldn't handle her. The bastard hadn't known the color of her skin until she walked in his door; if he had, he obviously wouldn't have offered the interview.

He didn't answer; Junie only looked at him, rage subsiding. And heard her *grand-maman's* voice, saying, Control to win, *mon titanfan* – you got to learn to watch your mouth. Because there was, after all, the slim possibility she'd figured him wrong. Okay, she decided, play it his way. Take a page from his waspy playbook and act like nothing had happened. Through gritted teeth, she asked, "Is the job still available?"

He took another half-step back. "I'm sorry."

"That's it, then – no more charades." *C'est la vie*, shithead. She grabbed her bag and turned to leave.

"Wait," he said, reaching for but wisely not touching her shoulder. Her head whipped around, braids spinning outward, and she stared at his hand, ready to rip it off. "I meant…"

"Meant what?" Junie asked. He wasn't doing a very good waspy-playbook job at all, his pigment-challenged face even paler than before.

"I mean, I'm sorry that I… that you thought I… but of course you would… of course you can have the job." He took a breath. "Tomorrow?"

Please. "Tomorrow?" She tried to read him – guilt or innocence? Guilt for sure, for what she didn't know, but on this matter… maybe… oops!… innocence.

Junie smiled, a little one, you're forgiven. Black's smile was bigger, so huge and so relieved he staggered, had to steady himself with a hand on the counter behind.

And as he did, Junie realized something else: while the guy couldn't be a complete dope, she was smarter than him.

Actually, she liked that.

5

DAVID DESCENDS

- or -

Prevegal Alcoholosis

DAVID POURED THE MINIATURE BOTTLE of merlot into the vibrating plastic cup on his drop-down tray. Outside the oval window, the Rockies unspooled in all their dark and moonlit majesty. The wine sent a pleasant flush down through him, though it might have been the altitude. Wedging his shoulder behind the bulging arm flesh of his neighbor in the middle seat, he settled back, thinking of the insanity of the past two weeks – how Sheyoni might someday be sorry, how sorry he still was, how Junie was turning out to be a rare stroke of good fortune, and how deeply strange it was for Oz to buy him this vacation. Starting with the merlot: nine dollars and covered by Oz's card. And even stranger, how something as enjoyable as the contents of his flimsy cup, releasing richly scented phenols as it warmed in his hand, could also be good for you.

It had begun with a very real-world observation that health statisticians promptly labeled 'The French Paradox'. The kind of catchy term that any good researcher knows will lead to more grants in the future, it brought to mind a certain Romance language David had been trying not to think about since that painful first interview with Ms. Junie Blanche. In any case, the paradox lay in how long the French lived, given all the goose liver and French pastries they vacuumed up. It was good news for the sybarites – Could wine reverse the damage of cholesterol? – and good news gathers money. Soon, vintners were sponsoring their own studies, studies that naturally discovered that their product's exclusive phenol, Reversatrol, was the key. But then non-vintner-funded researchers said it was the alcohol that made the difference, that drinkers had always had less heart attacks, so there.

He unwrapped a brick of dark chocolate he'd also brought with Oz's card, and did some sizable damage to one end. According to the *chocolate*-producer's studies, cocoa butter's saturated fats were somehow better than plain old butter, or any other heart-clogging saturated fat. He didn't find their conclusions entirely believable either – it seemed like every natural product special interest, from walnut wranglers to pomegranate pickers, now financed studies that 'proved' their products were the anti-oxidant best. Which to believe? Maybe it didn't matter, if just one would do the trick. He shrugged, deciding that the intoxicant he held in his other hand, potent and clear within its purple phenolic brothers, would be his magic shield tonight. It was the kind of move, simultaneously health-obsessed and self-serving, that would make a patient like Don Gilmore proud. If he was going to be an alterno-doc, he might as well enjoy it.

Desert now, and then more mountains, and as an otherworldly glow lit the horizon ahead, scattered lights appeared and, thickening, wound through the canyons and defiles to pool into the city of everyone else's dreams. Oz's dream, for instance – his dream for David and, as always, for his own profit. But other people's dreams, when so well powered by self-interest, are not easy to resist. The plane had started its descent. Passively, for he had no other choice, David headed down with it.

On the ground, the same lights, now dissected into colors, rivers of color washing over his car's front hood as he navigated the Strip. The shiny black hood came with the shiny black Cadillac he'd rented; Oz wanted him in a Vegas mood, and he was only trying to comply. His hotel was up ahead, a pyramid that beamed a vertical searchlight from its faceted glass apex, a defiant stab of pure-white power against the desert dark. David pulled under the portico, tossed the keys to a valet, and, proud to have achieved that one moment of Vegas cool, checked into the room Oz had reserved.

It was huge – Oz really *must* have wanted him in a Vegas mood – with a hot tub under a steeply slanting blue glass wall, permanently sealed against the bone-dry air. David threw his rucksack on the double king, pulled on a sweater against the climate-controlled chill, and headed for the first night of the Anti-Senescence Society convention.

Balcony-like hallways lined the hollow core of the pyramid,

numbered rooms on the outer side and a low railing on the inner, each carpeted strip cantilevered out over the invisible balcony beneath. Gripping the walnut rail with both hands, David bravely looked down through twenty-plus stories of smoky updrafts to the green felt tables and the bustle of the casino floor. It seemed to pull at him; he found himself leaning slightly outward, in no danger of falling but enough to be assaulted by a woozy surge that threw him back two weeks – back to the vertiginous sense of possibility he'd felt as he sat on his office floor, but this time tinged with more nausea than promise.

After that, he kept close to the numbered doors, circumnavigating the pyramid's lining to the elevators, which took him to a moving walkway set deep into the sands. Once underway, he was relentlessly serenaded by a panflute-and-synthesizer medley of Sinatra and Elvis tunes as he rolled through the wide-arched tunnel. David disembarked, stumbling slightly, at the edge of a vast and echoing glass-roofed conference center. Above him sailed a ghostlike crescent moon, pinned by that thick and almost throbbing shaft of light from the apex of the hotel behind. *Somebody* was proud, and it had to be a guy.

Grand chrome-balustraded stairs led down to the teeming conference floor, a mini-city of booths along carpeted pseudo-streets and cul-de-sacs on both sides of a marble-tiled avenue. All were manned by younger (and more attractive, and better-dressed) versions of the harried crowd that swirled between them. He stopped to find his name card – David Black, MD; Boulder, Colorado – clipped it on, and let himself be carried along. It was more dizzying than the walk from his room: thousands of scurrying eager faces beneath a visual cacophony of signs and banners that read *Amino-aesthetics, Bariatric Body Werks, Chlorotron CoreColonics, Derma-detox, Energic Fatigueostatics, Genophysix Geodyne, Himalayan Healthberries…*

AS DAVID SLOWLY TURNED, taking it all in, the occupants of two separate booths along that central white marble avenue took him in as well. Both were seasoned veterans of these sort of exhibitions, and both could spot, even at a distance, a true customer. Known competitors, they had independently arrived at the same definition of the ideal example of that species: a sizable free-ranging herbivore who either did not realize the sheer economic might he or she possessed or, for some minor ethical qualm, was disinclined to exert it. Separately, they watched their game descend the stairs and wander in their direction. The nearest of the two caught his eye first.

DAVID WAS IN FULL RECEPTIVE MODE, surveying the booths, senses unguarded, when he was arrested by a brilliant smile – suspended midway between a subtly pinstriped suit and a perfect newscaster haircut – that raised two fingers and gestured him over. Shrugging, if not visibly, he complied.

"You're a doctor?"

David looked around. "Isn't everyone?"

The salesman leaned forward and read his tag. "A *real* doctor."

"Oh." David shrugged. "Yes, I guess."

"And looking for an opportunity."

"Um... yes, again." David stood underneath the booth's banner, facing a set of illuminated displays, each with a simplified biochemical pathway that looked vaguely like something he'd memorized, if briefly, during med school. He stared at one, feigning interest. It featured a supplement with a chemical name too complex to decipher on the spot, and showed how a mega-dose could force adrenal glands to kick out totally non-physiologic levels of steroids.

"Steroids," David said. "Testosterone."

"Close to it."

"As in athletes, weightlifters."

A knowing nod.

"Isn't that... illegal?"

"Please. This stuff is harmless – just chemical building blocks. Don't get me wrong: they'll bump the hormones, and you can't match the quality, but anyone can buy them. It's not like you'd be writing prescriptions for real drugs."

"Then why do you need a real doctor?"

"Me? It's not what I need; it's what your patients' need. You've

got a trustworthy face, and I'm sure they follow your recommenda-
tions. And then, of course, there's what *you* need. " His gaze was
clear. "Do you need to take home half a million a year?"

"H-half?" David's mouth was suddenly the Sahara. "No. No... I
mean..."

The salesman spread his arms. "Okay, seven-fifty, if you work it.
But it'll take six months to hit that."

Yikes. "Oh... Ah... Thanks?" David eased rearward into the
close-packed crowd, but not quickly enough to escape that grimace,
which seemed to reveal the backside of every shining tooth, or the
glittering holographic business card that shot out and hovered inches
from his nose.

TWO BOOTHS; TWO OCCUPANTS. The first consoled himself with a
successful card-insemination, watched David turn away, and
thought: Doctors – all that *influence* and afraid to use it. Then
scanned the evening's ebbing tide for other possibilities. Perhaps a
snowy pompadour, or at least a balding crown – approaching
retirement age, when an inauspicious 401K trumped the finer points
of ethics.

Meanwhile, that second set of eyes, a few booths down and
across the aisle, continued to track our Boulder pilgrim's progress.

SHEYONI STEPPED OUT ONTO the cabin's front porch, looked down
through the black cutout shapes of the wooded foothills to a wedge of
city lights and felt totally, one-hundred-percent relaxed. Well,
ninety-nine percent. Just a tiny tight kernel of worry, down beneath
the thin and fragrant film of scented almond oil, beneath fair skin still
warmed by candlelight, beneath those ninety-nine-percent-relaxed
muscles, every single one of which had been touched and stretched
and soothed by the deepest possible therapeutic massage. A massage
so deep as to become almost sensual... well, not *that* deep, not one
of those college boyfriend massages. And it did stay away from the
tricky places, though occasionally getting pretty close, sort of
brushing by but still entirely professional.

As professional as her new best friend, Nancy, a bodyworker by training who ran the bookstore as a favor to its owner. And if her new best friend had seemed to get *into* the massage a bit, that was only natural, as she'd said her current job kept her from doing what she loved the most – bodywork, that is – and letting the feeling flow and being natural was what it was all about, right? Plus Sheyoni had let slip enough girl-talk comments about this or that guy (even, Krishna forbid, Don Gilmore, who was cute if old and kind of frizzy), that Nancy *had* to know where she was coming from, even if Nancy herself might be coming from an entirely different but understandably Feminist and completely Legitimate Place.

There. That put it in perspective. That and the cool night air – her clothes less fragrant, her skin less warm, her muscles less like putty, less pliable with every passing instant. Less and less like that one moment, in fact, when Nancy had climbed onto her massage table and knelt to press Sheyoni down with all her mature and womanly weight, two linked hands moving up and down her spine, manipulating – or womanipulating, if you were going to fair about it – each and every clunking vertebrae, before moving from fists to firm raking fingertips to the heat and smoothing friction of her palms, smoothing the adjoining skeins of interwoven muscle. All the while, those bare thighs pressed in on either side, although Nancy was still wearing her clothes, of course, or at least – having removed the rest to move more freely as she worked – one crucial piece of clothing, which was clean and flowered and made Sheyoni feel like hers were sort of smutty. It had been a moment that Sheyoni had dropped down into, down and down and down before she'd noticed that both the room and she had somehow grown too warm, *really* warm, and that she, in fact, had better get up *right* away if she was going to look for a new job for her new life tomorrow.

…INTEGRATED Juice Bionics, LiquidLife Science, Laserlucifer Faustronics, Mesomax Mutagens, Inc., Neuronaturolon…

David moved with the flow, trying to calm himself. He'd never had anyone actually try to buy him before – lock, stock, and ethics. The guy was like Oz's evil twin. Make that his more-evil twin. But why, he asked himself, had the offer rattled him? It's not like he'd *wanted* to come to this medico-holistic extravaganza. Though the whole scene was sort of interesting, and he was here, supposedly, to learn about this stuff – what to buy and what to sell and what would generate the most money. Of which, as Oz had said, there was plenty to be had. Enough to even finance (like Oz had definitely *not* said) the care of his nonpaying patients.

What was so scary about that? Somewhere in a dusty corner of his not-inconsiderable brain, a connection flared… a connection between selling and being bought, the great revolving mandala of commerce. It was a connection, unfortunately, that was easily forgotten as he reached for yet another brochure and noticed his hand's slight tremor. Alcohol: *that* must be why he'd been so rattled.

If alcohol was going to be treated as a supplement – if it was going to treated, really, as a life-prolonging drug – then this was the side effect, a side effect that annually terminated a small city's worth of hard-drinking Americans, no matter how many moderate life-loving Frenchies it saved. The other edge of the pendulum's sharp blade, swinging back now, even after a measly few glasses of wine. The depressant edge, the edge that made the crowd's noise and jostling more irritating than it should have been, the edge that had made him jump away from a friendly salesman who might have been offering exactly what David needed. The edge that made him, well, edgy. And the edge that now led him, like it led anyone, to seek relief in just a bit more of the same.

He looked to his right and saw the cure. Sweet fate had brought him to the Reversatrol stand, where, at a cost of only a few minutes of forced education, he could blunt that edge with a complimentary dose of an earnestly organic and soon-to-be-genetically-altered burgundy. The video on the booth's enormous flat-screen demonstrated the activation of an anti-aging gene in rats by the wine's purplish anthocyanosides, the same Technicolor compounds loved by blueberry and blackberry addicts. This was the original, non-alcohol take on the French Paradox – that it was the grape skins that did the trick. Believable or not, they were offering a sample of real wine, the whole package of grape skin and alcohol and phenoflavon-oid deliciousness, and asking nothing more than his email address. As he penciled it in, the video went on to inform him that the rats, who looked fairly healthy, considering, had been dosed with the equivalent of twenty bottles of altered burgundy per day. Wow – he'd never make a dent on that. But he was going to try, poaching a second plastic cup and pouring it into the first.

SHEYONI took another breath of clear night air. It had only taken a few friendly words to free her from that too-warm living room – to dress herself in filmy underlayers that slid, dragging slightly, over sweetly oiled skin. And then, of course, the filmy overlayers. All of which had brought her here, to Nancy's front porch, standing in the velvet darkness. Free to do whatever she wanted in her new life, uncommitted and free – free of husbands – hers and others – and, it looked like, free of girlfriends too.

A cool breeze stirred her gossamer hair, and she pulled a nubby Columbian swaddling blanket tight around her shoulders. The breeze was no cooler than Nancy had been at the end, though Nancy had looked as flushed as Sheyoni felt – the room *must* have been too warm – before stretching out a sturdy leg and, with undeniable grace, launched off the table to land on the pads of two broad feet.

Friendships were like that, up and down, warm and cool. Even relationships. Even marriages. The breeze passed, leaving only stillness and the distant, muffled sound of Nancy on the phone. Another friend, she'd said, as she'd ushered Sheyoni out. A friend she'd been planning on dropping into town to see, which was funny, as Nancy hadn't mentioned it earlier. Sheyoni didn't move, lost in a rare reflective moment, though exactly what she was reflecting on, she wasn't sure. That new life, perhaps, and the sense that its focus, or at least its orientation, might have just become a little clearer.

Sheyoni's reflections vanished with the snap of a twig in the shadows to her left; her breath caught in her throat and those melted muscles instantly tightened, preparing to flee. Until she saw the outline of a squirrel, or something small and frozen still on a nearby branch. Out too late – visiting a friend? – and probably as frightened by her as she was by it.

It darted away as a storm door slammed behind the house, the rumble of a motor started up, and a weathered van (for some reason, Sheyoni had expected a Subaru) came crunching around the gravel drive. Nancy raised a hand as she rolled by, her handsome profile in the dashboard light, not even *looking* at Sheyoni on the wooden front-door porch. Could she be... upset? Their friendship was supposed to be platonic; that had been clear from the start. Sheyoni remembered something that one of her college professors had said, a professor who had also been one of those massaging college boyfriends. About Plato and the ancient Greek friends that gathered around him, though they hadn't been ancient then. And how most of those friendships hadn't turned out to be platonic, after all.

With a sniff, she wrapped her swaddling blanket tighter, looked carefully into the dense pines beside the redwood-sided house, and, satisfied that not even a black-tailed squirrel was close enough to do her harm, stepped briskly to her car.

...NUTRI-OXYNEUTRALIZER, PhysioPharmic Therapeuticom, Pleomorph Protonick, Quantum Purifiers, Radiosurgical Revivathon, Symbiotic Surgeometrics...

David found a downstream eddy in the middle of the central aisle's traffic, stuck out his hand and stared at it again. The tremor was gone, taking with it that nasty edge. He could see why people kept drinking.

"Are you all right?" The voice, melodious, filtered through the crowd from somewhere on his left.

"I'm fine." He couldn't bear another pitch, but found himself too polite to walk away. Sighing, he looked up, and said, "Just checking out..."

The look that met him was open, mildly amused – and completely different from the scary rictus of the salesman who'd snagged him ten minutes before. Because it was *her*, the silver-haired woman from the cover of *Longevity Now!* And she was... he didn't know what. But it wasn't bad, not at all; every bit of her was strange and young and old and absolutely perfect. When his eyes threatened to wander in a way that was not at all professional, hers held them – dark eyes, dark pupils, dark dreaming depths that dragged him, arm now at his side, forgotten, to her booth. He passed through the slipstream of fellow attendees, pale doughy specimens clutching bags of giveaway swag as they rushed – late, always late – in the general direction of the day's last listed presentation, a lecture on 'Pheromones and Other Animal Attractions'.

His khakis bumped up against the blue drapes velcroed to her exhibit booth's front table. No banner, no displays, no pseudo-biologic explanations of how this or that worked, just a rack of scientific reprints and, mounted in the center of the fabric-covered rear wall, discrete brushed-silver letters that spelled out three words: Human Growth Hormone. Discrete because it was big money, and big money because this product, unlike that last supplement, could only be legally sold to doctors – doctors who would then inject it, quasi-legally, for even bigger money. The distributor's name was embossed on the simple white business cards on the table: HorTech. Indeed. Exactly the sort of thing he'd hoped to avoid.

David tried to back-pedal, to fade into the distance as he had before, but found himself powerless. He attempted an earlier resolve – something to do with Sheyoni and being wary of sheer beauty – but that was hopeless, too. Instead, he gulped at his remaining wine, choked, and spilled half down his front.

"You *sure* you're all right?" Pulling out an oversized leather bag, she found a pack of paper tissues and offered them; David had the feeling she'd had this effect before.

"Absolutely perfect – I mean, absolutely, um, fine." David coughed and pointed to the sign. "It's just... I'm really not in the market for, you know..." He took a wad of tissues and mopped the red beads that clung to his sweater, then blotted at the saturated regions further south.

"Hormones?" Leaning away, she looked him up and down. "No need for those."

"Gosh." He jerked the tissues away from his stained khakis, face burning.

"What I meant was, you're *tall* enough. Come on – *growth* hormone?"

"Oh," he said, cheeks burning brighter.

"Hey, relax. Nobody's going to make you buy anything." She checked her watch, then grabbed the bag and slung it over her shoulder. "Besides, I've got to go – I'm giving the last lecture."

"I should go, too." Maybe, he thought, he'd been too hasty. "To the talk, I mean. To hear about..." He pointed at the suspended steel letters again.

She shook her head. "Getting behind that podium makes me

nervous enough. And you, sitting out there, thinking I'm working a sale? Please, no."

"But…"

"Tell you what," she said, coming around the table. "I'll be packing this up in half an hour. Let me get you a glass of something to replace that. I'm sure going to need one."

"Y-yes. That would be… wonderful." He heard a distant pop as the last thoughts of Sheyoni, of wounds and resolutions, vanished.

She held out her hand, and said, "Paula." He stared at it, then took her grip, which was easily as strong as his, as strong as she looked. Peering at his conference pass, she added, "You're David," and turned and left.

Okay, he thought. Paula. Paula who really knew how to walk away. And who really smelled good, even after she walked away. Some kind of flowers, and… something else.

Then David noticed the purple map of Africa spread over his fly and, holding his various brochures in front of a point between Sudan and the Congo, headed back to his room for a less colorful wardrobe option. After dodging another joyless grin from the supplement salesman, who may or may not have seen the whole thing, he was in the clear.

JUNIE CORRECTED the angle of a battered gooseneck lamp, slugged some cold coffee, entered a few last lines of data from yet another scattered chart and placed it in the cardboard storage box on the front counter beside her. There was something about a small office at night, silent and dark, beyond the interruptions of the workday world. If nothing else, a break from the frustrations of transplanting her research to a new academic environment. The department's powers that be might have approved her work, but no one likes having to make room – on their lab bench or in their schedule – for someone new.

The office's computer wasn't much, but she'd brought it up to speed with spare parts salvaged from the wreckage of the Tulane lab. It had a Jurassic Era medical records program that helped her organize the charts, but man, it was work. The same software her Young Idealist docs (the few who'd let her in the door) had been moaning about five years ago – the potential to 'change the face of medical care', but requiring a full-time geek to load the info in. Which might explain the absence of entries after the practice's first few months, or the computer's nearly-new condition, other than a fine film of dust and the streaks of Patagonia Pink and Eco-Green nail polish on the keyboard's leading edge.

Maybe the program would have been better utilized if the thing had been able to dot its digital i's with little happy faces – to match the loopy script she'd been finding everywhere, which she could only hope was not her new employer's. Actually, she was pretty sure Black's writing was the scrawl below each entry, so illegible it proved the perfect, if unintentional, guarantee of patient confidentiality. The smiley-defaced curls marching across the top of each page, an exclamation point after every sore throat or ankle sprain, must be the handiwork of the mysterious ex-wife / employee.

Last week, Black let slip how the ex had been his 'practice partner' – partners in disaster. Still, he seemed to mean well, and Junie had even grown fond of the smiley-faces. The two of them had probably tried hard, hard as any couple, and just couldn't make it. She knew all about that.

She wasn't one to dig, but the past, everyone's past, did tend to seep out.

...SOMASYNERGY, Tachyon Massage and Therapeutics, UltraVibra Vitalometric USA, XenoWellness Specialists, YoungLovaVit, Your Name Here Marketing, Zenith Nadirlogic...

David climbed the sweep of stairs and turned to survey the conference center, brochures protecting his stained continent. Below him, the booths' banners and signs still shouted, but he felt immune, dreamlike, moving through an unreal world from one life to another. Maybe he needed one of Oz's favorite quadruple-espresso-laced-coffees – wake up, de-fog, snap out of the fugue he floated in.

Then again, he was supposed to be on vacation; why stop this one dream now?

6

THINGS LOOK UP

- or -

Myogleamic Strain

SHEYONI LOOKED UP from the brightly animated dashboard screen, swung her car back out of the bicycle lane, and glanced down again. Over 50 mpg, and on a neighborhood street – where stop signs punctuated every block! Her run down the long hill from Nancy's had left the battery fully charged, and if she only eased her right foot a little, she'd be running on full electric... there... 75... 100 mpg! Hypnotized, she rolled along in appreciative silence, the display bathing her in a warm green glow, until – Bam! – a sharp staccato hit completely ruined her mobile meditation, and she slammed on the battery-recharging brakes.

She peeled her fingers from the acupressure steering wheel cover and took a quick survey. No airbags had blown, and her little car was loaded with them – those magical five safety stars – so it wasn't *that* big a deal. The passenger-side hinged mirror had been knocked back, but it still looked intact, the plastic no more damaged than the last time. Like moth antennas, they stuck out a good long way; she considered them her impact driving guides.

Tempted to simply cruise off into the distance, Sheyoni considered the condition of the car that had so thoughtlessly interrupted her eco-conscious progress. It wasn't good. A primer-painted heap of an old Pontiac convertible, with its own mirror dangling feebly from a clunky chrome stalk. Which *was* good, actually – good that the mirror was all she'd hit, and good that no reasonable person would want to be bothered about a junkyard repair like that. Especially this late at night.

For all she knew, the car's owner was crashing in the low-rent duplex beside David's underachieving little office, which her car had come to rest in front of. Across the grass, a lone work lamp shone through the bay window of his waiting room. Even stranger, a cluster of black tight-knotted pigtails bobbed just above the raised reception counter. And just beneath them... Holy Sheyonisantavishnavarnu! Sheyoni immediately regretted taking her East Indian guru's name in vain – after all, he'd given her the best part of it, asking for *so* little in return – but the inch of brow she'd glimpsed was even darker than the warm chocolate of his Tamil skin. Tamil-brown there, but here? Things were different than in Mother India. If growing up on the safe-but-scared margins of Detroit had taught her anything, it was that.

She was certain a heavy-muscled body lurked beneath that ghetto hairstyle, a knife-tip working at the cash drawer's lock. He'd probably bulked up in prison; despite her natural alarm, she imagined him lifting weights in the central yard, his totally non-vegan pecs and lats and biceps straining, gleaming, as crowds of less developed, less frightening, less *impressive* prisoners trudged listlessly around.

Stealing the cashbox... or the computer? Or, if he was smarter than his hairstyle looked, the computer's not-very-protected (or up to date, admittedly) patient files. That was it – identity theft!

Sheyoni's cell was out, her thumb ready to dial 911, but she lifted it from the smooth glass screen. The contents of that drawer, of that computer, of that office, were no longer her problem. They were David's. And David, who really should have earned enough to provide her with a top of the line Prius – the one with the rear camera and Bluetooth, which made backing up while watching the display and talking on the phone so much safer – was no longer her problem, either.

Something else came to her: what if the car was that muscled hulk's – or, worse, what if he had a partner, waiting! Careful not to turn her head, she peered in the rearview mirror. Behind the wheel sat a huge, irregular silhouette. Dreadlocks – dreadlocks that had to belong to the tiny-pigtailed convict's driver! A driver who hadn't come over... who was watching her, dreadlocks absolutely motionless, even though she'd nearly knocked his mirror off. Now *that* was guilt – guilt and staring from the shadows, waiting for her next move. And so, lights off, Sheyoni pressed down oh-so-easy on the accelerator, and, heart pounding, glided electrically away.

JUNIE LOOKED UP from behind the computer. A certain sense of something moving, out the window, on the street. But no – only empty pavement and a silent midnight lawn. Craning forward, she made sure her car was still there, but what fool would try to steal Rosie? Junie shrugged and went back to Mr. Aaron Neville and his brothers' late-night iPod consolations. Returning to the open chart, she bent down close and peered at the scrawl, tilted her head to try it sideways, made her best guess and rapidly typed the information into the ancient computer.

There. It was the last of the fifty charts that had, on her arrival, carpeted every working surface in the front office. The messy progress notes and insurance forms had been given a fresh new life, an electronic life, transferable and researchable and neat as could be. But when she swung her office chair around to the deep-storage box, she was confronted with the close-packed rows of Black's previously *filed* charts, filling the shelves behind her. Fifty down and two thousand to go. Junie sighed; there had to be a better way, and tomorrow she would find it. But for tonight… she slipped the worn manila folder into the half-filled cardboard box, allowed herself a nice long stretch, grabbed her funky old hoodie and left.

Her car's mirror had nearly fallen off again; Junie wrenched it back onto its chrome base, then tested her repair with a cautious reverse twist – a little give and squeak, a flake or two of chrome, but overall as solid as before. She loved the old convertible, and Rosie loved her, on more than one occasion having nearly given her steel life to save Junie's. Rosie was an old-school girl, built of Detroit iron, the kind that protects the old-school way, even if about eighteen airbags and five safety stars shy. The door creaked as she opened it; she sat back carefully, the seatback's poking springs barely covered by the three thick beach towels she'd brought west with her. They were draped over the headrest, choked into a wrinkled, corrugated mass by a bungee cord.

The engine started, faithful as always, and Junie patted the cracked vinyl dashboard. It felt even rougher and more broken than it had been on their arrival in Boulder, as desiccated by this unnatural climate as she was. Hold on, baby – someday soon I'll do you proud: new leather, new paint, and a sweet ride back to where it's kind enough to rain. And when we swing your new top down, that soft southern sun won't try to bleach us white.

DAVID LOOKED UP, eyes narrowed against the desert sun that blasted through his room's slanted blue windows. Paula was truly excellent from this angle. Leaning back, her pecs and lats and biceps straining, gleaming; she was absolutely watchable, and so he watched until he didn't watch, or think or anything but move beneath her, following her lead until she collapsed beside him.

It was a far cry from last night, when he'd cautiously returned to her booth for a drink, just a drink, and conversation. A slow walk to the elevator bank, the surprise of exiting it together – her room, she'd said, was right along the hallway – and then a moment of awkward silence outside his door. A moment he hadn't had the nerve to act on, a moment followed by a restless, recriminating sleep, relieved only by the knock on his door this morning. Which opened to reveal Paula – she'd brought him breakfast after her workout, just for fun because here they were, neighbors.

A second chance, so how could he refuse?

The silver tray still sat untouched on the bedside table, loaded with a painfully healthy breakfast of tart blueberries, sharp green tea, and a large bowl of unsweetened yogurt garnished with a blooming sprig of jasmine, a flower that used to make him sneeze but this morning smelled just fine.

His cell phone buzzed beside his head and he automatically flipped it open. As his eyes focused on Oz's number, Paula's eyes focused on him, a steady look that stopped him. It buzzed again. She took the phone, slowly but firmly, and covered it with one damp palm as she placed the other, also slowly but firmly, over his mouth. David breathed her in and was lost – lost in the scent of her... one part jasmine, which must have been why he'd also lost the will to sneeze, and one part something else, at once feminine and mammalian but most of all *Paula*. Time passed timelessly: the distant, muffled buzz of the cell was no competition. Paula's eyebrows were raised, waiting. The open phone buzzed a fourth time, the call as yet unanswered. He nodded; releasing him, she snapped it shut with half a smile.

She eased off the bed and headed through the bathroom door – Paula really *did* know how to walk away, all parts moving with a syncopation any former student of anatomy could appreciate, her figure tall and curved against the tilted blue glass of the pyramid's walls. David realized that he felt, well, lucky. Lucky for the first time since... uh-oh. Lucky since someone he didn't want to be thinking of right now. He made an effort to banish Sheyoni and all their yogic, tantric moments from his mind – closed his eyes and whoosh, she was gone, an amazingly easy task. But he was left, oddly, with a color-reversed, black for white after-image of Junie, she of the shapeless clothes and critical eye. He'd been lucky to find her as well, of course, but that was business, an entirely different thing. Not the same kind of luck as with Paula – not at all.

As Paula clicked the shower door behind her and stood beneath an ice-cold blast... as Junie arrived at her first seminar, stood at the end of the long oak table, and committed each undergraduate face to memory, especially the smirking Afro-Adonis who would certainly *not* be getting a better grade on her watch... as Sheyoni sat on her new mountain of velvet pillows and gazed out at David's crummy furniture piled upon the curb... As all those things transpired, David lay flat, drained, and exhausted, a faint smile on his lips, congratulating himself on successfully placing each of the above in an appropriate category – lust, labor, lost – that made *sense*: sense of the past, sense of the present, and sense of a future that, he imagined, he could almost discern the shape of.

Three women, then, triangulated between. Did David feel crowded? Amazingly, not yet.

PAULA LOOKED UP though the shower's angled glass ceiling at an extra-blue morning sky and ran the soap along the carefully-toned hills and valleys of her body. A good night's sleep, a bounce out of bed for an hour of sweaty lifting – her pecs and lats and biceps straining, gleaming – and then a nice quick bout of extra-sweaty sex. All in all, the perfect morning. Especially as she already had the first draft of a contract roughed out. Young David didn't know it, but he was about to be a large – very large, she thought, smiling at a recent memory – part of HorTech's future. She'd done some research, knew how resistant the Boulder market had proved so far. Too young and too natural, until now. But those baby-boomers were aging, and were ripe for what HorTech was selling – as soon as they took a long stare in the mirror and saw what all those fruits and vegetables weren't doing.

Biggs was right. Boulder was ready to pop, would be their way out of California and into the major leagues. And who could help pop it better than David Black? A real live MD, a real live practice, and the kind of open, guileless face that patients trusted – and even better, that trusted her.

DAVID AGREED TO MEET Paula's boss on the last morning of the conference. After twenty-four hours of gradually lengthening sorties onto the sales floor, each desensitizing exposure to raw commerce rewarded by a session of ego-pumping bliss with Paula, he felt strong enough to resist any pitch, no matter how well slung. Following her into HorTech's business suite near the apex of the pyramid, he walked beneath the high ceiling and turned to face an open bedroom door.

Her boss looked up, smiling shyly as he worked to close an overpacked aluminum suitcase. Unfortunately, that smile was shy because he was nearly naked, with a shining shaved head, a hotel towel wrapped tight around his waist, and a solid mass of carved-teak pecs and lats and biceps straining, gleaming – something David found oddly disturbing – as he bore his full weight down until first one and then the other suitcase latch clicked shut.

Paula seemed comfortable, if amused, so David tried to be comfortable as well, or as comfortable as he could be while trying to exit the scene as soon as possible, stuttering an apology as he pulled her elbow out toward the cantilevered hallway. But she swerved and dropped into a leather couch, which wasn't great, and, worse, patted the overstuffed cushion beside her. David did as told, and, happily, Doctor Biggs , a name he was wide enough for, if on the stumpy side gave an embarrassed wave and disappeared into the adjoining bath.

DR. ERNEST BIGGS pulled on fine summerweight wool pants, then cashmere socks and polished loafers. Then a white shirt, fresh from its laundry box. He wondered if he should tuck it in, deciding yes, but no tie yet, and leave the top two buttons open. Let Paula's client know who he was dealing with – first the full sideshow, and not hiding it now. The power of the product was from the power of the sale, and he, who could press the weight of that couch with both its passengers, was very powerful indeed. Let that oversized Boulder puppy see what a *real* dose of growth hormone could do – keep you alive and happy to be here.

Though Dr. Black already seemed happy. Even Paula seemed… not actually content, not Paula. But possibly… satisfied. Temporarily, of course, but satisfied nonetheless. Had he seen that look before? Biggs frowned as he adjusted the relative height of his open collar points. There'd been a solid sale or two that lit her up like that, but nothing, well, personal. Four years ago, he'd learned (the hard way, from the fearsome Mrs. Biggs) that chastity was a necessary precondition for the workplace. If he ever wished to work – or walk, or other biologic things – again.

Thus, the bilaterally locked doors between the suite's two bedrooms. At least Black hadn't noticed hers – it would take some explaining, what with her running in and out of the suite, up five flights of service stairs every time she told her boyfriend she was going next door to brush her teeth. But Paula could pull it off, same as she pulled off everything.

Paula who bore watching. Talent, beauty, and enough ambition to run his company out from under him. As his haberdasher Daddy used to say, I might admire ya, but can still fire ya. Same as Paula would say, if she had anyone to fire – business required prioritization, and priority starts with Number One. The Biggest, as *he* liked to say, was the best.

Biggs pulled his eyes from the mirror and, after a brief admiring glance over the broad slopes of one Egyptian-cotton shoulder, went out to make the deal.

HOURS LATER, David found himself beneath an enormous LCD screen over the conference center's main auditorium, thinking about escape. Biggs, the contract he kept waving, even Paula: things were moving fast, too fast. The meeting's closing presentation was starting in one minute, starring a certain Cyrus P. Flint, Ph.D. The screen displayed a gentleman of later years, nailing the camera with a penetrating, practiced gaze. It reminded David, for some reason, of Paula's photo on that *Longevity Now!* Cover. Flint appeared as ultra-lean and ultra-fit as all the presenters – something David was getting a little sick of, except, of course, in Paula's case. *Stopping Cancer Dead*, the caption read, *Lessons Learned Along The Way*. In smaller letters below, unreeling script described the speaker's distinguished university career, his ominous mid-life diagnosis, and the subsequent scientific studies and techniques that had held his disease at bay for decades. Apparently, he'd been a founder of ASS – they'd gone ahead and used the acronym – before holding a long list of academic positions, an 'ever-glowing light in longevity research.'

David looked over the conference floor, saw Paula in the distance, and estimated his chances of making it back to his room unsnagged. Problem was, almost all the conference attendees were inside waiting to hear the final plenary talk, leaving the long blue carpets between the booths vacant, ready to expose him as the fleeing coward he was.

The emptiness seemed, somehow, forlorn. The bustle of commerce was gone, but also the pervasive atmosphere of hope. It was part self-delusion, part science, and part a clear-eyed, if not defiant, look at the big D. Part lie, but somewhere in the reams of bogus research and highly marketable conjecture, at least a few molecules of truth. Real hope, hope of progress against our greatest common fear.

The auditorium itself was packed. Outside the bank of doors, his sole company was a hunched, frail figure in a motorized wheelchair, waiting to roll in and plug the last gap between those who stood patiently in the back.

His scalp was at elbow height, only a foot or two away. The peeling skin was spotted with what had to be metastatic skin lesions, livid purple growths between patches of fuzzy post-chemo hair. Pure pathos… but also pure hope, by the simple fact that he was here. And why not hope? The old man must have heard enough bad news to last a lifetime – at least his lifetime, which David guessed was drawing to a close. Here, he could hear the promise of the new, could buy some optimism-flavored pills, and perhaps invest in a Grantawish-inator, a Balmilating Yearnatron, or a Revivinate™ Aspirelizer. Maybe the devices would arrive in time, or maybe not. Hope had to be an increasingly precious commodity at his late stage, and to keep it alive by throwing a few dollars into the wind seemed more than worth it.

Hope. That had been Oz's pitch from the beginning. Self-serving, but still… how much was hope worth? If pure hopelessness could kill – and it could, through the obvious routes of depression, self-neglect, and suicide – did that mean hope itself could maintain life? He'd told Oz it might. The studies he'd read were inconclusive: motivation to continue therapy and, perhaps, a lift to this or that immune function. What *wasn't* calculated, but what had to have an impact, was the undeniable value of happiness, of comfort itself.

Hope that brings comfort. Like the comfort of believing that comfort itself could save a life. The justification of any snake-oil salesman, the thing he didn't want to be. What happened when doctors, for the sake of hope, let themselves close their eyes, suspended their critical faculties, learned to look the other way? It was a blindness that had to cost, as all blindness's cost, even one that might serve a larger good.

The malignancy-scarred cranium cranked around, turned up, and surprised him with the same commanding gaze as on the screen above. The same gaze and the same face, except that lean and formerly white-crowned aristocrat of health looked way leaner, the flesh sunk deep around the eyes, the bloodless lips pulled back in an even more frightening grin than the most aggressive salesperson from the now-empty booths below.

David stared back, then croaked, "Hey."

An almost imperceptible nod. "You're in the business?"

"Um… yes."

"Good." Cyrus Flint's eyes narrowed, reading the nametag, seeing the MD. "Who knows? I could get sick, need some help." A skeletal hand covered a phlegmy cough; when it came away, the grin, which was really more of a grimace, was still there. And waiting for a response.

"Do all of this," David tried, looking around the vast hall, "And that'll never happen."

Lame, but Flint laughed politely, a laugh that turned into another cough, after which he stared up at the title of his talk and said, "You know the fool-proof, sure-fire way to stop cancer dead, don't you?"

This time, David was speechless.

Flint gave a happy wink and said, "Think about it." The cart powered up and with a whiff of ozone whirred toward the standing crowd. It parted for him and he spun down the long red-carpeted aisle as his wheezing laughter drowned in their applause.

David had lost more than a few patients, held a fading hand or sat beside a grieving relative, so he didn't need to think about Flint's question long. Cancer could be killed with chemo and radiation and surgery, plus diet and exercise and mental imaging and whatever else seemed to help. But what *always* kills malignant cells is the death of every cell around them. Cancer is its own worse enemy – no matter how triumphant, it dies when its host does.

Flint had powered his way up to the dais now, and his voice, amplified, grew strong enough to not only lead believers out of the wilderness, but to reach out through the doors to one doubting doctor who knew how dark that wilderness was. An old man providing hope when he no longer needed it, when his path was clear to the end.

Hope and reality: not a bad mix. And not that different from his old job, family practice. As long as you don't let wishful thinking – to maintain hope, a profit margin, or a clinic – edge into the territory of lies. And of course he'd never let himself do that.

David walked toward the barricade of shoulders, squeezed in, and closed the door behind him. Leaning back against the auditorium's rear wall, he closed his eyes and listened to the rest of Flint's plenary and, he suspected, final ASS address.

7

JUNIE, ASCENDING

- or -

Projectile Afflurrhea

WARMED BY A SUNSET LIGHT that bounced off orange clouds and through the front bay window, Junie arched back in her stiff new CU t-shirt – part of the welcome package from her grad school – and stretched her bare toes on the cool plastic of the rolling chair econo-mat she'd bought herself. Still out-gassing the clean, sinus-clearing scent of a toy store's worth of polyvinyl phthalates, it was the kind of small luxury any office laborer deserved.

Sighing happily, she scanned the contents of an elderly woman's chart into the office computer. Or, rather, into the office's new Turbo-MediMagic program. True to its trademarked name, both Black's scrawl and his ex's loops were magically translated into text on the screen. Soon every available bit and byte of the patient's medical history would be routed to its new electronic home, a proper password-protected file in a pleasant giga-neighborhood to be built from the data in the rest of the charts behind her. Glowing yellow boxes highlighted the few misspellings from the script-to-text translation, but Black could sort that out later. If he was really desper-ate, he could dig it out of the cardboard deep-storage boxes the paper charts were headed for. She added a brief note about the refill and watched as the medication list checked for interactions and then updated itself. Sweet.

Manually entering the data into the Black's old medical record program had driven her nuts all Saturday, so she'd brought in her old scanner, plus a few extra salvaged hard drives. After slipping into the wireless network of the vegan garden-supply shop across the street, she'd penetrated MediMagic's laughable series of firewalls and downloaded their newest software. It was an infinitely better designed program, which it should be at the price they were asking, an outrageous figure that nicely served to justify her borrowing it. *Temporarily* borrowing it – just a decade or so, at most. Something this important shouldn't have to jump any economic hurdles: good health care was a right, and this just made it better. Besides, with that kind of money, they really should upgrade their security.

The brass bell rang as the door opened and Junie looked up, startled – she might need to upgrade *her* security – as a pear-shaped figure stopped just inside. Placing two thumbs in the armholes of his vest, he pursed his lips and surveyed the waiting room, from stained couch to gummy carpet and then, of course, to her.

His eyes widened slightly, and hers did as well, as she mentally stripped off his suit (only the top bit, thank you very much), and dressed him in a voluminous, too-colorful shirt.

Maque daddy. The one on the mall, the one who *knew* her – as if. That was some case of first-day jitters, now that she saw him closer. Just another striver, with his too-formal clothes, enormous gold wristwatch, Bluetooth headset, and polished calfskin briefcase at his feet. Not yet middle-aged but trying to be; a shade or two darker, and she could see him marching in a jazz funeral, a hint of pompous swing while his full cheeks worked a trombone. No, he wouldn't be playing – he'd be leading the musicians, pumping his umbrella at the head of the Second Line. He looked like a guy who liked to be in charge.

What he didn't look was dangerous, and so she only raised her eyebrows.

He frowned and said, "Junie Blanche."

"And you are…?"

"Ozvaldo Garcia." Wandering over to the corduroy recliner on his right, he frowned deeper as he fingered the puffy wedge of batting exposed by a split seam.

"Then you're Oz."

His head rotated back. "What?"

"Black – *Dr.* Black – mentioned your name."

"Ah." A calculating look. "In the context of…?"

"Friendship. I think."

"Hmm." He nodded. "Good." Hands clasped behind his back, he strode into the narrow hall across the room.

"Wait a second—" She left her desk and followed, barefoot on the musty carpet. "You can't do that."

"Sure I can," he said, peering into a darkened exam room. "I'm the practice manager now. Here to check the square footage." He stuck a hand behind him; she shook it, if reluctantly. His palm was soft, warm, and faintly moist.

Junie wiped hers – discretely, though he wasn't watching – on her well-worn Sunday jeans. Then stood straight against the wall as he finished his tour, curling her toes to avoid his heavy oxfords. His next stop was her desk, craning over it to examine her computer.

"Got it running, I see. And you're trying out the MediMagic... Know how much that baby would cost?"

"The patients' needed it." Junie squeezed herself, toes be damned, between his prying eyes and the monitor. "All those diagnoses, the meds and lab results—"

"*Needed...* It's not a trial? He's already committed me to this?"

Junie gave him a moment to calm down, then said, carefully, "I got a deal."

"A deal?"

"A good deal."

"Go on..."

"A *very* good deal. A deal you don't have to worry about. Ever."

"Oh," he said. "That's different."

Junie saw no further need for comment.

He reached around her to hit a key and, before she could protest, opened up the last patient's chart. In the few minutes since she'd scanned in the data, the program had automatically searched the internet to complete the information Black and his ex had been either too polite or too distracted to ask for. The old woman's complete demographics and insurance coverage lit up the screen, including her retirement income, her husband's paltry wage as the designated ancient greeter at a local fast-food franchise, their credit scores and the bills they hadn't paid. A separate window opened to a full schedule of the screening tests, like cholesterol and bone densitometry, that each of them had fallen behind on – tests they should, in the program's opinion, soon submit to. Paternalistic, to be sure, but a way to keep track of patients, a way to keep them healthy.

"It's... beautiful," Garcia said. But he was looking at the column with the charges, each inflated number followed by the single best diagnosis code to motivate Medicare to pay for it.

"It *is*," she tried. "A way to organize, to slice and dice and really use the patient information in those charts."

"I couldn't agree more. Like they say, it's all about the billing."

"I meant their *medical* information: keeping track of problems, making sure their meds don't interact, and that they get whatever they need – screening tests, visit reminders, everything – to stay well."

"Hey, if that's what turns you on. Me, I figure the medical quality stuff's just thrown in. Get some federal underwriting, put some stars in doctors' eyes. But practice managers pay real money for these suckers so they can bill more, and that's exactly how the software companies pitch them. Every time a doc checks a tiny box, it generates a paragraph of text, and pretty soon every earache reads like a full physical. More billing, more income, to pay for this program and much, much more."

"Except you got it for free," he continued, actually rubbing his hands together. "Which I never, I repeat never, heard you mention. Though it proves one thing: I was right to let him hire you."

Suddenly, Junie didn't feel so wonderful about liberating the software, no matter how justified the hack had seemed.

"And like you said, there *is* the data." Garcia was gazing fondly on the thousands of patient charts still filed in the racks. "All those accounts, right at our fingertips."

When she looked at patient records, electronic or paper, she saw people, but Garcia – her future boss? Please, no – saw revenue streams. Junie wondered what he was planning. Put a nice high-tech shine on the practice, as shiny as his shiny shoes, then sell it to the highest for-profit hospital bidder? She'd seen it happen to the dog-eared solo practices on her old sales route, and now she'd made it that much easier. Junie puffed up, prepared to give him a nice solid piece of her mind, then stopped herself. What did she care? She might have hoped that Black was up to something better, but she'd done far worse in New Orleans.

If Garcia noticed her head of steam, he didn't seem to care. "Put your shoes on," he said, "I want to show you something." Walking to the front door, he held it open.

The shoes were next on her list anyway. She balanced against the desk, pulled on one and then the other sneaker, and shrugged. Why not? It was the end of the day, and he looked manageable enough, in a canny, watch-your-pockets kind of way. When she got to the door he bounced ahead, leaving her to lock it.

BY THE TIME JUNIE had thrown her keys in her canvas bag, he was halfway down the block, talking – either to himself or his Bluetooth, smartphone in hand and short legs moving, a man on a mission. After he turned the corner, she broke into a sprint, catching up just as he stopped, almost skidding on his heels, for an unbreachable slug of traffic on Broadway. She bent over and caught her breath, still not used to Boulder's altitude.

His voice, fractionally louder, said, "Check it out," then continued its businesslike mutter into the phone. She looked up and he was staring at her.

"Check *what* out?"

He pointed with his chin at a new retail and office co-op across the street, while simultaneously terminating his call and texting an email, thumbs flying over the candy-button keyboard. The empty building had three stories, the first two brick, the top story glass, and all very, very upscale. A hand-lettered sign on the maple-framed front doors read, 'Building For Rent – First Month Free', which seemed on the downscale side, considering.

But the sign was no competition, downscale-wise, for the seedy shop next door. Five green neon leaves sputtered in a grimy window, as a healthy if sedated-looking patron drifted out, swung into a Porsche Cayenne with a handicapped sticker, and roared away. Garcia watched and said, "That place won't be a problem for long. Just another biker who took his slip-and-fall settlement and bought some grow lamps."

"Nice attitude."

"You think so? In this case, it's true." A tattooed slab in a neck brace, chains, and sleeveless denim jacket emerged, lit an enormous blunt, and leaned against the doorjamb. Through the steady stream of traffic, he shot a grudging, one-crook-to-another look at her companion. Both nodded, slowly, and Garcia said, "Colorado's squeezing his crowd out with the new medical marijuana tax. Only the mob and the cartels can afford to pay, and all their outlets are downtown."

Garcia looked off into the distance, beyond the biker, beyond the medical cannabis-themed shops that seemed to have sprouted on every block. "Can't believe I missed the boat on that. An opportunity is a terrible thing to waste."

The light changed and he was off again, thumbing though his emails as he dug for the building's keys. Soon his leather soles were slapping the marble tiles of the atrium lobby, still fresh with construction dust. A perfect square in the middle of the floor was outlined by a yard-high glass wall, with a deep groove running close around it. As they approached, the center portion of the barrier slid back, welcoming, and soon their steps were hushed by the deep-woven Tibetan rug that covered the space within. Still looking at his phone's screen, he reached over to push an illuminated button on the rail. After a slight but disconcerting shake, the low sliding door closed and the unit ascended, magic-carpet style, towards the heavens.

He began typing again and leaned absently against an imaginary elevator wall, though the inch-thick glass barely reached his waist. As he tilted backward over the shrinking marble floor below, his self-assurance vanished for an instant – just an instant – before Junie grabbed a lapel and pulled him back to vertical.

"Thanks," Oz said, flatly, then straightened his jacket and put the near-lethal device away. When the platform came to a halt, he turned and swung his arm to the twilight-filled space.

"Too much in-town office development, and this is a prime example. The building itself was put up by some clients of mine, along with a silent partner. I tried to talk them out of it, but they insisted on going green: continuously filtered air exchange, yogurt paint, quadruple wool insulation, recycled wood walls, the whole eco-tamale. Truly, a labor of love... like most of the real estate projects that tank around here."

He shook his head, but didn't look all that sad. "No way they could make enough to break even, not in any market. So they sold their interest to the partner – very secretive, won't even meet with me – who's not only throwing in the first month but offering a year, a full year, at far, far below cost." He spread his hands. "His loss, my gain.

We'll sublet something appropriate in the units downstairs, to make everyone feel at home. There's a teashop interested, and a yoga mat store."

A yoga mat store, Junie thought. What a town. Another perfect retail solution to someone else's mid-life crisis, worth whatever they were rich or addled enough to pay. Maybe the mats would be custom-colored, or hand-milked from the latex tree. Unroll it and they will come. Though the woman next to her last weekend – the one who'd farted and then glared at *her* – had the prettiest cloud-pattern on hers...

The glass gates had slid open to a drawbridge of exotic wood. Oz strode proprietarily across – Junie followed, gripping the handrail – then unlocked a wide teak door that opened to mirror-polished floors, scattered prayer rugs, and kilim-covered furniture. The broad open room ended in a granite-topped counter and a hallway lined with frosted glass doors. Free-hanging stairs spiraled to a balcony jutting out beneath a skylight a good twelve feet across. It was tinted dark – were those transparent solar panels? – and angled open to reveal a deepening blue sky. The gear-driven glass cover blocked the sounds of Broadway; all she could hear was the faint susurration of the wind through the pines on the ridge above town.

Hold on... the air had been dead still all afternoon. Junie peered up and picked out the camouflaged speakers on either side of the skylight. Which also explained the birdsongs – but not the lingering scent of something burning. Sage, maybe, or a whiff from the stoner palace next door.

"Apparently, my mysterious landlord ordered a feng-shui thing yesterday, " Oz said, noticing. "I'm still trying to air the incense out. Maybe he, or she, figured the place needed a dose of luck. The original tenants – the ones who bankrolled all this interior work – bailed on their long-term lease. A transsexual surgery group, got stretched too thin and had to cut it off."

Junie looked at him sideways, but he was reading another incoming on his phone, dead serious.

"So why bring me here?"

"Come on." He led Junie behind the reception area to the flat panels and humming electronics of the records room. Beneath each workstation, a section of polished granite had been set into the woven Berber carpet – no need for her econo-mat here. "It's your new office."

"Not *my* new office," she said, her rebellious toes stretching in their steamy running shoes towards the cool granite. "I'm a part-timer, a temp. I've got research and a degree to complete this year."

"Sure you do. And a car – that heap in front of David's office is yours, right? – that really needs a new top and a paint job. Not to mention," he added, putting up a hand to fend off her glare, "a lab at Tulane that won't be rebuilt or hiring any Associate Professors for at least... one year. Don't you love it? The lease, your program, your future – all the same magic number."

He might have done his homework, but that didn't give this clown the right to shape her life. As Junie put everything she had into her glare – that farter's glare had been *nothing* – Oz pulled out his checkbook and added, "I figure a signing bonus to cover the car, and double your hourly after that."

"I'm not for sale."

"Triple," he said, as though he'd been planning it all along. "And three afternoons off for your graduate work."

Damn. He was already up to an Associate Professor's salary. "Benefits?"

He paled, then said, "Of course."

Junie figured she'd nailed her limit. "Why me?"

"Why you? Because you're good – I can tell."

"Already?"

He shot her a look. Please.

"But why move over here?"

He turned in the direction of the front wall of the building, bracketed his hands, and spread them wide. "The... Forever... Clinic," he said, drawing it out. "Catchy, huh? Longevity medicine, alternative care, a nice profitable stable of your holistic provider types... and, naturally, family practice."

"Oh – you'll see some sick people, too?"

"Hey, don't be that way. People need all kinds of care."

"Like this place needed a dose of feng-shui. I'm no stranger to juju, but I know science, and none of that's been proven." She twisted her face, thinking. "Except, I guess, the Seven Habits."

"The seven *what*?" He looked alarmed. In fact, he looked exactly like someone who'd just offered a job to the wrong person. A new brand of cultist, say, just landed in Cult Central.

Garcia could think what he wanted: it didn't change the facts, and if there was a cult that only believed in facts, she'd be the High Priestess and Chief Brainwasher combined.

"The lifestyle thing," she said finally, taking pity. "It's been around forever, forty years at least. From studying extremely long-lived people. Population researchers always find the same seven traits: daily exercise, enough sleep, a nice breakfast, regular meals, not too fat, no smoking, and some but not much alcohol. You know, the basics. Though breakfast was a surprise to me."

"Common sense," Oz said, relieved.

"Of course. And it works."

"Until you're eighty. We're talking a hundred or more."

She tilted her head. "You can do that?"

"That's what we're going to find out."

"And make enough to pay rent on this place?"

"Oh, yes."

"You don't look like a true believer."

He fastened the middle button of his jacket, not quite hiding his paunch. "Do I have to?"

As Junie once studied David – had it only been a week ago? – she took a step back and studied Oz. This one was a little smarter than she liked in a boss, but still. Predictably self-interested, and predictable wasn't bad. And 'longevity medicine'? Well, there had to be *some* science behind it, and any kind of science was interesting. Molecules in motion, doing – or not doing – their aging thing.

Having decided, she said, "Those benefits..."

"The usual: basic health, a week's vacation, five you-pick-em holidays."

"Trade me all that for two more afternoons off a week. Two plus the three you offered, which gives me half-time here, half-time for my research."

"Done."

He put his right arm out, but Junie found herself hesitating.

Slowly, his face lit with a pirate's smile. "Are you thinking what I am? That Junie Blanche's half-time is anyone else's fifty-hour week?"

Crap. She crossed her arms and said, "Yes."

"Relax – I've got plans for you. And they don't include working Sunday afternoons." He paused, gears running too fast for her to track, then said, "You want the benefits? I'm generally not known to be free with them, but still – why not? They're yours as well."

Her arms stayed crossed. O-kay… "What kind of *plans* were you thinking of?"

"Business plans. Do I look like I'd have any other kind?"

His hand was still suspended in the air; cautiously, she reached and shook it. Because, well, she believed him. All business, no personal… An able dealer who saw her true worth, who saw her as she saw herself. Maybe he did *know* her, after all. Junie felt a blush coming on, but managed to control it.

"And yes," he added, grandly, "you can call me Oz. In private."

"Which means you call me Junie all the time?"

A finger pointed like a gun. "Like I said, you're good."

With that he headed toward the door, then stopped. "One more thing. Look around."

He made another of those sweeping gestures and she followed it, taking in the affluence and the excess, but also the undeniable grace and beauty of the space. After a shared, respectful moment, he said, "Wear something a little sexier, okay?"

"Who the f—" she started, spinning back to face him. The teak door had already swung closed.

HAVING SUCCESSFULLY EVADED the wrath of Junie – hey, it was just a suggestion – Oz picked up dinner from the new Thai take-out place and negotiated the winding road to his foothills home and office. Then arranged the carefully orchestrated courses in front of the three flatscreens that spanned his desk, slipped out of his tight-laced shoes, unfolded David's sailboat printout, flattened it by tucking the top edge under his executive leather-trimmed blotter, and aimed the first forkful mouthwards. It was precisely at that moment that his phone began a vibrating sideways samba on the polished oak.

"David." Fragrant tendrils of steam eddied toward his flaring nostrils.

"You were right, Oz."

He checked his watch, almost dumping a tannish glop of *pra ram rong song* on the printout's azure sea and pure white hull, and considered David's schedule. "Aren't you flying back?" For safety's sake, he popped the forkload in. "And what was I right about this time?"

"About taking a break, about Vegas. It was exactly what I needed. And thanks for paying. Especially for paying."

"That's great," he said around the food. "Especially the paying part. Truly great." Though his mouth was full, the *thad mun pla* fishcakes looked lonely on their paper plate. He speared a two-inch disk and managed to wedge it in with the *pra ram,* masticating them together for maximum flavorosity. After briefly appreciating the intra-oral combination, he regained his focus. "But if you're in the air, you must be calling me on—"

"Air-to-ground. And not the old seat-back deal – they've got this new cell-phone booster thing. Pricey, and I had to buy it for a whole hour, but don't worry, I'm using it, catching up with my mom in Africa, and I figure we've got it covered."

"*We?*" Oz swallowed the bolus of food, getting it down but not before a gulping back-surge deposited a soggy red pepper particle deep behind his left nostril. When the tears and snorting had subsided, he asked, "When are you going to quit busting me?"

"Busting you?" David sounded almost innocent.

Oz blew his nose on a wad of paper napkins. "Never mind. But I'm taking the minutes out of your half."

"Half of nothing."

"It won't be nothing for long," Oz said. "You'll have plenty to pay me back with, for the call *and* the trip. Trust me on that."

Though expecting David's usual blather about trust and evil manipulations, he heard only silence.

OZ COULDN'T KNOW IT, but David's silence, while nearly filled, on his end, with the muted roar of turbojet engines, was also still echoing with those recently uttered words, 'Half of nothing'. By now, however, that echoed voice had mutated into Sheyoni's. Not her usual chirp, or even the hard-edged bark of last Saturday morning, but something considerably darker, the hurt and wounded voice of his Sheyoni-stricken conscience, repeating those three words over, and over, and over. Until, desperate, he decided to banish the memory by thinking, once more, of Paula…

Paula, radiant… Paula, self-assured… Paula, bouncing on top of him… Paula, who seemed to have laid claim to a fair portion of all the regions of his brain, cognitive and not.

Amazingly, it worked again.

BACK IN BOULDER, Oz waited through the long and quiet moment, working on another multi-flavored combination bite. But his gourmet meal-to-go was rapidly cooling, turning not very gourmet at all. After the tepid mass slid towards his gullet without further incident, he asked, "Still there?

"Sorry. Big weekend."

"What's her name?" Though David had been pummeling him with texts all weekend, they had been free of any hint of conference romance.

"Oz…"

"Okay, okay." Oz dumped the congealing Thai residue into its plastic bag, depositing that in his executive leather wastebasket.

"And don't worry – I snagged every business card I saw, just like you asked."

"Really." The idealist who wouldn't stoop to placing a phone book ad, now buccaneering through the crowded halls of commerce.

"Pretty much from everybody, or from everybody not obviously certifiable. Lots of free samples, and trial periods for the electronics and meters and magnets. If they offered, I said sure. Things should start arriving in a week or so."

"But you didn't have to sign anything."

David hesitated, then said, "Only for HorTech – for Biggs. At the end. I had to. Their samples were, um, harder to get."

"Biggs. You signed a contract with Biggs." Oz leaned back into the woven mesh nylon of his office chair, the burnished steel hinges reforming the taut cradle to his every move, and peered through the skylight over his desk. David's texts *had* mentioned HorTech, so he'd looked up Biggs, his company's site and a whole lot more, including the impressive covergirl who hawked the goods. Could she be the love interest, however hypothetical? Unlikely – not David's type at all.

It wasn't important. Biggs was what mattered, and Oz knew his type. Not so much the muscles, though he suspected they were evidence of how much Biggs liked jerking things around, but from the mirror each morning. An able dealer, stepping into the ring to fight for David's soul. Or at least David's segment – his potential segment, ever growing – of a very profitable market. David's soul, and the damage that could be done to it, was of no importance to Biggs. Though there were even times when its importance to Oz wavered, like that choking one a few moments ago.

"Hello?" David's voice came over the phone. "Did Oz have a big weekend, too?"

"No... unfortunately, I did not. But I wasn't prancing around signing contracts."

"I was *not* prancing."

"Whatever you say, big guy. I believe you. Scratch the prancing, or... whatever."

"You should, because... because I wasn't. Prancing. Or whatever." David sounded less than convinced. "Besides, Biggs said the papers were just a statement of mutual interest."

Oz listened as David read him the details, the limits and the bail-out clauses, and had to agree that it wasn't likely to come back around and bite them. Particularly as he and David had already hammered out the business plans for a little operation called 'David Black, MD'; David's name was, in fact, a corporation that Oz owned half of. Biggs's contract wouldn't be binding unless he had Oz's signature as well. And what Biggs didn't know was bound to prove useful.

In any case, David had apparently forgiven him, which was good on many levels. Once they'd hung up, Oz turned off the desk lamp and the monitors. Through the skylight, a scattering of pinpoint stars – and then, smoothly passing between them, the tiny wing lights of a jetliner. It could be David's, or some other group of wayfaring strangers, taking their chance against the dark and metaphoric unknown.

Metaphors. Each traveler a kind of poet, living in that hurtling aluminum metaphor, not knowing what would happen next. Whole mid-fuselage business sections full of everyday earthbound questions that, by their airborne context, became as tentative and metaphysical as anything in those hokey quantum books. Questions about contracts, no doubt, and profit and loss, plus a slew of less interesting moral issues. Or mortal ones, as in the wisdom of defying the combination of flesh-stripping velocity, near-vacuum, and thirty thousand feet of unhindered gravity, an issue that he found personally persuasive enough to keep him on the ground. All those questions were answerable only on those sojourners safe return to earth.

Even poetry comes back to the fundamentals, Down to solid ground, down to dirt. Which was his realm, a base of operations that had so far served him very well. Oz swung his legs off the desk, and, despite the disappointment of his dinner – a small tragedy that he would find the means to rectify from his well-stocked larder – considered himself a happy man.

8

BODY BY NANCY

- or -

Palpapeutic Hedonia

JUNIE LEVERED THE CARDBOARD BOX up onto the granite counter and looked hard at David, who hunched further over his cell phone, turning away.

The huge open space around them was quiet – she'd turned the fake breeze-and-birdcall thing off – so Junie could still hear him as he cupped his other hand around his mouth and asked, "Not for another *month*?" Pleaded, really. Since his return, Junie had been working next to him every day, progressing from Dr. Black to Please-call-me-David to a few blushing personal details (his, not hers) that first seemed like oversharing but turned out to be, well, okay. And while he had not been forthcoming about similar details from his trip to Vegas, she had a pretty good idea who he was talking to.

ONLY DAVID, however, could hear Paula say, "These products are incredibly regulated—"

"But a whole month—"

"—just the licensing alone," she continued, undeterred. "And you saw the registration forms I faxed... how many are there to complete? Thirteen per patient? The pharmaceutical company lawyers have to be careful, incredibly careful, that any hormone they sell us is used as intended, and only for patients that need it."

David looked at the phone, puzzled. "So we have to prove every patient has a physical problem? From not getting enough growth hormone?" He wasn't sure how he could do that – after adolescence, a deficiency wouldn't affect height, or any other clinical finding, at least anything major enough to document or measure.

"Not that," she said quickly. "Just proof that their blood levels are too low. You're drawing the levels, right?"

"Sure, but everybody's goes down with age."

"David. We've been over this. Of course the levels drop: that's why patients need it, why giving it makes a difference."

"But bumping up the blood level wouldn't necessarily im-prove—" He stopped himself: arguing was absolutely the last thing he wanted to do with Paula... Wanted to do, with Paula... "I'm sorry; you're right. Everything you showed me was absolutely great." ...Absolutely great, with Paula... "I mean, those research studies: the impact of the hormone injections were amazing." ...Amazing, with Paula... "And I'm – I'm completely ready to go."

"Hmmm." Her voice was warmer. "I bet you are."

David shifted on his chair and gave a painful grimace, praying Junie wouldn't notice.

"It's the paperwork," Paula said. "There's no way around it. It takes time, nearly four weeks before they'll ship. But look on the bright side: that's already given you two weeks to move into your fabulous office – Dr. Biggs loved the photos, by the way. Which leaves two weeks more to register your new patients before the first shipment arrives."

"Two weeks? That's better. I guess I can live with that." He swallowed hard and, out of the corner of his eye, saw Junie standing, arms crossed and waiting. A pause, then, "Plus an extra two weeks, the usual trial period, to start your registered patients on their injections."

"*Paula...*"

"I know, David – believe me, I know. Don't you think I want to see you? One more month, and I'll be there. Patients signed, patients started, and then a site visit. The way we always do it. No matter what I might want, or what I might *need*," she added, her voice lowered. "I have to be professional, don't I?"

"Oh... yes," David said, thinking of that first night, of Paula walking away, looking very professional indeed. Behind him, Junie sighed loudly, for some reason, and left. Once she'd gone, David pressed his cell phone to his ear, his eyes squeezed shut. "I'm just not sure... sure I can wait..."

The background noises of Paula's office increased – a door

closing, businesslike steps approaching – and she said, "Four weeks, then, as we agreed. You'll see, everything will be perfect. I'll call with the flight times and the date."

As David eased his cell closed and sighed a sadder sigh than Junie's, he wondered, not for the first time, what sort of leering fool he had become. The way his mind kept playing back their hotel moments, all those gleaming muscles, something he'd never really been into before. A wave of guilt: he was treating her like an *object*; not modern-thinking, pro-feminist, or right-minded at all. It hadn't been like that with Sheyoni. Her beauty had been something other men went nuts about – if anything, she'd seemed pissed that he hadn't joined the drooling crowd. With Paula, his big well-meaning brain got short-circuited. Basically, he couldn't help it.

FAR AWAY, a third and final sigh – another exasperated one, rather like Junie's, that echoed though her silent, empty office in Southern California.

Paula sat at her desk, hand on the receiver, and switched off the sound generator, the footsteps and ringing phones and background voices that proved useful at times like these. David was a sweet enough guy, and the sex had hit the spot, literally, the semi-mythical G and, when she'd rocked in her own special way, the supposedly even-more-mythical U and A spots. Not to mention the classic anatomic favorite, which she guessed you could call the C-spot. She let her mind drift for a moment, speculating on the rest of the coming alphabet; so many spots, so little time.

But still, that hunger in David's voice; ravenous, even more than she expected. A compliment, of course, and compliments could be useful, but she remained, if not skeptical, mildly surprised. Even this long after their first morning after, with the calm and detumescence that a solid stretch of post-contract-signing time and space provided to a boyfriend / client, David didn't seem to *get* it. Her body, for one thing. The fact that, like Biggs or almost anyone in their field, her body was an advertisement for the product. She knew how great she looked, at least from a distance: the shock of her hair, the artful tucks and implants, the whole shooting match. But the guy was a doctor, had to know the stories the skin's faint scars told. And then there was the effect of all those pecs and lats and glutei, revealed. Just her biceps, bulging Schwarzenegger guns that had driven more than one lover off. Particularly once the sweat, as it were, cooled. But not David, David the doctor, David who really ought to be acting a little smarter.

Unless...

Her eyes settled on HorTech's product list, pinned to the center of the office divider that kept Biggs, when he deigned to visit their actual workplace, from getting in her face. A single word leapt out: gynestenone, the very product she'd opened and held up for HorTech's 'Pheromones and Other Animal Attractions' presentation at the conference. The presentation she wouldn't let David attend, not wanting to spook him with the cheesier side of HorTech's product line, or to see her pose – leg back, hip out, a long-muscled arm poised gracefully aloft – like a glorified model while Biggs spun his spiel. The near-microscopic bottle's glass stopper had been loose, spilling a drop of amber fluid onto her palm. She'd rubbed her hands together, and then, curiosity piqued by its multi-hued scent, tried it out again the next morning.

Right before...

No...

It couldn't possibly have...

But still, if it did...

Bingo.

That first sample had landed on her desk the day before she'd left for the conference. She'd pegged it to become, at best, one of HorTech's minor earners. Just another pheromone; just another chemical that mimicked the scents that all mammals secrete from tiny skin glands to attract mates, win friends, and repel enemies. Unfortunately, none of the artificial products seemed to actually influence humans, no more than the natural ones from non-human mammals, like the near-infinite flavors of musk-laden perfume that had been sold over department store counters for over a century. You couldn't milk something from the come-hither glands of a musk-ox and expect it to attract an entirely different species. Especially our species, whose noses were hardly used for hunting any kind of game, fun or not.

Paula had read up on it, of course. Especially the Vomeronasal

Organ, a semi-mythical cluster of neurons between nostril and brain that pheromones were supposed to activate. In humans, though, it was atrophied, almost gone, a nearly-sealed door that required a hammer blow to gain admittance. Only a few studies showed signals getting through, the research Biggs's loved to tout at his presentations. Unfortunately, those studies usually involved very ripe t-shirts, worn for a week by male volunteers. When the *female* subjects were exposed to a small scrap for sniffage, they could pick the now-showered and presumably presentable male offenders out of the densest crowd, and the stinkier the t-shirt had been, the greater their mysterious attraction. Biggs, of course, played down the locker-room details.

But the new pheromone sample had been labeled *gyne*stenone – gyne being Greek for gals, as in gynecologists – in other words, a female smell to attract guys. The real money was in *andro*stenones – *andros* being Greek for guys – the fake chick-magnet scent their competitors filled the back pages of non-Greek men's magazines with. Paying through the nose for the smell of sweat. She'd yet to meet a woman who would cop to seriously liking *eau d'armpit*. Other than herself, of course. For her, the deep fruit tang was an aesthetic, work-out thing, and a smelly t-shirt was just fine. In any case, gynestenone was the mildest of the mild, a fine funk muted by jasmine, one of her favorites, with a hint of nutmeg and other, undeterminable spices.

The tiny bottle had arrived from a biopharmaceutical develop-ment lab in Columbia that she'd always figured was a cover for a far more lucrative product line. The accompanying letter (they really did not like e-mails) described some sort of spill between two adjacent vats, one fermenting your typical synthetic musk and the other in the final stages of refining a white powder that usually crossed the Texas border in the dead of night. The jungle-warped pages of hand-typed vellum, blanketed with poorly translated legalese, had gone to great lengths to assure HorTech that every aspect of the complex post-spill molecule could be sold, without fear of prosecution, on the open market.

There'd been something else, though... pulling open the file cabinet beside her, she shuffled through wads of similar papers – the Columbians really did not like emails – until she found it: a warning that the costly golden liquid could permanently saturate pigmented polycarbonate surfaces. In other words, dark plastic.

Paula's mind rolled back to her and David's very profitable morning: that second application, a bout of lifting, the treadmill, and then another kind of bout, once and twice and then again, every damp wrestle and flip perfusing the pheromone's aromatic oils into the whorls of her fingertips and her steel-weight callused palms, mingling them with all the salty drying layers of her sweet effortful sweat, a potent combination if there ever was one.

And after that, as they lay bruised and recovering, the cell phone call that bad boy had dared consider answering. She smiled, remembering how she'd brought him to heel, one hand over his face and the other over his open phone. Bought him to heel, and…

Could a residual trace of gynestenone have somehow 'imprinted' David's unthinking mammalian brain? And made a more literal imprint, a permanently scented stain on the coal-black plastic of his phone? So that every time he opened it – opened it and spoke to *her* – the tiniest molecular signal wafted upwards, was gently inhaled through his nostrils, gathered speed along whatever remained of his vomeronasal neural pathway and shot to the primitive regions hidden beneath David's over-civilized cerebral cortex? Straight to the real heart, the limbic brain-heart, the seat of all emotions and the seat of all desire – a blind and unreasoning desire that poor young David, it seemed, could barely control.

Hmm… Maybe. Or maybe not. Paula had been around long enough to know that there was almost always a likely story you could cook up, something to elegantly connect the facts you found most interesting and self-serving – the facts you wanted to connect. And that someone interested in a different product could come up with an equally persuasive alternate theory – a different likely story. It was true in the laboratory, she had heard, and it was definitely true in sales. But she also knew that, occasionally, it's your likely story that turns out to be true. And this particular story, likely or not, seemed to explain a lot.

One thing was clear: she had to come up with a different name for the compound. Gyn… Gynelure? No – still too legs-up-in-the-stirrups clinical… Guy-lure? No, too clunky… Something classic, even mythological… the lovely siren Lorelei, singing sailors to their doom? That was it… GuyLoreiLure!

And if it actually did work, even sometimes…

This could be good, Paula thought, very very good for sales. Not only in sales to lonely-hearted women, but in sales to *sales*women. Businesswomen like herself, who needed every asset to make a deal. It was a vast non-lonely-hearted market Biggs would never think to tap, not on his own. An idea she'd bring up with him, if their partnership talk went the way she wanted. And in the meantime, David might well be programmed, imprinted…

Hooked.

AFTER WEDGING a yard-wide box containing mixed paper supplies, patient gowns, clear plastic speculums, and a gross (in every sense) of disposable proctoscopes through the heavy teak door, Junie dropped it loudly on the floor, then bent over, recovering.

Once she parceled them out to the exam rooms on either side of the hall, they could start seeing patients. At least, as none of David's proposed alternative providers had been hired, his old family practice patients. Though they weren't getting that many calls from his poor and aging fans, which might have something to do with Ozvaldo Garcia's curious reluctance to send them the Clinic's new marketing flyers.

David's size-thirteen sneakers appeared at the periphery of her field of vision. "Wow. That was the biggest one. Why didn't you ask for help?"

She shook her head slowly, staring down as a drop of sweat fell from her temple to the precious pressed-wheatgrass flooring.

"Oh," he said, chagrined. "Before. When I was on the phone…"

"*Carrying* it was no problem." Junie peered up through a frieze of dangling braids. "It just took two of us to get it off the ground."

"Two?"

DAVID FOLLOWED JUNIE'S EYES back to the open door. Through it came a solid forty-something woman shouldering a box that was smaller but the heaviest of all, a wooden crate of medical books that had nearly crippled him when he'd bent to load it into the rear seat of

Junie's convertible. She crossed the room like a boat you wouldn't want to get in front of, slid the crate easily onto the granite counter, then turned, a handsome and not entirely unfamiliar package of Birkenstocks and dark-pressed jeans, an overhanging jewel-toned shirt, and short sun-streaked hair that fell boyishly over half an unlined brow.

"Nancy Ouvenstrasser," she said, standing tall. "I hear you're looking for a bodyworker."

"You didn't mention that down there," Junie said.

"A sister in need? I would have helped anyway." Her ice-blue eyes did not leave David's.

"Um... hello," he said, slowly. He *had* been looking for a masseuse, or thinking of it, but wanted to set things up for his former patients first. Still, Oz had been rushing him, and sent out that new-patient mailer... That was it: this Nancy character must know someone who got one and told her. Not surprising in Boulder, the motherland of massage.

Junie crossed her arms as the masseuse listed her experience and references and what she usually charged – a lot, though the clinic, she pointed out, would get half. It sounded to David like she did everything, which was great, as it meant they only needed to hire one person for the whole range of hands-on therapy. Saving money – Oz would like that. Then she started in on the equipment that the clinic, in her opinion, would have to purchase, the steel-reinforced deep-tissue platform, the drool-proof vinyl massage chair, and especially the Pilates torture racks.

Halfway through, David sat; Nancy put hands on hips and finished, still standing.

"A bodyworker, huh?" Junie said, "Can you bump out my old car?"

"She's not that kind—"

"I *know*," Junie said, but the masseuse was laughing, a sudden warmth that filled the room.

The clinic needed her, and needed that laugh as well. "I think we've got a deal," he said.

Nancy stepped close to shake his hand, then turned and pointed a close-trimmed fingernail at Junie. "You – joker. I've got a van full of my own stuff. Help me carry it?"

It wasn't actually a question; Nancy was already plowing toward the door. Junie made a face and followed.

DAVID SAT BEHIND the counter, made some calls and watched as they carried up Nancy's folding table, various pads and cushions, and a spare blond wood cabinet. Then came carton after carton of handmade candles and fragrant oils, far too many for the cabinet, and a tall set of shelves of the same hand-finished maple that looked suspiciously like a display rack.

"Excuse me," he said, cautiously. "Are you going to… sell all that?"

"All what?"

"In, you know… those boxes?"

She slowed to a stop but didn't let the burly shelves touch down. "You bet. My clients will need them, they'll be a bargain, and you'll still get half the profit."

"The *profit*? No, you've got the wrong idea – we're not in it for…"

By then she was continuing along the carpet, shaking her head. Junie, amused, followed her with a final box of folded sheets, royal purple, forest green, and lavender blue. She looked back as Nancy piloted the shelf unit into the vacant room she had apparently assigned herself. The one with the largest window, placed high enough not to reveal anything below the shoulders and opening onto an unbroken span of southern sky.

Once, David thought, he wouldn't have let a vitamin bottle in his office; once he wouldn't take free samples from drug company salespeople; once he'd carefully scoured each free patient education pamphlet to make sure its corporate sponsor wasn't using subtext to push products on his patients. Welcome to the business of medicine.

From the room came sounds of setting up, of boxes being emptied and a massage table unfolding, four legs faintly clicking into place. Followed by the snap of a door latch closing, firmly. David peered along the empty hall and listened, but heard only silence.

And then, from behind him, an almost inaudible, *"David."*

"Jesus!" He spun in his chair to face… Sheyoni. Who looked as tense and bloodless as their rare phone calls since his return from Vegas.

"She's already here?" Sheyoni whispered, and rose up on her tiptoes to look anxiously over him.

"Who?"

"Shush!" Moving to one side, she dropped her chin to the counter and peered around him at the door-lined hallway. *"Nancy – I saw her van, outside."*

"Okay," David whispered back, *"But the doors are closed – why do we have talk this way?"*

"Oh." She straightened, shook herself slightly, and said, "Obviously, David, I don't want her to know I'm here."

"Because…"

"Because…" Sheyoni glared at him. "Why do I always have to have a reason? I just wanted to get her off my… to help her out. Don't make everything so complicated. Nancy needs a job, you mentioned the clinic needed a massage person, what could be easier?"

"Well, sure. In fact… wait a second. She's not *living* in that van, is she?"

"No, David, she's not living in the van. She's got a lovely place in the foothills, and a job, or at least she had a job, at the Womyn's Bookstore—"

"The Women's Bookstore." Oh – that fit.

"The Wo*myn's* Bookstore," she said. "No *men* in it at all. Do you have a problem with that?"

"Um… sorry?"

Sheyoni glared again. "Anyway, she invited me up for, you know, a massage – she's really fantastic, legendary – and…"

A long, low moan came down the hallway, emanating from under the closed door.

"I already hired her." David found himself whispering again.

Another moan; they looked back along the hallway. David frowned, tilting his head slightly, as Sheyoni bit her lower lip. The creaking of a massage table, a long and silent moment, followed by the sound of movement in the room. And then, as the reflections on the small frosted panes on the door shook slightly, the snap of the latch, opening.

"Cover me!" Sheyoni hissed, and took off across the reception

area, bent low to ground. David watched her, then stood and turned, his broad shoulders blocking her exit through the office's teak door.

Junie, carrying her shoes and moving as if walking was a new and unfamiliar thing, made her way up front.

NANCY ROLLED HER SHOULDERS, sore but as yet unbowed, in the narrow space between her massage table and the window. She could see the Flatirons marching to the south, great red-gray slabs that baked and wavered in the midday sun. Two black specks circled above them, the ever-present crows. Even this far away, across a city filled with noise of its own making, and through a window closed against the heat, she could hear them crying, Welcome home.

But crows could be tricksters. Old Chief Niwot had probably thought so, Chief Niwot who'd leveled his famously benign-sounding curse: Once you gaze upon the beauty of the Flatirons, you will never be happy anywhere else.

In her case, the curse had worked. Dragged her back to bury her last parent – back from wandering the West, back to the lovely foothills cabin of her not-so-lovely childhood, and now back, finally, to the work she loved.

Supposedly, the long-dead Indian had intended that the swelling ranks of Caucasians would poison the fair valley they'd stolen from his people. And he could still turn out to be right, despite the desperately green efforts to keep its growth reined in by a ring of public parkland and open space.

The Boulder transplants within that greenbelt tried to ignore the curse part, to give his words a positive spin. They claimed it was the weather or the scenery that kept them, but in their hearts they knew the truth, knew they could no longer feel comfortable in the outer world. So here they came and here they stayed, imagining they'd made a Lifestyle Choice.

It was a common human failing, one that she still, if only sometimes, fell prey to. The belief that happiness depends on where you live. She'd read the magazine articles, The Ten Best Places To Metrourban Homestead, and Where To Recreate In Your Post-Millennial Years. But geography was not destiny, not happiness, not health. While there were certainly some things, like Chernobyl-level pollution or crazy stressful screaming crowds, that were worth avoiding, the real virtue had to lay in *connection*, connection with your people, friends and family, in a place you'd grown up in, a place that just plain fit.

As far as living somewhere to avoid 'stress'… The pollution down in town wasn't too bad, and she didn't hear that much outright screaming, and the stress was less, she guessed, than the *sturm* and clang of some bustling East Coast midtown. But if this berg was low stress, you couldn't tell it from the knotty muscles of her private clients. She knew from experience – she knew it in her hands – that they carried their stress with them, and as they evaded one set of geographic travails, they found another to replace it. New windmills to tilt against, splintering their lances against the already-tilting Flatirons.

That said, a nice massage always helped.

A nice massage. She used to believe that giving them would save her. It certainly had forced her to straighten out her act, cleansing her with a subtle energy – her clients' stress, transformed? – that flowed cool as quicksilver up her arms. But in the end, it was a job, even if the medium was the massage. The comfort of comforting was still there, but it wasn't her salvation. No more than the bad habits and broken hearts that had milestoned her careening life. No more than her parents, who had been anything but comfortable, a matched pair of bitter, hard-drinking academics who'd fled Manhattan for a Western university town. Where they'd raised their own bitter, hard-drinking, fallen-academic daughter and found themselves stuck for life – dazzled by natural beauty, bereft of connection, and suffering from a long-dead Chief's curse.

And now that both were gone, what was here for her, other than the calling crows? Precious little comfort or connection, but maybe she'd returned to a place that, this time around, just plain fit. Maybe geography *was* destiny, as long as – sorry, Chief – it bought you home.

Nancy absently wiped almond oil from her hands. Comfort or not, she loved the work. And Junie? For a moment there, she'd wondered. But there hadn't been that *connection*.

That said, a nice massage always helped.

"WOW." It was the first word out of Junie's mouth since Nancy left.

David, suddenly embarrassed, looked down and pretended to page through the work references the masseuse had dropped off on her way out.

A minute passed, and then another "Wow." Apparently forgetting she'd just said it.

"So..." David straightened the papers, tapping them on the counter until the edges were roughly aligned. "...is she, um, good?"

"She's... wonderful. I'm not into all this Boulder stuff – not personally, I mean. But what that girl can do with her hands..."

"You don't have to—"

"They're... magic."

With that, Junie rose and floated off, trailing aerial slipstreams of floral-scented almond oil, to start unpacking boxes. David wondered exactly what had gone on in there, and then chastised himself, as he often did, for being so predictable. Sex and massage. He'd seen it marketed that way – everyone had – but not in his sweet town. David scowled, grabbed the yellow pages from under the counter, and went through the local listings.

Nope. Not even an in-hotel service.

The problem lay in the middle ground between sex and therapy: pleasure. It sounded nice to call it comfort, but pleasure, he thought, was exactly what it was. There was something in the national character, some remnant of Puritanism, that frowned on buying pleasure on the open market. No, that wasn't true: you could eat and drink what you pleased, and buy stuff that was supposed to make you feel good, lots and lots and lots of stuff – the American pleasure-seeking engine that kept the economy rolling. But anything hands-on, physical, or skin-to-skin hinted at our forefathers' and foremothers' shame. Especially not in a doctor's office, where 'hands-on' had to also mean 'no-fun' or someone was bound to call a lawyer. Though labeling the clinic 'holistic' would probably get them around that one.

What was so bad about feeling good, anyway?

Maybe it was the passive part, of having something *done* to you, divorced from your own effort or work. But lots of 'body' therapies were active, like Pilates, a workout so hard it hurt. And there were some in which you lay passive and it hurt even more – deep-tissue techniques like Rolfing, infamous for its pain. He'd tried a free Rolfing session and even that had proved a kind of pleasure, a masochistic pain-pleasure, a mega-cluster of those brief moments when the masseuse really went for it and dug in. Pleasure welded to pain, and to the childlike faith that it would soon be over. Nancy had said she practiced all those hard and painful techniques – though not, apparently, today.

The thing was, basic massage pulled it all together. Hands-on and passively received, like medical care, and with a substantial amount of real estate exposed, like medical care, but also with a good-sized dose of pure physical good feeling. And, in that hands-on, passive, near-naked pleasure, way more *caring* than any other therapy. No wonder it seemed like sex. As an added plus, it worked, and not only for the obvious sports-type injuries, but also, in the studies he'd seen, for pain and anxiety, even nausea and fatigue.

Was pleasure a way to live longer? If not, living better seemed enough. As a completely different kind of health care provider – the no-fun kind – he was, well, jealous.

Picking up Nancy's resume, David gazed around the office, thinking how it was all beginning to gel. The Forever Clinic... he actually liked Oz's trademarked label. A place to get well, and more.

Over in a sun-bathed corner, Junie's graceful form bent, un-packing. She seemed to have struck quite the instant friendship with Nancy. A good massage, he guessed, could do that. Not that there was anything wrong with those kind of... friendships. Nothing at all.

He didn't mind, of course. In fact, he was sure he felt relieved.

9

DOCTOR DOCTOR?

- or -

Genderologic Fibulation

"HIS NAME'S QUINN," David said, fiddling with the layout of the appointment screen. The software Junie had found was amazing, though he couldn't imagine how much it had set Oz back.

"Like Dr. Quinn, the show?" Junie spun her seat to face him.

"Frontier Medicine Woman?" He looked over. "I guess."

"You know it, then." Her eyebrows ascended; below that long straight nose, the trace of a smile. "Must have been a favorite."

"I, um, might have registered a fraction of an episode or two. While studying – the set was always on. In the background; it helped me focus."

"Uh-huh."

"It *was* medical, you know. And historic, here in Colorado – what's wrong with that?" More than a decade ago, a biochem textbook facedown on his lap, yellow highlighter forgotten, memorizing every detail of the fictional Quinn's well-intentioned, old-time practice on the tube. Taking a chance, he turned Junie's unyielding gaze back on her.

Surprisingly, she looked away. "Nothing," she said, and studied her own screen – a proposed work schedule for the new providers, which basically meant an open field of blanks. "Not one thing wrong with it at all."

Ah-ha. "You brought it up." Hard-core inner-Orleans Junie, and a Hallmark actress in a buckskin dress.

Junie's face was lit by a faint but undeniable blush.

"What's your excuse?" David added.

"I watched it," she said, sitting straighter, "with my younger sisters."

A conveniently unassailable defense. David frowned slightly but Junie didn't notice. Luckily for him, she'd returned to musing on the doctor-applicant. "Quinn. What's his first name?"

"Er… Oz said it was just… Quinn. Just one name."

"Huh. Like Prince? And he had trouble holding on to that. So… Quinn Nothing, or Nothing Quinn?" She looked up. "Dr. Quinn Quinn?… Quinn Q. Quinn?" Her smile had returned. "They all sound fake."

"No faker than the—" David stopped himself.

"No faker than the *Doctor,* doctor?"

"Just watch for him, okay?" It wasn't fair; she always won. He knew he had a problem – a problem he'd thought he kept hidden – with the free use of the title that had taken him eight hard years to achieve. He didn't mind the psychologists, who'd trained as long as he had, or even the chiropractors, who put in at least a few graduate years. But some of the others, Doctorates of aura-this and aroma-that, were popped out in less time than a Thanksgiving tofu-turkey. He hoped there was more than that to the applicant due in a few minutes, who was either a naturopath or a homeopath; Oz wasn't sure.

In fact, after giving David the applicant's single name, Oz had refused to discuss him at all, only saying, 'You decide'.

Junie walked to the front window and David returned to his pile of resumes, the blanks he had to fill, the small crowd yet to be hired. Six doors along the hallway; Nancy had claimed the farthest, and he'd need two for his office and exam room, which left three. One – maybe – for today's candidate, one for counseling and meditation, and one the nutritionist and exercise coach could split. Upstairs were a score of yoga mats, the ropes and pulleys and sliding platform of the Pilates frame, even an EKG-monitored treadmill, all waiting to be used.

Mind/Body/Spirit, every base covered. He'd tried that out on Oz, who'd said he was missing home plate: Wallet. As in the profits from the supplements the naturopath or homeopath of whatever alternopath that came on board could recommend. Nancy's display rack would soon escape her office to be joined by many others, in a tastefully expensive pseudo-pharmacological display along the pale beech-paneled wall of the front room. A row of shaman power-objects (Oz had found a discount supplier) would reside above them, bright happy explosions of feathers and beads with a hidden inner knot of dried talons and thorns that Oz had been told – and asked David not to pass on to the clients – had been boiled in the blood-laced saliva of virgin jungle leopards, however the shamans obtained or determined that.

There was also a deluxe collection of fuzzy framed flower portraits, hand-colored with the powdered petals of the flowers themselves, already on display beside the teak door. Every book or bottle, everything hung or mounted – on that long wall, or in any public or semi-private nook of the many-crannied clinic – was for sale. David wouldn't be doing any shopping, but the flowers seemed the safest. They smelled nice, too.

Then there were the cool electronic toys from David's Anti-Senescence Society associates (his ASS associates, Junie called them), due any day now. He joked about the strange devices, the magnetic-field generator and all the rest, but figured they couldn't hurt. Not if he kept a medical weather eye on the patients, just to make sure no honest-to-illness medical problems were misdiagnosed or missed.

An anxious thirty-something male with chest pain, for instance, might actually *be* suffering from a magneto-energy pathway problem, but that was a diagnosis, bogus or not, that would only be applied after he'd been stethoscoped, phlebotomized, and stress-tested to the cardiologist-standard max. If those results were less than reassuring, David would shoot him over to the hospital ER. And if his heart looked fine? Then the Clinic could use the device's full-color electro-gaussmeter to persuade him of the need for a tune-up – maybe a nonrefundable ten-visit package of mediation sessions, exercise, and diet, knowing Oz. A walletectomy, to be sure, but also the help the patient needed to manage his own anxiety, the problem that had actually brought him in. Some might say the device's techno-showy middle step was unnecessary; was it any different, though, than an equally showy (and equally unnecessary) electron-beam heart scan at some hospital-authorized Imaging Center?

At least their patient would leave a healthier, if slightly poorer, man. And the magnetic field generator, with its lights and dials, hair standing on end and watches running backwards, *was* sort of fun.

Injecting growth hormone was edgier: it would be the biggest of the money-makers, the most medically aggressive and least-accepted anti-aging intervention. Still, just the possibility... a magic key to slow, to even stop, the physiologic processes of decline. The studies Paula had given him were certainly persuasive. Overall, the clinic's future looked to be a sunny one. Profit and benefit, doing well by doing good. Or so he hoped.

David still had his doubts: the cringe-worthy devices, the overpriced supplements, and especially the injections. But he'd largely signed off to Oz, doing what he was told so the Clinic, with its enormous expenses, would be able to stay afloat.

Despite Junie's complaints, the patient schedule wasn't entirely empty – he could see that a few old patients had already set up appointments. An economically viable clinic would make sure that they, at least, got what they needed. Their needs gave him license, he decided, to ignore the odd ethical qualm. To try something new, get creative, experiment a little.

"SOMEONE'S headed for the entrance on Broadway," Junie said.

"Does he look professional? Say 'yes', please."

"Well... *she* does, I guess."

"Oh. Of course."

She glanced over. Poor David – too nice to admit it, but getting that drowning look. Like her brother at every meal, surrounded by his mother and five sisters. Junie ran on estrogen, could swim through it all day, but having another guy around, some non-distaff staff, wouldn't hurt.

The elevator was rising; David took off for his consultation room as Junie slipped behind the counter and looked busy.

There was no knock, no hesitation, just heavy footfalls that passed from the echoing wooden parapet and through the Forever Clinic door. Which bonked against the rubber doorstop, ringing the meditation chimes, rattling the various spooky power objects and causing those stupid flower pictures to emit a thin purple mist of pollen. Dr. Quinn didn't notice, only stood inside the threshold, holding her purse and surveying the domain.

Junie took a quick inventory as she watched their potential whatever-doctor stride over. The sheer bulk, the wide-based walk, the thigh-thick calves, and especially her flaming hair, big southern five-alarm hair above a sapphire dress that clung to round shoulders and rounder breasts and tapered to a drum-tight girdled gut. Not obese, but... enormous. As Quinn drew closer, Junie also registered an alarming skin condition: hundreds of tiny bumps erupting beneath a layer of beige makeup that had been trowelled from the base of her neck to the bags beneath a set of uncommonly sharp green eyes.

"Dr. Quinn?" Junie didn't rise from the receptionist chair. She felt safer where she was.

"You bet," she said, leaning forward, massive elbows on the granite. "Got the 'dentist time' appointment... Tooth-hurty, get it? On the dot." An unmistakable Texas accent, but strained, oddly musical and high.

An office door creaked behind her, and the applicant looked over her head. Junie heard David gasp, then cover it with a cough, a dramatic paroxysm that lasted far longer than necessary. As it wound down, she gazed blandly at Dr. Quinn, knowing if she turned, she'd be a goner.

Finally, David asked, "Why don't you come back?"

Quinn shrugged and walked around the counter, the thick carpet of the hallway doing little to muffle the thunder of her linebacker steps. Wafting, as she passed, the smell of a hard-ridden saddle, of talcum power, and an eye-watering dose of essence of magnolia, liberally applied.

DAVID KEPT HIS EYES on the heavy crème-colored pages she'd handed him. "Dr. Quinn."

"Please," she said, in a rather froggy trill. "No need for formality. Call me Quinn, just plain Quinn."

"Of course." He flipped through the brief curricula vitae. "I, ah, can't help noticing a gap here, after your undergrad degree. Kind of a long one."

She drummed her fingers on the uncreased leather of her purse.

"Twenty years?" David added. "Not to be too inquisitive, but..."

"Just the usual," she fluted, finally. "A marriage, three lovely children, then off they went to college." Leaning forward, she fumbled her purse open, pulled out a well-worn folded wallet, and from that a well-worn picture. "Here."

"It's not necessary—"

"Please." A dewy look, with a glint of steel beneath. "I insist."

He took the photo, a former rectangle trimmed down to a square, as though a family member or two had been excised. After a perfunctorily glance at the three husky boys who remained, he said, "Beautiful."

"Yes, beautiful – a beautiful life. But not... not any *longer*." Placing a hand to her ample chest, she turned away. "My husband left a week after we dropped the youngest off at Texas State." A loud, wet sniff.

Oh no. David held out a box of tissues and she grabbed a handful. "I'm fine. Truly, I'm fine." She honked into the wad, then sucked in her gut and tucked it in the waistband of her skirt. "Better than fine. An opportunity, the opportunity to become what I always dreamed, to be..." She turned back. "Dare I say it? Dare I wish it? From Mrs. Quinn to Dr. Quinn – a *healer.*"

"A healer." Did she know, he wondered, how big Boulder's local chapter was? There had to be some other reason why Oz had sent this person over.

"Yes," she said, that steel unsheathed. "A *Healer.*"

"Oh. Very good." He looked down and read on. "So... you went to homeopathy school... and naturopathy as well. Why both?" Maybe that was what had hooked Oz – two degrees for one.

"They're quite complimentary – in fact, they're often taught together." Suddenly breezy, she swung sideways on her seat and hooked a beefy arm over the back of the chair. "One uses *tiny* amounts of chemicals, and the other, *natural* substances – or at least substances derived from nature: vitamins and supplements." With a flourish, she pinched her thumb and forefinger nearly together and peeked at David through the narrow space between. "Tiny interventions, with natural products: the perfect combo."

"But homeopathic meds – I mean, all those serial dilutions, one-hundredth of one-hundredth of one-hundredth – the doses must be absolutely microscopic, almost pure water. Do you end up giving anything at all?"

"Lovely question," she said, then fished out the wad, blew her nose again, and lobbed it into the wastebasket beside his desk. "The odds of getting a single molecule of medication can be vanishingly small. We like to say the water holds the 'resonant memory' of the molecules…" She stopped, eyebrows raised. "Seems unlikely, doesn't it?"

David nodded, carefully.

"I expect that a medical doctor would want to understand how that could possibly work. The same way you'd want to know how an antibiotic, or any medication, works." Her eyes were clear, family drama forgotten. "To understand, to know the world, to embrace it and be embraced in return. A kind of belief system, an almost religious experience and the basis, ultimately, of research."

Religion? Belief? "I thought research was all facts, no belief."

"Nope. Sorry." She shrugged. "Facts are what you find, belief tells you where to look. Your view of the world; what you expect to see – your hypothesis."

"But isn't research supposed to test that hypothesis?"

"Absolutely. And if a hypothesis fails the test, you'd expect a good scientist would be able to cook up a brand new hypothesis. Trial and error, getting closer and closer to that imaginary ideal, objective truth. Would that it were so, Dr. Black. Would that it were so."

She shifted her hydrant-shaped body – the chair creaking mightily – and sadly shook her head. "Unfortunately, the old hypotheses just get recycled, with a problematic corner or two rounded out. Maybe it's because the lab-coats are so specialized, aiming their microscopes at the narrowest segment of the big broad world that's out there. Within that narrow view, they can only search for *confirmation*, and why test something you're sure won't fit? No wonder they're not big on homeopathy's story. Like those multiple dilutions you were having trouble with, or the Law of Similars."

She stopped and looked at David. "You know, giving something that mimics a symptom in order to treat it, like a dose of cayenne pepper to cancel out a fever."

David nodded dumbly, still not getting it, and wondered if he ever would.

"But sometimes they slip up and actually *look* at a homeopathic remedy… and sometimes they find it works. For no good medical reason at all."

David had read one of the studies she was talking about, a test of a diluted-to-nonexistence homeopathic diarrhea treatment in Africa that had, remarkably, saved children's lives. But he'd also seen some in which homeopathic remedies were no more effective than a sugar-pill placebo. The thing was, they worked as well as the placebos, and placebos could work very well – the power of *patients'* belief. And homeopathic remedies, as far as David knew, were not potent enough to harm. The same old holistic story: unproven benefit, unlikely harm. At least some people felt well, got well, and stayed well. For no good medical reason at all. Was that good enough?

"It doesn't matter," David said, deciding. "What matters is what works."

"There you go." Quinn looked as pleased as David's old Bio-chem professor, when he'd finally mastered the awful Szent-Györgyi-Kreb's cycle.

We use what works, David thought. We might try to understand *why*, try to understand the mechanism, to dig down deep into the unknown earth, closer to the truth – the real, *non*-placebo truth. A pathway to the next discovery, a pathway through the dark. But she was right, it all begins with our beliefs, the bright linking stories that we weave. How many of those scientific stories, at the end of the day – or the century – will turn out to have been true? Perhaps belief drives everything: scientists' belief in the story they follow; patients' belief that the medicine they take will do the trick.

Quinn was still going. David put an elbow on his desk and planted the side his face in his palm, amazed he'd submitted to a full-on lecture in the middle of an interview he was supposed to be running. A lecture that, as Quinn moved blithely on to the wonders of Naturopathy, looked like it would last awhile.

THE VAST SPACE in front of Junie's reception desk was empty, the building dead quiet. Just the faint sound of Broadway's traffic making it over the roof and in through the skylight far above… and the murmurs coming down the hall from David's office.

Dr. Quinn – what a remarkably curious woman, Junie thought.

And what a remarkably curious woman I am. And how totally unlikely that anyone would wander in while I left my work area and took a few small steps, say, along the carpet-padded hall to my boss's door.

AS QUINN'S HISTORY of Naturopathy wound down, she crossed her legs, resting one ankle on a knee, her dress riding high. David turned his glance away, parking it on the photograph of her three children, still in his hand.

Apparently, the antique German discipline remained the most cruelly unexplored by science. Modern medicine might have gradually come around, Quinn said, to Naturopathy's emphasis on diet and exercise, but as to the rest of the *Medicatrix Naturae*–

"I'm sorry – what?"

"Nature's Healing Power, of course." Quinn's look instantly removed David's favored-student status. "Herbs, doctor. Fabulous, natural herbs. And I don't mean the herb sold by your neighbor down the street, elevating as it might be. I'm talking herbal supplements, which naturopaths virtually invented. Not only to fight illness, but for health."

David frowned into his palm. He should have known that. All those charmingly-named folk medicine potions, used for thousands of years. "Like valerian for sleep? Chamomile for an upset stomach?"

"I thought you were all about longevity," Quinn said. "Phosphtidylcholine for cell membranes, and querticin—"

"Those are herbs?"

"More… extractions, but yes. And don't forget ginko and vinkca for brain function, and nettles for immunity, and grape seeds and alpha lipoic acid and carnosine, another excellent antioxidant."

"Everything seems to be an antioxidant – didn't oxygen used to be a good thing?"

"Oxygen, of course: we can't live without it. But not the free radicals it forms in every tissue. Consider all your statin drugs, lowering cholesterol and saving lives. Antioxidants. So why not *natural* antioxidants, doctor? Red rice yeast, obviously, as it *is* a statin, but also all the others, a whole pantheon of harmless products – harmless, in my hands – from which to pick and choose."

Quinn had a point; in fact, a whole bunch of them. She was a natural teacher, one who seemed to have an amazingly solid grasp on at least two, if not all, of holistic medicine's arcane and branching fields. How, David asked himself, could she have possibly developed all that in a few post-grad years?

And there was something about her increasingly hoarse enthusiasm, something vaguely familiar...

He glanced down at the photograph again. As familiar as the face of the husky teenage boy beaming beside his older brothers. Two vintage cars in the leafy shadows behind them, that one child's face lit up for the camera, for his brief appearance, much as his mother's was right now.

His mother...

Lecturing...

And the Family Medicine Academy meeting, year before last.

Especially the keynote speaker, the famous Dr. McIntyre, flying in from the McIntyre Center in San Antonio, storming the stage for his ninety minutes and then gone – out the back, before David could snag him with everything he wanted to ask. A caftan-clad, Rabelaisian figure with an explosion of black hair and biker beard, winning over the conservative audience with the force of his personality, the legitimacy of his MD, and especially their envy for the empire the physician health guru had built.

The year before the fall, before the disgrace and, just before the indictments and – had the headlines been a month ago? Two? – his timely disappearance.

As David raised his eyes from the picture to the furry shadows he'd been too shy to examine before, he was not surprised to find the sagging, telltale seams of a seasoned pair of jockey shorts. Raising them further, he was unable to keep a slight smile from his face, as his illustrious fugitive's presentation slowed to a halt.

"What?" A pause, and, again, "What?"

"The Academy meeting, in Denver, two years ago. *Holism In Family Medicine.* I was there."

"That's fabulous, dear, but... Oh, fuck." The voice dropped an octave; McIntyre reached up, tugged on a thick hank of scarlet hair, and asked, "Do you mind?"

"Do I mind...?"

"The wig." He didn't wait for an answer, but pulled the flaming mass off and tossed it on top of his purse, revealing a close-cut scalp. "How can they stand them? They're *hot*."

He rubbed his face, scowled at the silly-putty color of the pancake makeup now covering his palms, then drilled David with a penetrating stare, bright below savagely plucked brows. "What now? Turn me in? Do your civic duty? Uphold the lofty standards of our profession?"

My profession, David thought. My profession could stand a change or two. And McIntyre, the old McIntyre, had offered them. Two years before, David had heard his broad view of medical care and been set on fire, burning with ideas. Until he'd returned to his small office, to Sheyoni's needs and the certain knowledge that he couldn't take that kind of risk.

So McIntyre had lost his license. And as for the outstanding charges… well. It *had* been consensual, as he recalled, and they all had been adults. And this was Boulder, not Texas. To have someone of McIntyre's talent here, to learn from his intellect and grasp, be it homeopathy, naturopathy, allopathy…

"Actually," David began, slowly, "How do you feel right now? Distressed?"

McIntyre snorted. "I like to run foundations, not wear them."

"Seriously."

"Okay, I'll admit it. It's been tough."

"And you're telling me that here, in my office."

"Yes…"

"Almost as if you were…"

"A patient?"

"Whose past would be have to be treated confidentially. And whose condition might benefit from…"

"A job. Perfect." McIntyre knotted his fingers together, each topped by a shovel-shaped pink nail. "I love it. An independent contactor – no liability to you, just an opportunity, a *therapeutic* opportunity. I like the way you're thinking, doctor."

Did David like the way David was thinking? The second thoughts came rushing in.

"Ethically," he said, "I'd have to turn in any patient who could seriously harm someone. And if that patient is a doctor, someone I happen to work alongside, I also would have to inform the medical society. If, for instance, there was any hint of…" He let it hang.

"Impropriety? Please. Everybody – the newspapers, the authorities – knew they weren't my patients."

"No, they were your *students*."

"A weekend program, Physical Counseling, at a seminary." And then, with a smirk that David didn't particularly like, "Well named, huh?"

"Physical or seminary?"

McIntyre deflated. "It would have been fine… a little sensitivity training, a little fun. They explore their sexuality, I happen to be in the line of fire, what's the harm?"

David wanted to stop him there, but McIntyre kept going.

"Until half the sanctimonious little twits – the ones who had *issues*, obviously – went to confession."

"Weren't they training to be priests?"

"That's it: you've hit it on the nail, exactly. The whole thing was the church, deciding to make an example, take the heat off. Protect its own pederasts."

David let that one go, and asked, "Wasn't there something about nuns as well? Novitiates?"

"Sweethearts, every one. And every single one of age – I made sure first, the little darlings. The D.A. gave me a pass on them – hey, it *was* Texas."

I KNEW IT, Junie thought. Knew it, knew it, knew it. Of *course* he was a man, and of course he was a sleaze. Maybe a little fun around the edges, but definitely a sleaze. Like Tony Curtis, dressing up in a flapper dress for that Billy Wilder movie. Except bigger. And uglier – as ugly as a white woman could get. Or man. Whatever.

They were quieter now, voices lowered as if plotting something. Junie looked back up the hallway to the counter, the reception area beyond. Still no one. Then put hands on knees and bent forward, face near the frosted glass, left ear close to the crack of the door.

Was David going to hire Quinn anyway? Unbelievable. But then, David *was* working for Oz. Oz who held the purse strings, Oz who'd sent this clown over to be hired. In fact, she was working for Oz, too.

Damn.

Junie bent even closer, reaching for every word.

ON THE OTHER SIDE of the frosted panes, David sat in silence and pretended to mull McIntyre's situation over, a man of the world, while actually recovering. In the distance, the faint sound of a ringing phone that for some reason Junie didn't get. His applicant looked around the office, as comfortable, despite the girdle, as in every other moment of his life. Then studied a Latinate diploma on the wall, and said, "Impressive."

"Not really." David blushed. "I was lucky to get in."

"Don't be modest – credentials are everything."

"Speaking of which…" He held up the resume that McIntyre had given him, still turned to the list of his/her graduate degrees.

"Those? Honorary, after I gave a semester's worth of talks for free. But the vellum and ink are real, and I've been doing this long enough to teach both the programs."

Quinn looked at David, then added, "What'd you think? I took one of those online courses?" A single laugh, a short deep punch at the air. "My site had them; we called them Hamburger Helpers, as in stretching out the bottom line. A few hours online, and your docs can start referring patients to themselves – 'I sent her to my consultant on the other side of the exam table' – and tack on any kind of fee they want. The only away they can get around the insurance companies, poor bastards. Make some money, have some fun, but it's not like we expected them to develop any skill. As opposed to this place," he added, gesturing towards the door, the clinic behind. "You're actually trying to get people who are *good*."

As David agreed, he casually eased an open medical journal over the printout for the Acupuncture course he'd been considering. "Like…"

"Me? Absolutely. And that colored girl you got – she's sharp, I can tell."

Shocked, David blurted, "Junie?"

THE DOOR BANGED OPEN and Junie almost fell into the room, stumbling as she cut around his visitor – it wasn't easy, as Quinn took up half the space – to stop at David's desk. "You called for your *girl*, Massa?"

David stared. "You were listening?"

"Listening? I could hear this gasbag from my desk, but wanted to get the details right. For his hearing."

Dr. McIntyre gazed at her, benignly. "Disciplinary, or sentencing?"

Junie stood, fists closed and seething.

A smile. "It seemed the only polite way to invite you in. My mother taught me that yanking doors open on sneaks was rude – not that you didn't deserve it, but rude."

"That was on purpose? Give me a break."

He spread his hands. "You know I'm open-minded. Just ask your doctor here."

David started to mumble something conciliatory; Junie silenced him with a glare, then snapped back to say, "Thanks. I heard. All of it." After which she crossed her arms, tapping her foot. "And if I ever, ever hear the C-word coming out of—"

"Scout's honor." McIntyre held up two fingers.

"Don't. Interrupt. Me. And *don't* mention Boy Scouts."

"Hey, they taught me everything I know." When there was no response, he dropped the salute, regretfully. "All right."

Junie sat back against the low cabinet behind her, still tapping her foot, considering. "Is he – she, whatever – really on top of all that stuff?"

David looked at McIntyre. "He wrote the book. Um, books."

"As if there was any rational... I must be nuts," she muttered. Then, more clearly, "You are absolutely the worst cross-dresser I've ever seen."

"It isn't easy."

"And you don't make it look that way. Take that wig – please. Take it home and leave it."

"Really?" McIntyre rubbed his head, smearing makeup over his shaved scalp.

"Call the bald thing chemo. For something... something female.

You're a doctor: you decide. With chemo you get to wear a scarf."
She couldn't believe herself, but what the hell. "If you're gonna lie, lie
big."

McIntyre looked up, impressed.

Junie fixed him with a pointing finger. "That's the attitude I want
to see from you. Keep it." She heard herself and thought, Attitude?
She must be channeling her grandmother. "And that rash on your
face? The answer's electrolysis, pal."

"But—"

"It's not like you're going to grow a beard."

His eyes widened, and she could see she'd stuck a nerve.

"You want the life, you got to commit." *Grand-maman* would be
proud.

David watched, amazed, as McIntyre sat obediently, looking
like he was taking notes for his next book. "What about the voice?"

She scrunched her mouth sideways, thinking. "You can come
down a little. Big women push their voices up to be more feminine,
just like little guys force theirs down, but you're all natural and
homeopathic and beyond that, so be the kind of girl you are."

He cleared his throat. "Thanks."

"Don't mention it." She got up, still wondering if she should take
it all back, call the police, whatever. David looked at her – she could
tell he had wrestled with the same thought himself. Kind of a relief.
Kind of. She shook her head and exited the room.

"WHO *IS* SHE?"

"I'm not sure I know."

"Well, tell me when you find out." McIntyre pulled himself
together, started to pull the raccoon-sized wig on, held it front of
him, frowned, and stuffed it in his oversized purse. Then got up and
leaned over David's desk, right hand out, pendulous breasts swinging
like the water balloons they probably were. "Do we have a deal?"

"Sure," David said, exhausted. "Why not."

"Why not, indeed – embrace the future."

Which was definitely from the last book, David thought, at least
the last one he'd read. "What's it to be?" He rose and took his hand.
"Just Quinn?"

"Let's keep it simple. And no contract – a handshake deal. See you Monday?"

David nodded and he left.

DOOR CLOSED, David took a moment for himself. A moment like the solo-practice moments he used to have, when a patient didn't show, or when Sheyoni was off on one of her guru days. A blessed moment without, for instance, McIntyre – oops, Quinn. Or Junie. Or Nancy, as of yesterday. Or Oz. Or even Paula, he couldn't forget Paula, Paula who he'd never say no to, but still, like all of them, even Junie, well, looming. Just... big.

Big... big... Oh no – another one: Dr. Biggs. How big would he turn out to be? If only there was just one soul he was a little smarter than. Or more forceful, whatever. Sheyoni, maybe. But she was gone. And even Sheyoni possessed a certain cunning that had – on more than one occasion – easily skunked him.

The thing was, he'd never felt quite so threatened. Or maybe it was... challenged. That was a good thing, wasn't it? Kicked into gear, and now he couldn't stop. Even if he wanted to, no one would let him. He was central to their plans.

WITH THEIR OUTRAGEOUS NEW HIRE GONE, Junie reconsidered once again. While it wasn't her nature to call the authorities, she could just walk out, walk out and not come back. She was tempted, but... no. Because the job was... interesting. Like a physics problem, with lots of brand new particles she could name. Like the rarely observed Quinnoid quark, in many ways similar to the Ozipositron, but strangely unaffected by the normal physical laws of sexual repulsion. Or the Shestrayino, drifting any way it wanted, though always in the opposite direction of the speeding Palmalevaloid, and easily knocked out of orbit by the hyperdense mass of any passing Nancilon. All of them loosely pulled together by a classic Davidial weak-force attraction, forming a malleable aggregation that itself hung in the vast field of patient matter – very little of it dark matter, unfortunately – that composed the hypothetical construct of Boulder's spiritual universe.

Hmmm.

Or, it was a job that paid more than she needed, had flexible part-time hours, and didn't involve anything that wasn't deniable, should those selfsame authorities intervene. Either way, it worked. There *was* David, though. And worrying about him getting squashed by all those collapsing particles, packed down tight enough to form the kind of mini-super-nova that could permanently toast a professional career. From physics to astronomy, Junie thought – science was so much fun.

At least David had gotten himself a guy to work with. Sort of. Now all he needed – and she was including herself here – was someone *easy*.

10

THE REAL THING, SORT OF

- or -

Free-floating Blissiety

NOT TOO FAR AWAY, Howie Krishna floated on his thoughts, legs crossed in a classic Lotus posture, a bright-tipped cone of sandalwood incense still burning – if slowly, amazingly slowly – in a ceremonial iron bowl before him. His rooftop apartment was otherwise empty, a spare, ascetic environment that he had not stepped from since the summer solstice.

Through his fine-tuned meditative state came a slow wave of actual cognition, the first fully-formed thought his carefully emptied mind had allowed to bubble up for a full lunar month. One by one, a small handful of words materialized behind his closed eyelids:

...time...

...to...

...go...

...to...

...work?

That querulous mentation floated on the still surface of his awareness, until he allowed it to pop as neatly as a fart in a Tibetan cedar hot tub, causing a secondary ripple to spread over the larger membrane of his perfectly focused mindfulness, the iridescent-but-invisible boundary that had isolated, protected and, in general, shrink-wrapped his existence for the last 29.53 days. The concentric waves reflected back on themselves in a beautiful and oddly harmonic dissonance, a vibration that dissolved every trace of that immaterial amniotic sac, traveling fully around his consciousness to ultimately answer:

Yes!

Howie opened his eyes, stretched, bent back, and back, and back, then placed his palms on the ancient carpet beneath him. After smoothly swinging his still-crossed legs up into an inverted handstand, he held the pose for an unmeasured but appropriate number of breaths, then unwound his calves and, pushing off from coiled fingertips, flipped neatly to his feet. After dealing with the expected colonic consequence of prolonged no-fiber fasting – a condition easily managed by a few little-known yogic postures, a bit of strained Vedic chanting, and a liter of soapy water hanging from the bathroom wall – he felt rested, fit, and, in fact, rather sprightly.

Yes... to teach, again!

Soon he was showered, comprehensively shaved from the curling lower margin of his luxuriant beard to the tiny reddish hairs that adorned the backside of his toes, self-anointed with essential oils, and dressed in a laundered set of robes that had been delivered, as usual and by one of the many prior arrangements that preceded his sabbaticals, to his doorstep last night.

Parting a fragile shoji screen, Howie stepped out on the sheer edge of the rooftop's redwood deck, extended his arms to each side and, with his toes curling a good fifty feet above an unpopulated alley, greeted the last of the sunset with a lion-like but not unmusical roar. Then he spun to cross his raked sand garden – stepping so carefully that the bare pads of his feet left no footprints – and descended, happy to be once more in the charming roil and play of the outer world, to purchase the local paper for that day's list of employment opportunities. He was sure, quite sure, that he would find something very near.

OZ SAT AND LISTENED to his speakerphone the next morning, watching the second hand precess around the face of his watch with agonizing slowness. After a full sixty seconds, which was really all he had time for on this or any other day, it was time to break in. He needed something simple, something to arrest David's soliloquy. A brief ponder and he had it: "It's a *good* thing."

"A good thing?" David asked, his tone aggrieved, or as aggrieved as he could muster after a long and sleepless night. "McIntyre goes through half a co-ed seminary in one weekend and you call it 'a good thing'? Then jumps bail, visits you in drag, and you pass him on to me? I can't believe I went ahead and hired him."

David switched on his own speakerphone so he could rub his tight-sprung shoulders, which seemed to be up around his ears. A glass of wine had helped late last evening, but his doubts had flooded back in the small and pre-dawn hours that followed. That alcohol-rebound thing again, and why it made a terrible sleeping potion.

"You did well," Oz said, soothingly. "I didn't know *all* those details of the good doctor's background, but still, think of it: for hardly more than slave wages, we've got ourselves a famous holistic physician."

"But no one knows who Quinn – I mean, McIntyre – really is."

"They will."

"When? Tell me you're not planning to blow his cover." David was nailed by a vision of Oz vs. Quinn, a bespoke-tailored Godzilla taking on a red-wigged Mothra in a battle of the titans, stomping Boulder to ruins as he ran for cover. His shoulders cranked up another notch.

"Everything comes out sooner or later." Depending on many things, Oz thought sweetly – like contract negotiations. "And when it does, it's free publicity… a cross-dressing doctor, pursued by The Man. Yet another victim of society's sexual persecution."

"Come on – *victim*?"

"Sure. Don't presume. Anyway, free publicity's like free advertising. And you're the kind-hearted doc who took pity on her."

"Or him, I guess. Depending on how serious he – or she? – is. About, you know, what he – or she – wants to be."

"Of course." Oz drummed his fingers on the polished wood of his desk, thinking. Then said, with an uncharacteristic lack of certainty, "The, ah, business and publicity angles aside, are you absolutely sure that she is… that Dr. Quinn is… biologically… really a…"

"A guy? Well, yeah… what did *you* think?"

"Me? I don't want to assume, you know. And I was reminded…" Oz hesitated again, for the topic was a troubling one – the *most* troubling one, and about the only one that could penetrate his steel-clad heart. "I was reminded of Beatriz."

"Beatriz," David said. Actually, Oz was right. Now that he

thought about it, it was uncanny. Not the wig or jockey shorts, and certainly less razor burn, but pretty much the rest. "I guess they're sort of—"

"Sisters," Oz interrupted. "I mean *siblings* – siblings under the skin." And what skin she'd had... and so much of it, acres and acres of downy haired skin... and the charm of that faint mustache, at least before the cruel world made her so self-conscious she'd borrowed his electric razor to attack it.

David closed his eyes, and also saw Beatriz, or at least his memory of Beatriz; trying, as always, to see her from Oz's perspective. It was tough, but then it always had been, even those twelve years – was it twelve years already? – ago. Oz and Beatriz had been a nearly-matched pair: Oz's lost love exactly the same height as her college boyfriend, more than meeting his girth, the two easily crowding David out of the tiny freshman dorm room that he and Oz had been assigned to. The love-struck couple had generated a hypercaloric happiness that David had never – before or since – seen in his friend. Until, of course, the first stirrings of Beatriz's unfortunate obsession, the shameful pseudo-sport that drove a wedge between her and her family and even, though Oz fought it, her otherwise true-blue lover. And then – a dark night, a hoop-shaped bag, the ear-imploding vacuum of her sudden departure, and she had disappeared from all their lives.

David was searching for something to say when Oz, recovering, beat him to it. "You can work with, ah, *him*, right?"

"Well..."

"Good," Oz said bruskly. "And don't worry – I'll keep an eye on our good Dr. Quinn."

The call ended soon after. David looked at the phone while, across town, Oz looked out his panoramic windows – traveling, if reluctantly, back down the years.

A THOUSAND MILES DUE WEST and two degrees of latitude south, a soft but steady breeze bonged stainless-steel halyards against a carbon-fiber mast. Beneath it lay a dark-haired and still relatively young woman, pleasantly round of face and built for strength and inertia rather than speed, though she did possess a dancer's grace that served her when the seas were running high. Beatriz Hanacanahuoli-palipalulu, formerly Beatriz Rodriguez, stared up at the sky above her, which was pretty much the same as the bird's-egg blue hanging over Boulder, only decorated with scudding clouds, and fresh with the sea's salt scent rather than sun-blasted asphalt and the intermittent emissions of hybrid vehicles.

Although not generally one for contemplation, especially when a breeze was calling her back to the South Pacific, today her heart and mind were tangled in the unlikely path that had brought her to this anchorage on Cat Harbor, an indention in the ocean side of Catalina Island, twenty-five miles off Los Angeles' teeming shore.

Her story, at the start, had been a familiar one, the classic and often tragic path of the hula hoop professional. Her gyrational fascination had, like that of so many other young women, begun in her high school years, when, rejected by a featherweight cheerleading squad, she took solace in more privately whirling endeavors. Unlike those amateurs who soon abandoned the trance-inducing rhythms of their hoops for a lifetime of conformity and yo-yo dieting, it had led – after a brief romantic diversion during her single year of college – to a tearful dawn flight to Hawaii, in an anonymous escape designed to leave her past, her uncomprehending boyfriend and her really quite astonished parents far behind her.

At first, her natural talent served her well – that and her natural circumference, which few other fields of dance or sport appreciated. After a brief and ceramically disastrous interlude as a hula-skating waitress at a fast-poi restaurant on the seedy side of Honolulu's railroad tracks, she climbed the artistic ranks from a rotationally distracting magician's assistant, through various semi-clothed burlesque and novelty acts, to finally attain a featured billing, just below the hoopless grass-skirt artists, at the largest of the torch-lit Waikiki hotel reviews.

Her ascension was followed by a storybook marriage to the reigning hula king of the time, but his supernumerary decades and unspeakable island perversities ensured that her stay at those rarified, flashing-paparazzi heights was short, an exit hastened by a personal overenthusiasm for pineapple wine which, although it had seemed a psychological necessity at the time, she now took full responsibility for.

But that was history, safely and happily behind her. She stretched and rolled sideways in the intermittent sunlight, her arm a solid pillow against the gritty painted fiberglass deck as she looked – through nearly-closed lids and a weave of long black eyelashes – at the reaching waters of the open Pacific, and sighed a heavy sigh. She was still safely insulated from her history, but happiness, for some reason, had been proving more elusive.

The obvious explanation was a lifestyle issue: a smuggling lifestyle. To be specific, and she had carved a very specific smuggling niche, the quasi-legal intoxicants sold in health food stores and head shops across the land. Lately it meant moving bales of kava kava from Vanuatu to Vancouver, where the mildly addictive sedative had been banned because of a hepatitis scare, with a stop along the way for a few burlap bags of the short-term hallucinogen *Saliva Divinorum* from a backwater port on the Gulf of California. But with each passing year, things had been getting uglier. Just last month there'd been a Tazer pointed at her, which was definitely impolite and also dangerous, at least for the pointer, who'd ended up dog-paddling as underwater sparks from the evil little device lit the icy black around him. There was big money in psychoactive herbs, and people, even Canadian people, were increasingly willing to do bad things to get it. Any good sailor knew when to bail.

A week, then, to rest and recharge batteries, solar and other-wise, while waiting for the last of her supplies to be trucked over the island from Avalon. Nothing going back this time, nothing other than herself, another long solo trip. Except for a dog, a new puppy snoozing in the cabin, whose understandable but liquid accidents were, in fact, why she was up on deck, taking a break from a stink she could almost taste. They said having a pet made you live longer: it sure got you out in the open air.

A friend had recommended it, telling her she'd been too long alone. Which was just plain stupid: this was the life she'd chosen, free of encumbrances, free of the past, free of pain. The little dog whined, and after a whiff of something alarmingly ripe wafted through the hatch, she groaned and rolled to her feet. It was a sweet little creature, but a boatload of trouble so far. She didn't need anything or anybody – a life unconnected was the pirate life for her. It had taken a decade, but she'd worked hard to trim away every weakness, every string that bound her to her past disasters. Each time she'd repainted a new and entirely random name on her ship's stern (a surprisingly easy way to avoid the forces of law and order and taxation), she'd added another layer of a completely new identity, to create a now totally unrecognizable persona to those who'd once known her, a totally clean slate to sail forward with.

Padding around to the rear deck of the Ozma – formerly the Oscarina, the Ozprey and the Om Zweet Om – Beatriz held her nose and ventured below.

"I AM HERE."

"Jesus!" Junie hadn't heard the elevator, the door, the little brass bell David had brought over from his old office, or a single footstep crossing the pressed-wheatgrass planks of the waiting area.

"No, but I thank you for your misapprehension. Howie Krishna."

She looked him up and down – the spotless robe, the narrow freckled face wreathed in springs of rusty hair, the pure white cotton turban wrapped around his head. And then there was the incongruous East Indian rhythm to the pale young man's words.

"I'm sorry," she said, although she really wasn't. "The sign, downstairs? You can't solicit here."

"Ah," he said, "Donations. For my cult. Of course." A small smile. "It is not Jesus, but it also is not *Hari* – Hari Hari, Krishna Krishna? It is, in fact, *Howie*." He placed a translucent vellum business card on the polished counter between them, engraved gold letters that read, Howie Elijah Wineman Krishna. "I have arrived to satisfy your needs."

Junie stared at him, thinking, this job just gets better and better.

Howie looked back calmly – thinking, intra-species communication was *so* difficult – and reached deep into the voluminous folds of his garment. As he did, Junie casually placed a hand over the very sharp pair of scissors she kept beside her, removing it only after he pulled out a copy of yesterday's paper, folded to the clinic's classified ad.

"Oh," she said, and pointed one elegant, dark finger at the couch. "You can wait over there."

He bowed – one must not antagonize the natives – and did as he was told.

AT LAST, DAVID THOUGHT, as he looked across his desk at the white-robed applicant, someone who listened more than talked. And did this guy *listen* – listened to David review both the Yoga and the meditation-coach positions, listened to David read out the interesting parts of Krishna's impressive resume, and listened to David's almost involuntarily frank description of the previous practice's failings, his divorce, and the aspirations and financing of the Forever Clinic. More than that, once David had slowed to a complete stop, they both continued to sit comfortably, listening to the silence in the room, from which emerged the sound of distant voices, the intermittent gurgle of insulation-wrapped plumbing, the shush and flow of moving air, and even, David could swear, the sound of electricity humming through the wires.

David was impressed: applicants were rarely so relaxed. Totally unlike Quinn. In the sandalwood-scented quiet, he glanced again at his prospective employee's qualifications. Krishna easily had the experience to take either of the available positions. Given his clear-eyed concentration, perhaps he could do both – once again, Oz would appreciate the two-fer.

Krishna, who Junie was already calling Howie, sat with the suggestion of a smile reposing on his face.

David found himself breathing more slowly, cranked-up shoulders dropping for the first time since he'd called Oz this morning. Still, he *did* have an interview to get through. He needed, for instance, to find out how Krishna had spent those frequent month-long intervals between the illustrious positions the applicant had held at what appeared to be every yoga center, meditation program, and ashram in this yoga/medi/ashram-thick town.

David looked up from the resume to find his applicant looking back. One of Krishna's copper eyebrows lifted a fraction of an inch, and David found himself thinking, what did it matter? Quinn's supposed resume had had that twenty-year gap, and he'd decided to ignore that. The eyebrow lowered and David felt, well, better.

But then there was his last name, which David doubted he'd

been born with. Not like Quinn's understandable evasion, but a sixties-style stunt that reminded him of Sheyoni, née Jessica. She'd changed hers on a whim, during her solo trip to India, returning with a brand new handle and a nasty flare of herpes – just a recurrence, she'd informed him, of a long-dormant infection she'd been too embarrassed to mention before.

Krishna's Buddha-like smile flattened slightly, and David didn't feel... quite as comfortable. But then he thought, that was Sheyoni, and Sheyoni could be, well, whimsical. Actually, inconstant – in changing her name, that is. It was obvious that Krishna was far more evolved, and certainly there were good reasons, cultural and religious and philosophical reasons, for someone so evolved to adopt a more spiritually appropriate name.

The flattening resolved, and David felt... well, even better than before. And he should feel good, for this applicant was ideal – ideal in his quietude, his pure reception, almost as if he could hear, in that quiet receiving silence, the very echoes of David's most private...

Whoa. Whoa, whoa, whoa. Mind reading? Not possible. Even the idea gave David an entirely un-meditative chill. Carefully keeping any apprehension from his face, he slowly, casually, rotated his chair around to his diploma-covered wall. Howie, seen in one diploma's glass reflection, hadn't moved a millimeter.

David decided, foolish as the whole thing was, on a kind of test. A few truly nasty thoughts – see if any got a rise. David, while basically kind, was no stranger to evil ruminations and could easily summon up a few.

Start with pure, unadulterated *cheapness*... Krishna might be able to fill both the yoga and the meditation-coach positions, but they added up to a full-time spot. If he was hired to do both, the Clinic would have to offer a full package of Oz's worst nightmare, *benefits*. David's oldest and most controlling friend might not be so happy with this 'two-fer' after all.

David snuck a look. Nothing.

Okay, he thought, try personal. Like the turban – what kind of stoner dreadknot might be parked in there? And those *robes*? David recalled flying as a child, when every linoleum-floored airport concourse seemed the territory of the real fake-Krishnas, pallorous and singing, begging in exotically patterned bedsheets and ringing their bells. Their robes, at least, were colorful; Krishna's nubby white cotton looked like the kind of pseudo-holy rags you'd see in some fundamentalist Armagedistan, with a Russian-built assaultomatic rifle – a *Karyshnikov*, or was that the ballet dancer? – slung underneath. Not that his new job applicant was scary, but he was kind of... spooky.

David peeked again, and saw only inner peace.

He found himself, however, on a surprisingly enjoyable small-minded roll – what about adding a nice fat dose of Western-world, Euro-centric skepticism? Meditation, for instance. All those different, varied *types*: eyes closed, eyes open, meaningless mantras, special kinds of breathing, Om-ing, sitting, walking, even praying... how could each and every variation accomplish the same thing? And what did any of them really accomplish, anyway? The research David had seen was... well, there was no better word for it – the research was simply *underwhelming*. A few proper academic studies, but mostly tiny little ones from far-off places, biased to suit the claims of the cult that paid the bills.

And Yoga? He didn't know where to start. There'd been plenty of articles that crossed his desk over the last five years, but nothing substantial enough to remember now. And how could anyone fill both positions, anyway? Who had the simple mental and physical *strength* to pull off that kind of intense concentration, pointless or not, for a full eight hours each day?

During this, he studied Howie's expression in the frame, and saw no reaction at all. Just my own crazy paranoia, David decided, as he brought his chair back around to face him. My own paranoia, of course.

He'd barely come to rest when Krishna said, "Of course."

David stared at him, mouth suddenly dry.

"Of course," Howie repeated, "there is an overlap between the disciplines, and the practice of each one serves the other, building the endurance, the competency... building, quite simply, the dual practitioner's strength."

"*Strength*?" David almost squeaked.

"You seem surprised. But you did ask."

"I did?"

"In your description of the two open positions. Implicitly – if I would consider taking them. And I did."

"You did?"

"Consider it. For the past few minutes, doctor. As we sat here. I would be pleased to accept both."

"That's... good," David said, cautiously.

"Yoga is the most physical of meditations, but should blend quite nicely with any other form over, say, an eight-hour day?"

"Eight hours?"

"Did you not mention that both would be half-time? And I imagine I would be an independent contractor, so..."

"Don't tell me," David said, "No benefits?"

"Ah, the employer's nightmare: *benefits*. We peoples must run our businesses, mustn't we? And profits never, one might say, come *cheap*." Howie Krishna's smile deepened. "Please rest assured, Dr. Black. Benefits are not at all an issue."

David nodded, speechless.

"Which leaves only the question of which *type*, which technique of meditation." Krishna's eyebrows went up, and stayed up until David found himself saying: "I guess they all... accomplish the same thing?"

"I could not have put it better," Krishna replied. "A certain deepening, a certain focus. Different students seem to be drawn to different techniques, and often quite successfully. As I am sure you know, however, the research is... What is the word? Under... under..."

Oh no. "*Underwhelming*?"

"Oh yes, indeed." Krishna cocked an ear in David's direction, and waited.

"All those little studies," David said, starting slow, almost compelled to fill the gap. "Most without control groups... and rarely randomized. But... well, it costs millions of dollars to run a decent-sized study, and who's going to pay for research that can't sell a product? The various cults – I mean, the various, um, committed groups – are usually the only ones that care enough to try."

Krishna's eyes held his. After the briefest hesitation, David added, "Though there does seem to be a trend. The strongest results are exactly in the areas, the critical areas, you'd expect – stress and anxiety. Less so with fibromyalgia and blood pressure and heart disease, but those findings are suggestive as well." David stopped, mildly puzzled at his recall of the individual studies, as if the pages were spread in front of him. Not to mention how that recall had put so many of his doubts to rest.

"My personal favorite, Doctor, was the one with the 'Happiness Measure'. Up quite a bit, as I remember. Health is, after all…"

"…more than the lack of illness?" It was an old line, but a line that David didn't mind being reminded of, even if he'd ended up saying it himself. "People do seem to feel better in every study I see – I mean, that I've seen. Maybe feeling good is enough."

"Just enough?"

"More than enough – to recommend something as benign as meditation."

Krishna nodded. "But what of yoga, you ask."

"I asked that, too?" Except for his bright eyes, Krishna seemed to be blurring around the edges.

"No, no, no, Dr. Black. Merely a figure of speech. One hardly knows where to begin with such a vast literature. Most of those studies are also quite small, as you noted, but many are from the finest Indian Medical Centers."

"The finest *Indian* Medical—?"

"Then you've read them?" Krishna's head began the slight, inquiring, not-yes-and-not-no wobble that Sheyoni had maddeningly displayed, in response to very question and at every opportunity, on her herpetic return from the subcontinent.

David began to shake his head, then recalled, with the same strange clarity, the details of every obscure article about Yoga he might once have thumbed though, even Quinn's offhand but incisive comments when he'd stormed the medical society meeting two years ago. David's headshake began to turn into a nod, but stopped halfway and ended up matching Krishna's wobble.

"I guess… I guess I have," David said. "The back pain findings were impressive – in fact, all the musculoskeletal treatments – and stress reduction, naturally, because Yoga is a kind of meditation, after all. And respiratory problems like asthma, which makes sense, given the focus on deep breathing, and—"

His listener held up a freckled palm. "Delightful. We are in complete agreement." The palm dropped, and Krishna sat quietly once more. Or should it be 'Mr. Krishna'? David wondered. Why not 'Dr. Krishna'? David could see he'd been petty about the 'Dr.' thing with Quinn, who'd turned out to have an M.D., if currently a compromised one. And wasn't there a Yo.D. in Krishna's resume somewhere? It didn't matter, he thought, with a sudden warmth: it was definitely going to be 'Howie'. David looked to the door, the squares of frosted glass, the dust motes in the thin rectangle of hallway light between the Berber wool carpet and the oiled blond wood. All of it so calming, so very calming. And to think that, only a moment or two before, he'd been worried about something as silly as 'mind reading' – or, almost laughably, 'mind control'.

"I have the sense, David – oh, excuse me. Your culture, so pervasive, sometimes I forget... But perhaps, being here, a full participant, as it were... would it be appropriate, that is, would you mind terribly if I followed your charming Western custom, and called you 'David'?"

David watched Howie, who looked an awful lot like the Jewish kids from his Denver neighborhood, and shook his head, slowly.

"I am honored. Deeply honored. How very gracious. It appears that I have read you – that is, the collegial relationship that your lovely clinic fosters – correctly."

David tried to nod, but once again found his head wobbling in a way he was sure he would not be able to replicate later.

"As I was saying, I have the sense that the way we think is quite similar. That, perhaps, if one of us – just one of us – was sufficiently receptive to the small clues of expression that any human displays, and if the other's display of intention and emotion was sufficiently transparent, he might almost anticipate the other's thoughts."

That was it – that had to be the explanation. But was he that transparent? He'd have to ask Oz later. Or maybe Paula.

"In fact," Howie continued, "I imagine we would find ourselves able to communicate instantly, were we to meet, say, as strangers in a strange land. In a distant airport, perhaps, or on the dusty streets of the most dangerously primitive – fundamental, as one might put it – and violent foreign state. However 'weird' we might initially appear to each other."

Robes, David thought. And *Karyshnikovs*, sort of. But definitely weirdness. "I don't know what to say."

"No," Howie said. "If I am correct, however, there is no need." He stood gracefully, interlaced his fingers over a nonexistent gut, and waited for David to have the last word.

Which, after a moment, David did, sending him down the hall to Junie, to fill out the necessary forms. Then closed the door and leant back against it. Not tired, as he felt more rested than he had in months. Just not any less confused.

11

COUNTING CALORIES

- or -

Hypocaloric Dropsy

A BROAD QUARTER-MOON of home fries framed one side of the plate, while four locally-processed and lovingly cooked sausages stretched around the other. In the middle, further bracketed by smiling melon slices and a varicolored field of berries, towered a column of English muffin, home-cured ham, drooling farm-fresh eggs, and a thick, suspended puddle of Béarnaise, topped by a quasi-religious cross of two asparagi, draped just so.

And all of it for me, Sheyoni thought. Oh my. David had never ever let her eat this way at home – more precisely, he'd never cooked like this for her, or woke her up with something this fantastic on a Sunday, much less a weekday, no matter how she'd hinted at her modest daily culinary desires. No crisp white linen tablecloth, no hefty silverplate knives and forks, no steaming French-pressed coffee in porcelain, no just-squeezed juice in crystal, nothing.

The waitstaff was seating one the morning's first customers at the small table to her left, but Sheyoni didn't look over. She was entirely consumed by the fabulousness in front of her, a gift that, consumption-wise, she fully intended to repay.

Then, from that table, a peevish voice, interrupting the waitress before she could fully describe the same extra-special special over which Sheyoni's fork was currently poised. It was the same as every weekday's special, Sheyoni knew, but still. Another businessman on his rushing way to the airport, another harried day, another dollar. Though dollars, she had to admit, could be consumed with as much enjoyment as the elaborate breakfast that so far remained untouched. And that voice was, in fact, familiar.

"No, no, no… just oatmeal and skim milk, okay? That's all my doctor lets me have."

My doctor? The voice was *very* familiar.

"Toast," he ordered, "but no butter. And tea – wait, it's got to be decaf. Do you have that? No? Then let it steep a minute, drain it, and add more water. Weak, I know, but it washes out half the caffeine. Caffeine," he said again, sounding plaintive. "Another thing I'm not supposed to have."

Still not looking – making a game of it – Sheyoni listened, working hard. Not quite there… not quite… Giving up, she peeked to her immediate left. And saw that last patient from the office; her last patient, *ever*. Gilmore, the hemp guy! To be specific, the world-wide market-leading Wall-Street-traded hemp guy who'd seemed to *like* her!

Dan Gilmore? Or Don? She wasn't sure, but suddenly her breakfast didn't seem to matter. She turned and looked openly, waiting for him to notice. But he already had, staring directly at… her food.

DON CATALOGUED EACH ITEM on her plate, circling inward, ending with those Béarnaise-covered eggs. As he stared, it came to him that someone, a female someone, was sitting just behind them. Surreptitiously, from under the camouflage of luxuriantly wiry brows, he raised his eyes to also register her sunshine-yellow sweater – not hemp, but entirely forgivable, considering the astounding symmetry beneath. Those rounded hills, a blushing plain, and then the faint, excited pulse at the base of a flawless ivory neck. He had barely made it to her strawberry lips and cornflower-blue eyes when, he couldn't help it, his gaze sank back down over each wonderful but now neglected topographic feature, back to the greatest wonder of all, back to the Béarnaise.

After a moment, she coughed delicately, and said, "Has David got you on a diet?"

Don forced himself to look up, and asked, "David?" Then saw her – or remembered her – in a starched white nurse's uniform, and blurted, "David!"

"Dr. Black. My ex."

"Your... your *ex*? But that means..." Suddenly, her breakfast didn't seem to matter. She extended her fair hand and he took it, lightly, her fingers warm in his, her skin soft, as soft as velvet, as rose petals, as the finest pumice-peached citric-acid-washed mock-chamois hemp...

Her skin – oh, no: Intrapustular Fidelopenia. Glancing down again, not at the Béarnaise this time, but at the sweater and points beneath. What dermatologic terrors might be lurking there, waiting to erupt?

"It's all natural," she said, with a suppressed but triumphant smile.

"I'm sorry... what?"

She gestured at her plate. "All natural, and all good for you."

"All of it?" At first merely making conversation, trying not to think about... about... The plate swam back into focus, a welcome distraction, salt and sugar-sweet and soothing fat, fat, fat. Salivary glands geysered as Don asked, "Even the sausages?"

"Especially the sausages."

She picked up the longest between two perfect fingertips, snipped the end off with her teeth, then offered it to him.

He hesitated, closed his eyes and bit, gratitude illuminating his face. Then opened them and looked back to the Béarnaise.

"That too?" he asked, voice trembling.

"Oh, yes." She raised an oozing forkful and held it, poised.

His mouth dropped open; the journey was short, cool silver-plate tines resting briefly on his tongue before sliding out.

"Umph..." His eyes had closed again. "Fank you."

"You're felcome," she said, and gently tucked his napkin in the collar of his shirt.

TWENTY-FOUR FEET ABOVE JUNIE'S HEAD, the first sunbeam of the day, at least the first that made it through dawn's East County shelf of cloud, bounced off the Clinic's glass roof to illuminate her work area. With a frown, she adjusted her monitor screen and took another slug of the black chicory sludge she called coffee. Tolerating no interference, there to do a morning's work.

Morning being from six to eight, a lovely time to work, once you'd had enough caffeine that drooping eyes and errant yawns were no longer an issue. And work? Work was all the things she'd been too busy for. That is, anything that did not involve the expanding cast of characters David kept hiring. The very crew – the very odd crew – that almighty Oz expected her to ride herd on. Two precious hours, one already spent, another to go before David's arrival. When she could excuse herself, still early enough to spend the rest of an entire 'day off' at the university. To wallow in the joy of holding her nervous undergraduates' hands during their physics labs, ghost-writing a grant or two, fine-tuning her own data, and generally performing the showy acts of hard intellectual labor that kept her academic overlords happy and her tuition grant intact.

But for now, time to herself.

Until, of course, the door cracked open. A squirrel-eyed head popped through and surveyed the room, followed by another, just above. On spotting her, both immediately withdrew. Conferring voices, and then the door swung wide to reveal twin wisps, barely spanning the entrance as they stood shoulder-to-shoulder, side-by-side. One female, the other male; she guessed but wasn't sure.

They clumped over in organic cotton shirts and shorts and cork-soled sandals, to place four sets of spatulated tree-frog fingertips on the counter. The rest? Pencil arms and knobby elbows, cheeks drawn enough to count every molar, sallow blue-veined skin, and matching Prince Valiant haircuts, pale as straw.

"And you are…?" Patients, obviously. Or survivors, though she hadn't heard of any recently rescued expeditions.

"Thomas and Adeline Thinna," they said together.

"Thinna." Really. "Mr. and Mrs.?"

The marginally taller one – Mr. Thinna? – said, "Dr. and Dr." Then added, "For the job… er, the position you need to fill." He straightened wire-hanger shoulders. "The exercise physiologist."

"And the registered dietician," his wife chirped.

Junie looked at the wall clock. "It's only seven."

"That's what he said – Dr. Black. 'Come in early'."

"*Early* is eight-thirty." Junie opened the scheduling window on her monitor, and saw the entry David punched in late yesterday. "Sorry. Early, in this case, is eight."

"Excellent – we haven't had breakfast." He held up a flat blue-and-white container.

"Help yourself. In fact, I've got a few *beignets*..." Two pillowy domes on a grease-stained paper bag, powdered sugar snowdrifts spilling off. Their eyes grew wide; shaking their heads, they shuffled backwards to the sofa, where they barely indented a single red leather cushion. Carefully unsealing the plastic lid, each took out a small square bowl, filled it with tannish piles of various grain-like substances, and added a few measured ounces of a translucent white fluid that looked alarmingly like watered-down skim milk. After a brief whispered squabble over the process of division, they greedily emptied their shallow vessels, plastic spoons clacking against the plastic corners.

Junie tried not to watch but couldn't help it. Which may have explained the newspaper when they finished – a single section unfolded and held up like a screen, Mr./Dr. Thinna's left hand on one side and Mrs./Dr. Thinna's right hand on the other, methodically reading every page before turning, with a pointed snap and rustle, to the next. Diet and exercise, Junie thought. Please let them be the last.

SHEYONI'S PLATE was clean, the porcelain between the streaks of Béarnaise shining, while Don's bowl of oatmeal sat untouched and cold. She wiped a dab of yellow from her chin, and then a matching smear of egg from his.

"I'm really a vegetarian... a vegan, actually."

A wave of guilt, but a brief one. "Me, too. Just not today." Today being her first day on this new and amazingly plum job; Nancy's old girl network had definitely paid off. The fact that she was the hotel's new Quality Inspector was something Don did not need to know.

"And on your other days?"

Ms. Sheyoni Flankenship, formerly Sheyoni Black, Jessica Black, and Jessica Flankenship, looked at him and said, "Except when I come here. But I come here," she added, throatily, "As often as I can."

Ordering absolutely everything on the hotel's various menus was part of her job, but he didn't need to know that either.

"No kidding." Don swallowed. "Me too. And I'll be back..." He pulled out a an enormous smartphone, tried to turn it on, peered at its blank face, knocked it firmly against the edge of the table and then, once the colorful software logo flickered and then steadied on the screen, hurried through various options, pull-down lists and tiny glowing windows, working his way towards his daily schedule. A frenzied, clicking moment passed, until he said, "...the day after tomorrow."

"Here? In the hotel?"

"And the restaurant – every morning for the next few weeks, when I'm in town."

Sheyoni nodded, thinking, Perfect.

"I'm fixing up my place." Don took a deep breath and launched into the conversion of his foothills palace to an energy-neutral dwelling, taking care to note that – while the city's engineer had told him he'd have to occupy it for fifty years to pay back the carbon cost of manufacturing the windmills, the solar panels, the geothermal tunneling, and the rest of the reconstruction – the way he was taking care of himself these days, that wouldn't be a problem. He had only started on the insulating properties of the various organic building materials when he happened to notice the time.

Sheyoni, who was fighting not to let her eyes glaze over, was as relieved as she was surprised when he tore the now-stained napkin from his neck, pushed back his chair and rose to his feet. Don handed her his card while telling her that if he didn't catch Lufthansa's over-the pole flight, a huge, bigger-than-huge, recycled-hemp NATO uniform deal would go down the drain. Already making excuses, Sheyoni thought – they really were *connecting*. She flipped the card and, smiling shyly, wrote out her number.

AS SHE LEANT FORWARD, Don could not help but view the acreage on display. Twin pale curves disappearing into lace, and not a bleb on either horizon. It must be early days, he thought, and in a rare incautious moment, had a vision of devoting himself to her... of rising, honorably, unselfishly rising to the occasion. Sheyoni handed it back, her fingers once more grazing his, looking pleased as she glanced at his otherwise loosely draped hemp pants.

He followed her eyes, then reddened furiously, swung his briefcase around between them, and, pretending even greater haste, made his escape. Both of them aware that, for a gentleman of a certain age, some embarrassments – spontaneous, unexpected – are a complement and a gift.

The embarrassment had dwindled, in fact everything had dwindled, soon after Don had climbed up into his all-wheel hybrid Volkswagen 400eBUS and pointed it towards the airport. The vehicle's current design was vaguely reminiscent of the vividly painted microbus in which he'd pre-exited the University for the larger world (a world even more psychedelic and definitely more entrepreneurial than that academic sphere) forty years before. The vehicle possessed the same suppository shape, the same white roof and split windshield, but that was pretty much where the similarity ended.

Designed for those with both nostalgia and the means to pay for it, the microbus's current iteration possessed more luxury and now-thundering, now-silent electro-boosted V-8 power than any executive, pony-tailed or not, could ever need. With the hybrid drive, it was way more efficient than his old Mercedes – 20 MPG! On the highway! – a figure that might not impress anyone who drove a Civic, but Don knew he wasn't a Civic kind of guy, and besides, it all added up, right? Anyway, the various battery displays and gauges gave him that special eco-feeling, a feeling that made cruising the forty miles to the airport, solo, not only acceptable but fun. Don settled back in fine perforated pigskin, switched on the massage-and-acupressure function, and gazed happily over the wheel. Life was good, life was *very* good, and thinking of Sheyoni made it even better.

He'd be back by the weekend... perhaps a 'chance' meeting at the following morning's breakfast, and perhaps a date for dinner, candle-lit and leading directly to a room service breakfast – who knew? That sensation, again, rising from the formerly briefcase-hidden region to an also-swelling heart and then his often-swollen head. All three working together, lust and romance and, as in the restaurant, the strangely intoxicating notion of Sacrifice. He *was* a good person, he was sure of it, and this would prove it to all those fellow former counter-culturalists, those coffeehouse poverty-snobs who were secretly jealous of his car, his new solar home, everything.

And then a hitch: would he be able to handle it when the IFP, that horrible mortal funkiness, appeared? The glaring landscape outside the curved glass windshield seemed to darken. But it soon returned to its proper, cheery, what-a-great-state-we-live-in light. IFP wasn't infectious, and posed no threat to his occasionally worrisome health. Why, it could actually be therapeutic, help him transcend those worries, mortal lessons from a disease he happily did not have. And in these modern times, the most tragically funky end, if comprehensively bandaged by the best nursing care money could buy, could be made, he was sure, tolerable.

He was no stranger to tragedy: funkiness of a different sort had certainly appeared in his three marriages – as inevitably, if not as quickly, as Sheyoni's would. Unfortunately, all his ex-wives were still walking around, each robustly healthy enough to bust him, one and then another in a hellish three-way tag team, on a near-daily basis. But this, short and sweet – too short for vows and too sweet to turn away from – could work. From Sex to Sacrifice to Soul-elevating eulogy, without the lingering sour symptoms of Divorce.

As the high plains and their sprawling suburbs rushed by, Don decided that, given her considerable charms, Sheyoni was definitely worth it.

DAVID EXAMINED his day's schedule again. "This other one – Mr. X – he wouldn't leave his name?"

"Nope. Said he knew you, he'd come at ten, and hung up. I've got to leave for the university, but you'll hear him come in. Just tell him we haven't opened and to come back in a week."

Bending over the counter, David drew close to her ear. "Those two on the couch – are you *sure* it's 'Thinna'? I thought I hadn't heard them right."

"I swear. Oh Lordy I do."

"Junie, please." He shot a quick glance back. "They've got the degrees, and those are the last two positions we have to fill. And I can't take much more of this."

"Tell me about it."

He considered that, briefly – he'd love to tell *anyone*, unload in any way he could. Oz was too wrapped in the middle of it all, and

Paula too busy to answer his calls. But this was neither the time nor the place. So David gave a small groan, private and between them, then levered himself up and, game face on, turned to welcome the Forever Clinic's potential new exercise and diet mavens.

As soon as David led them away, Quinn huffed in the door, wearing a major floral outfit and carrying a double armload of supplement bottles. Acknowledging her presence with a nod, he dumped the lot on one of the reception area's empty maple shelves and headed out the door again, presumably for another load.

Junie was left with half an hour of precious morning time, a seemingly uninterrupted series of interruptions, and the earnest desire *not* to overhear what was being said in the office behind her. Not after stumbling into Quinn's interview last week. In any case, the dubious doctor had struck again, leaving half his bottles on their sides and ready to roll off. With her own small private groan, she came around the counter to straighten up.

By the time his steps were thundering back over the elevator bridge, she'd arranged them by both size and alphabet, each hand-pasted label facing out. "Dr. Quinn Recommends:" and then, in smaller type, Joint Formula, Memory Formula, etc. To the educated eye, an older label could be barely read beneath: "Dr. McIntyre Recommends:"

She picked up an amber bottle up and squinted at the ingredients: …*Cetyl Alcohol, Stearic Acid, Dimethicone, Ethoxydiglycol, Carbomer, Diazolidinyl Urea, Methylparaben, Tetrasodium EDTA, Propylparaben, Triethanolamine…*

Man.

"Pretty impressive, huh?" Quinn walked up with another double armful, waiting for help.

"Pretty… artificial." She took a few off the top and began a new row.

"Naturopathic meds need preservatives, too," he said, and shoved the rest onto the shelves, packing them in with bare arms spread wide, ruining her careful order.

Junie pushed his bulk aside with a hip check and quickly reorganized them. "I thought they were supposed to be... different. You know, organic."

"They're organic – organic chemicals. At least that's what the manufacturer said. With the shelf life he guaranteed I'm not asking. Besides, everything works the same, darling."

Junie shot him a look but he missed it, instead rummaging in a new and even-more-enormous purse, this one garish pink. "Like I always say: one part effectiveness, one part belief."

"I've read about it – placebos and the benign fib, the lie at the heart of healing, et cetera." The opposite of science, in her opinion; just thinking about placebos gave her a headache.

"Why do they line these things in black? You can't find *anything* in here!" Quinn head was nearly buried in the purse. "The 'benign fib', huh? A poet who doesn't know it. But there's more to these babies than that. Because the whole show, and I mean show, depends on the supplement – or drug, or weird massage deal – being at least a little bit effective. Which would be a lot less confusing if the effectiveness didn't depend on that belief. Belief to effectiveness and effectiveness to belief: kind of your basic helical conundrum, which, if you're smart, you just let whirl away. There!"

Triumphant, he produced a semi-used cigar and a pack of matches. "Do you mind?"

"In here? *Yes.*" She could smell the bitter char from where she stood.

Quinn grumbled, put the matches away, and stuck the chewed end in his mouth. "Belief plus fact, darling. Look at those Skinnies, for example."

"The Thinnas?"

He seemed puzzled. "Haven't heard that one before. They're nutritionists, right?"

"One of them."

"That's usually all it takes – take your basic you-are-what-you-eat compulsiveness, add a master's degree, and they're off to the races. A little knowledge might be a dangerous thing, but with nutritionists, a lot is worse. It's obvious: they're Skinnies. You know, starvation artists."

Junie didn't know, and only looked at Quinn, waiting.

"The calorie-restriction thing," he said. "Starving themselves to live longer. Hoping that by not shoveling calories into the body's metabolic engine, they'll turn it down – turn down everything, from heart rate all the way to cellular activity, the rate at which their bodies age, wear out. Maybe switch on that 'longevity gene' they talk about."

"The one that makes telomerase?" Finally, something she might possibly know more about than Quinn. "We studied it – how the body's cells can replace themselves, but they can only do it few times, and telomerase fixes that. Little brain and heart cells you can't destroy."

"Uh-huh. Problem is, cancer cells multiply indefinitely. And they do it by producing…"

"Telomerase?"

"Bingo." Quinn crossed his arms, towering in high heels. "So if you switch on telomerase production, what kind of cells do you get even more of?"

Shit. You condescending… whatever. "Weren't we talking about the Thinnas?"

He frowned. "That's their *name*?"

"Bingo." June gave her warmest smile.

He cleared his throat. "The Thinnas. You couldn't make this stuff up."

"Tell me about it. Anyway, you were saying…"

"I was saying…?"

"Calorie restriction." Actually, Quinn wasn't any worse than her average blowhard professor.

"Oh. Right. Metabolism, genes, accumulated dietary toxins, it doesn't matter. They keep coming up with reasons, because they've decided calorie restriction is the key, the one thing needed – painful but rewarding, at least in terms of compulsiveness – to keep their narrow-gauge cabooses rattling down the tracks for a few extra decades."

He regarded her, then added, "You'll like this part – they've got evidence, hard and fast. Thirty percent less calories, forty percent longer lives. Study after study. Quite simply, it works."

"It does?"

"In mice." A nice, warm smile back at her.

"But people aren't mice—"

"Um-humm…"

"—which means they don't know if it will work. In humans."

"No one does. But those two *believe* it will. A belief I share – because, dear Junie, belief is what I'm all about." Then looked down and said, "That and this dress."

He pinched the yellow-and-orange flowered fabric halfway to the frilly hem, pulled it out and gave a beefy twirl. "What do you think?

"Think? I *think* that dress is beyond logic; I *believe* you should tone it down."

He looked hurt, was about to protest when David's office door opened and he led the Thinnas back up the hall.

DAVID MADE INTRODUCTIONS; now that Junie had a handle on the Thinnas' alarming appearance, she found them harmless. And friendly, in a sort of watchful and oddly old, or pre-old, way.

Adeline paled as she took Quinn's full Carmen Miranda magnificence in. Or perhaps she'd gotten a whiff of that cold cigar, which had been safely returned to his remarkably handy purse. She managed, however, to say something nice about Quinn's pseudo-post-chemo scarf, the same pattern as his dress; he stared over her head at Junie, knowing that she'd heard.

Then, from the other side of the door, came a rhythmic whirring noise, cycling from faint to loud to louder before ending with a solid thump that rattled Quinn's supplement bottles on the wall.

David looked at his watch, said, "My ten o'clock!", and ran to the door. The whirring was nearing its peak at the moment he swung open the heavy teak, yelped and leapt to the side. An electric wheelchair charged though the doorway, making it as far as the clinic's prize we-got-money Persian prayer rug before its elderly operator could hit the brakes. As their combined momentum easily exceeded the friction of wool against polished floor, the entire patient-wheelchair-rug unit continued onward, spinning in a graceful arc that came to a frictionless halt at the feet of the astonished crowd.

None were more astonished than David, gaping at a purple-crusted scalp, a patchy furze of hair, and a death's head grin that opened gleefully to croak, "Hello, everybody!"

Quinn leaned over and said, *sotto voce*, "We're in the big time, Junie. That's Cyrus Flint."

"So?"

"Another star from the holistic circuit – he *invented* longevity." By then, David was squatting at the wheelchair's side, immediately pulled into an intense but unfortunately inaudible conversation. To Junie's right, Adeline and Thomas swayed slightly, eyes wide and fixed on Flint.

Junie glanced back to Quinn. "Invented?"

"Just about," he said. "Research, teaching, every journal's emeritus editor, and most recently, as you can see from the expressions on our favorite Thinnas, the calorie-counters' hero. Flint's dying, obviously, but they say he's stretched even that out an extra ten years. So far."

As Flint scanned the Forever Clinic's partially-assembled staff, Quinn bent his knees, dropped six inches, and discretely side-stepped behind Junie.

That voice, again, this time more creak than croak. "Forgive my hearing, but did you say it's Dr... *Quinn*?"

Sheepishly, Quinn returned to view.

Flint's birdlike hand gave a barely perceptible wave. "Perhaps we've met before?"

"He just moved here," David interrupted, "From, um..."

Quinn waited, then grumbled, "Texas, dammit."

The grin widened, tombstone teeth protruding from receding gums. "A wise choice, I'm sure." The old man's laser-like gaze shifted to the two stick-like figures in front of the couch. "And Adeline Thinna! I enjoyed your article on—"

A soft, crumpling thump, leaving Thomas Thinna, oblivious and still staring, swaying alone.

"Vasomotor instability," Quinn said. "Part of anorexia, any kind of starvation."

Junie batted his arm, said, "Would you *stop*?" and bent to help Adeline. Flint watched, amused, as the two hauled Adeline and guided a shaky Thomas to the couch. Soon each hung limp over a thick-padded arm, an acre of empty leather between.

"Just a faint," Flint agreed. "They'll be fine. One of the reasons I got this baby." Leaning forward against his safety belt, he grasped the snug restraining armrests of his chair. "You can program in your daily rounds," he added, *sotto voce,* "I could be dead a week and still rolling."

And shot another harrowing smile up at David – who tried, unsuccessfully, to return it.

12

Do No Harm... Mostly

- or -

Erosive Amoralosis

"WHY'D HE PICK ME?" David said, "Because he lives here. Because Flint was – is – a professor at the University. I hadn't heard of him before Vegas; guess he keeps a low profile in his own home town." Elbows on his knees, he sat head down on the other side of Oz's execu-desk.

"Hey. It's a good thing. He's famous everywhere else – and coming to the Forever Clinic! The dean of longevity, seeing *you* to stay alive." Oz couldn't be happier.

That big, square head came up slow, a pale, befuddled sun rising over the polished oak between them. "That's the problem."

"What? Too much opportunity for you?"

"He doesn't want to stay alive."

"He wants you to *kill* him? That would not be good. Although..." In a move not unfamiliar to those who knew him, Oz went directly from joy to calculation, efficiently bypassing any intervening mood as he searched for the winning angle. Perhaps a branch operation: The Forever-After Clinic? Smaller, of course, and the lease was still open on the first floor...

"No, no, no." David's head was down again, swaying from side to side. "He's tired – tired of trying. Always planned on breaking a hundred, then got sick, really sick, with... well. You know I can't say."

"Come on..."

"He's a patient, Oz. My patient. He can tell anyone he wants – in fact he has, even gives lectures on all the ways he's fought it. But I can't, not unless he tells me to."

"Only curious – doesn't sound like *what* he has would make a difference."

"Not any more. All the things he did, worked. All the drugs and chemical tweaks he developed, and probably the supplements and the impossible diet, too. Gave him twenty years, he said, but it keeps on creeping, steady, and he's ready to let go. And I'm the one he's picked to be in charge – I wasn't that impressive in Vegas, but for some reason, I guess, he liked me."

"Lucky you."

"Actually, I am. Sort of… honored. He knows the interventions he wants to stop, and when, and we'll be there for any pain meds he needs. He'll feel comfortable at the Clinic, and we can keep him comfortable, probably more than anyplace else."

"But quietly," Oz said.

"Yes. As quiet, he said, as the…"

"Got it. But what if he changes his mind? Gets religion – sees the light, newspaper articles, a big hoo-hah at the end?"

"Oz."

"Publicity, David. A little warning and I can make it work for us."

"I don't think it's going to happen. We were back in my office and I asked him – about beliefs, that sort of thing. Normally I would have waited… I've barely met the man, but we can talk." David paused. "Know what he said?"

"No. But I know you're going to tell me."

"Right – *I had a dog, his name was Rover, and when he died, he was dead all over.*"

Oz scratched his beard, thoughtfully. "Nice."

David got up. "See you later?"

Oz nodded. "Three o'clock, as planned." Thinking, epitaphs for atheists… condolence cards… are gravestone inscriptions copyrighted? He'd have to check.

LUNCH AT A BAR. Nancy had come at Sheyoni's invitation, but she was more than familiar with the place. As a congenital if closet academic, Nancy couldn't help but think of it as the *Ur*-Bar: the bar that defined, by its very lack of definition, all other bars. At least all the bars she'd ever been in, anyway. Which used to be a lot.

Its real name was the Bar None – formerly Peggy's, formerly the Hi-Low, and before that the Broken Drum and Tom's and a receding catalog of names, all short-lived and most forgotten, that stretched back down the decades to long before her first fake ID. Each version completely remaking itself, working to take advantage of the prime Broadway location, and each time failing in months to, at best, a year or two. It was a particularly intense manifestation, she figured, of old Chief Niwot's curse.

Why manifest here? Two reasons, actually. The first was the frequent turnover itself – who better to sell a distressed property to than a returning refugee, one of the already cursed, hoping against hope to resume a better life. The second reason was the ancient tribal bones that had surfaced though the dirt floor of the basement below her barstool. A sacred circle of his followers, and probably the big chief himself, had been disinterred last year. Their identity was confirmed by the university's Archeology Department – before the Department of Ethnic Studies, in a daring nocturnal raid, seized the curiously intact skeletons and re-interred them in the basement below. But the landlord claimed he wasn't superstitious, and had publicly stated that the six inches of reinforced concrete he'd laid over their re-freshened graves was simply in line with Health Department regulations. And, he had added, if it continued cracking in the remarkably concentric pattern it was currently demonstrating, he'd keep pouring in concrete until it reached the top of the basement stairs.

SHEYONI SAT one barstool over. She wasn't aware of the bar's history – Sheyoni really wasn't much of a history person – but had picked it because she'd heard the Bar None was a place to meet new friends of all persuasions, the kind of place that Nancy and her *type* of friends might hang out. From what she'd heard, it got pretty lively around midnight, thought it was more than dead right now. In any case, she thought Nancy would appreciate the gesture enough to open up and tell her what she needed.

She *was* feeling a tiny bit nervous, the way she always seemed to feel in Nancy's presence, and couldn't think of what to say to get her started. Falling back on her usual and quite unconscious (or, at least, un-*self*-conscious) techniques, she scooched her stool a little closer to Nancy, the only other occupant of the five yards of battered and varnished mahogany that stretched to the flyspecked glass of the front door. They were both working their way through TeriVeggie Mock Tuna specials, the management's latest attempt to lure customers during the non-witching hours.

Nancy figured Sheyoni wanted to pump her about her ex's new clinic, but wasn't quite there yet. Still, it *was* nice to see this particular pretty face, and the Mock Tuna, with its sugary cucumber slices, fermented non-fish sauce, and thin schmear of wasabi wasn't nearly as bad as she'd expected. So Nancy gave the girl a break and sat there, looking in the long mirror behind the bar at the Broadway traffic that rushed beyond the plate-glass windows, squinting against the streaks of chrome and noonday sun.

Outside, the diesel pick-ups and the busted-muffler Subarus did their best to out-rumble and out-pollute the upstart mass of high-end hybrids. Inside, the muted echoes of that roar were oddly complemented by the smell of last night's beer, this morning's bleach from the toilets, and the smoking fry cook's griddle on the other side of the rectangular pass-through in the rear. The paint was chipped, a color somewhere between dirt and green, and only the absence of stale tobacco – which she missed, actually – separated the atmosphere from the scabbiest Wyoming bar her traveling life had ever pulled her into.

The remarkable thing was that it was all art and artifice, that they sat surrounded by a truckload of hard-drinking artifacts shipped in from the crustiest bankrupt establishments that she might, for all she knew, once have done her best to get kicked out of. Even more impressive, the new owners had somehow resisted temptation and performed the transformation without a fake enamel old-timey sign or busted saddle or varnished set of pointy-toe boots between them. Nothing cute, just a blast of almost-real authenticity, an extra meta-level to the done and redone Western mini-metropolis she lived on the rocky edge of. Except for the straining New Age menu, they'd somehow gotten it right.

"To think this used to be a fern bar," Nancy said. Back then, it had been Peggy's; same target group marketing, same otherwise inexplicable economic problems. She'd been a regular when she first returned Boulder, before she realized that the bar scene, straight or gay, wasn't her scene anymore.

Having offered that gambit, Nancy waited, monitoring the last fading tingle of the wasabi, until Sheyoni finally wiped those lovely lips, cleared her throat and said, "Okay – I confess. I've got to find out about the Forever Clinic."

Honesty, as unexpected as it was welcome. "Okay... why?"

Sheyoni turned on the stool, an earnest schoolgirl – she was *good*, Nancy thought – with her hands clasped before her. "My ex. He wasn't supposed to have any money."

"And now you think he does?"

"Look at the place."

"I don't know," Nancy said, then gave a little skitch out of the side of her mouth. "He seems sort of helpless. Like it's all happening *to* him."

"That's just David."

"If you say so. But there *is* this guy he didn't introduce me to – comes around every few days. Bossy, wears a suit, eyeballs everybody but gets out before you can say hello."

"Oz. Of course." Sheyoni turned to the mirror behind the bar and sighed. "David won't see a dime."

Nancy shrugged. "Sorry."

"Thanks. But how it is, really?" Looking as though, for some odd peri-divorceal reason, Sheyoni wanted it to be good for David.

"His old patients seem to love it."

"Oz is letting them in? Amazing."

"The few that found it," Nancy said, watching Sheyoni in the mirror. "Crew-wise, he's put together a nice team – everybody means well. Even one, I had a feeling... but no."

She pushed her hair back with her left hand, the other flat on the thick cool wood. Sheyoni put one of hers – so soft, so warm, she was *so* good – over it. "I'm sorry."

Nancy brought her other hand down over it. "How sorry?" The afternoon was young.

Sheyoni slid her hand out. "I... I met someone."

"Tell me it's a man."

"It is. That's better?"

"You bet. Now I'm not jealous." A pitying look. "But poor you."

"I can take care of myself."

"Then poor him." Sheyoni looked at her, laughed, raised her iced tea.

Nancy did the same. "Men." A clink of glass, ice cubes rattling, and they returned to the mirror. "Like those two," Nancy said quietly. "They must've shipped them down with the rest of this stuff."

FROM ACROSS THE NARROW AISLE, huddled in a booth beside the windows, the two cowboys watched the women finish their drinks and leave.

"Two of them, sitting at a bar alone?" Jeremiah shook his head. "I figured they was going to hit on us."

Wayne grinned. "Maybe it's not that kind of place." Knowing because he'd come by once, after dropping Jeremiah off for his night shift at the convenience store. He'd nursed a beer and found himself getting talked up by a lonely-looking fella – before he came to his senses and skitted out of there.

"I've been in a bunch of bars," Jeremiah said. "I can see what kind of place it is." Same as any in his home state, the state they'd just escaped from.

Wayne, who'd never mentioned his previous visit, decided to let it go.

Jeremiah turned and looked out the same window Nancy had, out at the busy street. He took in the rich-and-poor cars, the homeless crazies, the sorority-girl miniskirts and Lycra-suited bicyclists and alloy-punctured skateboarders, each and every one of them on the move. Not exactly crowded, but any street was crowded compared to where he came from, where every soul on a given sidewalk was either friend or enemy. All these strangers weaving in and out, acting like they were getting along, just missing each other, probably ready to blow up if they didn't. A mixed-up mash of people, so many different types it was weird; the whole thing gave him the jumping willies. It just plain wasn't *natural*.

"Sodom and Gomorrah," he muttered, barely audible.

Wayne heard. And was about to say something funny but

decided he'd better not. After all, this was still new, a kinda-big city, and if Jeremiah didn't like it – if it made him mutter truly stupid things – then they'd climb up into their old pickup, close those creaky doors and roll right out of here.

THE FIRST VISIT, David thought. Well, the first full-on holistic visit in his brand-new office and consultation room. Up to now, he'd been seeing his old patients in the smaller room next door, homey and crowded with his old green-enameled exam table, a cracked vinyl stool, and all the other stuff he still liked but that Oz said he shouldn't let the high-rollers see.

Anyway, here he was, seeing the first patient to sit on the hydraulic exam table the trans-urogenital surgeons had left, the first to crinkle the sharp-creased white paper strip down the middle, the first to wonder at the flesh-warm eco-foam padding, the calming subsonics that thrummed from the stainless steel base. Who cared if it cost more than any car he'd ever considered possessing? Oz had gotten a deal, and when things picked up, his old patients could circulate through both exam rooms. Every one of them, old or new, deserved the best that David could beg, borrow, or steal. Although, David had to admit, he wasn't one-hundred-percent sure about the stealing part.

In any case, who better to start with than Don, an old *and* a new-type patient, and the one who'd gotten the whole thing going? A little needy, a little demanding, but David knew that a lot of his future deep-pocketed patients were bound to be. They paid to have it all laid out for them, from illness care to prevention to every sort of life enhancement that could be dressed in medical white.

White. David looked down at the crisply starched jacket that covered his very best denim shirt, and felt… foolish. It was Oz's idea and, overall, the crew had taken it pretty well. Knee-length white cotton lab coats for everyone, emblazoned with the Forever Clinic logo: a red Swiss cross, a blue soaring bird, a radiant yellow sun. Everyone except Howie, who had only agreed to pin a small badge with the same design to his equally-white robes.

The long jackets were probably a nod to the high-priest doctor thing Oz had been spouting at the Triad that night. The night that he,

David, had said 'No' – followed by the morning he'd last seen Don, the morning he'd said 'Yes'.

And now, as that same patient slowly rose on humming machinery toward the ceiling, the circle had closed.

Don lay back, nervously noting the drop to the floor, ready to be examined. *Completely* ready, in fact, having stripped off every stitch of hemp clothing, including his organic green-tea-dyed antioxidant undies, before hopping on the table. At these prices, he didn't want his doctor to miss a thing.

David, a little embarrassed, unfurled a sky-blue sheet to cover the frizzy zone, as gray as the top of Don's head, then moved in and started his exam.

"I hope," Don said, "we're not too late to catch… anything."

David looked up from his stethoscope.

"It's been fourteen months – almost fifteen."

He pulled the black earpiece out of one ear. "Since…"

"My last physical."

"No problem."

"But I thought, you know, every year."

David nodded, draped his stethoscope around his neck, and stepped on the floor pedal that simultaneously morphed the table into a padded chair and lowered it to a more reasonable altitude. Then leaned back against the wall, raised his eyebrows, and waited for Don to tell him what he was worried about. Which was, as usual, not immediately forthcoming.

"Right," David said. If Don didn't want to talk, they'd have a teaching moment. Maybe if he bored Don enough, his patient might cough it up. "Adult physicals. Why we do them. Think of a physical, the classic health maintenance exam, as a bunch of separate screening tests, things we want to check. There are some that anyone over fifty should have: a quick once-over for skin cancer, that sort of thing. Plus a few that someone with hypertension, someone like you, might need in particular. Like checking the vessels in the back of your eyes with an ophthalmoscope, or listening to your heart and lungs. We throw the other stuff in because patients expect it. Those rubber-hammer knee reflexes, for instance; if you had a problem big enough to wipe those out, you'd be limping in here to tell me about it, not waiting for a physical."

"That's it?" Don asked, disappointed. "What about the blood work?"

Blood work. David didn't think that was Don's issue, but he kept on talking. "Most of it's pretty much a waste. Same deal – by the time something medical shows up, you're already so sick that both of us will know it. But there are a few... like the LDL measure in a cholesterol test. Or blood sugar, which can really sneak up on you. If either is high, you've got a classic silent killer. And a killer that can be thoroughly reformed, turned into a model citizen with diet and exercise and, your favorite, drugs."

Don frowned but kept listening.

"Other screening tests can be, well, iffy."

"What could be wrong with finding something early? Like... like a *cancer.*"

"That's the thing: cancer isn't always a problem."

Another frown, disbelieving.

"A lot are benign," David continued. "Just growths that stop themselves and don't invade. Like the tinier breast lesions that show up on mammograms. Some look truly awful, and cutting them out can definitely save a life. Others look more questionable, but it seems safest to remove them, too. We end up with a huge number of unnecessary surgeries, and each has its own cost, complications, suffering. It's not that we shouldn't screen... it's just that that, like most things in health care, screening is a double-edged sword, with the potential of decades of extra life on one side, and extra surgery and radiation and chemo on the other. That's why they're recommending less frequent mammograms: getting some is good – they're great, save lives – but more and earlier isn't always better. Which is driving women crazy."

"But that's their problem, not mine."

What a sweetheart. "Okay. What about a PSA blood test, for prostate cancer?"

"Every year, never miss it – though I hear prostate surgery is a big scam."

David shrugged. "Surgeons like to cut, but to heal, not harm. The thing is, every time doctors argue back and forth about something expensive, it looks like the ones who recommend it are trying to line their pockets. And maybe they are. Or maybe they're just trying to figure out the best thing to do. Because PSA testing is no clearer than mammograms. In fact, it's less so – the biggest prevention group is saying skip it entirely. Better not to know."

"I don't care. I still want to know."

David agreed, in general – what could be wrong with knowledge? – but he was fully aware that the driving force could be fear as much as curiosity and self-responsibility. In twenty odd years he'd be in the same spot, thinking about having some future screening test – say, a super-miniaturized handheld MRI to scan for pancreatic cancer, that and all the benign lumps that could look just like it. Would *his* desire to know also be motivated by fear, in a kind of anti-denial coping mechanism, drowning anxiety with too much information? Like Don, he'd be both the last to realize what was really moving him, and the first to suffer from unnecessary consequences.

Still, the PSA debate was by no means resolved, and Don seemed sure of what he wanted. "If I was healthy and nearing sixty," David said, "young enough that a slow-grower like that could put me in the ground, I'd probably want to know as well. Find out what might be there, figure out the chance that it might be something truly scary, *then* decide what to do. Let's go with it – but really think, and think carefully, about what to do next if your PSA level comes back up a bump." He touched his tablet screen and the test, ordered, lit up.

"At least," David said, "everybody agrees so far on screening for colon cancer... though a colonoscopy demands a bit more, um, involvement than a blood test." With a stroke of his finger, he pulled up the copied images of Don's old chart on the flatscreen mounted on the wall. "You did that five years ago, right?"

"Six, I think."

"Then you're good for four more," David said, turning back. "As long as it was fine, and no one in your family had it."

Don shook his head.

"You can do a lot to stay out of trouble, but aside from those, there's precious little that exams and tests can add. In any case, a physical is just a way of tying them together – a hard core of what you need, added to what everybody your physiologic age needs, all wrapped inside a fair amount of fluff."

"Why bundle them up at all?"

"To get a patient in, I guess, and hear what's bothering him." He put his elbow on the little wall-mounted keyboard desk under the flatscreen, cupped his chin in his hand and looked at Don. Holding it, he decided, as long as would take.

Until, in fact, Don said, "I'm in a new… relationship."

Finally.

"And she's, ah, *younger* than me." From his perch on the exam table, Don thought, this could work – there was no reason he had to tell his doctor who it was. "And I was wondering… you know…" He steeled himself. "Didn't we check my testosterone level last year?" David – thinking, oops, it was blood work after all – found the result and opened it in a new window. "It's normal, Don. Normal for your age."

"For my age. What if I was… thirty?"

Thirty. Not exactly cradle robbing, but it wasn't his to judge. "Then it would be, well, marginally low."

"Marginal enough to give me some?"

Primum non nocere, David thought. The first rule of medicine – do no harm. Liver disease, hypertension, explosive rage and every other reason athletes couldn't take all the steroids, in this case testosterone and its cousins, that they really, really wanted to.

"Or anything," Don added. "I mean, anything to feel stronger, younger. Anything I can do at all."

"Anything?" Then David saw it, amazed he hadn't seen it before. "There *is* something new. Human Growth Hormone, HGH. And it looks like it might be able to turn around some of the things that normally change with age. It definitely builds muscle, and as for energy… well."

"You mean…?"

"I've heard." From Paula. And for all he knew, Oh Paula Oh Oh Paula, had seen and felt it too. David wondered for an instant what he *hadn't* heard – or felt or seen. The unforeseen but expected side-effects of any new treatment, the things that went wrong that no one, especially anyone in sales, wanted to talk about. But then that instant was gone, flushed away in the excitement.

Don leaned forward, the sheet a rumpled band of blue across his thighs. "Can I get it here?"

"Absolutely," David said. "We'll be starting our program up next week. But it's expensive, and no insurance company's going to cover it." He paused, bit his lip. "It could be… it could be over twenty thousand a year."

"Twenty grand? For a chance to be young again? Please."

Wow. Was that all it took? Across the room, Don was beaming – the clinic's first patient, and his first HGH patient, too. This could be as easy as Paula promised, as easy as Oz had said. David quickly finished Don's exam, and then was occupied by ordering the extra bloodwork and printing out the information and releases Don would need to read and sign. All the while suffused by a certain warm and multi-hued glow, composed of one part simply doing, one part doing something new, and one part helping Don do what he wanted, as often as he wanted, to who he wanted to. Plus one part keeping Paula – and Oz, of course – happy.

Don was also caught up in the excitement, and only after it had passed did he recall exactly *who* it was he wanted to be doing. As David opened the exam room door to show him out, he said, carefully, "I didn't see, ah, your wife as I came in… how is she?"

Oh God, David thought. Don's last visit, Oz's absurd disease, the fact that Don had bought it. And the anger – justifiable anger – if Don ever found out. "She… she…"

Don studied his doctor's stricken face; Sheyoni really must have been the one who'd called it off, exactly as she'd said. What a woman, leaving everything her own personal *doctor* could offer her – all the soulless medical care, but not half the love she needed. Seizing her own life for herself, she'd said, leaving unspoken what Don already knew, that she was seizing it in the last healthy months that she could seize anything at all. And deserving, richly deserving, of all the help that he alone could give. A love supreme; a short and tragic love.

He put a hand on David's shoulder, and said, "I'm sorry. I won't speak of it again."

Nor did David, at least not then. Just watched, stunned by his great luck – no mention of Oz's confabulation, of any of it – as his patient crossed the sunlit waiting room and left.

LIKE HIGH SCHOOL ALL OVER AGAIN; skipping classes, playing hooky. Except this time it didn't involve basements or hand-rolled herbs or other sullen pastimes. Just a clean cold breeze that descended from the mountains to blow cross the Boulder Reservoir, as David floated a quarter mile from the nearest point of the rocky shores.

Ducking away had been Oz's idea, and so far a good one: rent a boat and see if they could remember a few of the lessons that Beatriz had once tried to drill into both of them, Beatriz who'd swung from one unlikely sport, traversing the constrained and gusty puddles that spotted these high plains, to an even less likely one. Oz had been talking about sailing since David showed him that sailboat printout at the Triad – an imagined passion that, for David, had seemed to evaporate in that same instant. Although floating out here was nice.

The mast waggled with each wavelet, loose sail luffing, as Oz settled back against the plastic cockpit of the tiny rented boat and – looking like an obese Rafe Lauren model in a double-breasted, anchor-embroidered navy sweater, perfectly weathered chinos, and sockless deck shoes – offered David a cigarette.

David stared at the open pack. "Give me a break."

"You liked it – you know you liked it at the Triad. Right out there on the sidewalk, puffing with the public."

It was a *lot* like high school, David thought, both of them busting each other. And the Triad, coming up again. Sometimes he wished that evening had never... No, he didn't. Lots of good things had happened. Like Don, today. And Paula. And Junie... all the staff, he meant. The whole crew. Which, of course, included Junie.

Oz shrugged, cupped his hand against the breeze to light up, then slipped his gold Dunhill deep into a pocket.

"Tobacco, my friend, is a crucial part of the Continental Diet, every skinny Parisian's trick and the perfect compliment to your vaunted French Paradox. Think, if you will, of what I'd weigh without cigarettes."

"Think of what you'd weigh without *food.*"

Oz directed a column of smoke in the general direction of the cloud-spotted sky, pointed the ashen tip at David and said, "Good one."

"Really, Oz – do both. Quit *and* lose weight; I'm worried about you." Crap: it really was like that evening at the Triad. Slipping into advice-mode again.

"You know I've tried – I even got Adeline to customize a diet for me last week." An involuntary shudder. "I just can't seem to do it."

"That's what everybody says."

"Because it's true?"

"Maybe for some," David allowed. "But if you could only..." He was about to start in on all the things that he knew worked – the daily exercise no matter what, simply eating less, the recognition that some ache of hunger was an inescapable part of the plan. All the things that Oz had tried and almost instantly rejected. Instead, David paused, then said, "Okay – one suggestion and then no other."

"I like the last part."

"Just listen. Consider it a business plan.'

"Now I'm definitely listening."

"Here it is: The Three-Hour-Cruise Diet."

"As in Gilligan's Island? That particular three hour cruise lasted three *years.*"

"It could feel like it."

A frown. "Just watching the reruns could feel like... never mind. Keep going."

"I drop you – I mean, the client – on a desert island, then pick you, um, him or her, up in a month. Lots of water, vitamins, books, sunscreen, a satellite phone if you get sick. Only one client per island, to discourage cannibalism. Success guaranteed."

"And you're going to do this when?"

"I don't know. When I get bored and rich and bossy. Like you. Which probably means never."

"Good. Leave rich and bossy to me. Still... a *potential* weight loss program. Might happen someday, might not. Like Schrödinger's cat, but starving." He extended a pudgy hand. "Sign me up."

David shook it, then hauled his friend back up to a sitting position. Oz tossed the butt into the water and, as it hissed and darkened and sank, pulled the sail in. The white nylon luffed again, then snapped full in a sudden gust of wind; David felt the same chill he had that evening at the Triad, as he'd handed the sailboat listing over. Not about being on the water, not about sailing, but *something.* He didn't know what, but did know it would come to him, eventually. Meanwhile, Oz was wrestling with the multifactorial balance of wind and sail and rudder, faltering at first but then almost steady, catching that fresh breeze back to the not-so-distant shore.

TWO LARGER HULLS, one spotless and the other well-encrusted, floating less than a yard apart in a placid inlet of a larger, in fact oceanic, body of water.

"Of course I'm sure," Beatriz said, as she held the cushy bundle, warm within its blanket, over the unforgiving water. It looked pleadingly at her, then rolled adorable brown eyes to the flannel-skirted Earth Mother stretching over to accept it. As the latter clutched it close, it emitted a sputtering wet squeak of happiness, which Beatriz could smell from where she stood but its new owner at least pretended not to notice. Despite the eye-smarting reek, Beatriz felt more than a small ache of loss, a surprise she quickly pushed aside.

The vessels were the sole occupants of a hidden bay on the open-ocean side of Catalina Island. The Earth Mother's life partner and fellow eternohippie worked the throttle on their chugging packet-boat, trying not to bonk the Osprey's pristine hull with its row of dangling scum-stained bumpers. They were Beatriz's favorite tie-died customers, and, up to her announcement a few minutes ago, the only ones left. She turned and reached back into the open hatch, pulled up two five-kilo bundles of *Salvia Divinorum,* and threw them over to the oil-stained deck, where they landed with a thump beside the pilot's sun-browned feet.

His great toe nudged the printed burlap. "I thought you said you were out of the game."

"I'm out, all right. Next Taser-wielding fool, I might have to break his neck."

"Then what's that for?"

"Good luck," she said. "They're the dregs, the last of the stock."

He rubbed his chin, evaluating the bales in a more precise manner than his torn cut-offs would suggest. "Four more states just banned it, Bea. Got any idea what that makes them worth?"

"It doesn't matter," she said, "Doesn't matter at all."

A steady look, followed by a not-ungrateful shrug. His less-calculating half handed him the bundle, then returned to lean perilously over the transom to wrap Beatriz in a final hug. "You'll come see us? Non-commercially, I mean."

The gap between the boats was widening; arms across the water, balancing each other before pushing off. "I promise," Beatriz said, but she didn't say when.

And that was it – away again; a clean break and free.

THE DAY was winding down, the clinic unpopulated except for Junie. After Don Gilmore left, David had rushed away for a super-secret conference with Oz – but wearing shorts, for some reason.

Outside the teak door, the elevator platform groaned, followed by a heavy tread. Ripples spread across the top of Junie's coffee, seismic permutations of every step. The man doesn't *have* to walk that way, she thought, then rolled her eyes after Quinn swung through the teak door, performed an ursine tippy-toe across the pale green floor and pirouetted in the last yellow light.

"What do you think?" Quinn opened the jacket of a deep-blue Thai silk pantsuit, revealing a scarlet satin lining and a frilly white shirt.

"Better, but I still think you're having too much fun."

"No such thing – read my second book: There's No Such Thing As Too Much Fun. That said, here's what *I* think: keep it reasonable, go with the androgynous look."

Jacket still plucked open, he spun again, then came to a surprisingly non-sloshing stop. His prior pendulosities, Junie saw, had been considerably reduced, down to what she suspected were nothing more than standard middle-aged man-breasts confined within a padded bra. "Note the absence."

"Duly noted." Somewhere, in a no doubt charming converted-garage rental in central Boulder, two extra-large water balloons were sitting in a kitchen sink, headed for shorter but less troubled lives.

"Then check this out." Reaching up to his tight-tied headscarf, he whipped it off with a happy, "Ta-da!"

Above the makeup, the big hoop earrings and the over-plucked eyebrows, his balding crew-cut had been replaced by a shining, perfectly shaved scalp. "Maybe it was chemo, or maybe I just like the gleam." A thick hand slicked imaginary hair straight back. "I'm having it all, baby. Society can't tell *this* lady what to be."

This time, Junie just shook her head.

Quinn didn't notice, was busy leaning over the counter to read her monitor. "So what's the scoop?" He pointed at the schedule. "Was that a paying patient?"

"An intake physical."

"The full meal deal? When do I get in?"

"Don't be so mercenary." She turned the monitor away and scanned the schedule. "Next... Tuesday."

"Excellent. And what I do *isn't* mercenary. Or not just." He wrested the monitor back, checked the 'problem' column next to the name. "Low energy? I got just the stuff. Hit him with some CoQ10, a little Gingko and a boost of Yerbalicious Mate caffeine. Bump all that up with some of that belief we were talking about, and old Don will be a happy camper."

Junie was about to continue the war of the monitor when a delivery man entered with a large Styrofoam container, had her sign on five separate dotted lines, and left.

She cut the plastic straps and lifted off the top half, releasing a cool-mist cloud from the chunks of dry ice that surrounded a modest white cardboard box. Quinn tilted his head to read the label and gave a long, low whistle.

"What?"

"That's the shit. The bad shit. HGH? He really does mean to make money."

"David?"

"Or the great and powerful Oz. If David *isn't* in it for the money, he better back off of that stuff," he said. "A few semi-positive studies a decade ago, and they've been pushing it since."

"Who?"

"Anyone in the business with a medical degree and more lifestyle needs than scruples."

"I thought this was the one thing that actually worked."

"Slow down aging?" He tilted his hand, one way and then the other. "Maybe sorta. Like anything, it depends on the parameters you pick – garbage in, garbage out. If you pick muscle mass, lean body weight, or feeling a tad excited because your head's spinning to a chorus of every oscillating hormone from your hypothalamus on down, then sure, it delivers the goods. Probably helps the aches and pains, too."

"What's wrong with that?"

"It's the parameters you *don't* pick that kill you – the ones you don't know about, or don't want to. Like diabetes, hypertension, everything else that can go wrong when a complex organism is being told to ignore its own rules. In other words, it's hard on the homeostasis, how the body balances all the countless things it does. And because they really are countless, or pretty much, you can't anticipate which ones you're going to jam up."

Junie looked at him, crossways; with Quinn, it paid to be skeptical.

"Look, this is my business, or used to be. I know this stuff, and I know this much: you don't mess with Mother Nature, even if you don't like the general direction she's taking you. Meds, supplements, sure. I've got no problem with a tweak here and there, like I've got no problem with making a buck, but…"

"But what?"

"This is going *deep*. Down into the primal mud, stirring it up, trying to remake the way the body regulates itself. Like trying to rebuild a house, but starting from the foundation up. Sometimes it works; sometimes the house falls down."

BEATRIZ was nine hours out of Catalina, making good time on a whitecap-dotted sea when it happened.

After clearing the shadowy bulk of the last of the Channel Islands, she could see the lights of Santa Barbara unreeling off to starboard, each blurred by the waves' trailing mist to a soft and incandescent glow. The wind was coming from the north, and she made it work for her and Osprey's moonlit sails, avoiding the unseen perils of Point Conception and heading out into the dark Pacific, cresting the wind-chopped swells that made these black waters even less pacific than usual.

From her hydraulic chair in the dry but tilted cockpit, she turned the knob that rolled her sweet boat's sails tight against the wind. Or would have rolled, if not for the grinding metallic noise that told her the motor on the jib had jammed again. Cursing floridly in Bislama, the language of her favorite impoverished West Pacific island, she zipped up, stepped into the salt-spray, and clipped her harness to the safety line that ran along the deck. It wasn't all that hard – always keeping a hand on one halyard or another, her soles lifting off as Ozma cleared one crest and plunged downward, then landing on the wet teak as her hull tobogganed up the wind-tattered face of the next.

Beatriz used her trusty pliers to wrench the cable from between the gears and back into the pulley's track, then headed back to the cabin. She was hustling towards the light and warmth when a larger lifting wave hit – not a rogue wave, not wildly unexpected, but the kind of roller-coaster mother that surfers wait all day for. Her hand slid a full yard up and down the stainless-steel halyard in a stomach-clutching thrill of weightlessness, a thrill that ended suddenly when her left foot landed sideways on a coil of rope and she swung in a broad and accelerating circle to slam against the mast.

It stole her breath but that seemed to be the worst of it, just an excuse to spend a restful moment curled around the base of the broad graphite shaft. The next few waves' driven spray pounded her back, a solid weight that came and went and pounded her again. Cold even through the layers she wore, but not bad cold, at least not until a lash of wet found its way between the layers and sent a shocking freeze up her spine. She hauled herself to standing and pronounced herself fine, then leaned into the wind for the few remaining steps of a short but difficult journey, one hand to her ribs and only slightly unsteady as she slid the hatch open, unclipped the safety line and fell into the warm and dry.

Tea – hot tea was what she needed. The boat was fine now, literally shipshape, once more sailing on full auto. She'd managed to land on the cabin's padded bench and was flat on her back, working her way out of her slicker and then checking for a fracture, her fingers cautiously palpating behind the full curve of her left breast to find a tenderized chest wall that ached with each slow and even breath.

After five minutes she was ready to stand, recheck the instruments, and walk carefully down three steps to the galley. Where she poured honeyed green tea from a thermos she'd filled hours ago and wrapped her hands around the plastic cup. They said the green kind was good for you – loaded with as many antioxidants as, it seemed, they said everything else they were selling had – and she certainly liked the way it tasted, but right now she was after the heat, to chase the chill from the beaten core of her.

Beatriz settled on the bench against the downslope galley wall and was cozy enough, considering. She was not prone to doubt or worry, sworn enemies of the solo sailor, but could not help a single flash of what might have been, what might have happened if she hadn't been stopped by the mast and had continued sliding, to tumble over the wire rail and be dragged at six knots underwater, choking and spinning on her safety line. Her harness would have held, of course, and she probably would have remained conscious, And could have pulled herself back in the same as once before, but still. Did life have to be this hard?

The puppy. The puppy hadn't been hard. Stinky, but not hard. And she'd turned away from the thing, because it fouled her boat and complicated her life. Despite the love – that ache again, the same as when she'd handed it over, deeper than her aching ribs – and the warmth it bought. Connection. But the puppy couldn't have hauled her back on board... a gristly thought: the tiny thing starving as Beatriz rotted on her line, a sporty chunk of spinning chum, entertaining sharks at six auto-piloted knots per hour.

Yuck. Beatriz shook herself, then winced. A cracked rib, after all. Finishing the cup, she gingerly climbed back up to the closed cockpit. The lights of the coast were gone, and the dark Pacific lay ahead. Six weeks to the extradition-free republic of Vanuatu; six weeks to her home base, though not her home. Six weeks for a broken rib to heal.

Or she could tack back to the north, where a slip could be had, she'd heard, for not much at all, considering what she could make taking dewy-eyed honeymooners for San Franciscan sunset sails. Not that different from the Pacific inter-island charters that had gotten her import-export enterprise started. Fresh faces, with money in their pockets and flowers in their hair. And, among the live-aboards that populated any urban dock, new friends... connections.

Beatriz set her dials, pushed her buttons, and waited for the grinding noise that this time, thankfully, did not come. A swing, a tilt, a new direction, headed back toward shelter. Toward journeys that never ventured into open waters; how long before the keening, random wind called to her again?

13

DON'S DAY

- or -

Therapeutic Assetosuction

EARLY THE NEXT MORNING, Junie removed the plain white carton from the freezer and placed it in front of David. No fog this time, no shipping company special effects, just a cold dry smell, an ether-like hint of sterile biologicals within. The smell of Science – Medical Science – she decided, and asked, "You're sure?"

"No, but as sure as I'm going to be."

Junie replied with a look, a look that said that that wasn't nearly enough.

A look that David found intensely irritating – after all, who was *she*? Hadn't gone to medical school, hadn't spent three years of residency and four of practice holding patients' hands and trying to do right by them, hadn't wrestled with the vagaries of medical knowledge: of benefit and harm, of meeting impossible expectations, of hard choices with too little information. She had no idea, no clue of what it took to be a doctor.

Actually, her look contained a bit of knowledge David wasn't aware of – those years before graduate school, hawking that minor line of pharmaceuticals. Working her little pool of doctors in any legal and semi-legal way she could, bribing them to prescribe vast boatloads of whatever she'd been told to push that month. And using all the charm she could summon, which might not have been her strong suit but was definitely helped by the prime box seats to whatever acceptable sports diversion her customers' might choose. Not to mention the fan of crisp $100 bills beneath each heavy napkin of a steakhouse dinner-and-lecture combo, which the clowns were welcome to spend on all the *unacceptable* diversions they might desire.

To David, it was a look that seemed fully aware, and not particularly approving, of the indecent profit the clinic would be making.

He turned away and opened the carton, removed one of the small white boxes within, and, from that, took one vial of white powder and one vial of clear dilutant, and unfolded a yard-long instruction sheet. After finding a clear plastic syringe and a large-bore needle in the drawer below, he hunched over to read the fine print and proceeded to reconstitute it.

David mounted the needle on the syringe and drew up the dilutant. His irritation almost completely under control, he explained – patiently, if pedantically – his rationale again. Starting with how Don had read every conceivable risk on the patient forms and signed off on them.

"So it's his choice," she stated. "You're a completely neutral bystander."

David injected the dilutant, perhaps a little more forcefully than necessary. "I'm *not* passing the buck to the patient, Junie."

"Oh?" Bach was playing on the sound system again – Goldberg Variations and very nice, but in her opinion adding up to at least one too many white guys, dead or not, in the room.

"He's trying it and I'm happy, okay?" He shook the vial, carefully, to mix powder and liquid. "The potential benefits are enormous. Don could feel better, feel stronger, fell younger, maybe even *be* younger. Sure, there's some risk – nothing's without risk."

"Would *you* take it?"

He drew out the now-milky solution, then removed the syringe, cradling it, point up, in his free hand. "In five, ten years? I think so. Yes."

At that point, a disembodied voice – coming from somewhere on the other side of the reception counter behind them – rasped, "Most commendable, Dr. Black."

"Christ!" David's hand had jerked and the syringe was dangling from the ball of his index finger. Gingerly, he pulled the needle out, then jammed the perforated digit in his mouth, a streak of blood across his lower lip.

Junie hitched herself up over to the counter and looked down at the wizened face of the wheelchair-bound Dr. Flint. "Where the fuck did you come from?"

"The employee door, young lady, as your good doctor suggested on my first visit. Much easier to negotiate." His wheelchair whirred around the reception area to David, who was still holding the offending syringe. "And you might consider a bit more respect for the Queen's English."

"You want it in French?" Junie thought of his age and how her *grand-maman* would have whacked her, and added, "Sorry."

"As I am. Unforgivable." He smiled, thin and dry, gently pulled the syringe from David's fingers, removed the blood-tinged needle, flipped its safety cap back on and placed on the counter. Then looked up to David and said, "How do you like it? Feeling younger already?"

David's eyes went to the syringe to the needle, the hollow core of which had, no doubt, delivered a microscopic dose of human growth hormone to his finger. "Oh."

Deep within Flint's venerable if soup-spotted tweed sport coat, narrow shoulders shrugged. "I didn't either. Six months and I stopped – nothing, for me. But others…"

David waited, then said. "I hope so, at this price."

"Yes." Another faint smile. "But cost is immaterial. Think of what we all gain by their courage."

David liked that. Courage. His finger still stung; he was tempted to suck on it again, but controlled himself and dressed it with a small round Happy Tortoise Band-Aid. Flotsam from his old practice: anything to distract a vaccinated child… or wounded doctor.

"Whatever the cost, win or lose," Flint added. "We all gain knowledge. And knowledge, as you know, is priceless."

"Spoken like a true researcher," Junie said.

Flint cranked his corrugated neck and shot her a knowing look, appearing remarkably similar, David thought, to the Happy Tortoise on his finger. He wasn't sure he liked what he was hearing – research was great, except for the researched. But Don knew the risks, as did the other three who had, so far, answered Oz's mailing. All male, all from fifty to seventy years of age, all absurdly affluent, and all responding to the carefully targeted linen-envelope mailing.

As Flint proceeded to pry out Junie's academic *bona fides* – he seemed impressed, actually – blood rose through the tiny band aid, the Happy Tortoise's cheerfully pink outline disappearing in the bloom. Junie took the lead and peppered Flint with questions, while

David pressed his leaking finger flat and listened. How many rich middle-aged males had taken HGH so far, she asked, and how often had it made a difference? Was anyone actually counting, or was it just a mass of free-range consumers opting on their own to take the drug, while their doctors kept their eyes and ears open for a general sense of good or bad things happening. Gradually compiling a list of anecdotal patient stories – the softest, least reliable, least objective kind of knowledge, especially when the parties involved wished to hear only good things.

In reply, Flint artfully evaded specifics, demurring agreeably and parrying her questions with the hoary, but consistently successful, academic technique of praising them.

He should praise them, because she was right, David decided. If no one was counting, or doing any more than collecting anecdotes – Mr. X felt years younger, Mr. Y lost his hair but gained ten pounds of muscle mass so it was worth it – that just wasn't enough. With a long-term, Hydra-headed problem like aging, you needed to track all the numbers, not only the nominator of the patients who do well but also the *denominator* of everyone treated. Otherwise, Don and his fellow lab rats would be paying to play a game that no one knew the odds of, taking all the risk and assuming all the cost.

Cost, David thought. And the fact that Don's cost was the clinic's gain. As Oz had said, they needed a profit center to keep rolling. David didn't like to think about that part, but knew it was that real-world business aspect of medicine that had torpedoed his last practice, and that he had a lot to learn.

Flint and Junie were still going at it, but their voices seemed to recede as David remembered how he'd felt about profit when he'd started out to be a doctor; when his old practice had turned belly-up; and when the mighty wheels of commerce had spun around him as he stood, shocked, on the ASS conference floor.

He shook his head to chase those doubts away, picked up the capped syringe, and peered at the thin column of milky liquid within. Flint and Junie could argue all they wanted: to a physician, this was exciting in itself. After more than a month of preparation, here he was, actually *doing* something to beat back the grim reaper. Exciting and, well, fun. Now that they were finally up and running, he'd have to review the current research. There was that big study, over a decade ago; somebody must have taken a hard, non-anecdotal look at HGH since.

DON OPENED the Clinic's massive teak door and was once again impressed. Just seeing this kind of money gave him confidence. The sense, if nothing else, that they did not need his. Which was illogical – of course they needed it, his and every other patient's, and especially if they were spending it this way. But it still gave him a glow, for he knew that Dr. Black, emotionally withdrawn husband or not, was spending every dollar with his best interests at heart.

He strolled in beneath the high glass ceiling, open to the fresh morning air, some sort of dignified classical music filling the open space. There, behind the counter, his doctor in conference with his associates. When Dr. Black headed down the hallway, Don realized he'd been speaking to his receptionist, the one with the sharp tongue. Who remained in conversation with someone else, hidden behind the counter. As Don drew closer, he saw a peeling, threadbare scalp, then bright piercing eyes, and then was stopped dead by a frighteningly skeletal grimace. Good Lord – Let that aged wreck be a *before*, not an *after*!

UP TO THAT MOMENT, Flint had occupied himself with being a happy fisherman, playing a line out to Junie, enjoying the fight. But this new fishie, dressed head to toe in some sort of sweater-like material and dropping a two-inch stack of paperwork on the polished granite, was obviously a minnow, there to be observed and definitely not interfered with. Thus, his warmest, least threatening smile. Oh, the wonder of a willing victim, a living experiment, actually paying to spin off a tiny piece of data. Because Flint, whose fame was great enough to open all doors in the industry, *was* counting. Someone had to. The HGH companies certainly didn't wouldn't. Sales were rippling along; why take a chance on bad news? But he would, and with a few more self-funding data-points (that is, patients) he'd be ready to publish. Posthumously, of course, as the companies' lawyers were the sort of deep-water denizens he really didn't have the remaining time or energy for.

He introduced himself; Don took his withered hand reluctantly, then said, "And you're…?"

Flint winked at Junie. "A consultant."

As Junie turned away and rolled her eyes, Don looked relieved. "Then you aren't…?"

"Taking the wonder drug? No, not for me, I'm afraid. Not right now." He glanced down and patted the general region of his stomach. "Just a temporary setback – a little problem with my appetite."

"Your appetite…" Don's alarm grew as Flint's hand pushed the buttoned tweed jacket further and further in, nearing the approximate location of the old man's spine. "I… I know a good restaurant," Don tried, clearly rattled. "At the hotel, a few blocks from here." He gestured wildly to the south. "The food's fantastic, really – did wonders for mine – go there every day I'm in town – breakfast, lunch, dinner…"

"Snacks?" Flashing the tombs of his teeth.

Don nodded numbly and Flint nodded back. Then allowed himself to wish, for one rare instant that came dangerously close to self-pity, that hunger was the only appetite he'd lost.

DAVID RETURNED with Flint's prescriptions, the doses tapering at his request. After a quick and professional hello, as he was trying not be a salesman, he led Don to his injection, and then from there to his osteoporosis scan and then his exercise electrocardiogram. He'd only overheard the end, about the restaurant – where, Oz had recently informed him, Sheyoni now worked. As he walked by Howie Krishna's closed door, after being distracted momentarily by an odd floating shadow behind the frosted glass, David could only hope Don hadn't run into her, hadn't asked her about Oz's imaginary disease.

NANCY AND HOWIE, time on their hands.

Time on *her* hands, actually – all Howie had to do was close his eyes to make time disappear. But Nancy's hands had only time to hold, weightless time and nothing else, no muscle or skin or sinew, and she was restless, her hands and all the rest of her, pacing the hall like the mountain lion that paced the forested edge of her property in the evening. Howie's door was open; she walked by as Howie moved calmly behind his desk. He met her eyes and gestured, Come in.

"Hey there, Guru Guy." From the workout space above came the rhythmic thump of Don on the treadmill.

"Hey there as well, my friend." Howie seemed to drift sideways, just a centimeter, then tugged on his desk chair's arms and settled in.

Weird, she thought, but so much was around here. "Want a massage?"

"I would want nothing more from you." He wanted nothing, ever, but why be rude?

Nancy shrugged, spun on the ball of one foot and left, a finger crooked over one shoulder as though dragging him along. Howie followed, so quietly she wasn't sure he had, until her office door snicked closed behind her.

"You can hang your robes on the wall," she said, from the other side of the shoji screen that discretely shielded her desk. "There's a sheet on the table."

"And it is the softest fabric."

Nancy turned; the top of his white robe, plus a few indefinable but pure white underlayers, were already visible over the screen. She looked around it to discover he'd already slipped beneath the lavender sheet. Shrugging once more, she intertwined her fingers, stretched her arms, and cracked all crackable knuckles. Then peeled the top half of the sheet back as he lay with eyes closed, and watched the regular rise and fall of his chest, bisected by a line of reddish curls.

Her restless hands, a body laid out on the sheet. Placid and symmetrical, perfectly symmetrical, but there had to be some tension in there, somewhere, waiting to be fixed. Not so easy, this one: she was going to have to *find* it.

This was going to be good.

"WHAT WAS THAT?" David asked, then heard another long low groan from Nancy's office. Flint had long since received his prescriptions and whirred away, while Don had moved on to Adeline's consultation room, where, no doubt, he'd be entering his diet diary into her special program – the one that flashed subliminal photos of ICU's and bypass surgery after every slice of pizza, but butterflies and flowers after every Brussels sprout.

"What do you think?" Junie answered. "She's giving him a massage."

The groan began to build again and David turned back. "But isn't that Nancy?"

Junie got up; David padded after her along the carpeted hallway, to find a waxing and waning glow behind the frosted panes of glass.

"Candles," David said.

"*Blue* ones?"

A brighter flash, also blue and perfectly soundless, that backlighted the Berber wool where it passed beneath the cedar door. Followed by the smell of ozone – not electrical, but fainter, fresh, a summer field after thunderheads had passed. Followed by another low but distinctly feminine moan.

A deep and heaving breath, then Nancy's voice: "That's the fourth time, Howie."

"Perhaps it would be better if you did not use the oil."

"Oh yeah? What if I *like* it?"

Junie looked at David, blushed – an overlay of rose on coffee brown that he could not label as anything but absolutely beautiful – and then snuck, David sneaking after, back up the silent carpet to the front.

MINUTES AND MORE MINUTES PASSED. The waiting room was empty, Don still in with Adeline, reviewing his lipid panel results, his bodyfat measurements, and generally being subjected to the kind of motivation that only a wheedling, manipulative, coaxing, cajoling, and entirely too-committed ninety-pound dietician can achieve.

Nancy's door cracked open. Junie and David took care not to look down the hallway – well, maybe a peek. First came Howie, an unperturbed passage to his office with his usual floating gait. Then Nancy's hand on her doorjamb, and then the rest of her, the first step marred by a small stagger but immediately followed by a near-complete recovery. Leaving behind a handprint, composed of equal parts sweat and almond oil, soaking into the pale wood.

Her white jacket was buttoned, the spread collar of her deep green cotton work shirt still pressed and centered – no, not that; *that* had clearly not been going on – but her face was illuminated by a look neither one of them had seen before. A look, and a laxity to her joints, a new laxity to her *intention*, her palms glowing, almost burning, her short hair standing on end. Junie watched, wondering how she had seemed on her own post-massage perp walk, back on the day Nancy had been hired. Then remembered that Nancy had just *gotten* a massage, not given it.

Nancy made it to the counter and stood there, slightly weaving, hands flat on the cool granite to steady herself. An inch-thick outline of steam formed around them, slowly shrinking inward as they cooled.

A pause, then David asked, "Nancy?"

Another pause and Nancy answered, sort of: "Hmm?"

Junie pursed her lips, shook her head and returned to her work. David continued to study Nancy, who was still staring off into the middle distance, appearing no less puzzled than he was.

NANCY HAD PULLED HERSELF TOGETHER – filed it away for review later – by the time Don returned, Adeline's frail form trailing behind. Thomas Thinna caught up and introduced himself to Don.

Don looked at him, confused, and then back to Adeline, then at Thomas again. "Are you… related?"

"We're *married*." Thomas said, with a glare. "She's diet, I'm exercise."

"Aerobic exercise," Nancy added, joining them. "I'm anaerobic and flexibility, upstairs." Don glanced up the sweeping glass and steel stairs at the racks of gleaming equipment, the bars and pulleys and… were those *hooks*?

"I've already got your data from the treadmill," Thomas was saying. "We'll come up with some sort of run-walk plan, take it from there. After I watch Nancy put you through the paces." Thomas smiled brightly from beneath his graying bangs – 'relatives', indeed.

"The paces," Don said, sounded worried.

"Oh, yes." Nancy flexed her arms and rolled her shoulders, getting ready. "Followed by a nice, brisk deep tissue massage."

Don paled. Nancy landed a knee-buckling clap on Don's shoulder – Thomas involuntarily ducked away – and the three were off.

HOURS LATER.

Don had descended, shaken, for a late teaching lunch with Adeline, consisting of untoasted grains, extra-virgin olive oil, raw diced fruits and vegetables, and a few slices of boiled chicken breast. Served, unfortunately, in her own signature style, mixed together in the bottom of a large plastic bowl. But Don hadn't complained, having learned the cost of complaining at that masseuse's hands – first on the racks and pulleys, and especially later, when he'd innocently asked if she could not press those iron-tipped fingers quite so deeply into the integument of his back. Following which, there'd been another vicious session on the treadmill, Thomas Thinna standing with an nasty glint beside it, fingertip poised over a tablet computer, goading him until his knees screamed as much as they had months ago, at the end of his single previous back-to-exercise run. Could that twig run half as fast? Don doubted it; not if *he* was limited to his wife's thousand-calorie diet.

From lunch, Don had moved on to the very unusual Dr. Quinn, receiving a bag of gel-cap supplements that gleamed like precious stones at only half the price. And then a training meditation with Howie (not Harry) Krishna, whose benign presence made a half-hour of sitting frozen, tailor-style, not only bearable but somehow transcendent.

Now Don walked slowly, sorely, and totally completely exhaustedly to the front reception counter, arriving at the same sweep of elevated granite he'd dropped his pack of papers onto six hours ago. To Don, it seemed like years – a whole epic fantasy of adventures, from escaping the evil wheelchair troll of death, to the triple trials of Nancy and Thomas and Adeline, to whatever exalted if painful state he'd just arrived from.

Junie was the only one behind the desk. Laying his forearms on the cool stone, almost nodding with fatigue, he asked, "Next month?"

"Next week, you mean." Thinking, Poor Don.

"*All* of it?"

"Don't despair." She patted his hand, hoping that poor George, Don's demographic twin filling out his own papers on the other side of the waiting room, wouldn't notice the need for sympathy.

"I'm not – I mean, it was wonderful, but…"

"But a lot, I know. Next week's only an injection, that and a quick check with Adeline and Dr. Quinn, see how you're doing. And back in two weeks to see Thomas and Nancy—"

Don tensed, about to bail, until she added, quickly, "And then a tune-up from Howie." Don shoulders sagged down again.

Times were agreed on, forms were signed, and a copy of David's transcribed summary notes placed in his hand. After a slow, half-limping passage to the door – poor George still had his nose buried in the legal papers – Don's big day was done.

ONCE BOTH OF THEM WERE GONE, David called the staff out of their offices and – to Adeline's approval, Quinn's scowl, and Junie's rolling eyes – opened a magnum bottle of the finest imported sparking water. They toasted the successful passage of the Forever Clinic's first fully functioning day. There was a glow between them, and one not entirely emanating from Howie: the knowledge that they'd created something, perhaps something even beautiful. A team, working towards a goal they believed in.

The others trickled out, leaving just him and Junie, closing up. David watched her efficient, graceful motions, thinking she was exactly what he – that is, the clinic – needed.

After, as they parted on the street, he stood awkwardly, hands in pockets, and thanked her. For doing my job? She asked, and she was right, though he felt he had not shown his gratitude enough. A bonus check was out – he still had no money, and Oz said bonuses were really raises and would kill the Clinic as surely as he'd done his old practice in. Perhaps a polite, Boulder hug… no, never that, and Junie was already walking away. Looking not at all like Paula. Not one bit, he told himself, not one bit at all.

The last of those thoughts vanished as he bicycled home through the falling light. Peach-colored clouds cast a pre-autumnal, almost sepia light; Mercury, Saturn and Mars were in ascendance, bright pinpoints penetrating the deep blue between. David moved smoothly through the first tendrils of cold air snaking down from the hills; it was his favorite time of day. Not too different from that first night at the Triad, but a whole emotional spectrum away. Pedaling up and then over the hill on Thirteenth, gliding right in front of Sheyoni's workplace and Don's favorite restaurant, and from there across the grid of 'downtown' streets. Quiet at this hour, for once not featuring the usual SUV-driving students, music thumping behind closed windows as they balanced latte vs. cigarette, phones pressed to the ear. Or harried mothers, minus the tobacco but plus two screaming kids. In any case, he made it safely to the bike path, handlebar-mounted light turned on, tires rolling in the sweet evening to his apartment beside the creek.

David left his bike on the matted shag carpet of his hallway and stepped into the single large room. Nondescript, but he was getting used it. The Spartan look, if Sparta had featured folding metal chairs. But still, a microwave pizza, the window open to the rushing waters just below, a cold beer, and–

The cell phone rang, lighting up the depths of the bike messenger bag open at his feet. He gave himself a break, finished a long swallow from the tilted amber bottle, and hoped for no good reason that it was Junie, to talk more about the day. It rang again, no hurry, two more rings to go. David stretched, leaned over, reached down towards the handset, and read the number on the screen. 303... no, 310... Holy crap, it was Paula!

He grabbed it and sat up straighter, heart pounding as he answered.

14

PAULA'S BIGG VISIT

- or -

Hyporequited Stimulosis

"YOU'RE COMING? That's great!" The thundering in David's chest was immediately matched by a black-hole hollow in his gut. *Appetite* – he'd overheard Flint say that, through his open office door this morning. Don Gilmore had answered as if the old professor meant simple hunger. David knew Flint had meant far more, knew it then and knew it now, knew it from the hunger *he* was feeling, a solid slam of yearning, Paula in his arms, the touch and smell and taste of her. A hunger that was in no way simple and was already heading towards regions below.

Paula held the phone away, admiring her recent manicure while giving the boy a moment to calm down. "David, it's a *business* trip. Even Dr. Biggs is impressed by how well you've done; he says he has to come." The paperwork was spread in front of her: five signed patients already. Ten grand a month, in perpetuity, with five thousand headed toward HorTech, twenty percent of which was hers. And that was just the first week.

David hardly heard her mention Biggs; his mouth was dry, his palms damp. What *was* it about Paula? That brief, unasked question passed unnoticed – it didn't matter, nothing mattered, he had to have her here. Maybe begging would work. He cleared his throat and croaked, "This weekend?"

"No can do. Sorry." And she was; he had his charms, after all. "The flights are booked for next Wednesday. We can stay in Denver, or…?"

"I've got the place," he said, up and pacing. "The St. Julio. It's this huge hotel they just, um…" His mind blanked, then was filled by a vision from the bike path: cranes against the sky, heavy counter-weights climbing towards the top. "…erected by the creek. I mean…" Oh no.

The corner of Paula's mouth turned up. "Erected. Huh. And huge? Make sure Biggs is staying somewhere nice, too – somewhere *else*."

He stopped in front of the bathroom mirror. What was happening to him? His pupils were big as saucers.

"Hello… David…?"

"W – what?" Sinking, with some difficulty and at least one wardrobe readjustment, to the white-tied floor.

"Do you want me to get on it?"

He closed his eyes and saw her above him, head forward, strands of silver damp and hanging. Then dimly remembered, though the fog of testosterone, that she was on the phone. "The reservation?"

"Yes, David."

"You… you better. There's also the Boulderian."

"Biggs can stay there."

"It's… it's almost as nice. He'll like it."

"Perfect."

Perfect. David sighed, struggled to get up – with further readjustments, searing and electric – then limped to the apartment's dog-eared phone book, lonely on the carpet near the wall. He read the numbers out to her, and then, her voice brisk again, she had to go. But still, at the end, the way she said goodbye: the hint of something, almost an endearment. He put the phone down and, elbows on the windowsill, sat and watched the creek, black waters flowing in the dark.

Back on the coast, Paula swung sheer-stockinged feet off the desk and slipped them, with a cool hiss of charcoal nylon, into a waiting pair of arterial-red high heels.

Pheromones, still working after nearly a month. She shook her head. You gotta love 'em.

SIX DAYS. He could do that. But those conversations on the phone, his reaction. As intense as, well, Vegas. Or close.

Only close, and not requited.

Time to think about something, anything else, David decided. And if he couldn't make himself *not* think about sex – baseball stats really weren't his thing – there was always his tried-and-true technique: thinking about it, or anything else that had him by the short hairs, *clinically.*

So... hmmm. Sex... appetite... arousal! That was it! Sexual arousal, if he backed up and put it in a properly rational perspective, wasn't all that different from any other kind of arousal. Like 'fight-or-flight', your basic caveman-versus-Sabertooth response. Except for one prominently featured aspect in the male, a feature that would, in some far distant past, have significantly impaired both the fighting and the flighting.

Better not dwell on that, he told himself. The impairment, that is. Better to dwell on... fighting and flighting! Both of which sounded, well, *stressful.* What if all arousal was a kind of stress, an adrenaline-charged uptick in the body's oh-so-carefully-balanced homeostatic physiology?

As the rushing song of the water came in though the open window's screen, his mind traveled back to medical school, a projected image in a darkened lecture hall. The Stress Score. How 'good' stresses, the birth of a child or a new job, counted as much as 'bad' ones, like being fired or losing a parent. Either way, if you scored enough points in a year – a marriage, a death, a new house, a few wrecked cars – the body would give it up and something truly bad would happen. A significant illness, or even death, predicted by the total score.

David shifted on his folding chair, crossed his legs, and was momentarily distracted by a particular aching sensitivity. Sex couldn't kill you, he knew that; if things went right, that particular stress – Paula Oh Paula – was soon replaced by the kind of post-stress bliss that was just what the body needed, mission accomplished. But if any stress, good or bad, continued unabated – Paula Oh Paula Oh Stop, he told himself, Stop – it would wear the body down.

Win the battle and it was over; slog on and on, and you were. It wasn't how good or bad the stress was, but how long it lasted: a time-frame issue, the physiology of constant stimulation.

What if that stimulation lasted for... years, even decades? A low groan began deep within him, then was truncated as another thought, a rather significant cognition, rose to the surface. Years and decades of stimulation, years and decades of alteration in the body's physiologic steady-state, years and decades of... HGH injections? Decades of forced tissue regrowth, renewal, physiologic change... decades of stress?

All the data he'd seen had been from the first six months of HGH treatment – feeling great, big muscles, more energy. All good. And the *story* was good, too... how muscles wasted with age, how declining growth hormone levels might be the cause, how the machinery of aging could be driven by that lack. But what happened when you stretched the time-frame, when you took the long look: were the effects still good?

He'd read everything he'd been given, but hadn't gone beyond that, hadn't gone off and reviewed the medical literature, all the HGH studies. David felt a flush of shame, the professional sort. Still, better late than never. If only to help his mind, and at least one appendage that seemed directed connected to it, resist the well-oiled tug of Paula.

His phone rang and he grabbed it off the desk, insanely hoping it was her again. No, the screen read Oz; David's thumb hovered over a bug-sized button but did not press it down. If he talked to Oz, he'd have to tell him Paula and Biggs were coming out. Which led to an image he didn't like: Oz and Biggs, planning the clinic's future.

He didn't answer. Not until he did his homework.

Better late than never.

SATURDAY MORNING. David hadn't seen much sleep the night before. The lingering buzz of Paula had been effectively dispelled by the arcane tables and graphs and medicalese paragraphs that had soon filled his computer screen. The hospital's medical library let him access a score of full-text articles he'd printed out and laid flat on the apartment's dun-colored carpet. Together, they formed two columns of stapled pages – microscopic black text, narrow margins smudged from reading – that marched across the funky rug. The positive studies reached all the way to the foot of his bed; the negative reports, perhaps a third of the distance. Reassuring, sort of. Still, there was something off about that good-news majority of the studies, something that did not look better in the morning light.

Enough. A run was what he needed. He slid open a louvered closet door, rummaged in the depths of the slotted light, and found the running clothes he hadn't worn since... well, since the day he'd hired Junie. A white synthetic t-shirt and ratty khaki shorts piled on top of his socks and running shoes, the whole stack a little ripe but good for one more workout.

It was another mercilessly sunny day, but the bike path and the tree-lined streets were shadowed, not yet scorching at this hour. Without thinking, he followed the same route as his last run, going up the creek by the now fully-built hotel – *Erected! Crap!* – then up through the neighborhoods and into Chautauqua Park, running in piney shade and then full sun, the air heating up but not too bad if he kept moving, big long relaxed strides that took him back down along that row of old cabins, heading towards shade again and home – heading there, at least, until his cell phone began to vibrate, a fat bee thrumming in the small of his back.

JUNIE, FINALLY SATISFIED, turned the damp dirt between the carrots and the flowers in her little plot of garden. It had taken her all summer to figure how often to water it – *twice* a day, a waste of water but there you were, the true expense of sweet orange Little Fingers and Wax Begonias in the peppery dry heat of Colorado's Front Range. The garden, square and rimmed with railroad ties, was out back of her cabin – an eight foot island of verdant southern land between the flagstone patio and the brittle yellow grass that grew along the gravel access road. Some previous tenant had knocked the patio together, that and built strange piled-stone 'furniture' from of the roughly fractured flagstones that littered the steep hillside across the gravel, the stony shed dandruff of the Flatirons above. A juniper tree on the south side of the tiny lot afforded a few hours of mid-day shade, without which her still-blooming babies would have needed watering from dawn to dusk. Twice a day she could handle, out there with a faded rubber hose in the shadows before work, and again on coming home from the university, the heat still rising from the ground at midnight. Or this weekend morning, when nothing else needed doing and she had, frankly, way too much time to play with.

The pounding footfalls of yet another Boulder sportaholic stormed down the gravel road; her little cabin's view was nice but came at a cost. She kept working – didn't look and hoped the runner wouldn't either – but the steps soon slid to a stop. Followed by the sound of panting, a deep gasp-and-wheeze that was somehow familiar.

She peered from deep shade into glaring light: it was David in running shorts and, Lord preserve her, a fanny pack, holding a cell phone open, staring at its unforgiving face.

DAVID snapped the phone shut, unanswered, zipped it back into one of the many handy pockets of his lumbar suspension unit – fanny-packs, indeed – and stood with sweat dripping off his face and a slowly calming heart. It hadn't been Paula, but Oz again, and he still wasn't ready for that.

"David," a voice said, and he turned to see that critical squint he knew so well, the tight-knotted pigtails that dangled in every possible direction, darks hands deep into the dark earth. And the way her tank top dipped low to reveal...

She got up and brushed the dirt from her knees. "What's it gonna be? Water, lemonade, or iced coffee?"

He looked away and nodded; still panting, grateful his exertion covered a sudden flush. But then again, why should he be embarrassed? Just an errant glance, an instant's indiscretion. Because... because he'd been thinking of Paula, that the call was from her. Of course: thinking of Paula. Otherwise, an employee... not good at all. But there Junie was, and here he was, standing just beyond the edge of what had to be her backyard. Sort of *visiting*, if inadvertently. Not employer and employee, but host and guest. He could do that.

But not do it all that well, guest-wise: he still hadn't spoken. Shaking her head, Junie turned and walked away, pointing at one of two heaps of irregular flagstones that were, upon further inspection, piled into a reasonable simulation of a deck chair. He stepped gingerly though thigh-high thistles and grass, then around her garden and across a tiny patio to park himself on the largest, its stone seat poking his calves but cool enough to drain the heat from his sore thighs. And then there was the shade, and a tall tilted stone that chilled the sweat on the back of his t-shirt as he reclined, and after one shuddering sigh that neatly summarized twenty-four hours of work and research, too little sleep, and a long hot run for the first time in months…

"RELAXED?"

"Hmmm?"

No answer – just cool stone against the backs of his splayed legs and, as he slowly opened his eyes… Junie!

David sat up quick, rubbing the sleep away from his face. Junie gave him a long look, then set a plastic tray on a stack of flagstones between them. Four tall glasses, ice ringing inside as the tray came to rest. One water, one lemonade, and two filled with a milky brown fluid thick enough to obscure the shadowed cubes within.

He grabbed the water and drained it, then said, "Big day, yesterday."

"Um-hum." Her face was bisected by the rim of the glass, blue sky and shining treetops behind, as a smallish ice cube bumped inside his mouth.

"Big night, too?"

David choked down the cube and the fluid wave behind it, coughed hard, grabbed the lemonade to drown the cough and downed half of that, though more careful with the ice. Then said, "Had to get through them a pile of articles."

"On…?"

A worried look. "Growth hormone."

"Old Don got you thinking."

"Yeah. Don and something Quinn said. At the end, when we were talking about how great it was to offer an intervention that powerful, an intervention that could make a difference. Just to me, quietly: 'As long as it pays the bills'."

"I heard, actually. Quinn's certainly not a believer – I got an earful about homeostasis, too, the day the package arrived. The Wisdom of the Body." She lifted the last two glasses and raised her eyebrows. "Can a prevention-type doctor handle some half-and-half?"

Her spidery dark fingers were wrapped around the top; his pale hand enveloped the bottom, the ice coffee a shade between the two. Even cold, he smelled it before it hit his lips: strong and sweet and something else, chicory he guessed, that rounded out any bitterness the cream had missed. "Just don't tell Adeline."

"You're no fun at all," she said, wondering if that was entirely true. Then backed away from that – *please* – and asked, "So what's the scoop?"

He shrugged. "Everybody's got an opinion, though it is more for than against. Three to one."

"It's not a vote, David. The data tells the truth."

"I tried to add the numbers up, but the studies were so different. I don't know how much weight to put to each."

"Try again," she said, and cocked her head, listening, as he verbally fumbled through the same sort of confused litany she got from her undergraduates. Once he was done, so was her ice coffee. As was her gardening, actually, and the day had hardly started. "Come on," she said. "You look like you need a ride back."

The contents of all three glasses – a good thirty-six ounces, plus one ice cube – sat cold and heavy in David's stomach. Skipping the rest of his run seemed an excellent idea.

"DO YOU *ALWAYS*," David asked, "drive with the top down?" The mid-day sun was roasting, heat radiating off every square foot of an expansive Motown womb of black leatherette.

Junie shrugged. "Do you *always*," she asked back, "work out in that shirt?"

He lifted an arm – the one away from her, to her relief – took a sniff and jerked his head back. "Yikes."

"Uh-huh."

David slid to the far side of the seat, lower thigh searing as it hit fresh leatherette.

"Stay over there, and I'll give you Junie's Five."

"Five what?"

"Five rules, so you can read those studies."

"I can *read* them, Junie."

"Sure you can. Just stay over there, okay? And watch my fingers."

David folded his arms, which closed down the offending areas and kept them away from the scorching gearshift handle and the oven wall of the passenger door. As she took the turns between her place and his with alarming speed, he worked to stay centered on the protective terrycloth of the beach towels covering the sprung seats.

"One." She raised an index finger, the creases darker than the pink. "B for Big. Got to be at least twenty to work. Twenty patients, twenty widgets, twenty whatever. Basic statistics, as I'm sure you recall from med school. Flip a coin nineteen times, heads each one, doesn't mean a thing. Personally, I wouldn't suggest a bet against it, but it's not statistically strong enough to, say, recommend a drug."

"Like HGH?"

"That's your biz – I'm not telling you what to do." Her middle finger joined its neighbor in the air, both topped with a translucent corona of fingernail, smooth and polished at the curve. "Two: R for Random. The classic drug study divides your subjects into two groups: half get the real drug, half get placebos – sugar pills. Nobody gets to pick which group they go into, whether they get the real medication or the placebo."

"So we ask patients to pay for a fake drug, at five hundred a week? And if they don't pay, who'll cover it?"

"Golly – the drug companies, so they can risk proving their profit center doesn't work? Guess not. But I'm talking about all studies, not just your HGH ones. You can still prove something without random selection. In fact, you can prove something without any of the rules. But every one you drop erodes the result."

David wondered if he could do his *own* study, track the Forever Clinic's patients. He couldn't randomize and give placebos, but if he amassed enough cases to overcome that weakness... No, he'd need access to every clinic in the country, and who was going to let him do that? It really would take forever.

"Head's up; we're less than halfway there." She unfolded her ring finger. "Three is P, for Prospective. Don't look back, retrospectively, but do something – give your drug, whatever – and move forward in time, measuring what happens. Don't just review old medical records and look at what's happened since. Or patients telling you, "I couldn't bend over before I took it", and you taking their word as gospel. Do that and you lose your chain of causality – memory is weak, as weak as your findings will be."

David waited for her little finger to pop up and there it was, palm open, pink-tan and inches from his face as she kept driving, looking at the road. "Four: D for Disinterested. No drug-company grants to fund the lab, and especially no lux lecture tours, a thousand an hour, for the docs who ran the study. And five…"

"That's a thumb – does it still count?"

"Shut up, boss; I'm in charge here. B again, but this time it's for Blind, and double-blind is best. As in, nobody sees who gets the real drugs. Not the patients, and that goes double – double-blind, get it? – for the researchers. Not until everything's recorded and you crank the numbers, figure out who got better on what."

"Big, random, prospective, disinterested, and blind… 'BRPDB'? That's the best acronym you could put together?"

"Sure. Who could forget 'BRPDB'?" She smiled, still looking forward. "You remember you can't say it."

"I guess," he said, then pointed out his apartment building's driveway. She swung her old car into it at speed, the sagging undercarriage hitting the raised concrete apron with a startling grind. Junie winced, kissed two fingertips and patted the searing dashboard for forgiveness. After a long firm push on the decidedly non-power brakes, the venerable convertible slowed to a stop, two tons of Detroit iron straining forward and then swinging back.

They came to rest in dappled shade beneath tall cottonwoods, a high breeze rattling silver leaves, the parking lot empty.

David popped the passenger door, then turned toward her, not ready to leave. "Do you… do you want a drink or something? Look at those articles?"

"I'm good," she said. Feeling oddly nervous and deciding to listen to it. Good, and staying that way. "You'll figure them better on your own."

"Oh… right. You're absolutely right."

Junie watched him cross the radiating asphalt and open a brown-painted door – one of a row of brown-painted doors, each brass number slightly askew, that marched along a brown-shingled wall. Deep inside, she saw a shining bright window, the creek's green aspen trees beyond, rustling in that baking prairie breeze. And in between, a folding chair, an empty space, and David, a white ghost disappearing into shadow.

OZ HEARD, OF COURSE. Not about Junie's chicory or David's extemporaneous research, but the coming site visit. David let it slip at their regular Tuesday lunch, a back booth at the Walnut Brewery, surrounded by oak and burgundy vinyl, echoingly high ceilings and a pleasantly anonymous post-college crowd. Oz heard about the visit, and was happy. Which was not surprising, with four more full-ticket responses to the Forever Clinic's mailing, and new ads in every holistic giveaway, organic grocery bulletin board, new-age magazine, old-fashioned newspaper, and regional cyber-marketplace up and down the Front Range. Life was good, Oz-wise. The books would soon be balanced, and now he would actually meet the most lucrative Dr. Biggs.

"I should be the one to pick her up." David said.

"No, no," Oz said, just as David hoped. "Play hard to get." Oz tore a steaming chunk from his complimentary mini-loaf of beer bread, fragrant with hops and yeast. "Think of it: the dedicated care provider, working late while she settles in to her fabulous suite at St. Julio's. Then a romantic dinner…" He let his words fade, the image hanging in the air between them, waiting for David to agree.

And David did agree, with the sort of pacing he knew Oz expected, hoping it might buy him a moment to figure out his thoughts. The thing was, he had gone back over the research again, and his doubts had grown. He wasn't sure, not yet: the data was spare on both sides, clouded by the preponderance of low-data, high-opinion pieces, the majority belonging to that long row of pro-HGH studies that still consumed the floor space between his desk and his bed. When you figured in the 'D' of Junie's rule of five – D for Disinterested – by stripping away the voices making money, there weren't many voices left. Noncritical voices, that is; there still were plenty of critics, and they weren't being paid a cent.

The image hanging in front of David hadn't been romantic at all – it was of the long drive back from the airport, of sharing all those doubts. Would Paula understand? Of course: she'd know he had to follow his conscience. But Biggs, leaning over from the backseat?

Yow.

Oz CRUISED at twenty over the limit, having bought the privilege by paying the brand new airport toll road's extravagant fees, as the Western wheat fields reeled on either side, the purple mountain's majesty rising up ahead. Behind him, the lovely Paula, a surprising example of David's maturing taste, watchfully resided on smooth leather in a muted mist of musk and flowers. Looking, he had to admit, almost as attractive as the general direction of their conversation.

"*How* many?" Biggs asked.

As pleased to amaze as any financial magician, Oz repeated his projections again. Then asked, in return, "And *how* much revenue will we each see, per patient?"

From the passenger seat, Biggs gave a subliminal hum of pleasure – in the isolated silence of the cabin, Paula could almost feel it vibrating back to her – and answered with a generous, wheeling flourish of one hand.

All three were excellent with numbers, could multiply A times B and come up with something very good indeed. Oz privately added the income from the Forever Clinic's other health-and-wellness services, while his passengers exponentially enlarged it by the many, many markets to be found across the vast and aging heartland their vehicle was currently ramming through.

Soulmates.

THE HACIENDA LOOK, Paula decided. Boulder was little too far north of Santa Fe, but she liked it, liked the arcing stucco ceiling over the lobby's costumed mariachi band, the blue howling coyotes carved into the elevator doors, the furry cowhide furniture, the rusty barbed-wire toilet paper holders that spoke of the kind of hygienic exactitude she favored, not to mention the burro-shaped basket of deep-gray pinion-ash personal care products. Paula, naked, paused in front of her suite's expansive window – the Flatirons before her, a few fraternity boys gawking up from the street – and placed a single drop of pheromone, mustn't overdo, between her breasts.

The ride in had naturally evolved into a business dinner, just the three of them, keeping young David at a distance to preserve, by unspoken agreement, his charming naiveté. A naiveté so useful when it came to the ethics of patient care, not to mention any pending governmental regulations. He'd agreed to wait, such a gentleman, giving her time enough for a quick post-prandial workout, a sixty-second burst of power meditation and then a cleansing needle-spray shower. And soon… showtime!

Paula donned a dense terry-cloth robe and, ignoring the small but gathering crowd below, reached with arms wide and drew the shades. After surveying the room, she took two quick tensile steps and sprung up to land in the exact center of the mattress, bouncing into a perfectly executed forward flip.

Better than the Cirque!

A knock; she liked promptness in a man. Paula jumped down and jammed the champagne bottle into the silver ice bucket that stood near the bed, knocking a few large cubes to the carpet but no time for that now. Then strode across the room, opened the door and watched his pupils dilate.

Yes – still working, and very well indeed.

DAVID had been keyed up in the hallway, but when he inhaled the first invisible tendrils of her musk and jasmine scent, a not-one-tiny-bit-forgotten flood of molecules rode his pulse to slam happily into the vomeronasal receptors of his hindbrain, that supposedly atrophic cluster of pheromone-sensitive cells he possessed an unusually healthy supply of. Once his pupils had fully dilated, as they are wont to when aroused, David fell into the room, fell into Paula, fell into what looked to be an endless swooning future. All doubts had vanished – about the HGH, about the hiatus in their relationship, about whether he was supposed to walk over and open the chilled champagne in the silver stand behind her. Doubts gone with the robe that covered her, gone with the shirt she ripped from his chest, buttons flying, gone with the shorts he happily hobbled out of, gone with any lingering thoughts about a certain intellectually demanding employee.

A two-handed shove from Paula sent him tipping like a lumbered redwood toward the bed; he hit the mattress and watched wonderingly as she followed, flying above to land on knees and outstretched arms that caged him as he bounced up into her, both laughing – why not? It was fun! – while they rolled along the downy too-many-threads-to-count king-sized comforter.

David, however, was slightly more than king-sized, and his last half-roll took him beyond the realm of feathers and springs and into the less-forgiving region of empty air and simple gravity. After a solid thump to the padded carpet, he rose and stepped two paces back, preparing to launch himself into his destiny or, at least, into Paula.

And why not, he thought. He wanted her, right? More than that, he wanted *to*... sex being the healthiest, most vital act – a rare moment, now that he paused to consider it, to lose yourself, to join and surge beyond the bonds of self. Assuming some protection, of course... And, naturally, at least some mutual affection... And then there had been that magical, almost chemical attraction, the thunder in his heart – a pounding rhythm that, curiously, had slowed to a much more steady beat.

The thing was, David was now standing a good six feet from her carefully anointed skin, and as the molecule count dropped with the distance, his congested vomeronasal receptors had stopped their frenzied firing, and his pupils began to rapidly contract. Maybe it was the distance, or maybe it was the thinking, or maybe the thinking was because of the distance. In any case, he found himself in front of an exquisitely toned, startlingly platinum-haired, tawny-eyed and hopelessly beautiful woman: a woman, he was shocked to realize, that he didn't actually, really *know*.

"Come on home, big boy..."

He hesitated, just an instant, and a flash of puzzlement crossed her face. Eyebrows raised, she swung a polished leg wide, a leg that stretched, toes extended, to land gently on the floor. David, who was raised to be polite – innately, involuntarily, unless something more involuntarily overruled it – looked away.

Paula stood in a single graceful motion and stepped close. "Feeling *shy*?"

"Um…"

She stepped closer.

The scent of her, again.

"Oh," he said, as every neurocellular axon and dendrite of his olfactory lobe snapped once more to attention, "Oh Paula Oh Paula Oh…" His hands found the small of her back and slid down, spanning her buttocks and, as she climbed up and wrapped herself around him, lifting her high, his head back, senses filled with her again, eyes closed, breathing her in, breathing in the harsh warm breath of all he'd ever wanted, her breath close to his ear, her heart close to his heart, all of her achingly close to a perfectly penetrating union when – stumbling slightly with the weight of every one of those beautifully toned muscles – his bare heel hit something very, very cold, something hard and square and slippery, and, after trying to correct himself with considerably less gymnastic skill than Paula possessed, David began to tumble, once more a lumbered redwood, blindly backward.

EVERY INCH THE NATURAL, if startled, athlete, Paula rode David down, twisting her mount a few degrees sideways to miss a full-on impact with the champagne stand – he wouldn't be much good, unconscious – even catching the spiraling bottle in midair by its cold perspiring neck. Just a minor hiccup, she thought, as he slid backwards on the carpet; rough play and nothing more. Until, that is, she registered the slightest shifting of the cork – a cork from which she'd removed the foil and wire earlier, to make sure that things moved smoothly. And things did, the cork proceeding to slide smoothly from the green glass and launch itself – as she watched in slow-motion, an accident unraveling – towards the center of her up-to-then unblemished brow. The impact didn't hurt so much as sting, and the sting wasn't really as bad as the gush of icily expensive French foam that missed her eyes but got pretty much the rest of her.

David was up on his elbows, astonished, moving to help when she warned him, throatily, "Don't… say… anything."

"But—"

A glare and David stopped, instantly.

Ripping the white serving towel from the horizontal silver stand,

Paula mopped herself off, her face and breasts and arms and the six-pack of her belly, leaving a little champagne below, where it might soon be of interest.

"Now," she said, eyes level, "Where were we?"

UNFORTUNATELY, the Champagne had washed the pheromones away, leaving David with a near-stranger again, the professional who he liked, who he admired in all aesthetic ways but that was it. He had, in fact, cooled off, both virtually and literally, the latter due to the melting slush his scrotum happened to be parked in, an Arctic experience he was eager to shift out of.

As David clasped himself and clambered to his feet, Paula frowned. Of course: the champagne bath. That and an overall comedy of errors guaranteed to drown any man's unmanipulated ardor. She didn't take it personally, because she didn't take anything that way. Her young friend, she reminded herself, was still most definitely an asset.

Gallantly, he removed one warming hand from his frigid zone and extended it to help her; Paula handed him the towel instead, got vertical on her own, and went for her robe.

Which left David with a damp towel, strategically positioned, trying to think of a way to excuse himself and leave. Until he was saved by buzzing from his abandoned pants, in the pile of crumpled clothing by the bed. Squatting to pull it out – now Paula, unseen, looked away – David saw Oz's number. "The hospital," he said. "The emergency room."

She snapped her robe's terry-cloth belt tight. The little fibber. "You'd better go, Darling." He glanced up and she wondered if 'Darling' been too much... no, not a trace of suspicion. Standing, an Adonis once more – problematic, but still an Adonis – he struggled into pants and socks and flapping shirt as Paula watched.

You're mine, she thought, and you'll know it when we meet again.

WITH ONE HAND ON THE DOOR, David remembered what he had to tell her. "Um… ah… now that the clinic's really getting started, I was thinking, well, I had review the research – you know, on HGH." It seemed only honorable to let her know.

Absolutely fucking wonderful, Paula thought, smile pasted in place. The perfect end to a perfect evening. "Oh, David; of course you have to. I wouldn't want it any other way."

She strode across the room to her shoulder bag, pulled out a card, and jotted down an address at HorTech's website, a few pages they'd set up for awkward inquiries just like this. "If you want, here's an independent assessment, a look at everything that's out there. Unbiased, *supposedly*." A wink, on the same team again. The articles were spun, of course, something he'd expect but probably accept, a way for him to neutralize his concerns.

A kiss – awkward on his part but she'd make up for it with more GuyLoreiLure when they next met – and she saw him out the door. Paula leaned on it and sighed, then grabbed a handful of half-melted ice off the floor, threw it into a drinking glass, and added two thumb-sized Manhattans from the minibar. A piece of carpet lint floated to the surface; she dabbed it away with a corner of the robe and fell deep into the sofa, rattling the complementary copy of the local paper she'd grabbed at the front desk.

It wasn't the Times, but not exactly the cat-in-tree local trivia she'd expected, either. More bear-in-tree, with two whiny cubs, and tranquillizer darts, and cops in riot gear, hands on the real guns. And another story just below it, about a mountain lion wandering through town, then throwing itself against a window's glass – hunting an innocent reader, much like herself, sitting in her bathrobe. Paula's eyes went to the hotel room's sheer curtains, the outline of moonlit mountains behind. She was on the third floor… no wild animal could possibly…

Ridiculous. Still, the far outline of those mountains. Craggy… foreboding… *nature.* Covered with those dark, randomly planted – not even planted! – pine trees. And twisty undergrowth. And cactuses… did they have cactuses here? She slugged down half her glass, laid her head back and closed her eyes, but saw herself running, a steep downslope, dodging nasty pointy rocks and trees with branches tearing at her shirt, and cactuses, of course, and a rushing sound behind her, or hardly any sound, just soft paws, *paws,* and coming closer, huge warm puffs of air behind her knees, and then the scratch of bristling *whiskers–*

Sitting up, she knocked the rest of her drink back; the ice rattled in her glass as she set it down. The mountains with their wild and rugged flora were bad enough – now she had to deal with *fauna*? Not only on those cliff-faced ridges, but in the deceptively quiet streets below? She tossed the local rag aside. She didn't need this. Not after tonight.

Paula cinched her robe tighter, picked up the remote. Fuck it. Fuck the scary wildlife, and fuck neutralizing David's concerns. Flicking the Select button, she headed for the more shadowy realms of the pay-per-view – That? No, not *that* – looking for a non-sexist, non-violent, and not-entirely-gynecologic way to neutralize her own concerns first.

15

BIGGS' BIG VISIT

- or -

Pharmacopenic Chiroplexy

THE NEXT EVENING: David, Biggs, Oz, and Junie. That day's few patients were gone, but every monitor and LED ecobulb in the place remained on, every office door invitingly half-open, every gleaming or subtle woven surface saturated with a professional, stage-lit illumination that only a bespoke longevity clinic could afford: pure and white and clean but also warm and alive. Burnished copper clouds drifted above the skylight, and a tray of fresh-cut fruit, recycled toothpicks, and various lactose-free cheeses sat, so far uneaten, on the granite reception counter behind them.

Oz's catering and cleaning crew had unexpectedly descended on the Forever Clinic like a hive of scary Germanized bees, teeming and buzzing and done before the minute hand had covered half the wall clock's birds-eye maple face. Once the stage had cleared, they were followed by Oz, expansive, and Dr. Biggs, angling his shoulders though the Forever Clinic's already-oversized doorway. Introductions and re-introductions all around – all around the above, that is, the rest of the crew having been magically whisked off with that day's accumulation of prairie dust and mountain pollen.

An evening of glances, beginning with Junie's thunder-struck one on first spotting Biggs.

"WHY AM I NOT SURPRISED?" Junie didn't look happy. "But didn't it used to be 'Biggers'?"

"The name lacked a certain… *panache*." He spread his square hands.

"It probably stuck in the authorities' minds."

"You think so? Now, Junie, that's a name to remember. Not too commonplace, once you leave the South. In fact, I haven't heard it in, oh, an easy three years. Until this morning, and I've got to tell you, it gave me a start. The name of a young woman I used to know – a woman who could walk into any clinic, cold. A woman who could really push the product along."

"The *product*?" Junie was furious, but kept her voice low. "I thought they were real – real medications. Purchased in bulk and then resold by a *real* doctor – you, supposedly – at your famous wholesale price. To real clinics, to help real patients out. Prescription drugs that really worked, and were really made in this country."

"I thought they were real too, sweetheart." That smooth *basso profundo* voice. "But I must admit, I didn't ask when I saw the price."

"A price I paid, *sweetheart*."

He looked around. "You aren't doing too bad. And I hear you're finally working on that degree of yours. All in all…"

"Don't start," she said, knowing he was right. And while he'd obviously known about a certain absent medical license – his – there was a chance he hadn't known about the luxury-brand sugar pills they'd been selling. There were other mitigating factors: the fake drugs hadn't actually killed anyone, may have even cured a few. And he'd only given her a sad-eyed look when she told him she'd helped Louisiana's finest with the case. That look, a misty Gulf Coast night, his Caddie's taillights fading as he headed for the Texas line.

Same as always: she couldn't stay mad at the man.

She glanced toward David, twenty feet away and going over last week's numbers with Oz. "This guy's all right," she said. "I can't let you take advantage."

"Junie, Junie, Junie," he said, smoothly segueing from Barry White to Cary Grant. "This drug really *is* real – everything's above board, everything's good. You can check the invoices; I sell and the doctor, a real doctor with a real license, prescribes. And your boss, Oz, he's unscammable, and is watching out for his pal. Who looks like he might need a little watching after."

"Don't you have someone already doing that?"

"Paula?" He laughed. "She stepping on your action?"

"Please. A white boy?"

He shook his head. "Reverse racism in the modern South. Not that it helped me. Except one time, if I remember correctly…"

"That never happened," she said sharply, and Biggs nodded. David looked over at them, puzzled, before Oz dragged his attention back to his fancy silver laptop's screen. She frowned. "I don't like any of this. If I laid your history out, he'd run screaming."

"I can only hope, dear Junie, you don't. For everybody. The way I hear it, your boss needs a boost. A completely legal boost. There could be a boost in this for you as well."

"No. No bribes, I'm not interested, never again." Another look; David was headed over. "He'll do well?"

"He'll be *buying* this place. Just tell him you know me – it's the truth, and I know you like that."

FOR SOME REASON, David thought, Biggs and Oz were on him like a tag-team. As the two heavyweights switched places, Oz shot Junie an oddly meaningful look, which she returned with a steely stare. David had barely touched on that conundrum when Biggs, as resplendently tailored as in Vegas, snagged his denim-shirted upper arm, turned him toward the empty office, and essentially demanded a tour.

It seemed the least he could do. David might have his doubts about HGH – in fact, he no longer had anything *but* doubts about HGH – but Dr. Biggs had taken the trouble to fly all the way from LA.

His guest made the usual appreciative noises, and lingered at nearly every rack-and-pinion station of Nancy's stainless-steel trail of tears on the balcony. They were on the top step of the sweeping semi-circle of stairs that descended to the main floor when Biggs stopped him and said, "Why no chiropractic?"

"Um…" It was a good question, one that, David realized, he really hadn't asked himself. Picking every other holistic 'specialty' had seemed so natural. "Chiropractic's great… I guess. The studies show it works for back pain, and no one knows backs like they do.

But I figured we had the whole alignment-muscle-ligament thing covered. Deep tissue, Pilates… and yoga, of course."

"Of course." Biggs crossed thick arms, biceps straining at fine white Egyptian cotton, stuck out his lower lip, and gave a thoughtful nod.

"Chiropractors tend to run their own shows." David added. "With their own teams, I mean. And they really *run* them."

"Uh-huh…"

"And have their own *view* of things. How every disease is only due to a problem with the spine. It just doesn't make sense."

"Sense. How about your Pilates, yoga, all the others – don't they have their own views? Views that might, say, not entirely make sense either?"

David thought of his brain-twisting interview with Quinn. "Homeopathy, Naturopathy, sure. Most holistic disciplines don't fit with medicine's take on how the body works. But each seems comfortable occupying this corner or that. Not really trying to, well, encompass."

"Like medicine does."

"Exactly. We've got science on our side, can prove that our view is correct. At least in bits and pieces of the puzzle." Bits of the puzzle, but only bits, extending them by inference, filling the gaps between with… belief. David's mind rolled back, again, to Quinn's mini-lecture on that interview day.

"You're right," he added, after a moment. "Medicine feels, I don't know, *justified*… justified to encompass. Calling everything else 'complimentary' – whether they want to compliment or not."

"Then why reject chiropractic? Because it encompasses? Because of the competition?"

David didn't like it, but… "Maybe. I still think the medical view makes more sense, way more sense. But if you're talking absolutes, it's true: two sets of theories, neither entirely rock-solid, fighting for the same patch of swampy ground. A competition between the medical and chiropractic, um…"

"*Weltanschauung, oder ihre ideologie.*" Biggs watched him and laughed, a deep subsonic rumble. "Don't look at me like that – you know, world-view, ideology. Four years of German Studies. Inexhaustible language and exhausting philosophy."

"Wow. Four years of German, plus pre-med?"

"Who said anything about pre-med?"

Biggs was gazing out over the room again, as David thought, 'Doctor', but not pre-med... Oh, crap. All those documents – just the 'Dr.', never the MD.

Having given David the time any reasonably smart physician needed to work it through, Biggs said, "Uh-huh."

"Jeez... Sorry?"

"For what? I haven't cracked a back for years." He stretched his arms, hands clasped Nancy-style, and produced a snap from what seemed like every joint from shoulders down. "Missed it, though. A lot of us don't get twisted up in any *weltanschauungs*." A wistful look. "We just like messing with spines."

Down below, the Clinic's door swung open to reveal crimson heels, a black form-fitting dress, the flash of silver hair. Walking in, Paula waved at Oz, best friends.

Biggs laid an iron hand on David's shoulder. "Not that I'd want a chiropractor taking over your show, either." A tectonic chuckle as he headed down the stairs.

David followed, thinking about that missing MD, about why Biggs needed someone like him. About writing prescriptions, about giving injections... and, most of all, about those studies he'd been going over and over and over since Friday night.

JUNIE SHOOK PAULA'S offered hand – it was strong and dry, efficient – and then the stunning, if older, woman spun to face the others, saying, "I thought I'd give you boys some time to talk." David was still on the stairs, lost in thought. Junie watched as Paula, a cougar from red talons to white teeth, caught his eye and reeled him in.

For all his talk about Paula, for all those whispered conversations on his cell phone, it seemed that David was holding back, dragging his feet. Until he got closer, when his eyes lit up and he leaned forward, gaining speed, almost falling into her. She stopped him with a brilliant smile, a smile that said, behave yourself.

Okay, Junie thought, that's the way it is. The woman obviously had *something* to keep him under control; if nothing else, a fella could get hurt on a body like that. A beautiful white ghost, like

David. And then remembered David as he'd walked into his apartment, a pale shadow swimming into darkness. Two white ghosts, but David swimming deep. Paula on the surface, cruising back and forth, twisting as she turned, patrolling silver waters. Mix those metaphors, Junie thought; a cougar, a shark, a ghost. The ghostest with the mostest.

Oz cleared his throat, double chin vibrating on the starched column of his collar. "I – no, excuse me, *we* – have an announcement. An announcement that I'm sure will please you all."

Biggs was positively purring, center stage, broad face calm beneath the polished obsidian of his shaven skull.

Junie pursed her lips. Here it comes, and no surprise. Not to those three deal-makers, and certainly not to her – Oz had laid out the deal's rough structure the moment David left on his little tour, presumably to gauge her reaction. All growth hormone, all the time, for the benefit of all concerned. At this point she couldn't care less: money was money.

But look at David, Paula's little puppy – Junie wanted to *pinch* him, but the idiot didn't deserve it.

Disgusted, she backed away and slouched over the end of the counter, chin in hand. And then, from the soft pink palm that had briefly pressed against Paula's firm tan one, a certain scent, the faintest trace, a scent that had drifted by her more than once before. Matching, somehow, a certain look, a look that the idiot in question got every single time he'd flipped his cell open to answer a call from the Terminatrix across the room.

Musk and flowers – jasmine, that was it… And David's eyes as black as they were now, each gray-green iris dilated to a narrow rim.

The phone.

That scent, when he opened it.

Paula.

Fucking *voodoo*.

She put her palm down to the cool granite counter and sniffed the empty air. Nothing. Nothing, that is, this far away from the lovely Paula. Okay… As Oz droned on about the coming organization, with Biggs and Paula in rapt fiscal appreciation, Junie manufactured a short dry cough. One cough, and then another, at which point Paula blasted her with a machine-gun burst of daggers before refocusing on Oz. While David, just behind her, dreamily – and finally – looked over.

A quick sideways motion of Junie's head: come here. After all, David seemed to be all about following orders tonight. She saw a dim awareness rising, and repeated it; no one but David had noticed, yet. Slowly, reluctantly, he shuffled back and sideways until he stood beside her, shoulders slack, still listening, passively consumed by Oz's glowing plans for everyone else's future.

Unbelievable. The plan, and David – who she *knew* knew better – going along without a whimper. Maybe it wasn't Paula, it wasn't voodoo, but only David, happy to be nothing more than these fools' unwitting tool.

But as she watched, his eyes began to return to their normal color, and the words of the man who David called his 'oldest best friend' finally seemed to register. Puzzled, he straightened up and even raised an index finger.

Oz slowed to a halt, and David said, "But don't you think—"

"David," Paula interrupted. "Why don't we listen to *all* of Oz's plan first?" A hand stretched toward him, come on back.

In automatic and obedient response, he began to tilt toward Paula, and she turned toward Oz, her long, bare-muscled arm still summoning her errant doctor, confident of his return.

Something, Junie knew, had to be done. Her lower body was hidden by the maple cabinetry of the counter; with elbows still on the polished stone that topped it, and chin still poised in hands, she swiveled her right foot to place a hard, narrow heel just over the occupied toe of the nearest size thirteen woven sandal. Then lowered it to full contact as she gracefully lifted her other foot completely off the ground.

"Stop!" David said, snapping nearly back to full consciousness. He began to look down to his throbbing toe, but was interrupted by the gaze of everyone – including Junie, with a convincing look of surprise – in the room. "I…" he added, recovering, for Junie had removed her heel, "…I think that's the problem."

Paula's eyes narrowed. "*What* problem?"

"Well…" After a perplexed glance at his now-unencumbered foot, he said, "…Here we are, moving on to an organizational plan, a full-on agreement between HorTech and the clinic… I mean, we're not even sure how much growth hormone we'll be using."

"How much we'll be using?" Oz asked. "Isn't it the anti-aging *dream*?" He still held the inch-thick stack of incorporation papers he'd been happily reciting from. "The stuff that works, the stuff that anyone would want… if, that is, they can afford it."

"Of course it is," Paula said. "After all, David – Dr. Black – has reviewed the research."

"Research?" Biggs looked surprised. "You mean *our* research, right?" And then, to all of them, "HorTech's independent research summary, that is."

"Well, sure," David said.

On Biggs's face, the beginning of relief…

"That and, you know, everything I could find on the internet."

…followed by the sudden end of it.

"You can't believe everything you read on the internet, David." Paula took a step closer, willing this evening's double dose of GuyLoreiLure to cast its net.

"Absolutely," David said, as the outer diffused margins began to work their magic again. "Like with patients, all those commercial sites the search engines lead them to…" He paused. "Plus every cult of crazed believers… so much spin, so much opinion…" He was tilting toward Paula once more, close to falling over. "There's even been research on the info… I mean, the medical info you find there… way more than half is *dis*info… disinforma… just plain, um, wrong?"

"There you go," Biggs said.

Junie nodded agreeably, and, unseen, swung her heel back into position and vigorously re-mashed his bruised toe.

"*But not…*" David grunted, shooting upright with a desperate look around him. "*Not… Pub… Med!*"

Her offending foot still hidden, she released his toe and David went into a brief backwards stumble that took him away from Paula, towards the door.

"PubMed," Junie said, pure innocence. "The National Library of Medicine? Too technical for me."

"For anyone," Paula snapped, "Who needs to make a decision this week."

"It's hard to read," David admitted, with a wary look at Junie. Between the second stab of pain and a strange freshening of the air that reached dilated nostrils, he was alert enough to remember that Junie had seemed to know all about PubMed only a few days ago – as well as note how her square heel was remarkably similar in size and shape to the patch of pain still pulsing in the swelling tissues of his great toe.

"And self-contradicting," he added, "and definitely confusing, but when you take the time to look at all the strands, you end up with something that's, well, fairly objective. No... um... pain, no gain." Hands nonchalantly clasped behind him, he put more distance between himself and Junie. And also moved away – not so incidentally, as far as Junie was concerned – from Paula's voodoo-flavored sphere of influence.

"You're not *leaving*?" Paula, Junie was happy to see, was beginning to show a little of the rosy color that the otherwise pigment-challenged could do so well.

"Hey, David," Oz said, as a concern for his friend's odd behavior wrestled with more pecuniary considerations. "I can see you're upset, but don't worry. Look, if you really—"

"—*are* concerned about your patients," Biggs broke in, "We'll take another look at the medical literature, all of us together. It's only ethical... wouldn't you say that, Paula?"

"Absolutely, Dr. Biggs." As they spoke, she slowly crossed the room, casually approaching David. Who continued to maintain the distance between his smarting digit and *any* potential toe-stomper in the room.

"I don't understand," Oz said. "Doesn't everybody – everybody who's getting old – need HGH?"

"Not *everybody*," David temporized, still easing toward the door.

Stopping, frustrated, Paula turned and stared hard at Biggs.

"As Dr. Black knows," Biggs started, "It's been broadly demonstrated that if a patient's growth hormone level is dropping—"

"If not everybody," Oz asked David, ignoring Biggs. "Then *who*?"

"Outside of pediatrics? I mean, if you're not a short kid?" David's hands, still clasped behind him, reached the door's handle;

grasping it between them, he pushed the brushed stainless lever down.

"Obviously there's a need with growth issues," Biggs intoned, working hard to seize Oz's, or David's, or in fact anyone other than Paula's *rapt* attention. "But with aging, virtually everyone's level will drop—"

"So... what if you're *not* a short kid?" Oz said to David.

"Um..." David felt the subtle click of the latch transmitted through his arms.

Paula closed her eyes, hoping.

"—a drop that is a clear indication—" Biggs said, still trying.

David grimaced again; this time it had nothing to do with his toe. "...If you're not a short kid... then... I guess... *nobody*."

"Nobody?" Oz dropped the papers to the counter beside him. Profit was critical, but you couldn't thrive, not in the long run, if something simply didn't work. Unless, of course, you had a provider who'd convinced himself enough to convince each and every patient who raised the question. Oz frowned, calculating, considering. He wasn't *married* to David... But no – actually, in the heart of his oldest, bestest friendship, he was.

Paula, meanwhile, had spun back to where David had just stood, only to watch the heavy door swing in, swing out, and then swing closed.

Thinking, Shit.

"HMMM," SAID BIGGS, a reflexive move to fill a silence – that is, a key player's absence and the resultant waves of silence that spread out from it – that could not possibly bode well for any future partnership.

Paula had ended up beside the corner of the reception counter, a few feet from Junie. She was deeply suspicious – it was her nature to be suspicious when her plans went awry, as her will was easily strong enough to override anything less than a lucky act of focused opposition. But Biggs had vouched for David's receptionist, and when she looked over, Junie only shrugged.

It didn't matter: Oz was tapping his closed lips, thoughtfully, with his index finger. He was the remaining critical player, their way back to the cold-footed and curiously resistant resource who'd just fled.

The cheese plate was virtually untouched; she moved in and placed a pale blue-veined morsel, delicate beads of entirely lactose- and gluten-free fat forming on its semi-crumbling surface, between her well-bleached teeth. Then stabbed another with a toothpick, held it out to Oz and, as Biggs watched admiringly and Junie with some amusement, began the process of damage control.

16

AT THE UR-BAR

- or -

Separatus Commingulitis

LATER THAT SAME NIGHT – a booth in a back corner, chipped plywood, rings of beer, cool red vinyl, an occasional gargling flush from down the narrow hall. And Sheyoni and Don, sitting on the far side, holding hands.

"That was…" An hour later, and Don was still stunned. "That was…"

"Shhhh…"

"But—" A look from Sheyoni, a knowing shake of her head, and he stopped himself. Even though he wanted to crow about it, shout it from the rooftops: Fifty-nine's the new twenty-five! His doctor said the injections wouldn't work for at least a month, but the results were clear and in hand. Her left one, or nearly, that lay so casually on his right thigh. Okay, he knew it might have been purely psychological, or related to the three blue Yippiagra!™ tabs he'd ingested, just in case, mere hours before. Or, maybe, it was Sheyoni.

She knew it was her, and knew why; she was a level-three mistress of the secrets of Tantric Yoga, knowledgeable in the most minute arcana of Kundalinic energy release. All of which had been learned, the hard way, from a level-four GrandMaster Yoginator over a single well-lubricated Baja weekend. If David had been paying attention, he would have realized she wasn't visiting her mother, at least wondered about the mid-winter Detroit tan she'd brought back. But enough of David – this was Don's night. A gift, as love can be, from her very core. As well as an investment, and one that could return a substantial long-term yield.

Sitting quietly, fingers intertwined, but each mind circling, making their own plans. All that perfect skin, Don thought, and so far uncorrupted. Time-limited by the dreaded *Intrapustular Fidelo-penia*... not for awhile, according to her ex, but eventually. In his present state of bliss he was certain he could live with that, at least as long as she would. And when that quick decline began, he'd find a way to do right by her. It wasn't like he didn't have assets, and she'd know – or would know when the sad time came – that a man had needs that must be satisfied, even in the absence of a fully functional Sheyoni.

Sheyoni was experiencing a remarkably symmetrical vision of Don's own last days, the retirement home they'd build by the sea, the hemp-lined master suite that would occupy its own wing. Easily transformable to a fully-fixtured sickroom for one its occupants – the aging one, who wouldn't last forever. Especially if he fully lived the active and sexually-charged life (the *exhaustingly* active and sexually-charged life) that a towering success like Don deserved. After which, in a masterpiece of recycling that would be her final loving gesture, the room would be transformed back to the perfumed and silken boudoir she'd intended all along.

Each with their own plans, but still, something else, connecting – invisible, human, superseding their mutual calculations. Two monsters of the self, but then again, two lovers. For they were circling, but they were also sitting quietly, side by side. Until Don, for absolutely no good reason, sighed and said her name.

His head bent even closer; a kiss that happened, unconsidered, a kiss matched by her near-involuntary response; a dance to unheard music. The two of them, alone, almost hidden from the room.

Almost.

"Look at that. Just look at that." Two booths down, near the door. "Could they be any more obvious?"

"Come on, Jer... give it a break, okay?" Wayne still figured Boulder as a plenty nice town, but that was the problem – the reason, in his opinion, Jeremiah was slowly going postal. A cowhand needed something to work against, like bad weather, a bad fence or a bad cow. Or a bunch of small-minded no-neck dry-country in-breeders who'd whip, drag, or at least vote against the slightest thing that made them nervous. And here his best pal was, without a horse, a saddle, or anybody to do him dirt. The town was too nice, too liberal. People needed a fight, or Jer did, and he hadn't anything to pick on but all that *niceness*.

Jeremiah said the ponytail guy was too old for her, but Wayne didn't care, they looked mighty sweet to him. As sweet as Jer looked when he wasn't grumbling up a storm. And you couldn't blame the mixed clientele; the clubs they'd hit in Denver were even worse, a whole next level of hey-there flirtation that drove his Bible-raised buddy to distraction.

The bar's door swung open with a gasp of exhaust-flavored air. Bumping in on an extra-large set of dirty pink low heels came a well-grazed heifer with, no kidding, a raggedy black cigar stub in the corner of her mouth. She surveyed the room with beady eyes, slung her double-wide over a barstool, and slapped a wad of bills on the table, loud enough for the bartender to hear. Then pointed to an amber-filled bottle and held up both hands, ten fingers spread. He seemed reluctant, but she neutralized that with a truly dangerous glare, and watched, carefully, as a row of stubby glasses were set down and filled to the brim.

Wayne was by nature a sympathetic soul, and while he didn't know what her problem was, he had a pretty good idea that all that whiskey couldn't help. The first ten, maybe, and she had the size to handle it, but they'd only lead to more.

Jeremiah, still staring at the smoochers, was the perfect example. A single long-neck, fine. But even two was dangerous, turning him into a whole different kind of animal. Like that time a couple years ago, back in Wyoming, not all that far from home. The place with the college kids, baby giant football players who looked way meaner than your average rancher. Mean enough to think they knew how people ought to live and not too shy to tell them all about it. By the time Wayne had noticed the row of empties on the varnished mahogany in front of Jer, his pal had his penknife out and was hunched over the rolled edge of the bar, carving away, getting through 'Jeremiah loves Wayne' before the bartender noticed. Who didn't appreciate the craftsmanship, or want a tiny bit of the trouble that was brewing. And had said so, sort of quiet and tense and not at all unreasonable, but then Jeremiah had banged out the door for the coil of barbed wire in the pickup, swing it around to make his point.

A gentle clonk upside the temple had made Jer see reason, that and the forty miles of asphalt Wayne put under the wheels before his pal began to stir. Still, it had been more than close.

While Wayne reminisced, Jeremiah was waving at the college-student waitress, who came over with another round, fuel to the fire. Before Wayne knew it, Jeremiah had sucked both down and turned his focus to the barstool-overlapping lady just down the aisle. Loose women, public displays of affection, Wayne thought; his buddy had his issues. But the crazy thing was, it was the immoderate use of alcohol (by anyone else, that is) that *really* drove Jeremiah nuts. Which explained his bugged eyes and the muttered 'Jezebel', as she picked up her third shot with two porky fingers, raised it without spilling a drop, and skillfully knocked it back.

Oh boy.

QUINN HAD THEM ARRANGED in a semi-circle, leaving a nice open space for laying his forehead down and moaning, something he took the opportunity to do now. Nobody watching but the rustics at the booth behind him, and screw them if they couldn't see the joke. Same for Don, his first pay-through-the-nose Forever Clinic patient, noogling with his girlfriend in the darkest corner. Didn't matter, though, because Don wouldn't be his patient long. Not after what Quinn heard in the Clinic's bathroom. Or *from* the bathroom. Take an innocent, restful half hour to empty the chutes and fine-tune the makeup – women had it tough, as tough as they were always saying – and by the time you're done, strangers in suits are walking around, everybody sharing secrets.

Not wanting to be impolite, he'd stayed hidden for the next hour to listen. What he'd heard wasn't good, especially at the end. One miniscule ethical qualm and David pulls the financial rug from under all of them. Okay, he himself had been gas-bagging about not fooling Mother Nature to Junie, but that was just ventage – medicine, holistic medicine, *any* kind of medicine was miles away from perfect. In the end, so to speak, everybody bends over to make a buck.

How do you make a hormone?

By not paying *me*.

ALL NANCY HEARD was the knock – soft, rhythmic – on the door. No crunch of tires on gravel, no slamming door, no footsteps on her wooden porch. Nor, and this was a first, the slightest growl from Nathan, her giant PitLabrador Bultriever, who would normally be flipping over in rage. None of the things that would get Nancy cocked and ready for the rare visitor that might dare to drop in, unannounced, on a moonless mountain evening. But by the count of five she was on the other side of an inch of solid oak, pistol hanging loose and pulse thrumming in a way she quite enjoyed. Though Nathan's silence was sort of troubling, broken only by a pungent doggie-fart of anticipation.

Nancy braced herself, ready for anything, and opened the door. To see an empty driveway, a starlit sky, and Howie, as collected as always, while her stinking terror Nathan applied a glutinous layer of saliva to his open palm.

"I am sorry, my dear Nancy, but I need you."

Dear Nancy, she thought – kinda nice. For a guy. And 'need'? Nancy was not entirely adverse to the occasional experimental consideration – guys were people, too, or sort of. And sort of unattractive, and sort of disgusting, but there had been moments in her drinking days... Still, Howie? Though the blue sparks had been interesting. And she liked to keep an open mind.

Dear Nancy discretely laid her Glock on the end table, gave Nathan a shove with one purple-legginged hip, and held open the door.

Howie smiled benignly. Behind him, a trail of footprints crossed the dusty road – halfway across, oddly – from the rough outlet of a trail. A nasty, pointy-rocky trail that headed straight up to the ridge, its tree-studded top outlined by the dull glow of Boulder's lights beyond. That explained it, except for the clean, uncalloused toes that poked, as usual, from under his pristine robe.

She was working on that one when he added, "In truth, it is our friend Quinn that is in need."

Ah, the mighty Quinn. Definitely disgusting – pansexually disgusting – and too open a mind for the lot of them. But people ought to be able to rewrite their story, any way they wanted. Nancy sure had. Plus, she had to admit she liked the way Quinn dressed. Right out there – no, way out there, unafraid. And if she, that is

Quinn, went hard-core surgical with the transsexual thing, would she, that is Nancy…?

No, no, of course not, no! She wasn't thinking clearly; it had been too long, too long without *anyone.* She needed to keep it simple. Simple, and definitely not that open.

Howie – who was, now that she thought of it, the least sexual being, male or female, Nancy could recall meeting – still stood quietly. "And you're here," she asked, "because…"

"You are aware of this evenings' meeting."

"The one they kicked us out of."

Howie nodded. "Indeed, I felt a certain sense of rejection as well. Most unwelcoming. But Quinn remained after you departed, remaining when I left to dine at the Sproutarian establishment across the avenue. Following a meditative repast, I happened to see her exit, in apparently great distress. Do you recall the bicycle security unit in front?'

"The rack that nearly blocks sidewalk? Uh-huh."

"She rearranged it rather creatively. Across the southbound lanes of Broadway, in fact. With that in mind, I followed her, righting the occasional newspaper box and recycling receptacle, to the establishment you refer to, I believe, as the *Ur*-Bar."

"The *Ur*-Bar… I've said that aloud?"

Howie's head wobbled, and Nancy found no answer there.

She frowned. "Quinn's a big girl." Or whatever.

"You have precisely pinpointed the problem. I believe our Quinn is in search of a profound if temporary oblivion, one that may require assistance. Physical assistance."

"Oh." She remembered Howie's corded muscles beneath her hands, but Quinn outweighed him two-to-one. Heaven alone knew why, but he'd walked over a small mountain for her help. A call to help a coworker in trouble – a coworker and a *sister*. Or sort of.

"I'll get my sweater."

NANCY COULDN'T BELIEVE she was here again. Of all the joints in all the… Worse, there was the coy Sheyoni, hiding behind their famous first patient's ponytail in the corner. The fun never ended.

And there was Quinn, lifting the next-to-last of the many shot glasses, some now on their side, arrayed in front of him. Cranking his head toward the flyspecked ceiling for the throw and, following the general fun-never-ends principle, tipping slowly off the stool.

Before Nancy could jump forward, a solid young interfering type leapt up from a booth and, putting his shoulder to the center of the that well-marbled posterior, shoved Quinn back to vertical. Short blond hair, worn but well-pressed jeans and well-used cowboy boots; a bible-bred Republican from Wyoming, down here to get to know the Enemy. She hated that. On the other hand, Howie, who had made it to the stool beyond Quinn, seemed to have settled in, enjoying the show. Nancy decided that she didn't mind not being squashed by two-hundred-odd pounds of drunken homeopath either.

As Quinn re-established a tentative equilibrium with the bar, the interfering savior placed a hand around the last full shot glass, and drawled, "Buy me a drink, pretty lady?"

Unbelievable. The guy must be blind, she thought. Then saw the extra-focused look in his extra-wide, extra-scary eyes.

"Great idea, honey." Quinn's beige base layer cracked in a crooked smile. "Except you might – just *might* – have the wrong one."

By which time, Mr. Wyoming's cowboy brother had hopped up to grab his crazed friend's hand, unwrap his fingers, put the shot back on the bar, and say, "Jeremiah—"

Jeremiah bristled and turned, face darkening.

Nancy moved in but his friend shook his head and said, "Come on, Jer... hey, buddy... come on now, hey now, hey..." The frigging cowboy-whisperer. Mr. Wyoming melted and, led gently by the arm, returned to the booth.

Oh.

"Doesn't mean we can't be pals," Quinn called after, swinging around on the stool. Two twin glares from the booth; deciding not to take it further, Quinn hooked a pink-shod toe on the rail below the bar and spun the rest of the way around.

And then some. Nancy snagged her on the second orbit and returned Quinn's elbows to the bar, then caught the bartender's attention and ordered a fully leaded coffee. On second thought, she made it a double.

BIGGS wasn't a connoisseur of Western bars and couldn't recognize one without the usual saddle-and-boot paraphernalia – a style that, although he couldn't know it, had last decorated the *Ur*-Bar about two iterations and twelve months ago. The current scheme reminded Biggs of the downtown holes of LA in the seventies, minus the winos. Dark places; places to meet. He pursed his lips and pronounced his judgment. "Nice."

As they headed for the single open booth across from the long bar, a huge, brightly dressed, and phenomenally ugly woman turned away. Must have been the couple in the back waving at her, as she and both the patrons that flanked her waved back.

"And friendly," Biggs added. "Friendlier than LA." He took in the two clean-cut cowboys, the graying ponytail glued to his trophy girlfriend, the white-robed Jesus at the bar. "Friendlier, and maybe even weirder."

"Remember," Paula warned, "It's a small town."

Beneath his suit, Biggs rolled massive shoulders and cracked his neck. "We're new here, Paula. Nobody knows us. Relax."

QUINN TURNED BECAUSE he'd heard the voice, the same bass tones echoing through the Clinic's bathroom door – the HGH distributor – and decided to keep a low profile, just in case. Unfortunately, that had brought him around to face Don, who recognized his HomeoNaturologist and waved happily. Quinn waved back, as did Howie and, if grudgingly, Nancy.

After the distributor and his saleslady slid into the booth behind him, Quinn listened, hard. On either side, his co-workers waited patiently for him to recover. Which he had, mostly, but had to hear this first. Just to make a plan, and then tell Howie and Nancy.

Later.

Maybe.

If they really needed to know.

"A CONTINGENCY PLAN?" Biggs said. "I can think of one or two. But Oz's clinic is dripping quality, and *someone's* going to have to write the scripts. What's the big deal? You hooked your boy before – just rehook him." He shrugged. "Use twice the stuff."

"I did, but even that only worked in close. I think he's on to it; you saw him back away."

"On to what? We're legal, babe. He was nervous is all, had to say his bit and get out. You know, show he's an independent thinker. Try again, and if doesn't work, I'll talk to his boss and his boss'll talk to him, remind him what his patients' want."

"What's that got to do with anything? Patients want to be told what to do."

"When's the last time *you* wanted that?" He lifted his eyebrows, waiting. "I thought so," he said, finally. "You're not alone. Most patients have their agenda and are there to make it happen. Even better, from our point of view, is that docs need, they really *need*, to hear all those Thank-you-Doctor-Wonderful's every day. Probably why they got in the biz. Once they start practicing, docs learn the old-fashioned Pavlovian way: you get more when you jump through the hoops. All we have to do is help patients pick the hoops we want – with the mailing, the ads, internet, everything. Like that direct-to-patient advertising Big Pharm does so well, the ads that roll right over the 'best practice' objections of penny-pinching doctors and drives their professional associations apoplectic. Don't know why, as most of the groups are on the tit already, but hey. And best of all, which I know you know, is that our stuff sells itself."

He paused. "When it comes to doctors, any kind of doctors, patient demand is where the rubber meets the road." Biggs clearly liked the sound of that. "You made it almost happen, Paula. Leave the rest to me – I'll close the deal."

A contented look, but a look she didn't like. A look that said 'No percentage'… no partner slot, not for a sales rep who couldn't close the deal. A look that Paula knew she'd have to change.

WHAT, NANCY WONDERED, was Quinn playing at now? Spying, obviously, on the couple behind. A business meeting, it sounded like, of the nasty kind.

What kind of business would Quinn bother her big fat head about? The business of health, she guessed – like the California suppliers David had said were coming out. Nancy couldn't get the details, but they were clearly into jerking him around. Which might not be a bad thing, if it kept the Forever Clinic going.

Better she stay out of it. Some kind of lightweight country-pop was wheedling out of the speakers above the bar. Give me Tammy, crying her heart out; give me Tammy, even Waylon, please. Heartbreak, shitheels, broken dreams, the songs a drinking bar deserved. Nancy shook her head and made herself listen, knowing that when her brain shut out that market-research-driven bullshit, it would shut out the conversation, too.

As WAYNE WAITED for Jeremiah to sober up, his gaze drifted to the three perched posteriors that lined the narrow aisle across from the next booth down. The first was muscular, nicely rounded if not exactly his cup of java, no matter how butch. Next was the corn-fed one Jer had saved from a slide to the linoleum, now stabilized and drooping over the black vinyl of the stool. The third was skinny, and... wait a second... Wayne leaned into the aisle, tilting his head, eyeing it at vinyl-level. A thin layer of light shone off the undulating, butt-polished surface – an inch or so of open space below the loose white robes. His eyes traveled up the robes, beyond the curly red-brown beard, to meet the robe owner's kind and thoroughly unworried regard. Wayne's eyes traveled down again, to find that that unlikely space was gone. Then considered his empty beer bottle, his third, and decided that Jeremiah might not be the only one with a problem.

Jeremiah was half-turned away, arm stretched along the padded top of the booth divider, sobering up but back to glaring at the smooches that had resumed, fiercer that ever, in the far corner. Near Jeremiah's elbow – dangerously near, though Jer had calmed down now – was a polished black scalp, shinier than that fat lady's at the bar. Did every other person in this town, Wayne thought, shave his head? Or, worse, hers? What other parts did they go hunting with their razors?

That gleaming scalp tilted forward, then back, animated as its owner talked – business, it sounded like – with the respectable looking woman that sat across from him, a female executive, suit and all. A *normal* woman with nice, silvery hair. Kinda like his Aunt Bessie, but really keeping herself up.

THEIR DRINKS ARRIVED – the martini Biggs always finished, the pinot noir she never did – giving Paula a moment's respite. She had to bring David around before Biggs did, and hadn't given up on her best break so far, his unexpected sensitivity to GuyLoreiLure. Her boss might be full of all sorts of shit, but he was right about using more. It didn't work with every guy – Biggs, for instance, seemed to be immune – but when it did...

Maybe she ought to do some additional research. One of the young cowboys in the next booth was gazing in her direction. *Primed* with testosterone, and she certainly still had enough GuyLoreiLure on board. Raising her glass, she gave the hayseed her most sultry wink and fanned the plunging edge of her business-plus blouse. His face froze and he stiffly turned away.

Nope, not everyone.

Biggs had stopped talking and was examining her, those damned eyebrows up again.

She stared back. "What?"

"You having a hot flash?"

"You know what I'm taking."

"Everything, right?"

"Right. So how could I possibly?"

"Oh. Sorry. My mistake." He dug for the olive in his glass and popped it in his mouth, then smiled and settled back with a barely-contained belch, eyes closed, contented.

Biggs. Good thing GuyLoreiLure *didn't* work on all of them – he was tough to manage as it was. As a dedicated sales professional, she knew that there was more than lust and attraction when it came to moving minds. That said, it was probably time to rethink the hair color.

MEANWHILE, Nancy was studying the mirror above the bar, a mirror that, she had discovered, offered an excellent reflection of the row of booths across. Of that silver-haired gal, in fact, who'd fanned her shirt like she was hitting menopause, though she didn't seem that old. Or David's type, if it was her that David had been mooning over. Nancy sighed; you never could tell. Though she could, and would, if that sharp but scary sweetie wasn't there with Mr. Clean.

"I JUST DON'T GET THIS PLACE," Jeremiah said. "Maybe we need to check out Colorado Springs."

"You're kidding." A town where gay priests were only forgiven if they blamed their crack addiction. And had a long-suffering wife – and a passel of long-suffering kids – to stand by them.

"Okay, then – Santa Fe."

Santa Fe. Hot and dusty, but Jer was right, there was probably some cowboying to be had. Plus the art scene. Wayne mulled that over, eyes drifting back to those posteriors. No hovering this time, and the beefy one had shifted over – enough that he could see, along the rolled edge of the bar, the first two words of what some drunk had scratched into the worn mahogany. The angled letters appeared strangely familiar: 'Jeremiah Loves...'

Golldarn it, Boulder *was* weird.

"Hey, Pardner," Wayne said, and Jeremiah looked up. "Santa Fe? I'm thinking you might have an idea there."

As DON AND SHEYONI hurried out towards his place, holding hands; as Biggs and Paula casually fought to hold the door open for each other; as Howie and Nancy, both effortless in their own way, assisted a not completely steady Quinn down the narrow aisle between the bar stools and the booths; and as Wayne, carefully blocking the mysteriously transported inscription, waited for Jeremiah to slide out of what he hoped was their last Boulder bar booth... As those small dramas transpired, Oz sat, oblivious, in his foothills fastness, contemplating the various spreadsheets on the row of LCD monitors that marched along his desk.

HorTech. All the proffered treats were nice, including Paula. There were negatives, of course, like that weird musky perfume, or the fact that his heart still belonged to Beatriz. On the other hand, there was the fragrant chunk of Vieux Boulogne she'd fed him – and hadn't even winced at the outhouse aroma, which showed a certain strength of character.

He lit a long and thin and very expensive Cuban cigarillo, the first and styling part of his new stepwise plan to quit, a personal initiative that he'd decided on as soon as David promised he'd stop bugging him. After thoughtlessly inhaling, Oz coughed violently, then placed it on a thick glass ashtray and lit up something kinder.

Well, he'd tried. Like he'd try – he really would, it wasn't easy but he would – again tomorrow.

HorTech's chief treat, the only one that truly captured his attention, remained the figures on the screen to the left, the business plan he'd been pitching earlier that night.

The middle screen displayed a less rosy scenario, without HorTech. It was Fallback Option One, and they'd still break even, barely – given a modest return on investment, reasonable salaries, and a continued rent reduction that only a skilled negotiator like himself could pull off.

On the third screen resided Fallback Option Two: a spreadsheet with the sort of red glowing columns David would remember. A spreadsheet based on all the worst assumptions, the one that would get David off his self-righteous ass. And the one, Oz decided, that he'd tell David was the *only* fallback option. After all, it worked last time.

As his friend, it was the least he could do. Or the most. Or something like that. Powering down the monitors, he clicked off his desk lamp, put his heels up, and gazed through the skylight at the night sky. His favorite view. But no twinkling wingtip lights far above tonight, nor stars – only a blank field of the deepest charcoal clouds. In the silence, a bubble of gas worked its way down and was released with a whispered hiss. And then a belch, more audible, the half-digested Vieux Boulogne at least as fragrant in the warm still air of the room. Another bubble, faintly chortling though the tubes of his gut, as Oz's eyes drifted closed and he slept the sleep, more restless than usual, of the less than entirely just.

17

ANIMAL ATTRACTION

- or -

Sylvan Vitamuskosis

LAST NIGHT: David numb, David confused, David wishing he'd kept his mouth shut. David knowing he'd only done what he had to, but also that he might have destroyed everything they'd labored to create.

Today: David at work, a full schedule of patients, his old patients, with actual real illnesses. Happy to be busy, too busy to be thinking of himself – other than the rare lulling moment when he'd be thrown by, say, a sullen look from Quinn. Best of all, miraculously, no patient or staff showed any desire to discuss the myriad and diverse fabulosities of Human Growth Hormone.

Until lunch.

JUNIE UN-BUNGIED the beach towels from Rosie's front seats and spread them on the grass, holding down the corners with various soda bottles and deli items – a veggie hummus sandwich for David, a Reuben for her; fresh fruit salad for him, macaroni salad for her – leaving room to sit cross-legged with some paper plates between.

David paced as she laid the mini-picnic out. She looked over his shoulder, the outline of the Forever Clinic, taller than its Broadway neighbors and two short blocks away. The huge solar-glass skylight was up and open to the perfect day. Next to it, a set-back structure she hadn't noticed from the street, its roof gracefully curved and with generous eaves, a roof that balanced – that forgave, somehow – the trapezoidal cut the gray glass made in the sky. But David and she were here, now, with North Boulder Park stretched out in front of them.

In the near distance, a woman's soccer team practiced, their shouted commands punctuated by the pneumatic thumps of hand-stitched kangaroo shoes on the finest vinyl-covered rubber. Further on, children played, with fewer rules and a less frantic enthusiasm than their well-heeled athlete-mothers. The grass green, the sky blue, severe and clear, the warm air sweet beneath the yellow September sun. Best of all, they were *not* in the clinic.

"Sit." She pointed to the Jamaican-reggae towel from the passenger seat – less butt-pressed and, because of that, reserved for anxious pacing picnic guests.

"I should be back there." He peered at the office roofline, then down at the food. "Couldn't we have had this at the front desk?"

She patted the towel beside her; it sank deep into the uncut grass. "Sit *down.*"

David sat, grumbling about how he'd left his cell phone, how Oz might call and he wouldn't be there.

"He hasn't called you yet?" Amazing.

"No." David picked up his sandwich and checked the plastic wrap for ants. "Not a word since last night."

"And you're waiting."

"Yeah." David leaned back on one elbow, almost relaxed.

"No wonder."

"No wonder what?"

"No wonder you've been looking that way all morning, when you weren't running from one patient to another. It's why I got you out here, boss. He's letting you hang."

"Oz? No. Or maybe. But that's not it."

"Then what?" Though she already had an idea.

"Paula."

Right, Junie thought, again.

DAVID TURNED BACK, considered the limits of co-worker relationships, and asked himself, Why not? She was a friend, wasn't she? And sitting right in front of him, and probably loaded with good – even better, feminine – advice. "We've got this, um, *date*. Dinner. At seven."

Junie looked at him, deciding. Should she tell him about the voodoo, that other-woman funk? It sounded crazy, even jealous, a ludicrous thought. And David seemed okay now. Okay and nervous, which he probably needed to be.

Instead of answering, she lay back, an arm behind her head, succumbing to the amazing force of gravity of a warm September day. The smell of grass, not the aching green chlorophyll of a recent summer mowing, but the mellow funk of verdant leaves and roots and dirt and growth that had slowed but not stopped as the season unwound. Propped in it stood half a bottle of root beer, beaded and still cold.

"*Anyway,*" she said, staring up at the infinitely blue sky, the sun peeking over the stout cottonwood beside them. "About the research."

No girlfriend advice from Junie, David thought. Of course. He shouldn't have been digging, was on his own on this. And of course she wanted to talk about the research – those stupid studies that threatened everything they'd worked for. Ouch. He paused, then said, "I'm sorry."

She squinted over at him. "Don't be."

"I had to. I just had to bring them up. But if I don't write those prescriptions... you know. The clinic. Your job."

His profile above her: human, foolish but somehow strong. She closed her eyes. "That list of articles you emailed, the studies that didn't meet my rules? I pulled them up: you were right. Every one."

"But..."

"Whatever you decide, and I'm fully aware it will affect my job – I was proud of you last night."

"Is that why," he asked, guessing, "you stomped on my toe?"

"Twice. And yes. To wake you up." A second wave of doubt: should she tell him, as crazy as it was? And once again, decided not to. He'd figure it out.

"Wake me up from what?"

A hard, long look from the corners of her eyes – that much she could give him. She closed them again, basking, the autumn sun warming dark limbs and dark clothes.

Wake me up from Paula, he thought. She Whose Name Must Not Be Spoken Again. "I had to tell her, you know."

"Uh-huh." David, she thought, was getting there just fine.

"I was going to mention it the studies right off. But I couldn't."

He asked himself why, and found he still didn't know, not for sure. Only that Junie had helped him. In getting a handle on the research, and perhaps in other ways. "Thanks."

Junie didn't reply.

He looked over and down at her, but didn't want to *look* at her – she was a co-worker, after all – and quickly turned his head away. Then continued with his sandwich, then wiped the inevitable smear of hummus off the angles of his mouth. Got quite a mass, actually, and was about to pop it in but stopped, his fingers halfway to his lips. Still looking in the general direction of the running mothers and their children, but even more aware of Junie lying beside him. Eyes closed, her arm up, shoulder bare, the sun playing in the hollowed shadows of her skin...

WHOA, David thought. Have to keep things... professional. Hunching forward, he wrapped himself around his knees, enjoying the sun but in his own *private* way. Just sitting here with a co-worker – a nice lunch-break, a professional lunch-break, thinking professional thoughts about, for instance, the adhesive tannish wet-dry glop that still clung between his fingers. Professional thoughts, and ones that, if he hadn't been a doctor with an obvious professional interest, might be viewed as, well, rather obsessive. The kind of thoughts that someone might think in order to avoid, well, thinking about something else. But he *was* a health professional, of course, and so it was perfectly reasonable that he think them.

Anyway, the hummus: it *tasted* good, but what was *in* it?

Olive oil – that was healthy. Lots of omega-3's, plus monoun-saturated fat, helping the cholesterol. And garlic – he could smell it, as would everyone else. Though garlic probably didn't help the cholesterol, not like the garlic-fans' claims. He'd looked at that research last year, and a garlic-loaded diet really hadn't done a thing for cholesterol or heart disease. But garlic or olive oil wouldn't kill you, and there weren't many rich, good-tasting things that could stake that claim.

It was mostly mashed-up garbanzo beans, which happily rolled his train of thought onward to the whole veggie deal, something Junie and everybody at the Clinic knew he'd been wresting with.

Junie... David looked down – still there, laying in dappled sun – then immediately back up.

Where was he? Oh... hummus... vegetarians! Who just plain lived longer, at least the most observant, quasi-religious ones. Problem was, they usually had a zillion other healthy habits, like not smoking, and lots of exercise and other good stuff, all those non-dietary habits that the non-veggie critics said skewed the longevity figures, made it so the incidentally-vegetarian would have lived longer anyway. But that was only speculation. One thing was for sure: vegetarians definitely ate less meat, as in zero, which meant less saturated animal fat, the classic 'bad fat' that raised cholesterol and shortened life.

Good fats vs. bad fats. To a vegetarian, Good vs. Evil. The classic dichotomy of any diet: what you ate, and what you didn't.

Unfortunately, the food industry, which was nondenominational except when it came to profit, needed saturated fats – animal fats and tropical oils – to give processed foods a nice long shelf life, no matter what it did to the shelf lives of those who consumed them. When the first wave of cholesterol consciousness hit in the sixties, the industry responded by switching to hydrogenated oils and trans-fats, a supposed laboratory miracle that turned out to be the Darth Vader of ingredients. And now that the label-readers had outed trans-fats, processed food's newest star was palm oil, which was really an old baddie, a saturated tropical oil, but organic enough for the most vegan fundamentalist. David supposed that the jury was still out on palm *fruit* oil, but those studies were funded by the Indonesians who produced it, breaking the most important of Junie's rules.

Junie... who, by her slow and even breaths, sounded as though she'd fallen asleep at his side. David clenched his jaw, stared at the distant soccer players – whose far-away curses over a disputed point barely reached them – and forced himself back on point. Palm oil... bad fats... processed foods! And how to avoid them.

The answer was obvious and simple but expensive. Smart vegetarians, or any smart consumer, could match wits with those sneaky-smart food scientists by buying real, unprocessed foods.

Boy. Vegetarian, unprocessed, then add low-sugar, low-cholesterol, maybe low-salt – every step to a healthy diet seemed reasonable it itself, but together, it seemed, they left hardly any dietary options at all. David was trying, but not finding it easy. He could live without the Twinkies, and salads had always been a staple, but still he hungered for the chunks of fat and protein he'd been throwing in the general direction of his mouth since his mom let him start aiming it himself. Cheese sounded good but was nuts, had as much bad fat as any greasy burger. And nuts were... great, up to a point.

He sighed, flicked the glop of hummus away, and sucked his fingers clean, no longer self-conscious. He'd be a good vegetarian for a little while longer – as good as he could. Which meant periodic, that is daily, falls from grace. Skinless chicken in olive oil and spices, salmon and tuna and, yes, the odd lean cut of beef or pork, red meat for the red-blooded omnivore that, at the end of the day, he was. Lots of olive oil, and even a little butter, all of it as natural and unprocessed as he could. A 'prudent' diet; a *semi*-vegetarian, a term that drove the non-semi veggies to distraction. He could live with that. And for a good while, he hoped, he would.

A gentle, susurrating snore from Junie. She shrugged her arm to her side – there was something about that arm, lean and cocoa – then settled her head further down into her towel-lined depression in the grass, remaining asleep, somehow, on the cool late-September ground.

David checked his watch: they had a few more minutes. Carefully, he laid down on the Rasta-man striped towel, his bare forearm as far away from hers as he could manage without exposing the other to the ticklish grass beyond the towel's edge. They *were* co-workers, after all; just co-workers. He could do this. The sun, the heat, the shadows of the leaves on his face. The bump of an acorn, half-buried in the turf beneath his shoulder blade, that strangely became less noticeable the longer he lay still. The children playing in the distance; that resonant thump of the soccer ball being kicked – then landing, fainter. Another, even fainter, as it was returned.

In the air, the barest trace of something... something mammalian, warm, not at all unpleasant – quite the opposite, in fact. The sweat of sun on skin, the smell of heat and breath and a deeper perfume, feminine. Almost like another, a fragrance that he couldn't quite place. Just that that other fragrance had been similar, if more insistent, driving. And then, somehow, the hazy memory of that really rather chemical musk began to amplify the delicate scent that oh-so-gently radiated though the air around Junie, amplifying it subtly, no, not so subtly, no, absolutely not subtly at all and...

David sat up, heart pounding. Time to get back, right now. Grabbing the Rasta-man towel, and leaving a matching depression in the grass that his body had made beside her, he snagged as much residua of their *al fresco* lunch as he could, cleared his throat to wake her and headed for the nearest bear-proof trash can.

JUNIE OPENED ONE EYE, groaned, and got up to her elbows, her front baking, her back a little too cool from the grass, both of which should even out on the two-block walk to the clinic. David was tossing the non-recyclables and folding the towel, but still looked worried about something.

It was always something, she thought, and sighed.

In the back of her mind, the residual sense of David at her side. A David calm, a David who'd managed to let go, flat and chilling on the grass. Which was good; he'd need it. To figure something – no, figure *someone* – out tonight. Or not. Because, Junie knew, that one was David's problem, his alone.

AS JUNIE AND DAVID began their walk back to the Forever Clinic, Quinn stood in its vast reception area, glumly contemplating the yards of close-packed *Dr. Quinn Recommends* supplements on the open shelves. The clinic, closing. Who was he going to unload them on? A nightmarish image came to him, of cardboard boxes in the back of a garage, a time-lapse movie of the flaps curling and gathering dust as the bottles within slowly expired, hundreds of thousands of golden gel-clad babies wrinkling, drying, little mummies turning to dust. Why hadn't he been able to sell them so far? Had he lost his touch?

A sudden snort, from just behind his left shoulder. Quinn didn't jump; he was too busy being in the moment, which in this moment meant being entirely bummed out. Besides, the horsy sound wasn't in itself unpleasant, and the small gust that blew by his neck was warm, even balmy, and smelled vaguely of fresh hay.

"Vitamins," he heard Nancy say. "A total waste."

What is it, Quinn asked himself, about the women in this place? First Junie, now Nancy – all so... *practical.* Practical and critical and probably telling the customers, that is the patients, not to buy his stuff. All except Adeline, but as a nutritionist she knew the true business of nutrition was at least half business, like it or not.

"Come on," he sighed, still examining his unsold product. "Ever hear of Beriberi? Pellagra? Rickets?"

"Yes, *Doctor* Quinn. All those ancient starving-kids' diseases. I bet you've never seen a single case."

"Because some not-so-ancient doctors discovered what our bodies need: vitamins." Like the ones right in front of him, totally organic and reeking of the quality you had to pay for.

"In small amounts," Nancy said. "The amounts you'd find in any non-starving diet."

Quinn turned to confront her square face, her wide-spaced, unblinking eyes. In the corner of her mouth – which lifted, challenging – resided a green blade of wheatgrass plucked from the ornamental planter next to the sofa.

"Who follows a 'reasonable' diet?" Quinn asked. "Real foods, raw fruits and veggies, the whole deal."

She snorted a second time. And while it certainly wasn't an attractive sound, it was not, for the second time, unpleasant either. In an also-not-unpleasant way, it suited her.

"In this town, at least half," Nancy answered. "The half that *also* takes these," she added, and gestured to his white-bottled babies. "Which all goes right through them, unused – the most expensive pee in the world."

"Let me be sure I get this: what you're saying is... they have all the vitamins and minerals they need to be healthy."

"Yes." She crossed her arms.

"Not to die... prematurely."

"Yes..." She frowned, suspicious.

"What if they could die... *post*maturely?" His eyes surveyed the sun-filled space around them. "What if they took *optimal* amounts? For *optimal* health?"

As he spoke, Nancy took in the room as well, every carefully-placed design element of which whispered, Forever... Then shook herself, looked disgusted, and said, "What a load of manure. Live longer by taking a vitamin? It's too easy."

He was about to start his standard reply but she beat him. "I read, you know. There's always something – some article, some study telling you it's the way to go. And then, a few years later, telling you it's actually *not* the way to go. But surprise, by the time that comes out there's a new vitamin you should take." She rubbed her palms together, kneading. "Give me hands-on care any time. You won't live longer, but you'll feel better."

Quinn found himself unmanned by those strong tan fingers, calluses soft with massage oil, the scent of almond and soap and skin. "Oh," he said. "Like vitamin E, ten years ago."

"Exactly. The miracle cure. First it's good for heart disease, then they find out it's giving people heart failure."

"You *do* read. But that was the alpha-tocopherol form. *Gamma*-tocopherol was what they should have studied."

"See?" Nancy said, "There's always something – some slippery way to get around any finding you guys don't like."

"I suppose you're not too crazy about A, either." People sure had long memories; no wonder he wasn't moving the supply.

"You suppose right. I actually got talked into those powdered veggie pills that give five-thousand-whatever percent of the 'minimum daily's.'"

Thinking ahead, Quinn eased slightly to the right, between her and his own after-market version of the same thing.

Nancy noticed and leaned around him, read the label and nodded. "That's the stuff. Anyway, back then I figure it's natural, ground up out of whole foods, you can't go wrong. Until I turn yellow and get these headaches that won't quit. My doc looks it up and tells they were loading the pills with extra chemicals, carotenes and retinoids – basically, vitamin A, enough to make your brain swell. Scary, but the MRI's normal and everything gets better after I stop. Then in the paper, I see they tried the same big doses on smokers and it *gave* them lung cancer. Nice, huh?"

"Yeah," he said, defeated. But Quinn never stayed defeated long. If anything, it made him realize he really wasn't doing a good job of selling his point of view. He turned to the shelves, his hand floating to the right... to the left... there! He snagged a good-sized bottle and handed it to her. "My treat."

Nancy balanced it on one open palm held out in front of her, as if it was radioactive. "Vitamin D? For bones?"

"For much, much more than that. For *everything*," he said, gaining enthusiasm with every word.

"Nothing is for everything."

"This one might be. The small studies show it works on cancer *and* heart disease. And when you combine them, add up all the numbers and check the death rate..." He paused, then added, conspiratorially, "That's the most important outcome, the thing actually happens in the real world over time – the biggie. And guess what?"

Nancy looked like she was going to take a guess but this time he got there first: "Take a thousand or so units a day and the death rate goes down by seven percent, which might not sound like much but it's huge, an extra year or two of life."

She held the bottle a little closer. "Doesn't my body make its own? From the sun?"

"Did you go to medical school?" A hand, the gentlest, warmest, lightest possible salesperson's hand, to her shoulder. "You should have."

Nancy actually smiled.

"I say that because you're absolutely right. Unless, of course, you're living at this latitude. And wear clothes. And use sunscreen. Then no, your body isn't making enough D." He glanced down at the clean white bottle. "Go ahead – try it."

"Does it do, you know, anything bad?"

Damn, Quinn thought. He didn't want to, but he had to say it: "Hypervitaminosis D." He hated the way that sounded, and was quick to add, "I've never seen it, and I don't know anyone who has. And it's the same as your headaches – all you have to do is stop. That and change your diet a little."

The smile was fading; she started to hand it back. "No. No. I'm not desperate enough."

"You mean you're not old enough." Quinn said, bringing out the big guns. "You haven't seen enough good people go down. Enough to know how much an extra year of life, healthy life, can mean."

Nancy hesitated, a phenomena as rare for her as defeat was for Quinn. "Okay," she said, and jammed them in one flannel breast pocket. Which made that breast, he noticed, twice the size of the other, a look that was rather interesting.

But the important thing was that he was back in action – he'd made a sale! Or sort of. And maybe... maybe his luck was changing, maybe this was the beginning of a roll. Quinn reached behind him, randomly grasped a small cool bottle, brought it around and said, "How 'bout this?"

"More? What is it?"

Luckily, he'd read the label by that point. "Vitamin C."

She took the bottle and regarded it as skeptically as the last. "Another oldie-but-goodie? One year they're saying ten grams a day, then nothing. Something about kidney stones."

"I only recommend a fraction of that."

"What? Nine-tenths?"

No, no – he was losing her. "Two hundred and fifty milligrams, same as you'd take for a cold. Never more, unless there's a deficiency."

"Like what?" Nancy asked, testing him.

Quinn tilted his head, examining her. "Well, your eyes... those dark circles. Kind of... sunken." A stretch, but maybe.

Nancy wasn't vain, but the lack of makeup didn't mean she didn't *care*. Her hand went to her face, involuntarily. "My eyes? What could cause..."

"If I didn't know better, I'd say—"

"Wait a second," she said. "Vitamin C... scurvy? You're back to those old diseases again? I'm *definitely* at risk for that – if I'd just spent six months on a whaleboat. In the eighteenth frigging century."

"I didn't mean you actually had scurvy, not absolutely," Quinn said, scrambling. "We could do some comprehensive testing..." That would do it – a nice big multi-tube blood draw – mail it to Geno-Smokies Labs, the chiropractors' favorite. Something *always* came back low.

"No way, pal." Nancy handed the bottle back, relieved. Sunken eyes, indeed; all she needed was more sleep. "I'll stick with a healthy diet, thanks."

Rejected and dejected. Quinn took it without a word, returned it carefully to its row.

Men, she thought, and fished the vitamin D out of her shirt.

"Not the D," he said. "You really *should*—"

"Tell you what." Nancy smoothed the plaid flannel flap on the pocket closed, "If it still looks like it works in five years, we'll talk."

Quinn nodded, looking down. Actually, his spirits were rebounding once again, as he gazed at the pocket the bottle had just been released from. All in all, he decided, he liked her breasts the same size best.

Nancy watched, eyebrows up, then said, "Hello?"

"Sorry," he said, but didn't sound it, just met her eyes and took the bottle.

"What's it going to be, anyway?"

A puzzled look crossed Quinn's face, stubbled cheeks pouching a little more than usual.

"With you," she said. "Guy or gal?"

His smile revealed a smear of crimson lipstick on a capped front tooth. "Whatever you want?"

Nancy rolled her eyes and walked back to her office. Quinn shrugged and, as Junie and David came in through the employee door, returned to his too-crowded shelves.

BIGGS SETTLED his shoulders into the driver's seat of the German *über*sedan that Ozvaldo Garcia had so kindly loaned them, checked the built-in stealth-mode radar scatterer, and smoothly accelerated uphill, headed for Monument Pass. The laboring trucks were a pleasant blur on his right, the occasional presumptuous SUV in the left lane no more than an amusing encounter. One persistent fellow – no, make that a Western road-hog mommy and her brood – forced him to place two and then four wide tires on the highway's shoulder, but the superb car self-leveled and hardly registered the change.

After he'd swooped back, Paula looked over with a noticeably critical eye.

"What?" Biggs asked. "What?"

She shook her head, turned a page of the prospectus for the

Church of Life – a combined prayer, medical, and longevity facility – and said, "It's a hundred miles, Biggs, not the Trans-America race."

"I know. But driving like this, after LA…"

The minute hand on the jeweled dashboard clock advanced with a tiny, audible click. "We're going to be half an hour early. Half an hour, with nothing to do, in Colorado Springs." The very thought seemed endless. "Think we can find a decent cup of coffee?"

"Check the GPS, baby!" When Paula didn't jump to it, went after it himself, working though the complex series of nestled windows on the dashboard's central touchscreen. A grumble of gravel, a trail of dust in the rearview mirror, and she grabbed the steering wheel and brought them back to the shoulder and then the left lane. Biggs looked up, winked, and dove back again, Paula still steadying the wheel.

After he returned his attention to the speeding asphalt, she held up the prospectus. "I don't like this. Tax free, I get that, but honestly – do rich people pray?"

"Down here they do." They'd crested the rise to see the monolith of Castle Rock in all its antenna-crusted glory. "If they want to stay in business. Rocking with Jesus, seven days a week. Like Salt Lake City, except different saints."

Paula stared out the windshield, ready to grab the wheel again if necessary. Her body ached, muscles building and knitting; she'd had her injection today, but should be strong tonight. For David. An entirely different business challenge, but she'd best keep her mind on the present one. "I don't know. Seems like the money's further north."

"*Now* you like Boulder, huh? Uh, uh, uh. David, David, David."

"Shut up, Biggsie." She jabbed him with an elbow in the ribs, not so hard as to send them off the road.

Even so, it hurt, as any jab from Paula hurt. After he recovered, he said, "Just teasing. And you're right. Maybe not the money, but the *idea* of Boulder. An idea that says health, wellness, new Age, spirit, eternity. An idea, a place, a name that we can ride, east and west and everywhere." He let go of the wheel – Paula grabbed it, ready – and framed the air with his hands. "'Boulder: where people take good, good care of themselves. In any way, at any cost.' Oh yeah." He definitely liked his way with words.

Paula didn't, not when it had anything to do with her failure to control David and the Boulder market. She paused, then said, "I know, and I know you're right about the Springs – another Colorado footprint in reserve." She pointed with a perfect, surgically enhanced chin down the ribbon of highway. The low, serrated hedge of its downtown buildings, bigger than Boulder's but smaller than Denver's, were reeling into view, Pike's peak on the right. "The Reverend Dr. Hedley Taggard."

She took out a small emerald bottle and applied a drop below each ear, then spread the top half of her blouse open and carefully placed two more in the sculpted valley between her breasts. Biggs watched, appreciatively, though he'd long since learned not to mix business with pleasure. Among other things, he valued his life: He might have gotten away with Junie – and one or two others – but Mrs. Biggs, his homegirl honey, solo squeeze, and card-carrying NRA member, could be... *demonstrative.* Personal feelings aside, Paula was attractive, and that stuff did seem to give her confidence. And sometimes, if erratically, seemed to work. Except...

"Excuse me, Paula?"

"Yes?" She buttoned the white satin to her neck – sensual but churchy, unlikely to offend.

Or in this case, Biggs knew, to attract. "Do they say anything in there about Dr. Taggart's fashion ministry and clinic up in Denver?"

"*Fashion* ministry? Denver?"

"Biggest style outpost between Omaha and Tucson."

She stared at him, waiting.

"An outreach thing," he continued. "Blessing the designs, treating bulimia, bringing lost models back into the fold."

"'Lost' models. What a guy." Perhaps she should leave the top button open.

"Um-hmm. *Male* models, Paula. Check the headlines. Church-wise, Hedley's been an extra-bad boy."

"Oh." The button stayed closed.

Biggs loosened his rep tie, hooked the collar of his undershirt with one blocky finger and, tilting his head away, leaned in her direction. "Better hit me with a few drops of that mankiller you got there."

IT WAS DAVID, finally, who broke down and called Oz.

Oz who'd meant to leave him hanging, it was true, but who was, in addition, experiencing a curious reluctance to wheedle and cadge and otherwise maneuver his childhood friend back into the deal, a deal that would be David's first-class ticket as much as his.

"Hey," David said, "Meet you at the Zan-Mei?" Neutral ground, and Oz's favorite blowfish palace, where David would pick at veggie rolls while Oz dug into semi-toxic Fugu until his cheeks were numb. Maybe Oz would overdo it, and David could save him – that would *have* to buy forgiveness.

Oz paused, then said, "No, not tonight."

David felt guilty – not so much about the fantasy, in which he did save Oz, after all, but that Oz was still upset, and it was all his fault. "Look, what I said last night..."

"Was what you meant, David." The day was fading, the home office lit largely by the desk's three spreadsheet-filled screens. Oz turned his chair to the east-facing windows, the golden light stretching out beyond east Boulder, out to the far bruised twilight of the plains. He didn't want to see David, for once didn't want to *sell* him, wanted only to tell him how it really was. "The thing is, running the Clinic without HorTech would be..."

He was going to play it straight and say 'difficult', but his eye was caught by the columns of scarlet numerals that filled the rightmost screen. "Would be... impossible." There, he'd said it. A justifiable lie. A lie that happened, just *happened,* to fill his pockets.

"Oh. I was afraid of that. Jeez. So..."

"Our staff is huge; without HGH, we can't meet all those salaries," Oz said, warming to the task. "Even if we let half go... you know the story: less providers, less charges, less income. It only gets worse."

"No chance at all?"

"There's always a chance. Always." Oz was relieved to throw that bit of truth out there. "But the risk is too great. I've got to watch *my* losses, too." Loss of ungodly profit, to be specific, but he didn't have to mention that.

"Oh." David knew how quickly a speculator like Oz could get cleaned out. And Oz, without success... not good. Not good for Oz at all. None of it any good, for anybody.

"But you have to do what you think is best, David. Your medical judgment. We're counting on that." The truth – his license, his established and earnest presence in town was critical. The truth, again, plus a little more.

After David mumbled that he'd think about it, sounding as pliable as always. Oz answered with his usual nonspecific encouragement and ended the call. Was that a twinge of guilt he felt? No. Couldn't be.

Out the window, the plains were looking a little more bruised, but the lights of the suburbs were beginning to wink on, vast fields of streetlights, a shopping center, a blaze of silver halides mounted over a ballpark that almost hurt the eyes. The future, Oz thought – the future looked bright.

"HERE? At my place? I though we were going out to dinner." David, who'd just read another cellphone-radiation-panic article, held his cell at arm's as he hopped off his single bed, his eyes traveling from the folding chair to the table to the storm of scattered clothes.

"I'll bring something *special* over." There was something about his voice, Paula thought. She frowned as she ran a phosphorescent line of honey-colored liquid down the underside of her upstretched arm, tracing it with a fingertip into a graceful nautilus spiral that ascended the augmented cone of her left breast. Stopping at the areola, for GuyLoreiLure, she knew, was noticeably bitter.

"But I've hardly moved in..." Another sort of panic had set in: Paula, *here*. After the disaster at her hotel room, then that awful clinic meeting. The thought of her striding into his self-imposed purgatory, his dreary one-room unit...

Paula was still frowning. The voice coming through her phone was audible but also tinny, distant – distant in a way she didn't like. "Are you there, David? I can't hear you."

"Sorry." He brought the cell to his ear. "I said, I'm still moving in – the place is pretty spare."

Spare she could handle, and his tone was now more to her liking. "I don't care about your *furniture*," she said, huskily.

His phone close, he breathed in and closed his eyes, remembered. What had he been thinking of? The mess didn't matter –

nothing mattered, nothing *could* matter except Paula – Paula, Oh Paula – Paula, *here*! He swallowed, and asked, "How soon?"

"Give me twenty minutes." A smile as she traced the same pattern on her right breast. "I want to be right for you." With a naked shrug, she dumped the rest of the small bottle's pricey contents over her flat belly and tanned thighs. She obviously hadn't used enough last time. David's apartment had to be smaller than the Forever Clinic, and GuyLoreiLure would saturate every corner he might try to back into. Why take *any* chance he could evade his destiny?

Silence, a breath, the inevitable assent – shuddering, as if the poor kid was here with her – and then the faintest click.

She finished rubbing the GuyLoreiLure into all exposed and hidden surfaces, behind her knees, between her toes, then ran her hands through her silver hair to absorb the last traces.

In the corner of the dressing area, a scraping sound too faint for Paula to hear, as the breadwinner of the newly-erected St. Julio Hotel's first mouse family threw himself against the backside of the faux-marble baseboard and tried to claw his way towards the richly perfumed light. Behind him, another tiny mouse, a female of the species, scowled, if mice can scowl, and gathered her still-tinier children close.

THE SKY was now dark enough to let the stars emerge above the distant rim of East-county smog, and Oz had business, personal business, on the internet tonight.

The array of desktop monitors asleep behind him, Oz opened his private laptop. Screen shining in the unlit room, he stroked the touchpad, positioning the tiny dollar-sign cursor over his favorite search engine, the one that automatically wiped its memory clean. Oz liked to keep the personal and the professional separate. He might run for office someday, and even the businessman's political party of choice could hide only so much *indulgent*, shall we say, behavior.

The doors were locked, and he lived far enough from his sub-suburban neighbors to avoid chance sightings through uncurtained windows. With that thought, he checked his property's perimeter security, and then the WiFi encoding system: all good, a row of green diodes that gleamed on the far wall.

His hard-working father would have been shamed; even David, the romantic, had long since grown beyond this foolishness and would not understand. Would Oz's fellow entrepreneurs laugh at his growing obsession, or be appalled? A fine house, they all agreed, was a reasonable business expense, and fine cars as well, but this sort of thing could bring a rich man to his knees. Was desire itself irrational, if unrestrained by cost? His peers would point their fingers, but simultaneously welcome him to the pricey private clubs of their own hell, happy that he had fallen, finally, as weak and human as they had proved to be.

Oz stopped, a fingertip hovering above the 'enter' button. Was he was going too far? All while staring at that screen-saver, her elegantly broad beam, her white hull plowing through azure waves. The original download of David's dream boat, though it was clear that David had never really cared, not like *he* did. And she was *nothing* compared to the other ships out there – and, with that thought, stabbed open the browser and dizzily dropped into an ever-branching virtual catalog, fingers dancing on the keys, bouncing from site to site to site to... Wait!

His fingers poised, frozen again, above the keyboard. What was more important, *length*... or *shape*? Mouth dry, sweat beading on his scalp, he began to type: 'Open ocean sailboat' 'Length...'

His hand trembled, but helpless, committed, he stiffened his resolve. Oz typed again: '40...'

No.

Delete delete.

'50...'

No.

Delete delete.

'*60* feet.'

FINDING THE SLIP, Beatriz had discovered, was as easy as advertised – even better, it came with its own tourist business, hers for a year if she promised to keep it alive. The slip and the business were being vacated by a homesick Chilean in a converted 12-meter, in exchange for a reasonable monthly fee and the promise to vanish on his return.

Beatriz coiled a mooring line on the dock – there, perfect – and squinted towards the dusk-shrouded pylons of the world's most famous bridge, the lights of a freighter sliding in between them, the shadowed sea beyond. It wasn't calling all that loud, so far. A full year's commitment had been tough, but she'd buckled up and signed the papers. After all, it was her boat, and she could do what she wanted with it.

She sighed and headed in to change the forward cabin's sheets – this afternoon's couple had figured their Honeymoon Special cruise was literally that, disappearing as she'd left the dock and hardly coming up for air. She'd been too embarrassed to protest, and the three-figure tip made up for the sticky spots. Not the pirate life, she guessed, for now.

After finishing off the chocolate strawberries and rinsing out the champagne flutes, Beatriz went up on deck again, up to the cabin roof, her favorite spot, and laid down on it. Marriages. A smile, but not a happy one. She'd almost drunk herself to death to escape her own – then found she couldn't stop, in a steep and sadly comical slide to poolside motel shows, auto-dealership openings, bat mitzvahs, and finally the public beaches, gyrating desperately for any *haole* who, wishing to enjoy an unimpeded view of the ocean and remove her sodden presence from his children's lasting mental pictures of their family vacation, seemed likely to throw a dollar in her direction.

Until, one rainy fruit-wine-flavored night, it happened: the event that changed her life. The same handsome sailing yacht, the same teak deck, even the same position, flat on her back. Beatriz closed her eyes and could see it, feel it all again: how she'd slipped onto the yacht basin, then hopped on a single bare foot down the dock with a fluorescent hoop twirling on one arm and another on a stretched-out leg, teetering wildly as her free arm held a ragged cap for change. Unfortunately, she'd been too inebriated to notice the inclement weather, the battened hatches, and the lack of any potential audience on the floating wooden walkways that creaked and shifted between the hulls. Unbalanced by a sudden gust, she'd toppled into an untended cockpit – the one just behind her – struck her head on the decking, and rolled beneath a crumpled tarp. She was still snoring peacefully as the vessel, in a unscheduled nocturnal departure, slipped silent from the harbor and, running lights unlit, out to sea.

Found by the sailboat's Vanuatu captain the next morning, she was marched through the upper lounge, down carpeted steps to the mess and chartroom, between the galley and the crew's quarters to deposit her in the owner's forward suite. A disgraced chief executive of a Christian charitable organization, his hasty exit the night before had been related to the increasingly hostile inquiries into his inventive investment schemes and overall compensation package. Perhaps it was his desire for spiritual regeneration, his own considerable hangover, or the prospect of an extra crewmember without salary or benefits, but in any case he announced, on the spot, to reform both himself and her.

And he did – which wasn't hard; Beatriz was plenty ready for a new life. Especially as the ship's hired captain, a variably observant son of Islam who was also the vessel's dangerously experimental cook and resident kava kava addict, had listened to his boss's resolutions and happily tossed every ethanol-containing beverage overboard.

So she learned to sail the Pacific, the captain imparting the skills, nautical and otherwise, that would serve her so well. Much of this depended on their frequent trans-Pacific migrations, ferrying the ship's owner to the mainland for another round of court appearances, the progress of which inevitably led to further nocturnal departures. While the owner's fortunes gradually depleted, due largely to a series of anorexic girlfriends who were constitutionally unable to secure a line or even clear their dishes, the crew's fortunes proportionately grew, not from theft, for Beatriz was not a thief and paid her debts in full, but from her and the captain's shared and very discrete trans-Pacific smuggling operation. At least Beatriz's fortunes grew – her Vanuatu friend always managed to consume his half of whatever contraband substance they had hidden for that crossing.

The owner's last court visit – bankruptcy court – had come more than five years ago, soon after which she was able to anonymously purchase her floating home and business. The owner's bank, urgent to justify its loans, had offered a substantial discount, based on the many flaws that the vessel's two crewmembers, obviously disinterested and soon to be unemployed, seemed eager to point out. Not too many months later, her mentor and former captain really did choose unemployment, and she deposited him into the arms of the South Pacific wife – at least one of them – and the many children – at least some of them – he had so labored to avoid.

Marriage, or, really, marriages. Despite their multiplicity, the captain had left and left again. He'd wanted to be unconnected, too. Beatriz had seen the separation was destroying him, but thought she was immune. And wasn't she? Beatriz scowled, a pirate to her core. Parking her boat at this slip had been an *economic* move, not an emotional one. She was plenty immune, and plenty unconnected. A few memories, was all.

The Honeymooner Specials, however, would have to go. Over on the cabin table, her laptop's open screen cast a multicolored glow against the custom maple cabinets. That was *her* connection – a new plan was all she'd needed, and the e-listings for the Ozma Open Ocean Sailing School were beaming far and wide.

"…MANY of the mammalian creatures in Our Animal Kingdom release a glandular odor that not only attracts the opposite sex, but compels demonstrable mounting behavior…"

David let the television drone as he ran about the room, throwing sweatshirts in the closet, squaring up the desk and chair, and frantically working his carpet sweeper over the matted brown shag. The apartment's ancient television had basic cable – the nearby mountains blocked most broadcast signals – and he'd gotten in the habit of leaving a nature channel on for distraction. And it *was* distracting, especially the mating behavior of two rarely-seen Red-Bellied Marmots on the thirteen-inch screen. First the female, sitting upright on her haunches and flapping her forelegs wildly to express her axillary secretions, after which the camera panned to the male, nose sniffing the air. Followed by a penetrating *Eeek!* and then a frenzied charge, to join in a tumbling ball of palpitating spiky fur. David escaped that particular image with a speed-cleaning of the bathroom, but could still hear the narrator…

"…While the presence of adequate vomeronasal receptors in homo sapiens is debatable, there appears to be at least marginal impact of pheromones on human…"

David looked up from the now-presentable toilet bowl. Paula had given that talk about pheromones, a part of HorTech's product line, the first night they'd met. Followed by that first morning – his senses flooded with the details, before and during and even after, the sweat cooling on their skin, her sheen of her palm as she'd reached for his cell...

"...scientists have demonstrated that even a molecule-deep layer of these potent biologic compounds can persist almost indefinitely..."

He moved on to the sink, thinking that Paula would probably appreciate the documentary, *Scent and Sensibility*. Drying his hands, he looked at his watch. Would she have left? Maybe, maybe not. Actually, he needed a few more minutes. He'd call and tell her she didn't really have to hurry.

"...although their effectiveness seems unlikely, crude mammalian pheromones have been used in fragrances since the early nineteen-seventies..."

David opened the phone, hit the redial button and held it to his ear, waiting for Paula to answer. His heart began again to hammer, his eyes grew darker in the mirror. Proof of love, he thought, while a somewhat less intoxicated part of his brain registered it as a physiologic effects of arousal – pupillary dilation. The same as that frenzied marmot. The same, except less fur.

Effects that, for some reason, were accompanied by the scent of Paula, as if she were here with him. He'd never really noticed it before, but there it was: a hint of jasmine, a floral note with a hidden whip, stinging – Paula Oh Paula – like perfume added to cover a deeper, almost chemical musk. But beautiful, of course, because it was Paula's. When had he experienced it last? That embarrassing flail in her hotel room, of course, and at the meeting... and also, oddly enough, earlier today. The picnic lunch with Junie, but it had been fainter, natural, unperfumed. At least at first, until the memory of *this* scent had come charging up within him – *this* scent, remembered, haunting and then amplifying and then ramping up and up and up as they'd laid innocent on the grass...

A scent, a memory, a burgeoning physiologic arousal, and a certain subliminal *Eeek!*

PAULA heard her phone ring from the purse on the passenger seat of her rental Camry and fished it from the crowded depths. David. Not a surprise, nor should it be. Whether it was the pheromone, or every other good thing she brought to the package that was Paula, it didn't matter. Results were everything, and she was still on top of her game. So let him wait; it would only make these last throw-down rounds between them even sweeter. She held her cell with two fingers and dropped it back in.

DAVID and the open cell phone.

Flowers.

Musk.

Paula.

Almost reeling – Paula.

What had Junie said, Junie who he couldn't care less about right now? Not on their little picnic – Oops, their *al fresco* business lunch. But weeks earlier, when they were still stocking the new clinic. Something about the phone, how he got that look in his eyes – the same dilated pupils? – whenever Paula called. But of course he answered. And how could he answer, if not on his phone? What had that narrator just said? '...*Even a molecule-deep layer...*'

Squinting close, David focused on the slight discolorations near the mouthpiece of the phone, the residual stain of oil on plastic, a blacker black, almost opalescent. With the angled, oval shape of two fingerprints.

Fingerprints.

No, couldn't be... Not possibly... No.

Paula in Vegas, Paula who would naturally have used HorTech's pheromone during her talk, Paula who'd grabbed his interrupting cell phone the next morning, hands sweat-damp with that musk, that perfume... that pheromone!

David yanked the cell from his face, his mouth, his nose, snapped it shut and stared at it, appalled, threw it on the white Formica counter and backed up against the tiled wall. Watching the mirror – It was true! – as his eyes regained their normal color, his pulse dropped, and the bright flush left his face.

And heard the knock on his door.

Damn.

HE STOPPED at what had to be a safe distance, at least three feet from the door. "Y – yes?"

"David. Darling." Impatient. "Let me in."

Her voice through the thin wood, and, as he stared at the inch-wide gap above the threshold, the first invisible wave of atomized molecules wafting through. His vision blurred, doubled; it was futile to resist.

In other words... *Eeek!*

Paula oh Paula, he thought, what nonsense had come over me? How could I let her wait out there? With happiness swelling his chest – and resuming its earlier effect on other regions – he strode to the door, swung it open, and held arms wide in welcome.

Paula nodded, approvingly, and folded in. As David found himself holding a beautiful, strong, very female body for whom he felt, suddenly, this close...

Absolutely nothing.

THAT WAS QUICK, she thought. David had pulled away, put his big pale hands on her shoulders, and stood with a goofy smile on his face, as if not sure how to react. Okay, she'd show him that part. He'd been a busy boy – a bad boy, looking up those research papers – and maybe he forgot. Grabbing one of those big hands, she walked by, dragged him into the room, and slung him on the single mattress.

David looked up at the cloud of silver hair, noting, for the first time, that the roots were dark. And why not? Paula was all about selling youth in age – how better than to make believe she's even older? Fifty, tops, and what a fifty; a somewhat distant admiration, considering that the entire length of her perfect fifty was pressing down on his far-from-perfect thirty-two. Weird, considering how *motivated* he'd been when he'd opened the door. At which point that perfume, the pheromone, had become, for some unknown reason, no longer intoxicating at all.

Then the kernel of a memory: his childhood dog, a foolish

puppy that had let itself get skunked. How David, as a puzzled ten-year-old, could hardly smell it as he'd let the puppy in – only a faint peppery odor, at least until it trotted away and into the living room, his overwhelmed nose had cleared and the stink magnified a hundred-fold, morphing into a hideous house-clearing funk.

But before he could apply that to his present situation, her mouth applied itself to his; a kiss, the taste not unpleasant – a toothpaste he liked, actually – but nothing more. Until David, as a puzzled thirty-two year old, was saved by a claw-like scraping, coming from the screened apartment window that he'd left open to the evening air.

"What's that?" Her head jerked up, cranking to look back at the windows.

Still pinned, he lifted his head as well, to see nothing more than dark gray sky through the skein of brushy trees, rustling slightly, that grew across the creek. "I... I don't know."

"What do you *mean* you don't know? Something's trying to break in!"

"We're ten feet over the water, Paula. Probably some branches on the screen."

"Branches? Water?" Nature: she hated it. "There's something out there, I know it. Close the window – please, close it now!"

Okay, David thought. If nothing else, a way out from under what had become an strangely dispassionate situation. The television was still on as he crossed the room, the same documentary, the same pseudo-academic voice...

"*...a persistent question, fanned by the perfume industry, has been the cross-species effect. Veterinarians have recently found that the scent of the female field mouse, when sufficiently concentrated, 'achieves something of an entirely unexpected magnitude in the bull elephant...*"

David peered through the screen, then jumped back as a narrow fanged snout launched itself against it. "Holy crap!"

"What!" Paula pushed herself up, yanking the comforter around her shoulders.

"Just a raccoon," he said, then heard a sound that he had never heard from a raccoon – on cable or in real life – a distinct, cross-species, '*Eeek!*'

The raccoon's head was swaying, swooning, and David found himself swooning as well, not from the close call but something else, something very familiar, something that was again taking hold of his brain now that he was across the room from Paula. A feeling that grew in intensity as those overloaded vomeronasal receptors cleared enough to register the scent of Paula – Paula Oh Paula – back on the bed. He gazed at her through again-dilated pupils, as did his furry friend on the other side of the screen. She looked... well, confused, but also... *wonderful*. Both of her – his eyes had crossed again.

"David..." She didn't like any of this, not one bit. "Turn around and close the window!"

"In a minute," he said, eyes shining, working at his belt. And with a running leap – identical to Paula's gymnastics at the hotel – launched himself to land, bouncing, on the bed. Straddling her bundled comforter, he bent close to breath every dense-packed molecule in, feeling completely, utterly ready...

And then, not.

Which was, for David, more than confusing.

Paula wasn't confused; she pushed him off the mattress, hard. "Get. Over. There."

"But—" Unfortunately, a new distraction had arrived. The scratching doubled as a new odor filled the room, an odor that was very, very reminiscent of... something very, very awful. As David struggled from the floor, he was assaulted by a stench that could only be dragged from the depths of a blood-warmed body, fermented and decayed and ripened, the fecal smell of...

Her eyes narrowed. "You *didn't*."

...anal glands? In here? Returning to the window, he found his answer – a second outline, jet-black and bisected by an unmistakable streak of vivid white.

Paula saw it too, screamed and pulled the comforter over her head as David ran back to the sliding window. The scrabbling built into a woodland frenzy while, with equal frenzy, David tried to pull it closed, the cheap brown aluminum frame jamming in its track. Behind him, the voice continued calmly, intellectually, boringly...

"...one has to wonder at the effect of man's commercial inroads into these compounds. If successful, might the resultant saturation overload – or extinguish, to use the physiologic term – the vomeronasal *receptors and, by that, short out the very mechanisms of attraction*?"

His fingers gave way; he stumbled against the television and knocked it to the carpet, where it expired with a terminal ozone-flavored hum. As he stood there, and as the scrabbling redoubled, three things came to him...

The first was how, once he'd reached the window, that over-whelmingly foul smell had disappeared, replaced by a faint and almost pleasant peppery odor. An odor just like Stinker's – finally, he remembered – on the childhood evening that Stinker earned his name.

The second was from that pompous narration – *nasal overload... blocked receptors... extinguish* – and how he'd been right so long ago. As in: the skunk stank over there, but not here by the window. As in: the scent of Paula called to him here, but not, he knew, once he returned to her side. Almost as if... as if... as if she'd dumped a boatload of pheromone over herself, to make sure the Clinic contract got signed?

The third, and most persuasive, was how Paula, even covered and coiled and defensive, had once again become deeply, irresistibly attractive. She wasn't cowering beneath the comforter, she was calling, silently calling for him, only him. A call that he could not help but answer with a resonating, loving, lusting, soul-shuddering... *Eeek!*

No, he thought, as he began to march, zombie-like, toward the huddled, trembling covers on the bed.

No way, he thought, as the scratching was replaced by a series of metallic tearing rips from the still-open window.

Uh-oh, he thought, as two furry forms, one brown and the other black-and-white, brushed against his legs in their pheromone-driven rush for the bed.

His head cleared once more, as predicted by both the documentary and his own long-ago experience with Stinker, in the moment that he reached the mattress. As did the heads of the raccoon and skunk, which, their noses shorted out as well, back-pedaled to a halt and looked at each other across the trembling bedclothes, puzzled as to why they found their normally un-fraternizing species in such close proximity, and in such a deeply unnatural place.

But not Paula's head, which poked above the comforter, howled piercingly, and then bounded – attached to the rest of her, of course – to the open bathroom door.

A resounding slam, then silence. Leaving David, the raccoon, and the skunk all staring, still stunned, at one another. Until the scent dissipated in her absence, their vomeronasal receptors de-jammed, the residual molecules re-stimulated that magical neurological organ, and... *Eeek!* ...all three rushed with flaring nostrils to thump against the hollow-core door.

"Noooo..." David heard her moan over the frenzied clawing and scratching by his feet. Which threw some sort of trigger for gallantry – a kind of lust, once removed. Managing to pull his face off the wood, he released his death grip on the flimsy doorknob and leaped back over the bed.

The bathroom window, he thought, over the parking lot: he'd save her and they'd escape forever, happy at last.

David shot out his front door, spun on a heel and scrambled up and over the low roof to a small square frosted window.

"Paula!"

No answer, just a low forlorn sobbing, the fuzzy image of a Paula-like shape huddled on the linoleum beneath. But though the unlatched frame came the intoxicating *essence* of Paula, the woman of all women, the woman he'd risk everything to save.

Happily, it was easier than that, nothing more than a few ripped fingernails as, heedless, he worked them under the narrow exposed lip and then, bare feet on either side, back straining, wrenched the window open on its corroded gears. With that his lovely Paula was free. David had hardly popped the screen and stuck his face through the open frame, inhaling the small room's concentrated essence ever more deeply into his brain, when Paula roughly shoved his face out of the way and scrambled through the narrow opening. With a running jump off the redwood shingles, she tore towards her rental car, working the fob on her keys as she looked, wide-eyed, back to his open apartment door.

David, whose last deep inhalation had forever toasted every one of his vomeronasal Paula-receptors, was free as well. Though not unconcerned: he might be entirely out of love and lust, but she was, after all, a guest. By now she'd made it into her car, the starter grinding as, wide-eyed, she stared at his neighbor's Great Bernese galumphing, leash trailing and tongue askew, towards the fragile barrier of the driver's side window – and then, worse, at the twin streaks of brown and white-streaked black that tore from David's door to speed between the dog's legs and leap to the hood – She's mine! All mine! – before their competition arrived.

The engine caught in the very instant that the freakishly over-sized canine went airborne towards the trunk, and her rental squealed and swerved and thumped over parking bolsters and speed bumps, throwing off the odd woodland creature – which the Great Bernese spontaneously decided would make far better sport – before lurching onto Thirtieth street to escape her nightmare business date.

18

PULLING THE PLUG

- or -

Recurrent Ethicitis

DAVID stood in the darkened atrium of the Forever Clinic's office building, bare feet on the frosted glass floor. Beside him lay a pile of skunk-stinking clothes; he shivered in his undershorts as he worked the teak door's hypersecure cylindrical key. Once open, he rushed across the front room in darkness, headed for his office's private bathroom. It was as lux as the rest on the place: a suspended stainless steel sink, a designer toilet, a slotted brass drain in the center of the granite tiles between. Arranging a circular dam of soaked patient gowns, he stood naked within it as he soaped himself head to toe and rinsed twice, three times, plastic cup after cup of sink water puddling on the tiles before sluicing down.

This was followed by a brisk drying with handfuls of recycled paper towels, which gave off a distant funk of their former uses as a sodden pile accumulated on the floor. If he could smell that, he figured, his blocked vomeronasal receptors must be back to normal. Locating a set of green cotton scrubs in the bottom drawer of his scarred oak desk, he slid his size thirteens into a pair of pale blue paper surgical shoe-covers he kept around on the off chance that a former hospital colleague would invite him to assist in the odd appendectomy.

Back in the office's reception area, he powered open the roof skylight to let the residual odor of his passage out, then closed it, quickly – Fall was coming, and the September night was mountain-cold. After which he put two bright red hazardous materials plastic bags to good use, one for his skunk-befouled clothes and the other for his trusty Birkenstocks, which might be recoverable. The tallest of the windows in the far wall opened onto a fire escape, and he stepped out, the steel gate like cold knives beneath his paper-covered soles. The bag with the clothes went sailing downward to the open dumpster below, a direct hit; the bag with the Birkenstocks was thrown with a lateral swing of the wrist to the pavement beside it, for inspection later.

A short stack of overpriced Guatemalan shawls occupied the open shelf space between the zinc mineral water supplement and the African Hibiscus therapeutic teabags; David slid them out and, lying prone on the red leather couch, unfurled all four and arranged them for maximum warmth and coverage. But the roof was too high, the moon too bright through the huge skylight, the leather arm of the couch too solid behind his neck. Eyes closed, he tried to drift off, the minutes passing... No. With a sigh, he grabbed the shawls and went in search of a better place to sleep. Yoga mats? Too short. And the vinyl-padded benches of Nancy's various devices were simply too forbidding.

Shuffling, he returned downstairs, wandering though the cool dark silence again. He almost – almost – wished he'd stayed at his apartment, done his best to scrub it down before collapsing in the redolent wildlife fumes. To be woken, no doubt, by one irate common-heating-vent neighbor or another every hour. Or the police, looking for a long-dead body.

His eye was caught by the nubby moonbeam-lit corner of the convertible futon sofa in Quinn's office, questionable but enticing nonetheless. David was asleep before he'd finished tucking the shawls around himself.

"LIKE AN ANGEL," Quinn crooned, his smile broad in harsh sunlight.

David turned a crusty eye to Quinn's desk clock. "Crap."

Quinn sniffed. "Yes, indeedy... no, not quite. I won't ask why, or why you picked my office. I might need the same discretion someday."

"Um... thanks?" A debt he didn't want, but would take.

"Don't mention it. Until I do."

David nodded, if reluctantly, still waking up. The way things were going, there wasn't much chance he'd be called on to repay it.

Quinn pointed toward the sink in the corner, the razor on its side. "Feel free; I keep one around for touch-ups." Then squatted at the sliding door to his closet, pulling out a breadloaf-sized pair of patent-leather flats. "Too conservative for me. But you? Perfect."

"Thanks, I guess. Again." Quinn started to ask something more, thought better of it and left. A minute later, a subtle knock; after David cracked the door, a thick arm thrust through, holding Quinn's Forever Clinic white coat. Another moment brought another knock, and David opened it to find a mug of coffee, almost white with milk, sitting on the carpet beside the doorjamb. It nearly burned his lips – more than hot and more than sweet. Not the way he liked it, but familiar, somehow, and not at all bad.

Sleepy, dazed, David stared at the razor, the iron-filament hairs caught between the blades. Running the water hot and holding it under the burning stream, he thought, this is how you cross the border. The border between us; the me-versus-you, blood-versus-world border. It didn't matter as much with the classic diseases, those caused by hardy organisms, parasites and bacteria and viruses strong enough to be spewed out, take a leisurely vacation on whatever surface they happened to land on, until they met a new volunteer kind enough to ingest or inhale them.

The really nasty, post-modern bugs like HIV and hepatitis C were actually wimpier, needing a special non-stop ticket to the bloodstream to get in. Sex did the trick, especially the backdoor kind – always a few microdrops of blood with that, the studies said – but a razor would do just fine. Problem was, if you put a condom on it, it wouldn't work.

He frowned in the steam above Quinn's corner sink, then shrugged, crossed his fingers, and lathered up, hoping that Quinn was as obnoxiously robust as he looked.

Eight-thirty. David squeezed his feet into the flats, carefully camouflaged them with his tattered paper shoe covers, buttoned his white coat, top to bottom, and tried to unobtrusively traverse the corridor to his own office. Tried – Junie was in the clean utility room making coffee, and looked up and winked. Making the coffee her way, which apparently had been his way this morning, with a pile of sugar packets and a plastic pitcher of microwaved milk. That sweat-drenched nap in the stone chair beside her garden... of course the coffee had tasted familiar, laden with chicory and cream; just not, this time, rattling with ice.

She started to say something but when he held up an open palm she stopped, amazingly, and looked at him with barely suppressed amusement. Proceeding with a measured, professional gait to his door, he whipped inside and closed it firmly behind.

FOREHEAD AGAINST the pale wood frame, David gathered his strength for what was shaping up to be a long, strange day. At least he had this moment, this precious moment to collect himself. Just the sun through the window on his back, dust motes moving randomly in the air beside him, and the sound of his breathing – slowly, calmly, in and out. His breathing, and something else's. Matching each of his inspirations with a long, steady hiss, followed by a solid mechanical snap.

He turned, slowly, to find Flint beaming up from his electric wheelchair, a pale green plastic tube from a rather noisy auto-feed oxygen unit plugged into his nose. He'd written the prescription himself, last week – Flint's newest general support device, a lovely addition to the overall effect of brown teeth and receding gums, beady squirrel eyes, and the rusty-hinge voice that creaked, "Surprised?"

David was, obviously, and Flint beamed even wider. Flint had found that he was pleased to make a dent – any kind of dent – in the world, as long as it added to his considerable, lifelong, but sadly decelerating tally.

David was too beaten down by the events of the last twenty-four hours to protest. Mindful of his bare ankles, he negotiated his way between the chrome wheelchair footrests and his desk before flopping onto his chipped and vanished oak chair.

"Of course you're surprised," Flint continued. "Your first patient isn't until..." He raised a liver-spotted wrist and consulted the black wristwatch-calculator that hung loose around it. "...Nine o'clock, according to your protective young associate up front. And here I am, scheduled for an injection, but certainly not for a visit. I had to beg her – I don't often beg, Dr. Black – to let me see you."

Flint's chart was open on his desk monitor – Junie's work, again. David crossed his legs and glanced at the grim display of indisputable facts. Slipping into doctor-mode, doing his best to look relaxed, open, and unperturbed. "Begged. You must be worried."

"No... No... What would I be worried about?" Flint gazed guilelessly across the narrow space between them, eyebrows up. Then noticed his doctor's absent sock, the odd blue paper bag, the revealed edge of a patent-leather slipper. A puzzle; he liked that. Puzzles kept him going.

"Well... your condition?" On the left side of David's screen was the list of Flint's active illnesses, long and not good. Starting with myelodysplasia, aging bone marrow that had simply given up. The stem-cell stimulants hadn't gotten any traction – transfusions were next, and after that... zip.

"My 'condition'. Ah. No worries there, no decisions to be made. The course is clear, has been since we met."

Okay, David thought, and waited.

Flint waited too, looked around the room, hummed a little ditty – the last bit of the Abbey Road album, the second side of which had been, in Flint's opinion, the best thing about the sixties – as he waited for David's nauseatingly doctorish concern to fade. Then stated, finally, "Growth hormone."

"HGH? If anything, it would worsen your... your 'condition'." Flint had to know that.

"Not for *me*, you—" Flint took an oxygen-boosted breath: the boy, he knew, couldn't help trying to help him. "Your other patients." He fanned a skeletal hand at the screen. "Their clinical information: how much they were given, what happened to them after that. Confidentially, of course. For a study." He tented bony fingers, pursed his lips. "The young lady happened to mention a certain supplier from Los Angeles, a man of known, shall we say, hunger. Biggs and you... my. This could be quite the center. All the data a researcher would need."

Oh. David sat back, disappointed. Junie had been right about Flint; she must have dropped Biggs' name to check her theory out.

"You don't seem pleased, my boy. Perhaps a co-authorship? I'm widely read." Posthumously, he hoped – let some other fool, perhaps this one, see the publication through the legal tangles.

This, David thought, was too much. Offering to buy his other patients' data – encouraging him, in fact, to risk their health – with the promise of some dry article that would put his name in lights.

He stood with all the dignity he could muster and stepped forward, tripping over that protruding wheelchair footrest and then hopping, with one hand clutching his scraped ankle, to the door. Once there, he took an even, calming breath and turned back. "It doesn't matter. I... I'm not going ahead with it."

"No?" Flint watched him, calculating. "Why not?"

"I'm not sure," David started, then realized he was. "Because it doesn't work."

"Really." That smile again. "And when did you come to *that* conclusion?"

"Just now. I mean, recently." His patient might be famous, wise and sainted – his patient might be dying – but David decided he really didn't like Flint's smile.

"Congratulations." The cadaverous smile even broader: such a good student. "I agree."

"You *agree*?"

"Certainly. The whole sideshow is driven by hope and profit. When woven together, they remove all obstacles in their path. But if add the benefits and risks together, and then look simply at the numbers, you'll see – you've *seen*, apparently – that the net effect, other than amassing muscle tissue, is quite unlikely to be positive."

"And you *recommend* it?"

Flint shook his head. "Not for years."

"But everyone thinks... I mean, you haven't..." When it came to HGH, David realized, he hadn't heard Flint commit himself in any way, shape, or form.

"First we need data, my boy. Hope and profit are not only close to unstoppable, but, in this culture, admirable in themselves."

"Well, hope, sure, but—"

"Hope, indeed. An indulgence I've had to discard, but highly commendable for others. Up to a point. The problem is this: no hormone is innocuous; they are, by their systemic pervasiveness, powerful biologic agents. Too powerful to be neutral – when there is no net benefit, one will almost certainly find a net harm. Hope, yes. And profit, undoubtedly. But also... injury."

"To patients." David wasn't happy.

"Disagreeable, but necessary."

"Necessary."

"To generate the data. Data as in, *proof*. Proof to protect the patients of the future."

"But not protect my patients, now."

"Quite the opposite."

"Then you know my answer, Dr. Flint."

"Ah – a romantic."

David opened the door, said, "You also know your way out," and left.

Flint watched him go, frowned pensively, then brightened. Sliding a finger on the trackpad built into his wheelchair's armrest, he motored out into the narrow hall. He may have lost an easy route in to the clinic's patient data, but suspected that, after brief and painless apology, he would again possess a reliably concerned physician. Concerned *and* ethical; how charming. And, in a mortal pinch – the kind of pinch that can come when pain meds stop working – likely to be useful.

"AND WHERE is the lovely Paula?" Oz asked, as Biggs settled into one of his office's black mesh chairs. The angled chrome arms and hydraulic chambers hissed faintly as they adjusted to his visitor's frame, dropping the seat to accommodate his short stature and broadening the fabric that supported the slab of his back. Office-furniture porn, and Oz knew – by his checkbook, if nothing else – he was an addict.

"Can't come out to play, not today. Won't leave her room, in fact. Something about your friend. And wildlife, oddly enough."

"Funny – she seemed quite the huntress."

"The 'huntress'. She'll love that. When she comes back; Paula always comes back."

"You don't actually have to tell her I said—"

"Believe me, I actually won't."

"Right," Oz said, relieved.

"In the meantime..." Biggs raised his eyebrows, tilting his head toward the monitors behind Oz.

Oz swung frictionlessly around to his desk and fired up a three-screen spreadsheet. "First, with the merger." The numbers – the same numbers they'd discussed on the drive in from the airport – really were impressive.

"And without it?"

Oz pushed a key and the figures changed, cascading down the screen. A zero less here, a digit more there, and at the bottom, a sum total that remained, Biggs was happy to see, essentially unchanged.

"Then we don't have to worry at all."

"No. A little less security, but I think we're all old enough to get by without that."

Another nod, and he settled back. Two bodies, an inverted triangle and a rather over-ripe pear, both entirely comfortable in the finest ergonomics the twenty-first century had yet to produce. Two coffees, raised in a collegial, if not entirely unwary, air toast. Two futures, planned.

"Which leaves your friend, Dr. Black. We do need him. He'll come around, once he learns we're willing to drop the merger?"

"No problem," Oz said, for he really didn't think there would be. "Trust me on that."

DAVID KNEW what he had to do, just didn't want to do it. Luckily, he didn't have to, not quite yet. Since Flint, his morning had been happily packed with patients; hours of obligation, the best diversion for the conscience-riven soul. And all of them, so far, veterans of his old practice, in for real medical things like colds and blood pressure checks, joint pains and diabetes. Except for his last excuse, Don Gilmore, sneaking under the noon-hour wire.

The clock above Don read 11:40. Fifteen minutes, David thought, then five to steel myself for... He didn't want to think about it. No more than he wanted to talk to Don about the injections.

His luck held: Don didn't want to talk about the injections either. Or, apparently, anything else. David clicked back to the schedule, the packed morning, the hypothetical lunch hour (more hypothetical today than usual), and – ouch – the afternoon held vacant for what was to have been another sailing afternoon with Oz.

In Don's narrow slot of time, Junie had entered, "Health Questions'. No specific problems, no pressing issues, just that.

Whatever they were, Don couldn't seem to get started, fidgeting as David watched the minutes roll over in the corner of the screen. 11:42... 11:43... This was worse than what was waiting for him in the clinic's front room.

Finally, Don uncrossed his jiggling leg, planted both handcrafted vegan pleather sneakers on the exam room's wool carpet, and cleared his throat.

"Yes?" David looked up, expectant.

Another pause. Going out to face the crowd in the front room was looking better all the time. Until Don said, "I've been... concerned."

This was more like it. "Concerned about...?"

"About... Sheyoni."

Sheyoni. Wow. David continued to look calmly at Don – or, rather, right through him. What he saw was a full-color newsreel of Don's last visit to the old office, starring Sheyoni, flirtatious as ever, standing by Don's exam table. Standing, as ever, too close. And now Don was asking about her. Asking *him*. Don and Sheyoni. Should be he jealous? But he wasn't, not a bit. Was that natural? Or had it been Paula... had the pheromone overload burned that out of him, seared away his ability to feel any attachment, for any woman, again?

As David wrestled with that unpleasant – no, horrible – possibility, Don was seeing his doctor entirely in the here and now, something Don generally liked to think he'd been good at since the sixties, when, in the aftermath of a few chemical adventures, he'd learned to claw his way back from being not really anywhere at all. Still, as he appreciated the younger (and stronger, and definitely larger) man's distant look, his flexing jaw and tensing shoulders, he found himself wishing, at least today, that his perceptions were less here-and-now and more there-and-then. As in, could David *know*? Watching him warily, Don gripped the compliant front corners of the exam table cushion and calculated the distance from the memory-foam padding to the door.

Meanwhile, David had moved on to an entirely different reason for the curious emotional vacuum where his attachment to Sheyoni used to be. Maybe she'd been right all along, right that it was over, completely over between them. Maybe it had never really been there; just a self-perpetuating obligation, momentum multiplied by doing the Right Thing. And maybe something could, well, *develop* between these two. Why not? He could almost see it. "You know," he said, finally, "Sheyoni and I have separated – we're divorced, actually..."

"Really? I mean, I'm sorry, so sorry to hear that. Really sorry. Of course I'm sorry. Terrible news."

"Thanks. But don't be. I mean, it was hard, but a good thing." David frowned. "I think."

"But what about her illness?" Don blurted.

"Oh. Right." Damn Oz and his fantabulations – David knew he must seem a total slimeball, abandoning a sick wife. There had to be a way... If she really *were* sick, what confidential patient info would he be allowed to share with Don? Nothing, really, but it was all a lie to begin with. What were the ethics of continuing a lie? Probably as mixed as hooking up his ex with a patient. Which would only happen if David cared about Don's happiness, and about Sheyoni's – which, oddly enough, he found he still did. And so, winging it, David said, "She seems to be... improving."

"*Improving*?" Up on the elevated table, Don swayed, a sudden pallor behind the crinkly gray chest hairs that showed above a heathered hemp shirt.

David jumped up and grabbed a heathered hemp arm – Don shied away, then eased as David wrapped a blood pressure cuff around it. "*Relatively* improving," David said, in his most calming voice. What was it that Oz had told Don, David wondered. Some nonsense – he'd better be careful, craft her a slow, believable recovery. "All the signs look good."

Don's vital signs did, anyway, with a rock-on blood pressure, a strong if modestly elevated pulse. That pallor hadn't been cardiac, not at all. Don's heart problem was one David knew too well, a heart problem of the Sheyoni sort.

David was almost correct, except for one almost-minor angle. Don's head was still spinning – from relief, certainly, but also, from deep within the core of his parsimonious being, a vertiginous recalculation of his future. The thing was, 'improving' sounded an awful lot like 'not dying so fast'. As in, 'lingering'. As in his own personal worst case scenario – a sick wife, forever; his brief sunset love fading to an unending fiscal night. A white-tiled sickroom, suction pumps and feeding tubes gurgling, at the far wing of the retirement home they'd no doubt spend his millions building by the sea. As Don stared out, forlorn on the balcony, across the gray Pacific waves.

With a peeling rip of Velcro, David removed the cuff; Don stood, still silent, and David did as well. David wanted to tell Don that she'd be fine, but he couldn't, not yet. He'd have to back out easy, a hint here and there, delivering her to a radiant and date-worthy future within weeks.

Don, without a word, grimly turned and marched out the door.

David cradled an elbow and tapped a finger on dry lips. Don seemed to have believed him, and hadn't he just given him a piece of very good news? Admittedly a partial piece, but still. Then David realized there wouldn't be another visit – not with Don, not for HGH, not with him – and took off down the hall. He made it halfway before he saw Don leave through the Clinic's front door and stopped; chasing a patient was never, ever a good idea. In any case, there was a more pressing concern: the full crew in the front room, already gathering for lunch. He couldn't duck it any longer. It was time.

They were milling around the front desk, busily discussing the merits of a mass meal, organic versus not, and who could afford what. The Thinnas not caring, as they were packing their own nuts and berries; Howie appearing as immune to hunger as always; Quinn and Nancy looking as if they could subdivide a horse; and Junie easing the unruly crowd toward a decision before the hour was up.

David took a moment – sad, proud, even... ready.

Would the clinic run without him? Probably. It was a going concern, and there was always some doctor who'd prescribe anything – who'd believe anything, or at least act like it – in order to live and practice in Boulder. He remembered that evening with Oz, a full season ago. But no downloaded ad for a boat, no need for an excuse or a plan, not this time. Just what he had to do, come what may.

Enough. "Everybody? A few minutes?" Quinn scowled but the rest looked over, curious. David never did this, was always with them in the huddle, pushing for the place with the cheap soup, under five bucks for a full meal!

He waited as they slowly filed over, Junie at the back, looking like she knew what was coming. She could, of course. Of course she would.

BY TWELVE-THIRTY IT WAS OVER, his audience pummeled, stunned, and, despite their generous attempts to understand his position, crisping at the edges with a persistent if low-grade resentment. They went off to lick their wounds over a meal that by this time would have to be fast-food Mexican, a forced choice that was generally agreed to also be David's fault, even if Quinn and Nancy were secretly pleased.

David, head in his hands, sat on the burnished red leather couch he'd been unable to fall asleep on the night before. Junie had remained behind, sitting on a walnut bench across the room. The skylight was open to the warm yellow light, and the birdcalls were real, for once. As real as the fragrance of the sun-warmed pines on the hills – she'd shut both the audio system and the scent-generator off.

"That's it, then?"

David looked over at her. "I can't let myself write the prescriptions, not for anyone who's signed on to be my patient, anyone I'm watching out for. Maybe another doctor can. *Someone* will have to." He looked around the airy clinic, too fabulous by half. "It's the only way the numbers work."

Probably, Junie thought. She didn't trust Oz, but she also had a rough sense of the Forever Clinic's daily financial burn rate. Most of all, she didn't want to get between two mutually disappointed childhood friends.

He waited for her to say something, to try to talk him out of it, but no, that wasn't happening either. Nor should it. He guessed he was grateful for that.

Grateful... and ready. Ready to quit; ready in a way he hadn't been before, sitting at the Triad on that twilit cusp of spring and summer. Ready for something new. A new life? That stupid boat, even if he could afford it? No, just a new way of living. Not sure what it looked like, only that it was there, ahead.

David rose to his feet.

"You're going home? Biggs and your friend Paula will be hammering on your door. They're pretty persuasive."

"Just to get some things." He pulled his keys from a pocket, made sure that a particular one, brass and corroded, was there. "There's a cabin up in Rollinsville – this doctor I know. He left town for a year, gave me a key. I was supposed to be checking the place every few weeks anyways. Been too busy."

"But not now."

"Nope. Not until Biggs and Paula leave – and then, I guess, after. All the cabin-sitting time I want."

AFTER BIGGS AND OZ had hammered out the final details – and there always seemed more than could possibly be expected – Biggs pushed back, extended his fists and, with a mighty groan, performed his patented backward stretch, arcing between the chair's back and the hardwood floor. Oz, to his credit, did not wish the wheeled chair would skitter away and across the room – he was more impressed by the chair's adaptive repositioning, though he did decide that here, in front of him, was one more reason why he'd never lifted weights.

Once Biggs's posterior had returned to its ergonomic home, he bounced up and strode, hands behind his back, to the diorama windows overlooking the city and the plains. The papers were signed, a lucrative partnership sewn up, and Biggs was looking, well, excited.

He spun on the slick sole of one Bally shoe. "Let's go over."

"Now?" Oz hadn't had lunch, and missing lunch was never good.

"I've got to see that place again. Just once more. Call it a... call it a spot inspection."

Oz was thinking about a quick pit stop at that Guatemalan hole-in-in-the-wall on the mall, crisp dollar bills in and delectable mole-drenched puposas out, when his cell rang. It was Junie, and the news ruined – as much as anything could ruin – his appetite.

"He's left?" Oz asked. "What do you mean he's left?"

Biggs took a step towards the phone; Oz held a palm up to stop him.

"Relax; I'll talk to him." A pause, and then a frown. "You don't know where he's gone?"

Biggs snatched the cell from his ear and gripped it, hard. "You did this," he told Junie. "I know you did this."

A tinny voice that Oz could hear: "All I did," she said, "was teach the poor child how to read a study."

"That's just as bad, and you know it."

"He was asking, okay? And it was weeks ago – before I knew it was you, *Dr.* Biggers."

Biggs slammed the wafer-thin phone to the desk; Oz picked up the near edge, gingerly, and was relieved to see the too-expensive-to-replace glass face still intact. Then looked at Biggs, thinking that his new partner might take some special care to manage.

"*What* did she call you?" Oz asked.

"Biggers? It's a pet name, from when we worked in New Orleans."

"No – the 'Doctor' part. What was that about?"

Biggs wheeled on him. "It's why we need this resource – the resource you said wouldn't be a problem."

"I don't get it."

"That's because you don't have to live with it. I'm a *chiropractic* physician."

"Which means...?"

"We need Black to write the prescriptions – I can't. It's not easy finding these guys; the docs who'll do it are usually the type who won't give a penny up. And local, and trusted? We really, really need him."

Oz looked away, through the windows to the pale blue mid-day sky, seeing David outside the Triad, all those months ago. "He's always been skittish under pressure. Not with patients, one-on-one, but when everything's on the line. You didn't happen to discuss the, ah, nature of your degree?"

A nod, and a particularly grim one.

Oh no, Oz thought.

"Night before last." Biggs had returned to stand before the windows, hands clenched behind a broad expanse of English summer-weight suiting, the fine wool perforated by an invisible mist of testosterone and the sharp sweat-like tang, if one was so foolish as to venture close enough to note it, of sudden rage. His head was tilted down a few degrees, his eyes fixed on the tiny, toylike outline of the Forever Clinic's roof. The glittering solar skylight, the odd penthouse-like structure, the whole package that the new partnership planned to purchase soon. A tiny toy that, Oz guessed, Biggs could not be refused.

"He's got to know how much we need him." Biggs added, turning with a glare. "If you're right about your boy, that means he didn't take a walk – he *ran*."

QUINN looked at Nancy, who looked over at the Thinnas. Howie, as usual, stared calmly straight ahead. The second meeting of the day, Quinn thought – What fresh hell was this? A nice hot one, judging by the furious homunculus pacing the floor behind David's friend and underwriter, Oz. Who was telling them they didn't have to worry, that the show would go on, that the patients would continue to purchase every bit of care they needed. The Clinic would find another doctor, somewhere, while the assembled staff, excepting Junie who was undoubtedly otherwise occupied at the University, provided excellent holistic care, same as always.

During this, the solid snap of leather heel-then-toe – four paces, five, then the spinning turn and back again, frowning at the polished wheatgrass floor. Despite that, the assembled staff, excepting Junie, concentrated on Oz, the *eminence gris* and potential David-influencer who might unravel and reverse this morning's madness. As for the interloper to his rear, their eyes tracked him at first but, with his metronome-like constancy, soon grew accustomed to his background pacing presence. And he did bring a certain power to the situation, perhaps enough to right a capsizing ship, an *eminence noir* to Oz's *gris*, his mood even blacker than their good Dr. Black's had been an hour before.

QUINN WAS WALKING back to his office and exam room – where a brand new middle-aged supplement consumer should still be waiting – when Oz tugged at the sleeve of his kelly green skirt suit, dragged him to a quiet corner beneath the sweeping stairs, and asked, "How much?"

"Double my salary," Quinn said, thinking quickly. "Double it and I'll stay, no questions."

"No, no, no. You'll stay either way: I know your story. I can blow your cover in any state, and Canada's not your style."

"Oh." He was standing, Quinn realized, in the presence of a master.

"How much, Dr. Quinn, to make the charges disappear?"

Oh, indeed. the Clinic's underwriter was offering him the price of redemption – a return to medicine, to his former life, sans skirts. San skirts? He wasn't sure about that, the light brush of cool rayon against the outer thighs.

Quinn pondered, then said, "A Texas lawyer, a firm big enough to know who to pay off in Austin... I don't know... two-fifty?" A quarter million – not that large a sum before he'd burnt his bridges, but an overwhelming one since. Plus a truly risky degree of exposure, the kind you couldn't evade.

"Hmmm," Oz hummed, numbers running in his head.

"I'd have to go back; there'll be headlines again, perceptions to change. It could be months." Waiting in a charmless motel, or worse, a concrete-block cell with an uncharmable cellmate.

"No, you're right. Too long – too risky." Too great a risk, Oz calculated, for lost income.

Oz had read his mind; returning was as impossible as ever. Even more so, given his newfound love of rayon.

"*However,*" Oz said, jamming hands in pockets and gazing up through the green glass risers of the suspended stairs. "What if you hadn't run *from* the law, but *to* a new life. After, say, an intense, no, an acute gender crisis... that's the term, right?" Deeply traumatized..." Oz continued, not waiting for a reply, "Deeply traumatized by a patriarchal... a patriarchal, police-run, Texas-*Ranger*-run state. And came to beautiful Colorado... and worked to save lives in any way that he – no, *she* – could..."

"That could get my license back, as McIntyre?"

"Not in Texas... like I said, too risky. But here, if we sold your flight as a move up? After all, you guys jump states all the time – a little trouble here, a new license there." A shadow crossed his face. "Still, the question remains: how long would the process take?"

"I already started filing the papers." Then Quinn remembered and hung his head. "But I filed them under... 'Quinn'."

Oz's mouth pursed. "Forged diplomas?"

Nodding slowly, Quinn slumped low and looked up from beneath downcast brows.

Oz lit up and clapped him on the back. "Perfect! You were frightened for your life... willing to make any personal sacrifice... take any risk... to provide the care the public needed!"

Quinn straightened. Was it possible? Could he get his license back, start his own practice, be free to do as he wanted?

Oz watched him, appraising. He hadn't planned this, not exactly, but the hook was definitely set. "Two hundred fifty..." he said, rubbing his chin. "Palms need to be greased – sorry, re-election war chests funded with voluntary contributions – in Colorado too, you know. Even with that, I expect a state licensing board would demand that a clinic, as in *our* clinic, oversee your rehabilitation. Of course, that clinic would need a security bond."

"Of course. You could trust me on that. Scout's honor." Quinn held up two fingers with, he hoped, a winning smile.

"Oh, I do. But I don't have to – *he* would be underwriting all of this." Oz looked over at Biggs, arms crossed, muscles pumped beneath his custom suit jacket, glaring. Just mad; not aware of what Oz was up to, for Oz was flying free. Which Quinn didn't need to know. "Remember," Oz added meaningfully, "You're frightened for your life. Willing to make any personal sacrifice – take *any* risk – to provide the care the public needs."

"I see." And Quinn did. Even so, it still looked good.

JUNIE might not have lived in Boulder long, but she knew there was only one way – one fully-paved way, anyway – up into the mountains. Accordingly, she parked in the tiny parking lot on the western nub of Pearl Street, and after a long, long thirty minutes, sure enough, David drove his little red car by. Pulling out from behind a smoke-filled student van, the occupants of which had yet to notice her presence, she aimed Rosie straight up Boulder Canyon Road and headed for the gap between the wooded cliffs that marked the western edge of town. After the first bend or two her cell phone stopped lighting up with Oz's and Bigger's numbers. She had every right to take an afternoon off – an emergency, even if it was David's – and Biggers had been plain rude, hanging up that way. Screw him and the Paula he'd rode in on.

Not that those two, all business to the core, were likely to have anything going. Or that she'd be jealous if they did – there'd only been that one Mardi Gras mistake, and the less said about that the better. No more than she'd been jealous of Paula and David. Please.

But she was glad to see him on the run from both those modern predators, his car disappearing around the turns and then coming into view again, climbing the two-lane blacktop towards the mountains. And pulling ahead, unfortunately – she pressed the pedal down and immediately hit carpet-covered steel, a plume of black smoke billowing behind her as Rosie cut a few yards, at best, from the distance that separated them. Had he noticed? Junie hoped not, and lifted her foot back up an inch, also hoping that Rosie wouldn't hold that brief cylinder-toasting injury against her, and that she wouldn't lose him on the road between here and Rollinsville, wherever that was.

"I DON'T LIKE IT that Junie wasn't there. She's screwing us, I know it." Biggs was pacing again, ignoring the few patients that had trickled in – patients who, wide-eyed, found their own way back from the empty reception desk to the open doors of their usual Alternopath providers.

Oz paced beside him, a yard or so away, turning where Biggs turned, trying to keep up. A little space, a little connection, progress. "She might be screwing you—"

"That was years ago," Biggs said, distracted.

"Oh." Now, *that* was interesting news.

"Years ago, and over." A lateral, hard-edged look that told Oz it really was, interesting or not.

"What I meant was, she's not screwing you – I mean, us. Ms. Blanche and I have a business arrangement. No matter what she told you, she helps me manage David, for the good of the Clinic and her own position in it. In fact, I'm sure she's out looking for him right now."

"She'd better, and she'd better find him. Because I need to be sure I can rely on Dr. Black." His right hand unconsciously drifted to the left side of his suit jacket – which seemed fuller, somehow – and patted it, as if for reassurance. "I need to be sure of it soon."

Oz nodded, agreeably. Agreeable was easy. But it was looking like Biggs might take some *very* special management techniques.

THE CANYON was a trip, sheer looming walls and hanging trees, a few groves of aspens on the flats along the rock-bound creek, gold leaves flashing in the rare sun that made it to the floor of the defile. It was a trip she hadn't made before, foreign to anything she knew but actually not too bad, as long as she didn't have to live up here. After ten miles or so, the road climbed beside a concrete dam and over the top; she expected a shimmering lake but got a reservoir, shimmering a little at the bottom but mostly dry sloping walls ringed by a thick band of gray rubble. Beyond it lay the Continental Divide, a bony broke-back spine beneath a glaring blue sky.

Like a postcard, but something was missing – the snow in all those pictures. There wasn't any now, not yet, which must be why that mile-wide reservoir had been almost emptied, drained before the winter, before the snow and then, come spring, what would have to be a huge snow-melt runoff.

Having completed that little exercise in Western water puzzle solving, she searched what she could see of the road that ran along her side of the wasted shore, looking for David's little car. And saw a tiny red pixel, entering a bare and hard-blown hamlet smeared around the far end of the reservoir. A half-mile later, a green and white road sign, shaking in the steady wind, identified it as Nederland. Another half mile and she was passing though, panicking for an instant when she realized there was one road in but two roads leaving, but she guessed right and soon spotted a sign for Rollinsville, south on the rather sweetly named Peak-To-Peak Highway.

Junie rolled through town under twenty; other than the med-pot head shops, Nederland looked as poor as the speed-trap bergs in her steamy former corner of this great neglected country. She'd learned that Western racism didn't run much deeper than a certain nervous avoidance, but still, a black woman in a rusty old car? Why take a chance.

Anyway, she figured Rollinsville couldn't be big enough to lose him. After passing a last post-hippie restaurant, she gave Rosie the gas her steel heart craved, climbed a winding rise to glide along a high road through the alpine forest. On her right, the bare Divide; on her left, a procession of gap-toothed hills, vertically wooded hogbacks that occasionally yielded a straight shot out to the great tan grasslands and desiccated farms of Eastern Colorado, even giving up one reassuring if distant view of the stacked-Lego towers of Denver. Soon after, Rosie swept down one side of a shallow U-shaped valley to her destination.

Junie pulled off into a railroad town, just big enough for a dusty handful of maintenance buildings, a closed gas station, and a seasonal snack bar and general store, all closed for the fall. Stores and sheds but pretty much no homes – no manageable cluster of city-like blocks to cruise around and spot David's car. Damn damn damn.

Her fists slammed into Rosie's steering wheel, which instantly expressed an offended and startlingly loud beep into the thin dry air. She apologized, had the sense that it was grudgingly accepted, then peered out the starred windshield.

Okay, a few homes, and some roofs in the hills, sparsely scattered in what she suspected was a classic example of Western keep-yer-distance neighborliness. But no little red cars in sight. It was hopeless. Except...

There, on the other side of the Peak-To-Peak. An unpaved road heading straight toward the divide. And hanging over it, the faintest pall of... *dust.*

Junie hit the gas. This time Rosie seemed as eager as she was, kicking up a high-yellow roostertail as she jumped the hump of asphalt and powered down the loose gravel after whatever vehicle – and there weren't many others, not up here – preceded her.

TEN MINUTES LATER. Bumping over and sometimes into potholes, the wheel nearly vibrating out of her grip over washboard corrugations, Rosie's big Detroit ass swinging wide on more than one dusty curve. The dust grew thicker, coating the windshield; Junie wondered if she'd lost him again until she saw, on the far slope of a long, right-curling vista, a spot of tan-caked red turning left onto an even *more* secondary road.

She eased up, hanging back: no need to spook him. By the time she made it to the turn, there was only more dust, but that was good enough, she had him now. Climbing, always climbing, as the pot-holed dirt and gravel grew narrower and narrower, dry grass and needled braches scouring Rosie's flanks, and then another glimpse of the little car, clearly David's, and she slowed before he could spot her. Soon the shining golden aspen were gone, and then the bare grey ones; climbing through the alpine zones like climbing through the seasons, into dark conifers now, green shadows then blasted with too-bright sunshine, feeling like she must be getting close to where the trees would dwindle to the dwarf treeline pines of her Plant Biology texts. But the road, now hardly more than twin ruts, leveled out and opened to a scrubby wetlands field, rusty barbed wire on one side and weathered low telephone poles over them, spaced so far apart that the single wire almost dropped to touch the higher bushes. Up ahead, the ruts veered left into a last tall burst of pines, so dense she could only see one window of a cabin showing through. Turning the key, she let the car drift to a stop a few hundred yards back.

Junie set the brake and got out, careful not to slam the door. A cloud of dust and Rosie's motor pinging randomly, cooling in the late afternoon air. She leaned against a fender and wondered why she'd come. Tracking him for Oz? Sort of, but not really – she hadn't told Oz about the cabin, and she could of. No, she was here for the classic stupid reason, that it seemed the right thing to do at the time. But she still wasn't committed to any course of action, didn't have to go forward, could release the brake and silently roll back down the road any time she wanted.

A tickle in her throat; a cough; a particularly loud ping from Rosie's engine block. And then David, walking across the field toward her.

Shit.

19

At The Cabin

- or -

Nocturnal Thermophilia

DAVID stopped a few yards away, standing in the high grass in heavy canvas shorts and a tattered sweater, squinting in the sideways light, the air dead still. Behind him, a bank of clouds was rising over the raw sharp peaks. Dust still hung above the car, an otherworldly amber glow.

Junie coughed again, an eddy in the haze of floating dirt.

"Come here," he said.

"Why?" Almost afraid, something new for her. She wasn't afraid of anyone.

"Why? That stuff you're breathing. It doesn't like your lungs. Silicosis."

Junie crossed her arms, the dust like silk on her skin. "Like miners get? I thought that was a lawsuit thing, until they all turned out to be smokers." Another cough, a little deeper.

"That was radon – but sure, maybe they were. Or maybe the dust is bad for you."

Mr. Medicine strikes again. She didn't move. She wasn't afraid or anyone... or anything. Especially dust.

He waited, then, "Suit yourself. I'm going in to make coffee."

As the last of it settled, fading her jeans and covering the rust spots on Rosie's fender, she watched him pick his way back across the field, unlaced boots squishing in the wetlands mud as he maneuvered between the leaning thistle stalks, the wilted skunk cabbage, and a low scrub with tiny-orange-red leaves that looked like blueberry but, at this altitude, she was pretty sure wasn't.

JUNIE STARTED ROSIE, who seemed to cough as well, and followed the twin-rutted track to park behind his now sand-colored Civic. He was unloading bags of groceries from a crowded passenger seat; she got out to help.

"You didn't have to follow me," he said, carrying four over-packed vinyl grocery bags toward the cabin, two per hand. Junie pulled the now-empty seat forward and leaned deep into the rear to find two more, perched on top of what she suspected was every warm piece of clothing David owned. Beneath them lay a few neatly-packed boxes of books – novels! How unDavidian! – beside a long scuffed case that looked disturbingly like it might contain a banjo.

She backed out, shoulders straining as she took the full weight of the can-filled bags, and turned to find that David had propped open the cabin's weather-beaten door and gone inside.

David was on the other side of a tar-papered mudroom, facing her from the threshold of a pine-paneled kitchen, bags still suspended.

"I didn't have to follow you..." Junie was still outside, the bags' thin vinyl straps cutting into her hands. "Okay – why not?"

"Telling Oz would have been enough."

"And what would I have told him?" Trying to sound pissed, but her face growing hot.

"That I was headed for a friend's cabin. The latest news flash."

Oz, her real boss. "You knew... about my reports?"

"It's not that much of a leap," David said, talking over his shoulder as he passed into the kitchen. "Oz covers himself for every other bet he makes – why not with me? For that extra bit of information that might prove useful, whether I chose to tell him or not. Like this one. Just 'cabin' would have done it. Enough for him to correlate with, say, a few names I may have mentioned, then go from there to doctors who might be on sabbatical, and then a quick check of county records, who owns what up here."

"If you knew," she said, moving after him, "why'd you tell me you were coming here?"

"I can't figure that either – I was kicking myself afterwards."

The kitchen was warm, windows sealed, air musty and neglected. "I didn't." She stopped in the middle of the worn pine floor.

David put the bags on a water-stained wood counter and faced her, eyebrows up.

"I didn't tell Oz about the cabin. I called him – it's my job, David – but only said you'd left."

"He didn't hammer you on where?"

"He did. So I told him the truth – that I didn't know."

"Thanks. I'll take that as an apology."

She tilted her head. "What's with you? You seem... different."

He shrugged. "Something hit me. Guess I had to kill two practices for it to get through."

"Nice work." Her hands were screaming; Junie stepped forward and dumped her bags next to his. Then leaned over the counter to an varnished wooden window and, taking care not to knock over the condiments lined up against the spotted screen, cranked it open. "What was it?"

"What hit me was... stupid. Forget it."

"Can't stop now, pal." Through the window, she heard a breeze cut through the pines; fresh air on her neck, cool on the meandering tracks of bare skin between her nearly random braids.

"Just this line in my head. From a song my parents used to play." He paused. "Okay. 'Nothing more to lose'. Happy?"

"Delirious."

David crossed his arms, sweater pushed up to his elbows. "Maybe I heard it the first time, too. After Sheyoni left, my solo practice crashing down around me. Thought it was all about freeing up, having an adventure with Oz. An adventure I'm glad I had, but this time it's, I don't know, like you said. Different. This time it's my own."

"Your own adventure?" She was tempted, more than tempted, to make a joke.

A crooked smile. "Yeah. Even if it sucks."

Junie thought of New Orleans, the sodden books and papers of her basement lab, the twisty journey that had taken her to this high strange place, standing here and looking over – and up, as he was only a few feet down the counter – at the pale broad face of a formerly wounded man. Then moved away, quick, toward the humming white refrigerator, as David cleared his throat and went in the opposite direction, having suddenly decided to stack a single can of crushed tomatoes on a shelf across the room.

"So," DAVID SAID, parking a box of Oreo clones – no hydrogenated fats, pure sugar but what the heck, they're natural – next to a tall cardboard cylinder of oatmeal. "What's next? You could go back, say you reconsidered. You should, you know. "

"Go back to what, a clinic without a doctor?"

"He'll find someone. You could still be... whatever. Clinic Director, I'd guess." A note of bitterness he couldn't quite get rid of.

She folded the bags and jammed them, hard, into an open shelf beneath the counter. "I'm a graduate student, David. It was a salary, not a career. A salary I couldn't say 'No' to." Her hands were fists, knuckles pale as his. "A salary that's over."

He frowned, looked around the room, then studied his boots and said, "I'm sorry."

She turned back and loaded the refrigerator. "Forget about it."

He looked up. "But Oz knows where you live."

"And I know how to lie."

"I'm aware of that," he said, and met her eyes, steady. "If anyone's his match, it's you."

"And if I'm not?" She let that hang, pushing through a swinging door to the tiny living area, crowded with an *über*woodsy plaid couch, pine captain's chairs around a much-abused round table.

He held the door open, behind her. "I need a day. A day to let things settle down. For Oz to cook up a plan that doesn't include me. So he doesn't weigh in with all our history, history that I can't say 'No' to. He'll still find me, of course, but a day should do the trick."

A window in the log wall behind the table showed the gray-bellied clouds had arrived, and that the breeze was no longer a breeze, the ragged treetops swaying from side to side. "A day. And where am I supposed to be between now and then?"

"There's lots of bedrooms," David said, resuming the close study of his boots.

A gust blew down the chimney and the bitter smell of ashes filled the room. Two brown-painted doors flanked the fireplace;

beyond the sagging couch, a yellow-varnished railing spiraled down.

"What's down there?" Junie pointed at the stairs.

"Another bedroom." As he spoke, the temperature in the cabin dropped another five degrees, a returning gust having blown in through the still-open cabin door to whistle *up* the flue.

"Then that one's yours," she said, as the first fat drops hurled themselves against the picture window. "And you cook."

IN THE END, she did the cooking, more for her survival than anything else, emptying the windowsill's pepper shaker and a nearly empty tin of paprika, plus half the fresh garlic bulb and the onion he'd brought up – because, no doubt, they were *healthy*. It was just enough to turn the boneless skinless chicken breasts he'd also bought into something you could taste, as well as something that could generate heat faster than the fire he was laboring to urge into being.

Before that, he was busy with the propane furnace in the basement – busy cursing, mostly, as he burned his fingers with matches that couldn't get the pilot lit and banged his head on the maze of valves he wasn't entirely sure of anyway. In the end, he decided the fireplace would have to do. After all, he said, it was only the end of September.

Junie thought that sounded reasonable, having never lived above the Mason-Dixon line and certainly not spent a fall night this near to treeline. And sleeping by the fireplace sounded cozy – alone, of course, with David in the basement bedroom. Naturally, the power was off. The problem there was unpaid bills, bills that David, reluctantly, revealed he'd agreed to pay in his friend's absence, before empty pockets and then the distractions of the new clinic intervened. Ditto for the phone.

But all of that was fine, even kind of romantic, which was also fine as long as David stayed over on the red-plaid couch, a safe distance from her corduroy recliner. They dragged the furniture close to the fire and sat, tailor-style, faces lit both by the flames and her semi-Creole chicken over Uncle Ben's White Rice (racist but still comforting) on a steaming plate balanced over crossed ankles. Her feet were clad in thin white socks, his in thick wooly ones – he'd offered his spare pair but she'd declined, thank you very much.

And then they were done and David went to make hot chocolate, which also helped and also was cozy and was probably better, all things considered, than the bottle of Port he thought was out in his car but she didn't, thank you very much, really want tonight.

It was all very *companionable*, a nice male-female feeling she wasn't sure she'd ever known – certainly not with any of her disastrously self-absorbed bad boyfriends, and certainly not with her one intoxicated mistake with the very bad Dr. 'Biggs's Biggers. With that, a chill down her neck; David saw her shake it off and tossed the throw blanket he'd been sitting on, still warm from his butt – yuck – but just what she needed.

Sitting there, reading feather-edged copies of last year's New Yorker, Ascent, and Nederland' Mountain-Ear, like some rural, back-country but slightly literary married couple. Not only companionable, but *comfortable*. It almost made her understand why people spent so much energy looking for that elusive special someone, a usually fruitless search that she was so totally and completely *over*. Almost every top-40 song, plus all those books and movies, all that wailing and flailing and railing against the lonely night, every lonely heart looking to fill some needy hollow space. Not her, though – she had her family, her city, what she was and who she was and what color she was and all of that was just fine. Thank you very much.

Like David – coming up here to be alone. That had to be a good thing. It gave him some stature, made him less the fool. Realizing he didn't need Paula, Biggs, Oz, didn't need anybody.

The fire was burning down to embers but still throwing off a nice red-orangey heat. She let the throw slip from her shoulders and looked over at him, David in profile. It was true – he seemed calmer, stronger…

That sudden pulse of fear again, like out in that field, when he'd told her what to do. Not fear of him, of course – David wouldn't hurt a fly – but something else, something she wasn't sure of. It was colder than she'd thought; she pulled the throw back up, tucked it behind her and stared at the fire.

Now he was watching her, watching her watch the fire. Had he seen her staring? She didn't let herself look back over, not until he said, "More wood?"

Junie nodded.

David stood up, all six-feet-whatever of him, and crossed to stand in front of the fire, the curling hair of the calves above his wooly socks back-lit and golden – gold today, all day, dust and sun and fire – and threw on as much wood as she expected the fireplace could handle. Then rose again and stretched, facing the crackles and sparks and growing flames, which meant she could look, or continue to, up and down, look and wish, for a brief unobserved if observing moment, that he hadn't come in so entirely the wrong skin tone.

David turned. "Guess I'll head down."

"Sure," she said, eyes safely back to the magazine. "If you're tired."

He checked his watch. "It's almost ten. Big day today. Maybe another one tomorrow."

She looked up.

David checked his watch again. "You'll be okay?"

Junie shrugged.

"Lots of split logs if you need them."

She nodded.

"Well, then. Goodnight."

"Right." Junie's smile was tighter than she'd intended. "Goodnight."

David hesitated – was there something he could or should do? – then grabbed one of the two flashlights on the mantle and clumped down the narrow spiral stairs. As for herself, Junie was fine, cozy, warm and lit by what was now her own personal fire, all that heat for her, just her. Thank you very much.

THE PLACE, Oz thought, stunk. Not only in that it was a crummy apartment, yet another instance of David's pseudo-austere divorce-guilt flagellation, but stunk as in… skunk. *Bad* skunk. He got a whiff from under the door, from the angled bathroom window over the low shingled roof beside it, even coming out the open door of the adjoining apartment, where white-suited workers wrestled thick HVAC hoses while tenants monitored their progress from outside, arms crossed and definitely not happy. No wonder David wasn't there.

On to Junie.

He had her address somewhere. Chautauqua – nice. Up the hill and into the park, leaning across the front seat to pick out the numbers of the tiny rentals that lined the road. And found it, but no lights, and no answer to his knock. Taking care, he lowered his well-cushioned *gluteus maximi* to the topmost wooden step.

Junie and David, both missing. Junie and David. Unlikely, but not impossible. A little getaway: if nothing else, it might help David see the light.

There were other options: Quinn remained an excellent possibility, albeit one that came with legal costs, uncertainty, and months of delay. And the defrocked – or was it frocked? – doctor was, not unreasonably, looking nervous. Which was why Oz hadn't shared their sub-stair conversation with Biggs, who'd been surprisingly excitable today, giving off a whiff of LA Gangsta that was more alarming than David's skunk. The man would obviously be heavy-handed with any potential asset Oz allowed him to come close to. And then there was that budge, high up under his jacket on the side: another excellent reason enough to keep him clear of assets who were also boyhood friends.

Oz tried each of their cells, again, but still no answer, which could mean neither David nor Junie was deigning to pick up the phone, a thought he found personally insulting but entirely plausible. Or they were in a place the signals couldn't reach. Like the mountains… Bingo! It had to be David's friend's place, the doctor that had gone off with his family to see the world. Oz could call the hospital, wheedle the name out of a lonely operator, how the Clinic really, really had to reach David. There couldn't be more than one internist on sabbatical. Then reel in a favor with the county assessor in the morning (love those campaign donations!), delve into the property records, and he was there.

His glass-fronted phone vibrated in his hand; he looked down and lightly slid a finger across the screen to answer the call. It was Biggs, asking if he'd found him.

"No." On those rare occasions when he could use it, Oz loved the truth – it was simple, elegant, and easily remembered.

"I've got an idea," Biggs said. "A good one."

"Yes?" Oz buttoned his suit jacket. Far above, a rolling bank of clouds had crossed the Divide to blot out the stars. A mountain wind, cold as night, flowed down around Junie's little hovel.

"He's up there, hiding. And I am going to find him."

"Up where?"

"In the *mountains*. Know why? I bet you don't. *Nature.* People, animals, everything heads uphill when they're running. I've got an instinct about these things."

"I think you're on to something." Everything heads uphill except fish, and bugs and snakes and, for that matter, smart people. But this was no time to be a stickler.

"You and me – we'll flush him out tomorrow. Find where he went, go get him."

"I'll figure it out, no problem. There's only a few places he could go." Namely, one.

Biggs seemed satisfied with that, and after planning to meet at the clinic at nine-thirty, signed off. Oz looked at the phone, put it in his jacket pocket, stood up and brushed a few pine needles off his well-rounded butt. *I'll* figure it out and *I'll* go get him – or deliver Quinn, ears stuffed with promises and eager to help.

DAVID LAY ON HIS BACK and stared at the ceiling, or at least where he knew the ceiling must be. It was dark, pitch dark, spots-dancing-in-your-staring-eyes dark. Through the faint and coalescing blobs he pictured Junie, curled on that chair, skin washed with firelight, a graceful, variable glow that loved her features. A glow, in fact, that fell into midnight eyes and was never seen again, that pooled in the shallows between her neck and shoulder, that flowed down the soft-draped throw – the throw that he'd *thrown*, like an idiot, over her. An idiot who, if that idiot had had a speck of non-idiotic sense, would have gotten up to *place* over her, even tucked it in a little, smoothed it down as the light flowed in dull velvet gold around and over…

He shivered, almost violently, then pulled up the heavy wad of blankets that covered him, up tight to his chin. There'd been a two-foot pile of them folded outside this chilly dungeon of a bedroom, with its rock walls, monk-like iron bed, and door that had been removed to lean, half-painted and casting crazy shadows from his flashlight, across the otherwise empty basement. Next to it was a sliding glass door – the land sloped sharply down behind the cabin – that led to a creek he could barely hear the music of, a trickle that was not quite frozen yet.

The blankets worked, and soon enough his thoughts returned, almost automatically, to Junie. A certain warmth, as warm as he was now, her fire-warmed woolen throw protecting an inner heat that radiated out from deep within... deep within...

No. She was an *employee*. Although, technically, if he was no longer working at the Clinic... No. They hardly knew each other, not personally. And he'd always be, at least in memory, her boss. But this was Junie; had he ever been her boss? Actually, given Oz's manipulations, she'd been *his*...

No. Their current situation was pure circumstance, an accidental juxtaposition of two bodies in time, two bodies that just happened to be occupying... occupying a single, tiny, rustic, isolated...

No, he told himself. Stop it. Stop it right *now*.

David lay quiet, arms along his sides, hands half-tucked under his hips. As if laid out for the grave. Which he should be, in regard to desire, at least – should be after Paula.

His eyes turned to the open doorway, looking for distraction, any kind of distraction, but found only the faintest square slider-door-sized shadow, or anti-shadow, a box of cloud-filtered starlight that really was no light at all. Darkness, the sum of our fears, but he didn't feel afraid, not in this cold dark cabin, oddly enough, a new strange place that, for some reason he could not fathom, felt like... home.

Home. A thought, a feeling, that occupied his mind until it faded, gently descending to a place where neither time nor space mattered, miraculously juxtaposed or not.

"PAULA?"

It was late – after nine – and the first call she'd answered since... last night. She held the phone out and peered at it, doubtfully. Even at arm's length, Biggs's voice somehow managed to sound as deep, as assured as always.

Paula took a moment, then cleared her throat and said, "Am I still working for you?"

"Of course. You're HorTech's good luck charm, lady. The reason we get the new accounts."

"Not last night."

"That why you haven't been answering?"

"Sort of." Paula looked at the suite around her, from the emptied tomato juice cans – for scrubbing off skunk, not drinking – to the trail of open minibar bottles that led from her feet to the screen on which an extremely pleasant woman, radiant in a perpetually early middle age, chatted with her audience.

"Sort of. Okay. I can live with that. Your job isn't easy, Paula, but you've been knocked off your horse before.'

Western metaphors aside – please! – Paula listened as he coached and coaxed and reassured her, listened while she half-watched those reassuring round features on cable, now telling a single standing audience member, unfortunately shot from the rear, that yes she could do it all – a reassurance that seemed as unbelievable as the ones that Biggs was throwing at her.

Until, gradually, hypnotized by a kind of stereo from the cell phone's tiny speaker and the pantomime on the huge flatscreen, she thought, well, *maybe*. And then, as maybe-type qualifiers really weren't part of Paula's overall game plan, not 'Maybe', but 'Yes! Yes I can do it, I can do it and I will!'

She stood up – her aching body gleaming beautifully, she knew, in the television's varicolored light – and began to gather up the towels and bottles and red-smeared glasses, her cell pinned between a perfectly sculpted shoulder and a perfect surgically-trimmed ear.

She *could* do it all – way more than the wide-hipped troll being coached onscreen – and would start by actually leaving the hotel, tomorrow. Or the next day. Either way, a step up from today, when she'd only ventured down the hall to the executive workout center, ventured once and then again and then hourly until her screaming torn lactic-acid-saturated muscles told her she had to stop herself. Cheaper than therapy, but it hurt.

Biggs finished up, then asked, "Pick you up at eight?"

"Tomorrow morning?"

"Of course, tomorrow morning. Where's the old Paula? I need your magic. Your boy – our client – is up in the mountains. Garcia says he'll find out where."

"The mountains? No, no, no. There's *wildlife* there." Paula walked naked to the picture window and, ignoring a gaping dog-walker, looked over the phosphorescent streetlights and through the night's gathering clouds to where, she was certain, a malevolent menagerie awaited. Bears, mountain lions… skunks.

"You want wildlife?" Biggs asked, voice toughening up. "Here's one: that horse I mentioned."

"Would you stop with the horses? And a horse isn't *wildlife*—"

"Get back on it, Paula, or you'll be stuck behind a desk in Anaheim. You had your day off; now you got to ride."

"Ride? I can ride the best you've got – clients, anyone – until they beg for pity."

"That's my Paula."

"I'm not 'Your Paula'."

"*That's* my Paula."

"Biggs…"

"See you in the morning?"

"Depends. Partners don't get stuck in Anaheim."

"You're not a—"

"Partners don't get stuck in Anaheim."

Biggs sighed. "Yeah." A pause, full of history, the past against the future. "We'll talk about it."

"Nine, then. Nine sharp."

Paula snapped the phone shut, thinking, Back on the horse, back on the horse. Then dialed down for room service, have them clean away this mess and bring something decent up. Euro-water and raw veggies, a steak with a pulse, and if I see a carbo on the plate I'll kill you.

Julio – like the hotel, he said – took the order well, with a young, careless laugh, and said he'd bring it up personally.

Good.

OZ CLOSED his front door and sagged down to his walnut foyer bench. With a low grunt, he bent in half to unlace his oxfords, then sighed – freedom – ten toes happy in argyle socks. No lights, no need, just the city's glow coming up through the windows and the stars down through the skylight.

A late-nite snack would be good. Very, very good, especially if it would keep him from... No. Not again, never again, or at least not now. Oz dragged himself to his feet and slid Scottish cashmere over Brazilian rosewood, trying to avoid the slightest sideways glance into his unlit office, especially towards the always-beckoning red LED of his most personal computer. And succeeded, until the blanketing silence was torn by a familiar *Cha-ching!*

What now? What incoming interest-rate flip, late-breaking commodity embargo, foreign market plunge or other wingnut of potential profit had arrived at this late hour to whip his fading energy to one last arabesque of alphanumeric swordplay – a twist-and-thrust at once graceful with expertise and flailing with fatigue – before his anointed hour of rest?

Wearily, Oz shuffled backwards, away from the calling outline of the walk-in Sub-Zero's humming doors, sliding one diamond-patterned foot and then another back to his office door, back to discover which of his *sanctum sanctorum's* many screens had sprung into demanding life. Not his triumvirated towers of desktop power, not the various recharging phones and pads and touch-screen tablets, but there, on the far corner of his expansive partners desk, his favorite screen saver was glowing above that beckoning LED, a white bow breaking azure seas!

Suddenly, Oz was wide awake, prancing across the rosewood like a cartoon tutu-wearing hippopotamus, to plop smoothly in his favorite black mesh and stainless chair, and, as its industrial-grade hydraulic cylinders recovered and he spun to face the desk, opening the message window.

Just as he'd hoped – an answer to his online plea. And oh, oh, oh, my pecunious Lord... she was *perfect!* Sea-sleek but comfortably wide, a fully-fitted fifty-eight, sea-worthy and sea-proven, having recently crossed the Pacific to San Francisco. The vessel wasn't for sale – not that he was buying, not yet, but if David could dream, why couldn't he?

The owner, the fool, was leasing it out as a day-sailer – a *day-sailer* – a boat like that! The ship came with a crew... a certain Captain Hanacananahuolipalilulu, who must be that squarish smudge on deck in one photo, a rock-solid seaman in overalls and slicker. Kind of Bluto-shaped: all he needed was a beard. Did

Polynesians grow beards? Didn't matter. Oz knew he could stand a few lessons. But he had every confidence in his ability to wheedle a purchase price far less than the boat's true value. Perhaps the captain would help convince the owner, in exchange for a modest payoff and a future commission.

The daily rate was outrageous, but what advantage might it bring? Rubbing his palms together, Oz began to compose an irresistible email offer.

BEATRIZ LAY with hands behind her head, gazing up and out the open hatch of the master cabin's fully-sanitized double bed. Feeling as reflective as in Cat Harbor – in fact, more so, as the evening had faded into night, with the night's propensity for the longest-reaching thoughts.

In particular, she wondered what had really brought her here. A bit of importing, a change in her business plan, but also an impulse, and why *that* impulse? An impulse to let memory resurface, to roll back the silken wave-borne years and uncover a drier, rocky land she'd once called home; an impulse to return.

A faint *Bing!* sounded from the galley. It was barely audible above the not-distant-enough murmur of San Francisco traffic, but all her ship's sounds were known to her, and in an instant she was staring at her laptop's screen. A response; the first she'd received. OhBoy@filthylucre.com, which reminded her, for no good reason, of someone long ago. The corner of a smile, but no, that little history was over. Plus, OhBoy soon proved low-balling weasel, trying to screw her on the day rate. She'd let him cool a day or two, let him toss and turn and reconsider. Then send one back, how she couldn't hire out Osprey for the single hour he must have meant, and that her rates were and would remain as published, though a generous luncheon was provided.

Beatriz looked at her refrigerator, how she'd never get through her Delux Honeymoon Special supplies, the *foie gras* and the Champagne, and especially that oozy blue-veined brie. Pretty freaky food, in her opinion, but she went ahead and listed every luxo item. Maybe a little added value would bring OhBoy around.

JUNIE WOKE, shivering, to a blank and stygian darkness. A dim memory of stretching the thin square blanket over her head, of warming herself with her own damp suffocating breath as she huddled deep in the padded hollow of the recliner. But now, the smell of ashes again... *cold* ashes. Gathering her courage, she popped her head out to peer in the general direction of the fireplace. Nothing, not the faintest glow. There was, however, some small light in the room itself – the moon must have risen behind the clouds, which had apparently descended to a tree-obscuring fog outside the windows.

Okay, she told herself. It wasn't going to get any warmer. But the bedrooms... Junie's mind was filled by the image of a gingham-skirted bed, thick down comforters, even flannel sheets, cold at first but warming as she'd snuggle in – all waiting, waiting for her, behind the brown-painted doors beside the fireplace.

Grabbing the throw, Junie levered the recliner forward and jumped out to bang her shins on the coffee table, then recovered and gingerly advanced, zombie hands sweeping for the heavy security-guard flashlight that David had left standing on the mantle. After nearly tipping it on her freezing feet, she pressed the rubber button in to see the sharp-shadowed room.

Jesus, it was cold. Still, those flannel sheets were calling. Or, as it turned out, the bare mattresses illuminated by her shaking round spotlight in first one and then the other bedroom.

Body temperature falling, Junie dashed back to the fireplace, crumpled two sheets of newspaper and shoved them into the ashes, searching of an ember, but finding them cool against her skin. Thinking fast, she piled on kindling and swept her hand along the mantle for the...

Matches.

The *missing* matches.

No.

Please no.

After an icy pee break – Yikes! – Junie made an increasing frantic and numb-fingered round of kitchen counters and drawers and wall shelves before jumping, tiny blanket sailing behind her, back into her former nest in the upholstery. A nest that had, unfortunately, grown so very much colder in her absence.

This was followed by a another round of shivering, which did little to help except to allow another image to surface, that of David slipping the matches into the right front pocket of his shorts – shorts! – after lighting the fire.

Fuck, fuck, fuck you David.

Junie rose and went to the slippery stairs, refrigerated oak under ridiculously thin socks, and descended to a subterranean Styx that had to be ten degrees frostier than the freezing room above. She followed the shaking cone of light across a flagstone floor – was that shiny white glaze *frost*? – into a gaping door that had to be the downstairs bedroom. A quick jab of light revealed David, his uncreased, sleeping brow covered by a fall of lank brown hair. Next to the bed, a pile of neatly-folded clothes topped by his shorts and, even better, a sweet, fuzzy blanket that had slipped to crumple, free for the taking, free for her.

Clicking off the flashlight – please don't let him wake – Junie snagged the blanket and wrapped it around herself, threw down the throw and stepped onto it, twisting the threadbare wool around achingly numb feet. Then squatted next to his clothes, breathing into the tent-like space, hoping to warm it with her breath. It had worked upstairs, sort of. And it did help, at least a little, enough that she could snake an arm out and rummage through his pockets for the matches. Wallet, keys... but no matches.

Crap.

Ransack the kitchen again? Hope the added blanket would get her though the night? She certainly couldn't squat here till morning. Junie stood, surrendering, too tired to do anything but let the cold penetrate her elegantly thin limbs to her elegant but uninsulated bones.

MEANWHILE, David was swimming up from his dream – a chase, pursuit, a dreamlike slow-motion fall into open space – to find the doorway's faint box of gray was slightly brighter, enough to register, through those far sliding doors, the mist-blurred outlines of spindly trees. The box was different, though: slightly irregular on one side, which, as he lay on his side, peering, he realized was the partial outline of a mummy-like form, standing just inside the doorway.

Normally, between the dream and the apparition, David might have found himself, well, perturbed. But this shape was somehow... familiar. So familiar he wasn't afraid. Like a parent, coming in to check him.

Add to that a faint sound of breathing, slowly, in and out, and the smell of cinnamon, of pepper, of all the spices they'd consumed last night – all mingling with the scent of...

"Junie?"

"Y-yes." Shivering.

"Um, hello. Good... morning? But it's dark, real dark. Aren't you cold?"

"What do you think?"

"There weren't any blankets in the bedrooms? Christ, I'm sorry; I found these down here."

"W-wait a second. You're... *warm*?"

"Well sure, I'm warm." He started to get up, to build a fire – *she* could have the blankets, in fact already seemed to have one of them.

"Don't move," Junie said, thinking: Warm... *warm*. She could almost feel the heat beaming out from the shadows. Why not, she thought – why shouldn't she? After all, she was fully dressed.

Junie was in mid-flight, having pulled up the covers and launched herself towards the indeterminate gray-shaded blackness when she remembered the neat pile of clothes – at least four separate items, sweater and shorts and shirt and uh-oh – she'd gingerly picked through. By then, however, it was too late.

"Turn around!"

"Well, okay." David, ever polite, was already spinning to face the wall, but reluctantly stopped and began to roll back.

"The *other way*!"

"Oh. I wondered."

"And stay on the other side."

"Junie," he said, knees pressing against the cemented stones beside the bed.

"What?"

"It's a twin mattress."

"Just shut up, okay? Shut up and stay as far over as you can." She turned away, butt to butt, and worked her single blanket around behind her, a wad between them. The rest of the blankets – four or five – lay thick and heavy on her shoulders, her hips, her legs. Junie gritted her teeth, thinking of how he'd snagged every one in the house. At least now they'd keep her warm, too.

Another round of uncontrollable shivers and they almost did, enough that the shivers stopped, but still nothing compared to the furnace of his broad back.

All that heat, wasted on her now-warm posterior. She couldn't stand it. "I'm rolling over."

"You sure?" David didn't move a muscle.

"There's a blanket between us, so don't worry."

"Um… good."

"And don't get any ideas."

"Hey."

"Hey what?"

"Hey… alright."

She turned quickly, trying not to lose the air trapped beneath the bedcovers, so quickly that the modesty layer between them was unfortunately shoved downward. But then was easily pulled – his butt was almost *furry* – back up. Junie slipped both jean-covered, blanket-protected knees under his, thigh to thigh, shin to calf, back to front, of course taking care not to lay too close, not press too hard, her arms bunched at her sides like an old-time boxer's, elbows close, protected, ready to jab.

DON'T GET ANY IDEAS.

He tried not to. Really. But Paula had been an education. Mostly an education in what he didn't want, but also an education in… Vermostimumonics? Autosexual Pheromology? Whatever. He'd never had to pay attention to his *nose* before. First Paula, and then that picnic in the park with Junie. Though Junie's had been imperceptible – had he even noticed the faint warm musk now suffusing through the air beneath the heavy blankets? He wouldn't have admitted it, not then, but was sure he had, echoing down neural pathways that had been dosed to hypersensitivity by that time.

And now, pheromonically-toasted or not, echoing right back up them. More a slow quiet song than a hit-upside-your-head crescendo… an elegy, quiet, so quiet… until it slowly built and grew and grew until it was actually crescendoing pretty well. Crescendoing and building in all ways. Not that Junie had to know: he could just lie here, aching. Until first light, which couldn't be more than, oh, three or four hours away.

The trouble, he decided, was the shape of her – thighs up against the back of his, fitting just inside his knees, breasts against his back, separated by the crumpled blanket between them but still more insistent, more *prominent* than he'd remembered. Like two points of heat, two hot and burning insistently firm points...

Oh, god. Maybe he could find the will to meditate – that was it. Yoga breaths. Breathe in, starting deep in the belly, up to the chest, stretching, filling, then out, slow, all the way, all the way out...

JUNIE EXHALED, the fine hairs below the nape of his neck tickling her upper lip. Not so hairy otherwise, just that furry butt she'd inadvertently discovered. Fuzzy butt. Fuzzy fuzzy fuzzy butt. She almost laughed – it was late and she was fading, getting loose – but didn't want to wake him. Because he must have fallen asleep, was breathing slow, so slow, slowing filling the huge bellows of his chest with big, deep subterranean breaths – deep, long, slow, big...

Stop.

The blanket ended at her chin. Her back was still freezing, but her front was nice and warm. As long as she stayed close. She could pull her head back and away from his neck, but as soon as she relaxed there she was again, lips nearly on his skin, nose brushing if not outright touching it. A nice smell, actually, the soft dry dust of the day, plus the saddle soap she used to rub into the leather of her shoes, plus honest sweat, a good man sweat, the top edge wine-sharp but low notes playing underneath. All of it a melody, connecting up, connecting with its own dark singing voodoo to her sleepy punchy brain.

Come on, Junie – she pulled away again, but a layer of colder air slipped between them and she didn't like that. So she dropped back closer, wondered if his breathing had changed but no, he was obviously still sleeping. She tried to nudge the modesty blanket up between them with her chin, to lay her face against that, but the old wool wouldn't stretch any further. If only the blanket was a little bigger. If only she was a little taller, could get her face above the level of his shoulders. If only he wasn't quite so tall, so very, very tall and long and big and...

Stop.

THE LITTLE WIGGLES were killing him. As soon as he started to forget the overwhelming, ever-present *sensation* of her – as soon as their mutual, shared stillness allowed him to pretend she was nothing more than, say, an exceptionally warm and close and curved and sweet-woman-smelling pillow, she'd do something like move the point of her chin or, worse, some other part, and...

THIS WAS RIDICULOUS. Close and far; huddled and avoidant. Grow up, Junie. This is only a *sleeping* arrangement. Perfectly natural. And she was getting warm, except her hands, the left one deep on the mattress between them, and the right... uh-oh. No blanket – it had slipped a few inches down, was only held between them by the steady if slight pressure of her thighs. The whole process occurring so gradually it hadn't registered. That her hand was on his hip, his bare hip. Underneath her open palm. She didn't dare move it – she'd wake him, then he'd know. It was so long since she'd moved it she couldn't feel it anyway. But, now that her attention was focused on it, there was something, the muscles tight, in fact all the muscles of his body tight, almost... hard...

Stop!

She tried, but still could feel it, a kind of deep, barely palpable tremor, a fine fasciculating tension. Cautiously, she increased the pressure of her palm, pressing down, his hip hard beneath the heel of her hand, but the muscles under her splayed fingers stayed hard, tense, rigid...

And then, so quiet that at first she wasn't sure an audible sound had slipped through her open lips, hardly more than a thought, a slow soft, "Ohhh..."

"DID YOU SAY SOMETHING?" Just a sound, the softest sound, but David couldn't pretend he hadn't heard it.

"You're not asleep?"

"Of course I'm not asleep." Did she think this was *easy*?

"Yes, you are." She pushed the modesty blanket down to the mattress, her hand sliding from bare hip to bare waist.

"*Now* I'm not."

"You are," she said. "You are *definitely* asleep. And this could be a dream. A dream we shouldn't have – a dream we wouldn't talk about... because, as far as each of us knows, it's only our own dream, the kind that neither of us could remember even if we tried to."

"Dreaming..." Her fingers were cool on his burning skin, cool and fine and close and it *was* okay, okay and banishing every previous petty worry that, in fact, he couldn't remember and definitely wasn't trying to. "I guess I could be dreaming. If you say so. I mean, whatever you say—"

"Shhhh." Now both her hands were unbuttoning, unzipping, pulling, twisting out of every intervening layer.

After each brief shuffling separation she returned warmer every time, whole new stanzas of a warm silk song that included those two pointy parts, still there but only parts, parts buried in the whole, buried in the same sweet music she was hearing.

"Jesus. You feel... wonderful," he said, all of her now pressed against his back.

"Shhhh. I'm sleeping." Those cool fine fingers returned to his waist, and began to slide forward and around, along a tight and lightly shaking plain, to locate – a bit sooner than expected – and brush against absolutely non-fuzzy skin, stretched tight along an anatomic structure that she hadn't forgotten, not at all, that was rooted in place and sprung back against her.

"Junie," he said, voice choking, "*Stop*."

She pulled back. "I'm sorry. I—"

His hand shot down find her retreating one, found it and brought it back to hold firm against him. "No. *Don't* stop. It's just... I'm, um, almost there."

"Oh." A pulse, thrumming; a pulse beneath her fingers.

Now his hand left hers, sliding up along her forearm, up over his waist and down between them. She pulled away to admit it to that damp soft curling region, then swung her hips back to hold it in place.

His knuckles against those curls, a plunging hot line along the back of one. "But shouldn't I...?"

"No. I'm there, too. *Now*. I'm ready."

"You mean—"

A hand over his mouth as she pulled him flat and climbed over in the inky darkness, her kneeling legs spread to find David as she said, "Shut up," and he slid into a greater heat than either had imagined at any time over that cold night. And then, her voice muffled in the hollow of his neck, "We don't have to do... or... say... *any*thing... we're... *dreaming*."

MUCH LATER.

She'd ended up on top again, half the blankets still on; with one hand, he reached and found and flipped the heavy mass of the others over them, pulled it to her shoulders but could only cover her left. Junie didn't stir, lay with her arms stretched out on the mattress, one of those little pigtails under his chin – softer than he'd thought – and snoring gently.

Straining, he lifted head from pillow to look at her, but even with the coming dawn there was only a faint gleam on her exposed shoulder, and a corresponding crescent on his, beneath. Burnished silver, not like the golden arc of reflected firelight that had traversed her face from temple to cheek to full lips earlier that night. No color at all, nor could he discern any difference, any change in the indistinct densities of gray-to-blackness, between the shoulder that lay above and the one, larger but anatomically and physiologically identical, that lay below.

In the shining dark, the same.

20

THE MOURNING AFTER

- or -

Traumatic Vehicular Populitis

DAVID heard the busy sounds of a fire being built, and then the rustling moans and pops and snaps of damp pine burning.

He rolled toward the open doorway, felt a very cold spot beneath one thigh and scooched back off it. If it had been a dream, it had been a wet one. Gray light, a pack of matches that had slid into a dusty corner, the ones he guessed she'd been looking for in the dark. From the sound of it, she'd found the other pack he'd placed so carefully on the kitchen windowsill after lighting the propane stove last night. David smiled.

Out the far glass doors, the trees remained obscured, now not by darkness but the opposite, a bright glaring fog, those gathering clouds having lowered to envelop them. There was a strange reflective quality to the blurred bark and branches – ice, a thin coat over everything. Something he'd never seen in the mountains, though he knew it sometimes happened at the freeze-thaw margins of the winter months.

Groaning at the prospect of the cold – and then the brute stone-floored reality of it – he whipped the covers back and jumped into yesterday's clothes. Maybe the shorts hadn't been such a good idea. But the fire was. And breakfast.

JUNIE stood close to the flames that jetted and flared from the still-green wood, the two blankets she'd stolen off their bed wrapped around her shoulders. *Their* bed. She didn't want to think about that, and so she didn't. And if she did, there was always the dream bit.

Directly in front of her, a beveled mirror hung over the mantle. She looked up: the same as every morning, maybe a little less tired around the eyes. All things considered – or carefully not considered – she hadn't slept this well in ages. Hadn't slept this well, in fact, since... some other dream?

David's big boots were clumping around in the kitchen, a place she'd avoided since discovering a lace of frost covering half the linoleum, a lace that instantly melted into her cotton socks. She'd scrambled back to the warming bricks in front of the fireplace, thinking, this was not the thing to pull on a Deep-as-Deep-gets Southern girl.

Supposedly, he was making pancakes. Or some presumably healthy food-like substance that resembled them. But the floors were frozen, and he was the one in there cooking.

As the fire became almost too hot to stand this close to, her fingers played absently with one of her braids, the little red ribbon at its end. And untied it on their own, just like that. Okay. Looking back in the mirror, she teased the braid apart, brushed it a few times with a row of fingers, and liked the way the little patch of hair sprayed up and outward. Then did the same next door, just for fun. All those months of weaving and tying, she found, had concealed a billowing length she hadn't gotten to before, and pretty soon she had herself an Afro – a whole *different* kind of retro pride, take your irony and stick it.

Then – yikes – David walked back in, carrying two chipped red plates piled with fairly realistic-looking pancakes. Looking away so she wouldn't see her blushing, she hopped, cloud of hair bobbing, back into her favorite recliner, and tucked her still-damp socks under her. The pancakes, actually, weren't half bad. Kind of slatey, probably because she couldn't taste a milligram of salt. Maybe there was a whole different, slatey realm of no-salt tastes, compensation for those high-blood-pressure unfortunates doomed to a low-salt life. But the maple syrup covered a multitude of sins. One good thing about these healthy types: once they decided it wasn't going to kill you, they did tend to go with the real stuff.

David had clumped out and returned with coffee, steaming in blue and white-flecked enameled cups. He put them down quick, steel handles burning, and sat on the edge of the couch, watching the fire, warming his knees. Smiling slightly and, after the cup cooled, cradling it between his hands. That vacant, morning look, thinking of absolutely nothing. Different, again – he was always thinking of something, unless he was jumping up and *doing* it. Junie sat back and pulled her shawl of blankets up around her.

He hadn't mentioned the hair; she wasn't sure he'd noticed, a relief. But he must have seen it when he'd placed her cup beside her. Maybe his mind had been floating then, floating off to where it floated now, but maybe, she thought – for no good reason, just a thought – he'd been seeing something deeper. Deeper than the hair, deeper than her skin, deeper than the South; seeing something deeper than she was used to anybody seeing.

The fire, the ice outside, the two of them sitting there. Almost as if life could be... easy.

BIGGS GLANCED OUT his hotel restaurant's plate-glass window at the monster occupying one and a half parking places. Which really meant two, and a good car, in his opinion, deserved a full two spaces. He'd been waiting for this ever since he'd seen Schwarzenegger cruising down Hollywood Boulevard in a military-green model, and was happy for the excuse. The broad square hood, beading with moisture from the fog; racks and lights and wheels studded with rows and rows of big hard-edged rubber chunks that you knew would have to hurt whatever they ran over, even pavement. When you go into the mountains, he thought, you need a vehicle to do the *job*.

Oh yes. He glanced at his watch. Equally big, relatively speaking. And equally impressive; if only Hummers came in 18-karat gold. The plan was to meet at the clinic at nine-thirty, but Biggs was thinking nine, in case Oz planned to jump the gun and work their soon-to-be-mutually-owned crowd on his own.

Either way, time enough for a nice big breakfast – steaming mounds of hash browns, gravy-covered biscuits, and organically fried bacon, which must mean no petroleum products. As he attacked it, he noticed a familiar face. On the other side of the white-linen table next to his; a familiar face he couldn't quite place. Pushing sixty, looking as gloomy as Biggs would be if he was old and

Caucasian and saddled with that ponytail, plus dressed in hemp pajamas. Except with pockets. And a belt. But the belt was woven, too. As were, as Biggs confirmed by discreetly leaning over, his slipper-like hemp khaki shoes.

"Can I help you?"

Biggs looked up, thinking, not discrete enough. "Sorry," he said, and then it hit him: in the bar, smooching in the back with Blondie. And more – the 'before' picture displayed above an electronic patient record Oz had proudly shown him, the first example of HorTech's before-and-after marketeering. Which meant that this fine specimen must be growth hormone Patient Zero. "I must have seen you at the clinic."

Don's long face brightened. "The Forever Clinic? Are you a doctor?"

"Indeed I am." Biggs settled back with a broad smile.

Don fumbled with his napkin, looking as troubled as before, then said, "Can I ask you something?"

"You're our patient?" *Our* patient – Biggs liked the sound of that, liked it very much. "Of course."

"It's just, well, that Intrapustular stuff—"

"Excuse me?"

"Fidelopenia. You know, IFP. Dr. Black was telling me – I mean, about his wife. His ex?"

Biggs was puzzled; Don leaned toward him, lowered his voice and cast his eyes toward the lovely blond – Blondie, from the bar! – checking off items on a clipboard with the maitre d' across the room. She noticed Don, winked, and Don shot back a pseudo-happy grimace. Before continuing, *sotto voce,* "I'm sure Dr. Black told you."

"Ah." Biggs still hadn't a clue, but could recognize the scent of blood.

"Exactly. The thing is, at first all he talked about was how she would... you know, the end."

Don looked stricken, and so Biggs nodded, gravely.

"And then, the other day, he said she might get a *little* better."

"Just a little," Biggs repeated. A little was good, wasn't it? No matter – he nodded gravely again.

"I looked it up but couldn't find it – I should have known because it's rare, extremely rare. But you're a doctor."

Biggs nodded a third time, less grave but thoughtful, another physician ready for one of the out-of-office questions that patients reliably nail their doctors – allopathic or chiropractic – with.

"Anyway... how long? I mean, she deserves every day she has left, but... if she gets, you know, *pustular*... I mean, first *there*, then everywhere... How long can something that awful... I mean, can something like that go on?"

Biggs tapped the side of his nose, saying, "I see." And if he read this right, he did. "Let me check my database." Reaching for his trusty wide-screened phone, loaded full to bursting with the medical diagnostic guides that had often seen him through a similar knowledge crisis.

A tap, another, and then a flurry of them, jumping from Epocrates to Pepid to PubMed, the whole shooting match. He found precisely what he'd expected – absolutely nothing.

Laying his tiny electronic brain flat on the table, he drummed his blunt fingers on the smooth plastic back and pursed his lips to thoroughly suppress a smile. David, David, David. A man of hitherto unappreciated depths – in this case, an entirely new and completely bogus diagnosis, one that managed to both taint a former lover and beat back her aging boyfriend. Nothing actionable, no actual malpractice, so it couldn't hurt the clinic. Just a strange, if understandable (to a man of the word like himself), breach of ethics. A breach of ethics that, if revealed to, say, an ex-wife's new lover, couldn't happen to a more deserving guy.

"Your friend?" Biggs looked over, and Don did as well. "I'm afraid..."

Biggs looked back. "I'm afraid that Dr. Black has been experiencing some, well, *difficulties*."

"I'm sure he is – I mean, the divorce."

"Exactly. I'm glad you understand. But the good news is – and I hope you'll take this as good news – there is no IFP."

"No IFP?"

He shook his square polished head. "No intrapustular, no fidelopenia. Nothing like it, anywhere."

"She's *fine*?" Don smiled, the sun coming up. "You mean, she'll *be* fine?"

Another nod, this time not grave at all.

Don began to get up, then stopped. "You're telling me he lied to me? My doctor lied?"

"Well..." Biggs spread his hands.

Don's pale face darkened nicely, after which he threw his napkin on the table and stormed out of the restaurant.

Biggs watched him go, amused, and started in again on breakfast, at least until Blondie broke away and came over to the table. "Excuse me," she said, "The gentleman you were speaking to... Is he okay?"

"I'm not sure, but I think he got some very good news."

She looked puzzled, then smiled tentatively, and, digging for her cell phone in her purse, walked out to the hotel lobby.

It was good to be a healer.

THE CREW, ASSEMBLED. Except David, of course. And Junie, who Quinn figured was doing her usual Friday gig at the University, a smart girl taking the smart opportunity to stay away. But everyone else was there on this oddly bleary, fog-cloaked morning, ready to see patients and wondering how many dwindling days they had ahead. Milling about, doing this or that pre-patient task in sullen silence. Most had spent the better part of yesterday afternoon bitching about David, and guilt was in the air.

Quinn put two fingers in his mouth and blasted out a New York taxi-whistle that shattered the uncompanionable quiet. It got their attention – even Nancy stopped tuning the gleaming hooks and steel cradles of her infernal exertional devices and came to the edge of the balcony above.

"Look," he said, as Nancy leaned over, forearms dented by the beveled glass, and the others gathered around. "Oz Garcia – the man who signs your checks – has some ideas."

He paused. How much to say? How much was he sure of? Would he take the job, the risk, the compromise? Contrary to appearances, Quinn was not entirely immune to guilt – while he hadn't betrayed his admittedly flexible moral principles in Texas, he knew he'd left everyone at the McIntyre Foundation high and dry. He'd shed his regret like a snake – or a butterfly, he reassured himself

– but there had been a few unpleasant moments, roughly the time it took to get from the Courthouse to his ritual guilt-shedding beverage, which was anything and as many as it took.

This was different, though; he was feeling weaker, less determined, and wondered if he could achieve that blissfully guilt-free zone.

"Garcia told me he may have a line on another doctor," he continued, not mentioning who that doctor could turn out to be. "Someone who knows this stuff, who's done this sort of thing before."

They didn't look happy. Neither, in fact, was he. Quinn looked down, feeling their eyes upon him, particularly the heavy gaze of Nancy, falling ten feet to his shaved scalp and rayon-draped shoulders. Fuck them – fuck her, he thought, but then fingered the smooth synthetic fabric of his dress and felt, somehow, even less determined to preserve his own hide, no matter what or who it cost. Was it his feminine side, he wondered, or even... his *butterfly* side? He knew he was a master at morphing, knew it from Texas and all the other states he'd lived and practiced in; morphing as he moved from one petty license-snafu or another, from GP to cardiovascular surgeon to psychiatrist to the gig that really clicked, holistic doctor-guru. But the transformations had always been *after* screwing everybody – what if he morphed *before*?

Could I...? Could I...? Of course I can!

What a guy I am, he told himself, caught up in the moment. Or what a gal. What a *person*. And personal transformation is what I'm all about! Standing straight, he met their eyes, Nancy and the rest of them. Fuck them? No, not today, at least not *en mass*. Instead, fuck advantage, the deal, the sideways slide. And so he said, surprising himself far more than even Nancy, "Fuck it – we've got to find David. I tried his place, and don't know where he's off to. Let's turn the place upside down, see what we can come up with. There's got to be a way to reach him, talk to him, get him to come back, make this crazy place work."

Blank faces, unconvinced. Howie's curious, but Quinn had expected that. He didn't dare look up at Nancy's.

"Go... go!" He waved his hands, shooing them. "Find something!"

The Thinnas moved, if slowly, then gathered speed and began

to sweep the office space; Nancy shrugged, descended the stairs, and followed Howie and Quinn towards David's office.

"THERE HAS TO BE SOMETHING," Quinn said, as Nancy, with a discrete and unobjectionable fart of effort, lifted one end of the motorized exam table off the floor. As Howie bent seamlessly to peer beneath the stocky steel pedestal, Quinn rifled desk drawers, then headed for David's computer. When a window on the screen asked for a password, he tried the birth date off the license on the wall beside him and it worked, big surprise.

Calendar, address book, email, all yielding less than zip. Then a kind of diary, 'Mistakes I've Made'. Which sounded good but, on opening, consisted of a self-flagellatory ramble about divorce and failure that soon, after a brief and painfully nonspecific entry about Vegas, trickled down to a line or less per week. Not even the makings of a decent self-help book, or, failing that, a memoir; all of it hopelessly mundane save a few tart comments about his co-workers. Quinn scrolled to the date of his own interview, read it and looked down at his frock, the same one he'd worn that day. That bastard: how *could* he? David had no sense of style, of color, of cut at all. Or, as he'd discovered, a decent secret.

"Hello?" Oz's voice echoed down the hall and through the open door.

"Krishna Fucking Vishnu," Quinn muttered, and, ignoring Howie's unusually sharp glance, closed the file as Nancy returned the various pieces of office furniture to their original arrangement. He hurried after Nancy, but Howie remained standing, eyes closed, by the wastebasket Quinn had already checked twice. Quinn shrugged and shut the door. A silhouette through frosted glass of Howie bending, robes fanned, one bare sole levitating toward the ceiling, as a freckled hand swam downwards into rustling, crumpled papers.

"AH. Hard at work, I see." Hands clasped behind his back, a benevolent look lit Oz's jowls, plump and pink above a deeply-trimmed beard, an immaculate white collar, a perfect Windsor knot.

Today's dark suit featured a barely visible chalk-white stripe, while rows of tiny boats sailed across an azure tie.

Behind that benevolence – and what was more benevolent than saving jobs and making money? – the alphanumeric wheels of Oz's mind whirred and spun. He noted Quinn's continued presence, as well as his carefully closed expression, which could only mean that the Forever Clinic's new backup doc was ready to negotiate yesterday's unrefusable proposition. Even better was Biggs's absence, an absence that should, as planned, provide the lead-time Oz needed to remind *all* the staff who their true benefactor was.

On the broad polished floor in front of him, the crew had assembled to either side of Quinn. Whose expression closed down even more: they were attending to Oz, Quinn thought, with a lot more attending than he'd just received. And being attended to used to be *his* job. Was it the dress? Had he been on the run too long? Completely lost his chops? As Quinn pondered, Howie padded from the hall and slipped in front of him. So this is what he'd been reduced to: another face in the crowd.

"So..." Oz frowned. What he needed, Oz realized, was a St. Crispin's Day speech! He cleared his throat and started, slowing building. "Today is... the day... the *big* day... the day we, um, hoist our petards, scuttle our butts, put three sheets to the wind..." He studied their faces, then suddenly beaming, leaned forward, thrust out a fist and said, "...the day we sail forth and *win*!"

Quinn scanned the small crowd from within; incredibly, the Thinnas, even tough-minded Nancy, were lapping it up! Had he, Quinn McIntyre, ever been that obvious? Well, maybe. Pacing the stage in floor-length robes – *male* robes then, and priestly white – swirling in his wake. Working the crowd, selling the idea, selling the product. The product being him, and by extension, whatever he might choose to recommend.

Oz had moved on to his ten-point recovery plan, which to Quinn sounded eerily reminiscent of his own Ten Supplements for Optimal Wellness talk, or for that matter any ten-steps-to-anything talk he'd ever heard, and he'd heard plenty. But Oz was rolling and still held Nancy's and the Thinnas' adoring gaze.

The message almost didn't matter, Quinn figured, because the media was *love*. As in, Love me and I'll take care of you. Love and *hope* – the hope that Oz was spreading thick, the same consumer emollient that Quinn had once laid in a smooth buttery layer across this grandly affluent death-and-disease-obsessed nation.

And Quinn did miss it. He may have just morphed into a butterfly, but he was still a butterfly that needed attention, that longed to lead, to be loved and followed unconditionally. His eyes teared with longing; he could feel it in his gut, his massive thighs. He missed the love, missed it coming at him, missed it more than anything.

Oz peered around Howie's turban and noted Quinn's incipient moisture, thinking he had Quinn exactly where he wanted him. "Our course will be much smoother," Oz continued, "if we can locate Dr. Black. Just a clue, any seemingly inconsequential bit of information he might have mentioned – a favorite spot in the mountains, say, or a *cabin* he liked to visit – anything to help me go to him, talk to him, and put the Forever Clinic back on track."

Despite his optimism last night, Oz hadn't been able to locate David's friend's cabin. Oh, he'd called in a favor to get a single-digit address on a certain Mountain View Road, but it seemed like every other dirt track was called that up there, half of them too inconsequential to be labeled on the satellite imaging systems he'd just been poring over at home. Still, he knew that David's friend, being a doctor, must have left a map. And David, who probably remembered the way and really wasn't as careful as he should be, could easily have left it behind.

The Thinnas looked almost convinced, the masseuse less so, and the fake East Indian was as inscrutable as ever. But Quinn, his boy – Quinn was raising a beefy arm above an armpit pink with razor rash.

"Yes?" Oz asked, delighted.

'We're with you," Quinn fluted, hoarsely. "And we've turned this place – his office, his computer, even his wastebasket – upside-out and inside-down."

"Finding…?"

Quinn shook his head. "Nothing. Absolutely nothing." Sorrowfully, Quinn cast his eyes downwards, and was surprised to see a crumpled piece of paper, *wastebasket* paper, held behind Howie in two freckled hands.

THE CLINIC'S MASSIVE DOOR swung wide, easily overpowered the new doorstop and hammered into the artfully hand-plastered wall, shaking but happily not toppling the outrageously-priced Zuni *Bruha* medicine pots balanced on the floor-to-ceiling shelves. Biggs stood framed in the opening, muscles quivering beneath a suit even finer than Oz's, and demanded, "Where is he?" His narrowed gaze moved from one to the other: the Thinnas now frightened; Nancy now defiant; Howie still unreadable; and Quinn, face neutral once more.

But not, apparently, neutral enough. "You," Biggs said, advancing toward Quinn. "I'll begin with *you*."

"Me?" Quinn squeaked, his voice finally finding the soprano register he'd been straining at for months.

"Dr. Biggs," Oz said jovially, moving between them. "Dr. Quinn and her associates were just telling me how hard they've been looking for Dr. Black."

"*And?*" Almost a growl; Oz might have them in his hands, but sometimes, Biggs knew, fear worked quicker.

"Sadly, they—"

Biggs stepped around him. "That's not good enough. 'Good enough' is finding him, and I need to find him, now."

"Might this, perhaps, provide enough good for your need?" Howie held up a much-injured scrap of paper, torn and tape-repaired, and handed it to Oz.

"'Map to Cabin'?" Oz looked up, amazed, and Biggs ripped it from his grasp.

"Let's go," Biggs said, heading out.

"We don't *all*—" Oz started.

But Biggs was gone; Oz hustled after him.

"TWO OF US SHOWING UP WOULD OVERWHELM HIM," Oz called out from the elevator platform. "He'll talk if I go alone."

"Alone works for me." Biggs had taken the lobby stairs and was almost out the building's rear metal door. "Let me try it first."

Shit.

Oz pushed the glass gate open and hurried after Biggs. He made it to the blind alley behind the Clinic to see Biggs climbing into a full-on Hummer, loaded with chrome and diesel stacks. The thundering id-mobile's engine gunned and a cloud of acrid grey smoke billowed over the parking lot, which Oz escaped by diving into his not-inconsiderable VW 500eBUS.

As Oz slammed his door, the Hummer's huge knobbed wheels gave a loud chirp on the smooth concrete and the vehicle lurched forward, not back, slamming into the Clinic's cement block wall, then back, then toward it again.

Having a little trouble? Oz thought, and put his own vehicle in gear, easing nearly three tons of plush German eco-engineering forward to block the alley's only exit.

He could see Biggs turn and look back in silhouette, could see that pure white grin, a study in contrast, shining from the depths of the dim interior. Could see it from ten yards away – and then less.

He wouldn't, Oz told himself. He just *wouldn't*.

The rending, when it came, was emitted as much by Oz's tenderly materialistic heart as by the hand-enameled steel that had crossed the Atlantic just for him. A rending followed by the strange sensation of a big car moving sideways, groaning and shaking but still a pretty smooth ride, considering. Contemplating his insurance coverage, Oz crossed his arms, settled back, and watched the weedy chain-link fence that lined the far side of the alley unreel in front of his windshield, followed by a longer view of the paved alley that intersected it, and finally the bright red taillights, a good three feet off the ground, as Biggs maneuvered around him and gunned his way into the distance.

Shit, indeed.

"HE TRASHED MY CAR – and took the only map." Oz suit was looking a little dusty as he sat on the couch, elbows on his knees.

"Ah, yes. The *only* map that we found." The others glared at Howie again, and again those glares bounced easily off his Teflon white robes. "But still, it is identical to this map, is it not?" Howie pulled a single smooth sheet from his robe and pondered it. It was covered with directions, a sketch of branching country roads, plus the photocopied dark gray outlines of scotch tape and the random angled traces of a flattened piece of crumpled paper. "Is a copy of the 'only' still the 'only'? An interesting conundrum."

Quinn hand shot out and Howie graciously passed it over. "Why'd you make a copy?"

"Because, my friend, it needed to be done."

"And why'd pull it out in front of Biggs?"

Howie considered. "The answers are as the maps. Two answers, identical in spirit: the thing needed to be done."

Quinn and Oz both stared at him.

Howie shrugged.

"Whatever." Quinn turned to the others. "We've got to get up to..." He peered at the map. "Rollinsville. Who's got a car?"

"We rode our bikes," said Thomas Thinna.

"For the planet," added Adeline.

Quinn shook his head, then asked Nancy, "What about your Subaru?"

"Broke," she said. "Thought I'd try walking over the ridge."

"In the fog?" It did explain the muddy boots outside the door.

"You want the full report?"

All eyes turned to Oz. "I'm not even sure it'll run," he said. Then sighed and headed for the door.

THE PASSENGER DOOR wouldn't open, but Howie came at it from the driver's side, managing to somehow flow over the leather-padded center console to sit in the broad seat, hands cradled in his lap. The rest piled into the back, the Thinnas sharing a seatbelt, Quinn half-bent on the hump in the middle, and Nancy squeezing herself in with a solid hip check to all concerned.

Oz gunned the engine, which sounded fine, then took off down the alley. No smoke, no screeching – except in stereo from the Thinnas when he turned left, sharply, and Quinn's perched bulk was thrown heavily against them.

Less than ten minutes had elapsed on the dashboard clock since Biggs slid Oz's luxomobile sideways. If Oz took the back route through the wealthy neighborhoods that hugged the ridge fencing Boulder's western border, it would cut Biggs's lead to five minutes, and Oz's fine vehicle could easily demolish that on the long but well-paved climb to Nederland and Rollinsville.

Oz turned up the canyon and pressed hard on the gas. The V-12 gave a teutonically-muted roar, the hybrid's auxiliary electrics whined, and the big car threw itself into the sweeping turns, moving fast if slightly crabwise from the damage. This could work, Oz thought, and pressed harder, as Quinn's head tilted like a metronome across the rearview mirror, his rayon-clad butt sliding between the cowering Thinnas and Nancy's unyielding, blocky hip. While Howie sat calmly, centered within the big car's movement, watching the streaming trails of fog outside.

THAT FOG thickened as they climbed, coating the small and scrubby pines that grew along the roadside with an iridescent sheen of ice. Despite his calculations, and despite his injured mega-hybrid's rapid progress up the canyon, Oz had yet to see the slightest indication of the Hummer's squarish taillights.

Miles ahead, Paula crossed her arms, scowling slightly as Biggs had his fun, the knobby tires doing a fine job on the pavement, drawing two black lines through the thin slush with an ongoing wet hiss like a wave on sand, a no-doubt satisfying demonstration of his vehicular prowess. More satisfying than the over-excited first spurt of their little expedition, when he massacred first the starter motor and then the transmission of his rental. Premature Eshiftulation, Paula thought, and nearly Drivus Interruptus. Testosterone was nice – she was a fan herself, when it came to the needle – but please. Like those chirping tires, that ridiculously over-charged engine: too much horsepower, getting in the way. But the four-wheel drive had been smart, she had to give him that. Maybe overkill is underrated.

And Biggs was definitely in overkill mode. Feeling good as he swung the paramilitary iron brick into the turns, feeling the road, an occasional stuttering release-and-slide but who was counting. On route to destiny, destiny being a never-ending and completely-enforceable signed contract with the good Dr. Black. A contract that would let him – and Oz, if the friendship-addled chub could step up to the plate – make the millions that Biggs really, really needed. No one seemed to realize the position he was in, how high the stakes really were.

Another swinging turn, solid on all four, solid right down through the muck to the pavement; driving this beast was nothing to a man like him. The windshield wipers slapped the condensed fog away as he thought, more than confidently, about what was coming. What had Black been weaseling about? 'Professional ethics'. He knew about those; it wasn't like chiropractors didn't have them. Ethics were tricky things, complex, every decision depending on the situation. Situational Ethics, something he knew the medical types were particularly into. Like that 'intrapustular' thing: that was way, way situational. Maybe he'd work that angle, bring it up and threaten a little reputational damage. That and whatever else it took to make Black sign. Biggs knew he could make it happen, because he'd do what had to be done. Smiling grimly, he unconsciously took his right hand off the wheel and patted the bulge beneath his suit coat's breast pocket.

"Both hands on the wheel, Biggs. Or I'm driving."

Biggs didn't look at her, kept driving with his left, nice and loose, until the vehicle slipped a squealing yard sideways and, what do you know, his right just jumped up opposite the other one, gripping hard if not white-knuckled.

Paula shook her head, but he didn't give her the satisfaction of looking over.

"YOU'RE GOING TO *what?*" Junie asked, eyes popping.

David finished lacing his boots and pulled his parka on. "Go for a walk. It's freshening up – look."

She had to admit it was, the fog blowing by in patches outside the window, sky mostly blue, the crackling varnish of ice already melting from the pine needles, falling plates of sugar glaze from damp brown steaming trunks. There was sun on the shingled roof, the cabin already warming up. A clean cold smell coming from outside, the wet wood of the old log walls and the quarter of firewood piled up below the window.

"I need to think. The ice is melting off the ridge; I'll be fine, just need to look down on the clouds and think." Think about what had happened yesterday. And especially last night.

Okay, she thought, not wanting to go there yet herself. Then asked, "What if someone comes looking? Biggs, for instance. He must be freaking."

"No problem. Those clouds blowing by up here are solid fog down there; the roads will be covered with ice all day."

"But not the rocks?"

"Nope. Check it out." Placing a palm on the rough wood above the window, he leaned to peer through the glass, underneath the eaves.

She walked over and saw a stone ledge that angled up out of the ground a hundred yards from the cabin and climbed like a ramp, if a steep one, toward the divide. Ascending not into cloud but out of it, its shining bright edge aimed straight at the tundra-covered slopes beyond the curtain of pines.

A more significant cloud, the cloud of her hair, brushed against the line of his jaw as she stood close, soft and filling his senses, less than the bath of sense and touch and taste last night but more than any prior contact, an increasing sensitivity that was building to Paula-like proportions, or would if he stayed a second more. David backed up, hit his head on a low beam, zipped his parka fast and clomped out through the kitchen.

Junie smiled and shook her head much as Paula had, two thousand feet below and still a good ten miles distant. Thinking, What now, Junie girl?

David wasn't there to notice.

OZ DRUMMED HIS FINGERS on the leather steering wheel, waiting for the officer beside the car to access his admittedly interesting driving history. Though all the fines had been paid, and his license didn't carry a single point. At least not recently.

"Am I detaining your party, sir?" A wide farmer's face, puffy-eyed and dead calm, now filled the driver-side window.

Oz's fingers froze. "No. No, not at all. We were just—"

"Speeding along."

"Well…"

"With more passengers than seatbelts."

From the rear, the metallic snap of the Thinnas' shared belt, releasing to twinned sighs. And then, to Oz's right, the low euro-thrum of the passenger window opening, followed by the hush of hand-woven cotton sliding over a rounded steel sill.

"Passengers need to stay in the vehicle." The head bobbed up to look over the car.

"But I am already out," Howie said, eyes staring hypnotically across the ice-crusted roof into the officer's. "And now, as you can see, there are five: one for each personal safety device." Adeline started over Quinn's bulk at the beckoning first-class open seatage – Quinn discouraging her with a ham-like forearm – as Howie added, slowly, "You must agree there is no need for my presence."

"I must agree..." the officer murmured, looking off into the middle distance. Howie gathered his robes and backed through the fog, disappearing between the ramshackle wooden buildings of downtown Nederland. Once those white garments had blended into the surrounding brightness, the office seemed to snap awake and bent back down to the window – taking in, as if for the first time, the variegated backseat group. "And *where* are you folks from?"

While they blurted out their street addresses, Oz dug into his wallet and produced his lifetime membership in the Boulder Police Department Benevolent Association.

The officer, just an overgrown farm boy with a mean streak, handed them back. "Nice to know you care, but I'm from Greeley." He tapped his badge-emblazoned cap. "State Patrol."

Greeley, Oz thought, the slaughterhouse of the plains. Which would explain the feedlot smell coming off that ballistic nylon jacket. The smell of money, they called it, a stink carried west by upslope winds every time bad weather came in. Plus a whiff of Eastern Colorado resentment.

Two washed-out blue eyes drilled into his. "And you were hurrying to...?"

"Dr. Black," Adeline Thinna piped. "We really have to hurry... because we have to... have to..." Oz dropped his forehead into an open hand.

"Dr. *David* Black?" A sudden, nicotine-stained smile. "The family doc?"

"Yes!" Opportunity, Oz reminded himself, always knocks eventually. "We're his... well, we're his office staff."

"He got himself a new office? That's great!" the officer hunkered down, nylon-encased arms folded on the lower edge of Oz's window, face filling the space again. "I was worried – a good doc's hard to find. Worth the drive, even into Boulder." He looked into the back again. "But why so many...?"

Uh-oh. Oz cleared his throat. "Perhaps you've heard – the Forever Clinic. A holistic clinic, longevity and prevention."

"*So that's* what he's doing." Chewing on his lower lip. "Keeping people alive?"

"Yes," Quinn's voice came, hoarse and high-pitched from the rear. "Keeping people alive."

A thoughtful nod. "Like seatbelts." Those puffy pale eyes narrowed, swept over each of them. "You want to stick around, you've got to wear your seatbelts."

Oz nodded helpfully.

"Wednesday's my day off. An appointment at eleven would be good." Two very pale blond eyebrows went up, waiting for confirmation.

"We'll be waiting," Oz said. "Every one of us." Not including David, but no need to go into that right now. Behind his right shoulder, Adeline made a sudden move for the now-unoccupied front passenger position, her bony pelvis clumping over the seatback without touching the perforated pigskin roof liner. Thomas definitively snapped his seatbelt closed, luxuriating in a pool of buttery leather, as Quinn, still stuck on the hump, grumbled, doubly foiled.

Luckily, the state trooper had missed the commotion, having stepped back to put away his ticket pad. "Drive safe," he said. "Twenty miles under in this weather, and I don't care how many airbags this baby's got. I want every one of you alive next week – anyone who isn't gets a ticket."

Forcing a smile, Oz waited, also forcing patience. And when he'd gotten the final, watch-out-next-time nod, forced himself to drive sedately – in fact safely, tires no longer sliding on the slush – though the little town.

"What about Howie?" They were Nancy's first words since

they'd been stopped, in accordance with her general vow of silence when it came to authoritarian males. Silence – until the point at which actions speak for themselves.

"He'll be fine," Oz said, eyes on the rear mirror, letting his right foot ease down on the pedal as the road opened up ahead, climbing through the glare. "It's not like he would have added much."

Nancy didn't comment, having cranked her head to the steamy rear window, trying to focus on a lighter patch of fog, a patch that that flowed like white water between the scrabby houses and the trees.

IT HAD BEEN, David knew, a bravura move, but happily he'd been right. With altitude, the weather just got better, one of those strange, non-common-sense inversions that sometimes happen in the mountains.

The full sun had melted almost all the ice from the rocks, removed the harsh bite from the air and bounced off the slick black wings of the wheeling crows above. Beneath his boots, reddish-orange and lime-green lichens covered the randomly sloping stones that formed his stone pathway to the sky. Over the edge on his right, a sheer drop to a slope of autumn-yellow tundra, and then a narrow valley of dense green trees, marked only by a curling column of wood smoke from the cabin. Not far beyond it, the forest was occluded by a sea of milky white; a sea broken only by the tips of the Flatirons and a few of the highest foothills – mountains, anywhere else; a sea that then extended to the blue horizon. All of it glorious, but also temporary: more clouds were rolling in behind him. That ocean of white might rise again to wrap him in cold and damp, but its fleeting nature only made the sun on his back warmer.

He'd come up here to think but soon found himself pushing it, trying *not* to think, to feel the work and sweat and joy and pain of being, the still-cool air ripping around and through him, blowing out every guilt and disappointment. Maybe this was why exercise worked, he wondered, how working muscles hard – the pain of being – drove the stress away. Maybe, but wouldn't any kind of labor do the same? Which could be why we hungered for work, at least some of us, a way to put the complications of our lives away.

Work – he thought of the work he'd left behind yesterday and grimaced, seen only by the crows above. And then moved on to *hunger*, as in last night... quickly followed by *complicated*... Ouch. David pushed harder, quadriceps screaming – the Paula cure, although he wouldn't have liked to think of it that way. A myofascial fiber-twanging harmonic howl that, silenced by an intervening layer of skin, passed unheard by anyone except the happily suffering David, unheard even by those too-observant crows.

BIGGS rolled his vehicle's chunky wheels right up to the back of David's car. The ice and slush had been nothing – he had to *have*, to *possess* a steel beast like this. But then, Mrs. Biggs... Hmmm... In any case, the splendid chrome bumper seemed to override half of Black's toylike hatchback. An old Civic from the days when subcompact really meant subcompact, it was parked in the dirt and gravel beside the cabin, next to an abandoned, ruined convertible, top sagging, that had obviously spent one too many winters at altitude.

"Let me get my hands on him first," Paula said.

"I thought you already tried that."

"No jokes – you know exactly what I mean."

"Hey, go for it." Jokes aside, she needed it, needed to win one for the home team. Biggs watched as she climbed down from the Hummer and started towards the peeling pine door. He could do what had to be done, no doubt about it, but here was a fine, fine woman, about to do it for him.

21

INTO THE CLOUDS

- or -

Hallucinatory Levitosis

"YOU," PAULA SAID. A too-rustic kitchen, and that black girl, the receptionist, from the office. The one Biggs had talked up at the clinic. David could do better – in fact, Paula knew he had. And, having missed some recent opportunities, was consoling himself with *this*.

"Me?" Junie asked brightly, hoping the silver-haired Amazon would not notice her hand as it drifted, oh so slowly, towards a small paring knife on the edge of the battered tin counter.

"You. Where is he?" Paula kept herself between David's pathetic consolation and what had to be the cabin's only exit.

"He's busy." Grabbing the knife, Junie moved away from the counter. She had absolutely no idea what she'd do with it – probably toss it out of reach of both of them if that musclebound witch got close – but Junie could see it stopped her, at least temporarily. In the meantime she let it dangle, like Billie Holiday with a straight razor in some old race movie, happy to work whatever preconceptions her unwelcome visitor might have.

"Busy?" Biggs popped through the open door behind Paula. "Where?"

"Sleeping," Junie said, but her eyes had already bounced in the direction of the kitchen window and the ridge beyond.

"I could always spot your tell, Junie – thanks." He winked, then asked his partner, "Keep her here?"

After Paula nodded, he patted an alarming bulge under his suit coat, turned and headed out.

"Biggs!" Junie yelled, but he was already framed in the window, halfway along the path to the ridge. Paula pulled a wooden chair over, leaned it against the log wall beside the door and sat, legs stretched out, ankles casually crossed. One hand cradling her elbow, the other cradling her chin as she pondered Junie. Who put her back against a similar log wall, next to the doorway to the living room, and the circular stairs that descended to last night's rock-walled basement. Junie sank to the ground, still holding the knife in front of her.

Damn.

THIS WAS GOOD. This was very good. David and him, alone. *Mano a mano* – one of them being a tall, floppy, not-so-very mano. Biggs's weight-callused hands gripped the rocks, his rubber-soled oxfords holding surprisingly well. Sweating up the suit but still looking sharp, business-like, and that's what dry cleaners are for. After all, there was a contract to sign, a life-path to alter beneath the mighty wheel of commerce. He did allow himself to loosen his tie – what the heck, go with casual, we're all in this together.

That crazy fog had blown back in but a patch of blue was overhead, right where he was going. This mountain shit was magical.

UNBELIEVABLE, David thought. A half-mile down *his* stony ledge, wearing a suit and yelling, though too far away to hear. Telling him to stop, probably, stop and reconsider. Which he was already doing, plenty, and still coming up with the same answer. The sea of cloud had changed its mind and decided to creep back up the valley – enough that Biggs, having achieved the ramp-like ridge, was framed by glowing wisps of white. Not that Biggs looked in any way angelic.

David got up off the flat rock he'd picked for reconsidering, cupped his hands and bellowed, "Go back!" Naturally, Biggs kept picking his way along the angled rock. Fine, David thought, turned away and, with a dismissive wave behind him, began climbing again; Biggs would *have* to get the message. If he didn't, he'd deal with Biggs on the way back down.

THE CREW CREPT single-file across the soggy, fog-bound meadow towards the column of smoke. Oz's hand-sewn shoes were soaked, but he guessed he'd give them up for David, give them up to keep the boy unperforated as he moved David gently back to economic reason. Pausing for a few deep breaths and to wipe the cooling sweat from his brow with a linen handkerchief. Up ahead, the Thinnas moved like eerie puppets, a little friskier than usual, as though thriving in the attenuated air.

Inside the cabin, Paula stood up, tried to look through the dense undergrowth and trees, and said, "What's that?"

"Bears," Junie answered. Screw her.

"*Bears?*"

The brick-built Valkyrie was trying not to show it, but was obviously scared. It fit, actually. The night before, David had revealed a few carefully-edited details from his recent adventures. Wildlife being the fearsome Paula's Achilles' heel.

"Or mountain lions." Or the wind, but this was fun.

"Mountain lions."

"They hunt the bears. You know, in packs."

Paula, who clearly hadn't been watching enough nature shows, backed to one side and stared at the door she'd come in through, looking like she very much wanted whatever was out there to stay away.

Junie stood herself, and pretended to peer out the window. There was nothing out there, of course, but she was thinking of the sliding patio door on the lower level, behind her – she could run through the living room, downstairs and out, try to warn David. If she kept this up, Paula wouldn't dare follow her outside. Kind of a Brer Rabbit thing – Tales Of The Honky South gone soul girl.

"Do you see anything?"

At that precise moment, Junie did, but she kept her face impassive, squinting and searching though the returning fog. Impassive wasn't easy: the skeletal outlines of Thomas and Adeline Thinna sneaking across the misty driveway, holding their Birkenstocks and stepping high to place each ragwool-stockinged foot carefully on the gravel. Behind them, Nancy, shaking her head. Behind her, the rotund shape of Oz picked a way through the trees toward the back of the cabin, closely followed by a blurry silhouette of Quinn, hem held high around thick thighs.

A TWIG SNAPPED outside the door and her captor's eyes went wide. "What if it comes in?" Paula asked, moving away from the door, moving closer. "Is there another way out?"

As Junie calculated – a little too long – Paula easily snatched the knife from her hand – *damn* – and stood holding it, looking over Junie's shoulder and straight through the living room at the stairwell leading down.

Rattling glass and then a sliding noise from that unknown region; Paula's breath came ragged and fast.

"The bears," Junie said. "You're right – they're coming in." Anything to rattle her.

"No…" she moaned, and then, a plaintive, "*Why?*"

"That pack of mountain lions, of course. Wouldn't you?" She shrugged. "Don't worry – it's better to have bears in here than mountain lions."

"In the *house*?" Another noise, from the cabin door behind her. Paula spun back and steeled herself, feet apart, arms spread wide to each side, the knuckles of one hand white around the tiny paring knife.

"Hey, Paula," Junie said, well aware of the damage the tiniest blade could do in the wrong hands. "Wait a second—"

Paula might have waited, but the Thinnas didn't, the door ripping open to reveal two dark forms against the mist – forms that, combined, in fairness did present a rather bear-like (if eight-limbed) outline. Forms that froze and emitted a totally unbearlike but disorienting scream, or rather twinned ear-splitting screams an oscillating octave apart, the instant they spotted Paula's knife.

It was too much for the already-unnerved Paula, who screamed as well and dropped the knife; Nancy came up behind the Thinnas and pushed their ululating mass ahead of her, rushing Paula and managing to knock her off her feet.

Man. Junie kicked the knife aside and tried to get around the tangle, looking for an opening, a way to get away from Paula and catch up with Biggs – Junie *really* didn't like that bulge under his jacket – before he caught up with David. Less than a yard away, Paula was fighting and wiggling her way to the surface, face up, bound by three sets of hands and arms reaching from beneath. Junie could tell it wasn't going to be easy; Paula would be out of there in less than a minute, with no imaginary bears or pumas to keep her from running Junie down.

She needed duct tape, anything – Junie turned toward the nearest cabinet but Paula ripped an arm free, snagged her ankle and yanked her into the heaving scrum. Twisting in the air, she landed flat on Paula.

Somehow, Paula swarmed up and around and on top of her, until Junie found herself mere inches from Paula's straining face, a face that went from red to purple and then paled slightly as she – as all of them – heard two sets of stomping footsteps thunder up the basement stairs.

"NO!" The Thinnas howled, but it was too late: Quinn was already airborne, landing with a lung-compressing, back-cracking weight that was instantly transmitted down through the interwoven layers of humanity.

"You are *not* a girl," Paula protested, as Quinn's generalized and typically indiscriminate excitement made itself known against her perfect buttocks. While he was not operating with any particular intention – never, unless invited – he grunted amicably back. Immediately below them, the stunned crowd fell silent, listening to Oz's now hesitant and circling footsteps.

Form the periphery of the squirming mass, Oz decided that Quinn's leap seemed to have done the trick. Furthermore, Oz was reluctant to apply any portion of his coddled mass to Quinn's equivocal and far-from-perfect buttockal region. But as Paula shifted even Quinn aside and tried once more to rip her limbs from their Velcro-like appendages, he felt he had no choice.

FROM THE MIDDLE LAYER of the scrum, Junie listened to those final footsteps pounding forward, and, as her ears were shattered by yet another wail of protest from the Thinnas, felt the cabin shudder from the spine-warping impact of an additional hundred-plus kilos of Oz flesh.

Enough. Junie let herself be pushed down and downward, until she was between Nancy and Adeline, cheek pressed into the grain of the rough floor. Deep in the warm compressed depths, she held her breath against the noxious gases being gut-squeezed from the human circus, looking for daylight. And found it, a squat triangle between Adeline's sticklike shin and Nancy's furry calf. Taking advantage of the undulating populace above her, she worked her way between and, after squeezing the last foul air from her tortured lungs, slipped free.

The knife – there, by the wall. As she scrambled for it, she caught sight of Oz seated like a Pasha, his broad posterior spread for maximum coverage over Paula, Quinn, and a mound of animated limbs. The knife and then the door – freedom, a portal to trees and wind-tattered fog and wonderful fabulous fart-free cold clear air. She stopped on the threshold, foolishly, for a single deep inspiration when she sensed a sudden uptick in the general level of protest and then a voice, undoubtedly female but also monstrous and enraged, blasting, once again, "You!"

Junie turned, even more foolishly, and was too stunned to move from the spot – the spot towards which Paula advanced, haltingly, with shuffle-and-thump eight-hundred-pound steps, Nancy and Quinn and Thomas and Adeline clinging on her shoulders and extended arms like so many wolves on her bloodied-but-unbowed silver-crowned queen-elkiness. In the background, Oz rolled away towards the living room, his sport coat gathering splinters on the spruce planks.

One massive step, and then another; Paula had halved the space between them by the time Oz regained his feet and correctly appraised the situation. Ever the pinch-hitter, he scrambled up the dangling Nancy with surprising agility and, having tipped the scale to an apparently crucial half-ton weightage, brought the entire cast and crew – Paula groaning, ligaments protesting with the strain – down to earth, or at least the kitchen floor.

Junie, not so foolishly at all, sprinted toward the rocks.

WHAT WAS *THAT*? David thought. A muffled thump, coming though the cloud behind him. More a crashing sort of noise – a car wreck, way back on the Peak-to-Peak? Or something nearer, perhaps Junie bumping into the precarious pile of pans and dishes he'd gradually constructed on the counter after breakfast. Every single one in the cabin: washing, then rinsing in bleach and then water and then drying, the excuse being the single mouse turd he'd discovered under the sink, tiny and black and innocent but possibly harboring the oh-so-deadly Hanta virus. The real reason, of course, being what they'd both been afraid to talk about.

David groaned, slid off Reconsidering Rock #2, and landed on the flat stones below. The patchy sun had moved behind the peaks, the air was cool; he pulled on a knit cap, grabbed his parka off the rock and tied the sleeves around his waist for the trip back.

If nothing else he'd made some progress. As in, Junie. As in, if it had been a dream, he liked it. As in, no matter how unlikely a pair they were, she was the best thing that had ever happened to him. As in, he wasn't a *total* idiot.

Regarding the Clinic, nothing had changed, no matter how often he turned it over in his head. He'd made his decision, trashed everyone he worked with, and that was that. He simply had to leave – if he didn't, patients would continue to get suckered in, pumped full of hormones they didn't need, and gradually relieved of their wallets. His old patients wouldn't know why he'd left, but would probably forgive him. All except Don, who'd already started the whole pumping process – hormones in, assets out – and would be particularly disappointed. David made a mental note to offer him a heartfelt apology as soon as they next met.

One last look around. He'd stopped where the ridge jutted out above the valley, a high prow over undulating grass slopes and a tongue of the last tall pines that lined the unnamed stream, a mile above the cabin. His lookout was backed by the Stonehenge-like rubble from an old failed mine, an excellent place to stop, sheltered by the man-high rocks. A last place of isolation, they blocked the view down to the ridge that Biggs had hopefully abandoned, but faced the valley and, beyond it, the full march of the Divide, up the Indian Peaks, Arapahoe and Pawnee to Long's Peak and beyond. David's friends had taken him here before, when all three dared themselves to sit and eat their sandwiches close to the edge, where the flat stones gradually curved down beneath their legs and, just beyond their Vibram-soled boots, fell away to nothingness.

Silence. And then a gust of wind, fresh with the still-melting ice of the ridge. Just a gust, but something… the short dark hairs on his forearms tilted up on thousands of tiny *arrector pili* muscles, caught the breeze, a chill, and then… the sound of heavy breathing, coming closer.

David sighed. Biggs.

And there he was: a blocky hand on the edge of one of the tall shards of rock, followed by a blocky head, carved obsidian, beaming despite the sweat that ran down to soften the collar of his snow white shirt. The suit, however, still looked immaculate – a strange way to dress for exercise at altitude, but David had to admit he pulled it off.

"It *is* you," Biggs said. "All I could see was the top of your hat."

"I didn't see you." If he had, he would have circled the rocks and headed down. Maybe slowing enough so Biggs could safely follow, but far enough ahead that he wouldn't have to talk to him.

"Figured you were waiting for me."

"No." David was tired of lying, tired of trying to satisfy Biggs or anyone else's needs. "Just thinking."

"About?"

"You know."

"And?"

"Same as before: I can't do it." He turned to start down.

"One minute, okay? Just one minute. I came all this way." Biggs moved from David's route of exit – best not *seem* to force the client – and crossed over to the flat stones in front of him, framed by space, by possibility itself.

"One minute? Sure." David folded his arms and leaned against cool granite.

"Imagine, just imagine, you're a young chiropractic student in Los Angeles – studying hard, trying to pay your bills, working toward the day you can take care of those who need you." He stopped, then asked, "Want to hear the rest?"

David hesitated, then nodded, his skepticism beginning to be overcome by the first pull of a narrative that was not entirely different from his own.

"Graduating, you go back into the trenches of Compton—"

Compton, David thought. Wow.

"—hoping to provide for the honest working men and women you grew up around. Only their aches and pains, of course – nothing as impactful, as dramatic, as life-saving as the medical field. But enough to make a difference, to get them through their through their days, get them going, back on the job."

Nothing as dramatic... Biggs might be talking chiropractic, but David was thinking family practice – the poor stepchild of the mighty engine of the medical field. Treating everyday problems and referring the scary ones onward, surrendering them to the glory hogs with scalpels, caths and stints, with mortal chemicals and radiation and the whole invasive, pocket-lining, self-aggrandizing panoply of the twenty-first century medical hit parade.

"But you can't keep it up," Biggs continued, sensing the hook was set. "The bills keep on coming, and the patients who need you most can't pay what it takes to cover your expenses. The practice closes – you want to reopen, soon, but you're forced to look beyond your initial goals, to figure a way to come back and make it work."

Biggs knew he had to bring Junie into the story – who knew what she'd murmured to young David? "So you try New Orleans, working with a remarkable young woman to bring affordable prescriptions to that city's poor."

David listened, nodding. Junie *had* mentioned something about that, though she'd certainly seemed a lot more *critical* of the whole affair. Still...

"Years later, on returning to Los Angeles, you discover a way to restart your little storefront office with something that has a chance, just a chance but what a chance, to be more impactful and dramatic and even life-saving than *any* simple medical intervention—"

He straightened up. "Growth hormone? *More* impactful? Come on..."

"You've got me there," Biggs admitted. "No argument." Biggs raised both hands in surrender and bent his head, eyes closed as he stood halfway between David and the tilting ledge, surrounded by blue sky, wind whipping at the tight-woven wool of his suit pants. That had been the hinging moment, the sale-killing moment but he was going to make it through, he knew it, because David hadn't rolled his eyes and walked away, because he'd made his young prescription-writer *believe* in that poor gritty practice, believe in that and the rest of the lyrical (if not exactly factual) picture he'd painted in the thin, clear air between them.

"But no matter what the intervention," Biggs added, "You want to *help*." And then, recalling what Oz Garcia had first said, at once ironic and glowing, about David Black: "You *need* to help – you can't *help* helping. An admirable goal, but not an easy one. Money, David." Biggs looked right, then left, searching fruitlessly through the empty blue, then stared directly at his small audience. "You can't get around it. I couldn't. Which meant... *financiers*."

Biggs paused, waiting for David to make to connection, to come to the inescapable conclusion that the two of them – not David and his financier, Oz, but David and his true partner, Biggs – were brothers in arms. "You may have noticed the color of my skin."

"Please. I don't let that—"

"Of course you don't. But bankers do. Who has money for a black man in LA? Don't answer that." The wave again, one-handed this time. "You probably don't know. I didn't, until I looked around. Until I found it."

A pause, waiting for his listener to *want* to know, and then, "Hip-hop, David. Producers. Talent. Strong men who want to stay strong – that and convert some size to muscle. Men who are willing to try a taste of whatever's out there, side effects be damned. And if they like it... they *invest*."

David pushed off the rock. "You're running on hip-hop money?"

"Worse," Biggs said, because sympathy was what this was all about. "I'm running from it – those kind of investors demand returns, immediate returns. Huge, drug-like returns. Investors, sadly, who like to play with guns."

JUNIE CLIMBED, steady, her laser focus distracted only briefly by a patch of white, seen from the corner of an eye, drifting between the trees that lined the slope below. A figment of the fog, no doubt, but a figment exactly the same pristine white as Howie's robes. She stopped, looked over her shoulder, and was about to cup her hands and hoot out his name when she came to her strained but not completely exhausted senses. Too far away, and she shouldn't squander the only weapon she had: surprise.

The fog cleared again and she sped up, breathing hard as she ascended the wide if slippery surface between the precipitous edge and gnarly treeline forest. Soon she heard their voices, if not what they were saying, as they bounced around the obelisk-like stones ahead. Biggs might not be half the gangster he pretended to be, but he had his little gun collection; if that bulge beneath his arm was what she thought it was, people could get hurt. If she could only sneak around the backside of that mini-Stonehenge and heave a rock, *anything...*

Junie stopped, uncertain, then took off through the Junie-sized treeline conifers that grew up the mountainside to her left.

"GUNS?" David asked. No wonder Biggs was desperate.

"You see my situation." Meaning, be my brother-in-arms against them.

David looked Biggs up and down, trying to decide how much he was being played. Hard to tell – and, after his experience with Paula, hard to know if he *could* tell. As always, Biggs radiated confidence, but he was also radiating vulnerability, standing at ten thousand feet in business shoes – the smooth rubber heels of which were alarmingly close to a blackish, shiny varnish of ice. A varnish, shaded by the Stonehenge rocks from the morning's sun, that coated the tilted, vanishing stone precipice where David had once sat and picnicked with his friends.

Not good, David thought, and took a step forward, close enough to catch Biggs' elbow if he slipped. But as David moved closer, and as the valley came into to view over the lip of the precipice, his attention was caught by something equally distracting: a small pale patch of white that looked remarkably like Howie's robe between the treetops far below.

"So... can you see my situation?" Frankly, Biggs had counted on a more sympathetic response at this point. Instead, David was not only crowding him, but looking off to his left.

"Um..." David's gaze refocused on Biggs. "You bet." His vision shifted once more to Howie's distant robe – a robe occupied, in fact, by Howie, who now, through some strange illusion of perspective, appeared to be floating, legs folded into a perfect lotus position, high among the evergreen branches.

"People could get *killed,*" Biggs said, taking half a step backwards to center himself in David's errant view.

Not liking where Biggs's heels had traveled to – that ice-coated rock – David decided to snag that elbow.

Unfortunately, it swung out of reach as Biggs dug into his jacket, going for something jammed beneath one arm. "Even *you* could get killed," he said, twisting, but whatever he was trying to snag was caught. "If you don't... if you don't..."

David froze, astonished, as Biggs writhed, bound in his cocoon of worsted wool until, with the sound of ripping liner silk, the hand whipped out, empty. Unfortunately, that uncoiling momentum spun Biggs round on the ice, to stare at the emptiness awaiting him – as he slid down the tilted slick shelf and, with a triumph of frictionless gravity, dropped completely from view.

David launched without thinking, belly-flopping on the rock and ice, heading over the curve until, luckily, he was able to stop himself by pressing his bare arms, sleeves dragged above his elbows, into a thin band of ice-free stone. Eight square fingertips decorated the tilted edge a yard in front of his own, digging deep into a rounded crack that ran along the precipice.

"DON'T LET GO!" David shouted – unnecessarily – then winced as a head-sized rock, dislodged by his sprawling leap, rolled over his back and shoulder, gaining speed but missing Biggs's grasping hands by inches.

'*DON'T LET GO*'? Junie was sure that was David, after which she heard the bang-and-echo of a rock crashing into the scree below. Was Biggs dangling him off the ridge? She couldn't see over the broken wall of rocks she'd climbed behind, and even Biggs wouldn't... On the other hand, maybe he would. At least she hadn't heard a shot. And she could count on Biggs not dropping him; the over-dressed thug could lift twice his weight, and David was too valuable to waste. The best plan, she knew, was to let David agree to whatever and Biggs pull him up; when they were both on safe ground she'd do what she had to do to defuse the situation.

All very rational, but not enough – she didn't like this, not one bit, and was still ten yards upslope from the action. Heart pounding, Junie threw herself into the brambly dry brush, eyes squeezed nearly shut against the snapping twigs and piney bristles as she rammed her way down toward the ledge.

'DON'T LET GO'? Biggs thought, and closed his eyes, counting to ten. Which he had, at least, in minutes – hell, he could probably hang for twenty. Trouble was, his purchase was too marginal to do anything *but* hang. Even swing a leg and he'd sail into the great wide open.

David was also considering his options. The right thing or the smart thing? As it was, he had barely enough friction to keep himself from slipping down and over. In mid-consideration, he felt a sudden catch-and-give and slid forward a few more inches; David could only stop himself by pushing his cheek, his jaw, even one numb ear into the rock.

How to live forever... right. Although the few brief seconds of his transit would probably feel like an eternity, even if he spent it holding hands with Biggs, cartwheeling though the sky to meet an abrupt and definitely eternal end.

The smart thing was easy.

"You up there?"

Crap. "Uh-huh." Mumbling sideways into wet stone, but he figured Biggs could hear him. *He'd* sure be listening.

"Think you could give me a hand?"

"That's kind of a problem." He couldn't safely move his head a centimeter, but could still see the tips of Biggs's fingers, tan nails nearly white from the pressure. And also see, not that it mattered at a time like this, that the pale spot of Howie seemed to have vanished from the valley beyond.

"Forget the deal, okay?"

"That's not what I mean. I'm nearly upside down already, and it's slippery. Real slippery."

"Oh." As in, Oh shit.

David, on the other hand, was going with his favorite, crap, a single syllable that passed through his forebrain a whole rosary of times, every virtual bead popping between his virtual fingers like, well, little crappy deer poops. During which, having made a decision that had a whole lot more to do with who he was than the life he'd planned to occupy, he let himself slide – crap crap crap – down the remaining – crap crap – icy inches, grinding the heel of his other hand – crap! – into an exposed patch of cold wet rock to – crap crap crap crap CRAP – stop once again.

Biggs heard him slide closer, heard the many muttered craps, and knew he'd have to contribute something from his end to have any chance at all. He tried swinging a foot, carefully, but his unsecured hand slipped off the rock and he shot it back to grab the ledge. "I don't think so. But thanks for the gesture."

"You're welcome," David grunted into wet stone, polite as always. Then listened to the silence – or, rather, the wind blowing round the rocks behind him. The wind that gently tousled Howie's beard as he rose slowly, still in that perfect lotus, from somewhere beneath Biggs to a otherwise empty spot of sky a good twenty feet out. The wind-blown silence was pierced by the fence-gate cry of a crow as it flapped away, frightened, but Howie didn't seem to mind, only regarded David, calmly, and held both palms open to the sky.

Howie didn't say a word – in fact, David wasn't sure he was breathing – but those cupped palms seemed to semaphore a message: *Perhaps I may be of assistance?*

Okay, David thought – stress, hallucinations, and secret messages. And assistance. Uh-huh. He looked up to the cloud-torn sky, then back to find Howie, or at least his hallucination of Howie, still there. Worse, there was something in that image's level gaze that added, *Either way, Dr. David, the choice is up to you.*

Up to me. Of course. And he'd been doing so well with choices. But were those really choices, or just his idea of what the rest of the world thought the 'smart' thing was? Closing the practice had been the smart thing, and look how that had turned out. While Junie was the entirely non-smart choice, and maybe his best ever.

David wasn't a big fan of hallucinations, but the Howie-vision hanging in front of him looked pleasant enough, even reassuring. More than that, it was leaving it all up to him. One option was safe, reasonable, and freed him of Biggs forever. The other, unfortunately, was the only one that he could live – and die – with.

Without so much as another 'crap', for this was far beyond the crap-level, he let himself slide farther and, grinding one bare forearm into last inches of exposed rock, stuck a hand out over Biggs and said, "Grab it."

"You're kidding."

David sort of wished he was, but wasn't.

A moment's hesitation, during which David noted that Howie, or his illusionary doppelganger, was no longer present to witness his unlikely bravery, and then a sudden pulling weight as Biggs surged up and grasped his hand.

And then, miraculously, nothing. No scrape of stone and howling mutual free-fall, just the sound of Biggs's deep and manly grunting as his shining, perspiration-beaded cranium hove into view. That and the pain in David's arms as his biceps contracted, somehow levering a boatload of extra-wide chiropractor in a purely vertical direction. All of which drove David's bare elbow into the rock, removing skin but keeping David nicely anchored. Well and good, though it still didn't seem possible – not, at least, until the bone-breaking load was halfway above the lip and he saw Howie, robes ruffled by the breeze, pushing from beneath.

David struggled to his knees and then his feet, heels slipping but then cracking the scrim of ice and catching, back bent double as he snagged Biggs's wrist with his free hand and, sinews straining, cranked and lifted until two polished leather toecaps made it to the icy edge. With worsted butt stuck out in a major squat over open space – or, at least, over the empty inch of air that magically separated that fine suiting from Howie's gently cradling hands – Biggs rose further.

"I don't believe it," Biggs said through gritted teeth. In fact, he'd found David's unlikely actions and even more unlikely leverage a virtually religious experience, as if the hands of some unseen being were orchestrating his unlikely passage.

"Me neither," David agreed, as a beaming Howie dropped from view.

"Or me," Junie added, who just then emerged from the thicket immediately behind the tallest stone, her hair transformed once again, this time to a spiky crown of leaves and twigs and poking pine needles. "I thought Biggs was dangling *you*."

"Um... can you help?"

Junie planted a foot on the last of the dry rock and stretched to snag David's nylon belt; strength combined, they began to drag Biggs, feet sliding, up the varnished rock.

"Stop," she said, and did, all three fixed and balanced in a paper-doll cutout against the clouds, a cut-out that ended with Biggs standing nearly upright, if tilted backward and still only halfway across the glazed ledge. "So – that voice from over the edge – did I happen to hear you say, 'Forget the deal'?"

"Junie, Junie, Junie..." Biggs's free hand reached into his jacket, the lining now torn and no longer able to catch, retain, or otherwise impair the free passage of anything.

Oh no no no... Junie closed her eyes and grimaced, until David said, "Excuse me – can we finish pulling him up?"

She opened one to see Biggs, shaking his head sadly. "What'd you think?" And then, "A gun, David – she thought I had—"

"A gun? You said it was the *other* guys that—"

"Uh-huh." Biggs held the unsigned contract, all forty iron-clad pages rolled tight into a substantial cylinder that had previously occupied the his jacket's right inside pocket. He brought it close to his face, snared the rubber band with brilliantly white salesman's teeth, worked it free, then let the pages flutter from his hand, carried by the wind.

Okay, Junie thought, and started pulling.

LATER, as David went ahead, leading them down, Biggs grumbled, "I'm black, I'm bad, I must be packing. You're such a racist, Junie."

A blush that luckily he couldn't see. "Black and bad? You set the stage, big man. Fooled even me."

Another sad shake, and, once again, "Junie, Junie, Junie."

"Asshole, asshole, asshole." Said laughing – she even liked him when she hated him – and with a shove to the small of his back. Where her palm was greeted, under layers of fine wool and silk and pure Egyptian cotton, by nothing other than a heavy metallic object, the kind that makes loud noises and puts holes in things.

He took a few more steps over the rocks before he said, "Self defense, babe." A quick glance over his shoulder, almost apologetic – then back, concentrating on his slick shoes' footing.

Now it was Junie that shook her head sadly. He didn't see that either, but he knew her and didn't have to.

22

ARIAL NON-BOUNDARIES

- or -

Regenerative Indignitis

STILL LATER – though hardly past noon – in the cabin.

Paula simmered in the corner, arms around her knees, surrounded by a scuffed but unrepentant quarter-circle of the Forever Clinic's finest.

Junie had passed Biggs and David and scrambled down from the ridge ahead of them, her thoughts increasingly on Paula, the way the heinous body-building whatever had barged into the cabin – her cabin, *their* cabin – after David. Until Junie made it to the weather-beaten front door and barged in herself, kicking it open to announce "It's over," with the kind of showy drama she usually avoided but was too mad to hold back.

Wooden chairs scraped as the crew got to their feet; Paula, seizing the opportunity, pushed through the phalanx to confront Junie. Nancy and Quinn reached to restrain her but she shook them off and stood her ground, a fiercely upright glaring tower of rigid muscle.

As did Junie – at least as fierce and upright, if not the muscles.

A classic standoff, until Oz, who was entirely ready to return to his spreadsheets in Boulder, decided to break it. "Love your hair," he tried. Women seemed to like that.

Both turned slowly, like twin solar mirrors, to focus their rage on a point just over the bridge of his nose.

"The afro," he said, unsinged, to Junie. "And the tiny leaves? The broken twigs? Very Autumn." Then turned to the surgically perfect if smudged face that stared, nostrils flaring, from beneath a tattered mane of silver. "Yours too, Paula. Sort of Darryl Hannah-ish, if you don't mind my..." Oz words slowed, wisely.

Their rage undiminished – except, perhaps, by a shared amazement that Oz had not been reduced to a smoking cinder – the two confronted each other again as the rest of the crew took half a step back.

Biggs walked in from the mudroom and, taking a riskier but more effective tact, inserted himself directly between them. "It's over," he said to Paula. His voice, a carefully tuned instrument at all times, was especially low and musical, having the necessary charm, he hoped, to soothe the savage breast. "We are off to greener pastures," he added.

Paula looked down at him. "You *failed*, you mean."

He spread his arms. "That's why I need you, partner."

"Partner?"

"Uh-huh."

"*Partner* partner?"

Biggs nodded, slowly.

"Okay, then," Paula said, recovering. She tucked the torn hem of her shirt beneath her leather skirt, raked back her hair and powered around him, heading out through the mudroom. "Let's get to work."

He hustled after her, leaving Junie. Who shrugged and followed, the others pushing behind. Outside, they found another confrontation in progress, this one between David, who'd clearly hoped that hanging back to take a last appreciative look at the valley would somehow save him.

If he'd begun with something conciliatory – and knowing him, Junie was sure he must have – he'd been smart enough to stop. As had the wind, the dripping of the melting ice, and the noisy passage of their small crowd, leaving only the slow, controlled inspiration and exhalations of Paula's measured breath. Her eyes tight, David leaning back, Biggs's advising touch on her sleeve, her sharp glance and its removal. And then, from the rocks at the base of the ridge, the sudden cheep, both harsh and birdlike, of a rare red-bellied marmot – currently unmotivated by his helpmeet's pheromones – who really did not care for this much human company.

Paula heard and gave a subtle shiver, but did not cringe or even break eye contact, standing stock-still for an extra mettle-proving moment until she spun away and, striding toward the Hummer, said, "Get me the fuck out of this zoo."

With a parting wave to the assembly, Biggs hurried around the steel monster, closed the driver's door with a solid slam and, with a choking diesel roar and his new-found mastery of the transmission, exited in a graceful slalom that threw a demonstrative roostertail and showered his audience with more than a few bits of partially-composted woodland matter.

"Just what I needed," Junie said, for pretty much all of it seemed to have magnetized itself to her hair. She picked at this latest insult, waited for the rest of the staff to retreat to a decent distance, and watched David.

"Wow," he said, when he turned back from the trailing dust on the road, "She's *tough*."

Junie smiled. "You want to know tough?"

David smiled back, and then, as her expression remained unchanged, thought, Uh-oh.

She nodded, slowly, then said, "We'd better get these kids back home."

David gratefully agreed.

"WHAT ABOUT HOWIE?" Nancy asked, from the cramped back seat of Junie's convertible.

"We left him in that little town by the reservoir – we'll pick him up on our way through." Quinn stretched his beefy legs and examined the proliferation of runs that laddered, ankle to thigh, up and down his panty hose. All those internet hours to find Midnight Smoke in a Plus Plus size, and now they were ruined, totally. Frowning, he watched two sets of red taillights glow diffusely and then dim, as David's Civic and Oz's Luxmobile descended into the fog.

"Maybe he's not there anymore," Nancy said.

Junie thought of Howie – or a Howie-shaped wisp of fog – floating between the trees in that upper valley, floating as she'd rushed up the ledge to David. She studied Nancy in the rear-view mirror and asked, "Where would he go?"

"Without a car? From Ned? Nowhere." Nancy met her eyes, then looked away.

There was something about the way Nancy had said that;

something Nancy also might have seen. Junie shrugged and returned to easing Rosie down the rough and rutted mountain road.

THE CABIN DOOR was open, the sun bright again outside, the fireplace blazing within. Howie squatted in his robes, feeding the recovered contract, one page after another, to the flames. Snatched from the air and now returning to it. Always the balance: on one hand, carbon and unneeded heat; on the other, scattered papers littering this otherwise unmarred valley. In this case, he decided, pure aesthetics won. Although, in all cases, impact of some sort was unavoidable. Life was damage, his teacher had once said – an accumulation of metabolic insults to the pure, unmarked *soma* of the infant. Evidence of adulthood, evidence of having lived. Every act of living an act of dying.

And with that internal damage came similar external impacts – starting with the simple act of breathing, the generation of carbon dioxide – on the surrounding world. But with harmony, with care and consideration, the damages of both sorts could be minimized in tandem. Less damage to the world, less damage from it – health reflected, within and without; the subtle and manifold rewards of maintaining a healthy planet.

Corpore sano in sanus orbus. Howie extinguished the fire with a cold but not unkind glance, then walked out, the door closing itself behind him. In the dimness that remained within, the waxed spruce planks' daily accumulation of dust remained unmarked by his passing.

Outside, the smoke above the cabin coalesced to a single coal-like chunk of carbon, which fell to rattle down the shingles, along the peeling gutter, and down the drainpipe to enrich the sandy dirt. One way to minimize, Howie thought – all things, all damaged things returning to the soil. He pulled up a muslin sleeve and, angling his wrist to the north, consulted his sundial watch. Time, like energy and even mass, was immaterial. And there was plenty of it for him to arrive in Nederland before the others.

As Junie drove back through the mountain town, Quinn adjusted his floral headscarf and watched, with the anxiety of any ex-near-prisoner, for the State Trooper that had detained them on the way up. There – the blue-and-silver emblazoned SUV parked tail-in in front of the Shining Star I. Junie saw it too and slowed as Howie, robes gathered around him, stepped outside.

A State Trooper emerged, clapped Howie on the back, and looked in the direction of Oz's receding vehicle; by the time Quinn scrunched forward to let Howie in, the trooper's SUV was gone.

"I am pleased to find all of you intact." Soft brown eyes traveled from Quinn to Junie to Nancy at his side. "I trust that a most successful outcome has transpired?"

"Yes, it has 'transpired'," Quinn grumbled, then cranked to face the rear, his rayon dress stretched near breaking. "Just where are you from, partner?"

"Ah. The cadence of my speech. My origin lies in the Far East, my friend."

"The Far East? Please. I've broken bread with Six-Pak and the Dollster." A quick aside to Nancy: "The bigger they are, they more they love the nicknames."

An understanding nod. "The Far East, good Quinn, of the Western Half of the Long Island. What you hear is the music of my people."

"Your people? But you sound... I mean... if you're from..."

"My *chosen* people," Howie added, with a gentle smile.

"But..." Quinn gave up, flummoxed, as they passed an irradiating display of flashing lights beside the dam below the town. The State Trooper, nylon jacket collar up around his ears, was interrogating a shivering Oz in the mist.

Despite a small but whistling perforation in the rear of Rosie's vinyl top, the air was close in the overheated convertible. Quinn smelled sour from struggle and exertion, as did Nancy and probably her as well. But from Howie's corner came green juniper and pine, cold clean air, and a trace of exactly the same rich dark scent of last night's roaring fireplace in the cabin.

"*TWO* TICKETS," Oz moaned. "One for my car and one for yours."

"I tried to stop," David said. "The trooper waved me on."

"That's what I thought. And told him. So he nailed me with the points for both of us."

"I'll make it up to you."

"Great." He swept his arm to encompass the Forever Clinic, empty save those who showed up – including David, by special request – for the emergency Sunday evening staff meeting. "Do it by coming back."

"Not and pitch those hormones."

"Is there any other way?"

"I don't know of one," David said, watching Adeline and Thomas Thinna console themselves with tepid cups of medicinal tea – warm not hot, mustn't bruise the herbs – behind the reception counter. "I wish I could do it for you, Oz."

"So does Biggs."

"Tell me about it." David sagged down to the leather couch and rubbed a sore elbow.

Oz leaned over, lowered his voice. "You heard about his backers?"

Junie, facing away but obviously listening, snorted. "What? The hip-hop backers? He tried that on me in New Orleans."

"You mean he didn't...?" Oz shut his mouth, too late.

"Take their money? Of course. But the only thing Biggs is afraid of is his wife – and from what I've heard, for good reason." Junie paused, remembering a Crescent City hotel room, dawn light on an ashen Biggs, squawking telephone in his hand; Junie had never learned how his wife had found out. "Whatever he did, whatever he owes her, she's hot for him to buy her a place in Beverly Hills."

"Well," David began, "who wouldn't want to leave—"

"Sherman Oaks?" Junie dropped onto the couch, not too close. "That's where they live, the whitest part of the Valley. Not Compton, not South Central, not whatever crock he told you."

"Oh."

"Supposedly," she added, "the Hills have better schools."

"Absolutely," said Oz. "Dr. Biggs told *me* about the Sherman Oaks schools, and I entirely understand."

She peered up at him. "He didn't sell you the busing thing, did he? How they had to buy up because of that?"

Oz turned away, fat cheeks glowing above a closely-trimmed beard.

"They haven't bused kids in decades." Sometimes, she guessed, you *can* shit a shitter. Even play an ethnic card on an ethnic player.

David looked from Junie to the back of Oz's sport coat. "Biggs didn't say anything about schools."

She stretched over and patted his hand. "He didn't need to, David. He had you with the rappers. "

David heard her tone and didn't mind – she was right. Besides, he liked the feel of her hand, warm on his. A warmth she pulled away as Oz finished his close examination of the far wall, turned back and asked, "Where're the other two? It's a quarter after."

He was answered by a mechanical creak from above, as the huge glass skylight began to lever open, twin electric motors humming, revealing a bright sliver of moon in a navy sky.

"No!" a distant, panicked voice came through the opening. "I'm not doing it. No matter what you say."

"But it is like your Walk With Me fire walk experience, my dear Quinn." The second voice was Howie's, speaking calmly. "A fear one must pass through to know there is none."

"That was different – those were clients, and they *paid* for it."

"You may pay; it would be amusing if you pay."

"I'll *amuse* you..."

David and Junie stood and all of them listened, craning up to see. Absently, Thomas reached to rub Adeline's birdlike neck; she reached reciprocally to his, bony elbows nestling below winged shoulder blades.

"My friend, you will place one foot *here*." Howie's voice was subtly firmer. "And the other *here*."

Surprisingly, there was no answering protest, only the sound of another electric motor, larger and straining, as a tall white hydraulic arm moved into view. David remembered its outline – for window-washing, he'd figured – from the park that day with Junie.

And then, swinging out of the shadows and into the penumbra of the clinic's low-energy lights, came the ghastly sight of Quinn's razor-burned legs. It was the same view as that first interview in

David's office, although this time, unfortunately, without benefit of jockey shorts. They were sturdy but pale and trembling, wrapped in a fluttering white terrycloth robe, and ended in a pair of ruby-red pumps that were jammed and twisted, toe-over-toe, into the narrow eyehole of a cast-steel hook.

The hydraulic apparatus came to a halt, the suddenness of which swung Quinn, a man of undisputable momentum, in a stately if terrified loop, spiraling downward as the motor, now grinding in reverse, began to let the cable out.

By the time Quinn cleared the skylight he was swinging his linebacker's backside with a maniacal grin, whistling around the room as steel hook descended to the level of their heads. The Thinnas squawked and crawled beside the counter, Junie ducked, and Oz dove for the couch cushion vacated by David, who stood and grabbed the cable. This whipped Quinn close and closer, leaning back like Biggs on the cliff, his centrifugal mass dragging David's feet, the prayer carpet David happened to be standing on, and ultimately Junie and the Thinnas and even Oz in a sliding group circuit of the polished floor before swiveling to a stop in the center of the room.

Quinn hopped off the hook as the Thinnas peeled themselves from David. From directly above their heads came a flash of white robes – Junie and David looked up again, each wondering what they might or might not have seen on the mountain – to find Howie spinning down the now-perpendicular cable, braided steel sliding smooth between bare feet and hands.

"Holy fucking *deus ex machina*," Oz said, and Junie snorted – not David's favorite sound, but he figured he could get used to it.

Once Howie touched down, Quinn immediately enclosed him in a bear hug, then partially unwound to leave an arm over Howie's thin shoulders. His bathrobe unfortunately unfurled to reveal a hairy belly and even furrier points south. As David tried to pinch a painful metal fiber from his palm – unlike Howie's palms, which seemed completely uninjured – everyone else stared at the couple in white.

"What?" Quinn stared back, for once innocent. "There's a *hot tub* up there." Then yanked his bathrobe closed and tied it.

Behind him, David heard a tap at one of the door-sized windows at the end of the room. It was the one, in fact, that provided egress to the fire escape at the rear of the building. In the dim light he saw Nancy, wrapped tight in a matching bathrobe, wet hair hanging close around a face that gave nothing away.

"Nancy," he said, opening the glass.

"David," she allowed, walking by.

Back in the middle of things, Quinn held his other arm out and said, "Baby."

That stopped Nancy in mid-stride, Oz and Junie and the Thinnas now staring from both sides. Slowly, Quinn dropped his arm, after which she nodded, then crossed over and put her arm around his substantial waist.

"But aren't you...?" Junie started, more than familiar with Quinn's old headlines.

"Only sometimes," Quinn said, happily. "I'm an equal opportunity kind of gal."

"But Nancy—" Oz added, before Nancy's blazing glare cut him off.

"I'm not a sexist," she said definitively, pulling him closer with a possessive tug. "Quinn happens to be *my* kind of gal, equal opportunity or not."

"But all *three* of...?" The Thinnas chimed together, both thoroughly confused.

Howie gave a modest smile, easily lifted Quinn's beefy arm off his shoulders, and took a lateral step away. "That was not indeed the case, but I thank you for your kind assumption. I was meditating in my private studio when our two associates graced my terrace with their company."

His terrace, David thought, looking up through the skylight. His terrace and his studio. The other structure he'd seen from the park that day, low and plain and hidden from the street. A mini-penthouse, and Howie had somehow managed to rent it without any of them knowing. The International Guru of Mystery strikes again.

David heard a faint rattle from the fire escape, turned back, and registered an outline in the darkness, dressed in Ninja black but topped with silver in the moonlight. She held her shoes in one hand, her feet indented by the outdoor stairway's serrated metal grid as she padded down the fire escape. Pain, David knew, was nothing to Paula.

She stopped on the other side of the glass but ignored him,

raising a hand, instead, to Howie, who tilted his head in acknow-
ledgement – though not enough that the others, still facing the center
of the room, would notice. On her face was a look that David had
never seen... Paula, satiated. Like all her looks, it was kind of scary.
David sighed, relieved, as she continued down to the parking lot in
back.

Oz had left the show to join David at the window, and seemed
dangerously close to proposing another difficult-to-refuse
opportunity when they heard the heavy slam of a car door, the thrum
of a diesel motor, and saw a gleaming pseudo-military vehicle ease
out into the throat of the alley.

"Curiouser and curiouser," Oz said. "Where do you think *they're*
off to?"

"Probably to hook up with someone else," David answered.
"That Reverend in the Springs?" Then thought of his primary care
compatriots in town, all of whom were undoubtedly good and
honest and ethical, but also, probably, having no easier economic
time that he'd had. "Or another local doc."

"He'd better not."

As Oz watched the Hummer turn onto Broadway, David looked
at his friend's reflection, wondering.

Oz put a hand on his shoulder. "Don't worry," he said, glancing
back to Junie and the others. "You'll be the first to know."

WELL, MAYBE NOT THE FIRST. But David would not discover that until
he passed his second post-cabin night in Boulder, laying on a cheap
new mattress in his now-sanitized apartment and breathing the
lingering trace of skunk, a funky undernote to the eye-stinging
chemicals the management had used to deodorize the carpet. As he
watched the lights of Thirtieth Street bounce off the ceiling, he
thought of Junie, a single mile away. Hopefully, she was doing the
same – thinking of him, feeling the same drawing cord of connection,
an immaterial line that stretched out the window, soared between the
streetlights, and arced like an attenuated umbilicus through the
midnight sky.

And she was, almost. Not experiencing the mattress or the fumes or the moving lights on the ceiling – her cabin being too far into Chautauqua for vehicular illumination – but thinking of David, of a life that was not going to be as planned, and the parts of the old life that, with luck, she could salvage and still have this new life she wanted. Thinking of him, and pulled by that same cord, almost but not quite to the point of throwing on her clothes, driving a cranky cold Rosie down through the sleepy residential blocks, passing by wandering dazed students and under blinking red traffic lights to slide in beside that body who had so recently warmed her through and through, slide beside and seal the deal.

Soon enough they slept – burdened with yearning but also with sufficient exhaustion to close their eyes against their needs. Each entering a velvety unaware state, as free of dreams as the night before, their initial post-cabin night, in which both Junie's and David's poor overloaded brains had been far too tired to wander. But tonight, as they tunneled down below the constraining physical world into the lyric, as fatigue faded but that yearning only strengthened, our two dreamers were rudely sent flying from their beds, out their windows and across the black sky on that tight-stretched cord, snapping by each other and then back again, back and forth through a realm of possibilities, barely sensing the irrational machinations of one imagined future life before being yanked into another, in a endless succession of feared or hungered-for but always haunting scenarios that was terminated, finally, only by the songs of the morning birds, by the thrum of a small city climbing into gear, and by the searing projection of spindly branches and dangling leaves in trapezoidal patches of yellow sunlight on their respective walls.

AND THAT WAS JUST the intervening night. Before he would discover the newest iteration of Oz's plans – which resembled David's and Junie's dreams in both inconstancy of detail and constancy of desire – David would be summoned once more to the Clinic. This time it was an early-morning call from Adeline, who had apparently decided that, even though David had twisted the tourniquet on the financial life-blood of the Clinic's operation, he remained its true pumping heart, and that his absence was by no means noble but in fact disabling.

"Come in? But haven't all my patients been cancelled?"

"Well, we were going to..."

"We?"

"Sure. Mr. Garcia talked to me Friday – before, you know – and then he came over this morning when Tom and I were doing our stretches, which we always come in early for and I hope is okay because no one else is using the space, and anyway, what he said was that we should, no... that we *shouldn't* talk about... Uh-oh. You should probably come in."

"Adeline..."

"And tell Junie," she added, sounding eager to go.

"She's not there?"

"That's why *I'm* calling."

"But I don't know—"

"Where Junie is?" Now Adeline, an inveterate gossip when it came to co-workers, seemed to have all the time in the world. "Really?"

He didn't answer.

"Then I should try her... at home?"

"Yes." David sighed.

"Oh. Did you two have a—"

"No, we didn't have a fight, but—"

"Good!" she said brightly, and hung up.

THE FIRST THING David noticed was Quinn's pantsuit – a dull, medium gray wool number in a size, for once, that appeared large enough to fit. No flowers, no satin lining; it was, in fact, something David would expect Nancy to wear, if Nancy was a totally non-New-Age bank vice-president in Philadelphia. And it was easily the least flamboyant thing he'd ever seen Quinn in, including that black-maned and berobed appearance in front of the Family Medicine Academy, two years before.

The second thing was the nametag. David leaned forward and looked close – it appeared to have been glued together from two previous nametags, each with the same white plastic surface, each laser-cut with letters to reveal the darker layer beneath. The left half read DR. QUINN, that recent *nom de practice*, and on the right, McINTYRE, M.D. – the name abandoned, months ago, in his flight from the long arm of the Longhorn State.

"Well?" Quinn asked. "What do you think?"

"Very professional," David said, noncommittally.

"You really think so?" Quinn planted the polished leather toe of a size-twelve Mary Jane an performed a signature twirl.

"Absolutely. But I meant the badge."

Twisting his nametag up to examine it, Quinn frowned. "Think the seam's too obvious?"

"Not really, but now that you mention it... wasn't that last name thing supposed to be a secret?"

Nancy walked up and nudged Quinn over, their shoulders blocking the narrow corridor. "He's not afraid anymore."

David retreated a step. "That's good, but—"

"Not afraid of an oppressive, sexist justice system, and anyone who'd take advantage, unfair economic advantage, of his plight."

Junie arrived and stepped in front of him. "David didn't take—"

"*Plight*," Nancy repeated, crossing her arms, as Quinn shrugged beside her. "The plight of an expressive, creative, female soul trapped in a man's body... trapped in a seminar full of young men, and after they'd had their way with her—"

"It's definitely 'her'?" David just wanted to be sure.

Quinn looked noncommittal, but Nancy paused, fixed David with a squint, then said, "—*pursued* by a predominately male, white, conservative state police force, tradition-bound in the service of... in the service of..." She looked over at Quinn.

"The Man?" Quinn tried.

"The Man," Nancy nodded.

"I think that one was from Oz," Quinn told her.

She pinched his cheek between two knuckles, hard. "You would have thought of it, cupcake."

"Excuse me," Junie said, "'Unfair economic advantage'?"

"We're just trying it out," Quinn said, rubbing his face.

David looked perplexed. "This was Oz's idea?"

A moment of silence, until Quinn said, "Hey, buddy," and laid an oven-mitt hand on his shoulder. "It's only for the press. You know, so I can get my license and... stay here."

"*Only* for the press?" Nancy's squint was aimed at Quinn this time.

"Only halfway, peaches. The other half's all true, and you know I—"

"Wait a second," David interrupted, removing Quinn's hand. "You're the new *me*?"

Quinn had no answer; David stared, then slipped around Quinn and Nancy toward the hand-stitched black calfskin toes of a pair of regulation business wingtips he'd spotted protruding from his office door.

"David," Junie said, but he was turning in his door.

OZ HAD ALREADY RETREATED to the other side of David's desk, and was about to sit when he saw the slow shake of his old and hopefully current friend's head.

"Okay, okay." Oz went round the other side, keeping the desk between them, to squeeze between the arms of the room's other chair. "It's not what you think."

"I was trying to tell him," Quinn's voice came from the open doorway, where he stood flanked by Nancy and now the Thinnas, their pinched faces curious; Junie leaned against the wall across the corridor and closed her eyes. David reached back, shut the door firmly, then sat on the edge of his desk, facing Oz.

"*First to know*," he said, frowning.

"Excuse me?" Oz shifted on the padded fabric seat.

"Yesterday – you told me I'd be the first to know."

"Oh, that." Oz found himself starting to get comfortable. "I might have stretched that a bit."

"How do you stretch '*first*', Oz?"

"Hmmm. First person in the room? Other than me, of course."

David didn't look happy.

"Okay, how about 'first medical person'? No, can't say that – Quinn's a real doc again." He admired his new wingtips, swinging the tips from side to side, legs straight and heels planted on the carpet. "Is he a family doc? Quinn isn't, is he?"

David breathed in and then out, even and slow.

"Good – then you're the first *family* doctor to know. First to be informed in our Family Practice Department."

"*What* Family Practice Department?"

"I like to think of it as Oz Enterprises' Family Practice Department. Though formally, the name is GBK. The entity that *used* to be known…" He pulled a dog-eared contact from the briefcase beside him. "…as Garcia and Black. Until you decided to bail."

"So you're asking me to stay, but not as management."

"You don't want to be management; you've made that very clear."

"Who *is* management?"

Oz held up three fingers. "G, Garcia. B, Biggs—"

"Looks like I got it right on Friday," David said, pushing off the desk. "I'm out of here."

"Okay… but if you go, Biggs does too. You're the condition."

David stopped. "I appreciate that. But it just brings us back to last week again. I told you I won't write prescriptions for that stuff."

"You don't have to – we're got another doctor, a new clinic in East Boulder." Oz glanced at the door.

Quinn, David thought.

"A brand new, satellite clinic," Oz continued. "The Ever Better Clinic? I'm not sure. In any case, it won't have anything to do with you. As for Biggs, he says it's personal – if this isn't good enough for you, he's gone. If it is good enough, he'd like to drop in when he's in town and crack some backs."

David slowly shook his head, then asked, "Who's 'K'?"

"K's the landlord. Owns professional properties all over the West. Remember this building's 'mystery partner', the one that didn't sell his half?"

"The one you never met."

"The one I *thought* I never met. You probably didn't think so, either."

"I've met him?" David crossed his arms.

"*Deus ex machina*, pal."

"You said that when… Wait a second… *Howie*?"

"K for Krishna. He likes our operation. Likes your operation, in fact. Only one problem…"

"Another problem? Poor Oz."

"He's also a conditional partner," Oz said, ignoring him. "Same deal: you need to stay for at least a year. No growth hormone, but everything else is the same."

"It all depends on me?"

"It always did. Oh, and Junie." Oz craned his neck and called out her name, then added, "She's got to stick around, too."

The door opened; Junie slipped through and closed it behind her. A look, apologetic, and then, "Oz called me this morning – after Adeline told him I wasn't at your place. Begged me to let him and Quinn run it by you first. I tried you anyway, but…"

"I was driving down, didn't answer my cell."

"Safety first," she said.

He ignored that. "You'd do this?"

She shrugged. "Depends on who I'm working with."

David turned back to Oz, who said, "What's not to like? Quinn will operate across town, and I'll be out of your hair, not to mention Junie's, getting the other clinic up and running. Me and Biggs – he even hooked in this retired physiology professor from the university, to do the data thing, give it that gloss of science. You know him well: it's Dr. Flint, your patient."

David met Junie's eyes – Junie, who only watched him, waiting – and crooked a smile.

Oz sat up. "You'll do it?"

"Maybe…" He rubbed his jaw, realized he hadn't shaved since getting Adeline's call. "It just doesn't seem, well, right."

"Not that again." Oz made a face. "The firewalls are in place, David. You may not like what Quinn's writing prescriptions for, but it's legal, and has nothing to do with you. You decided what you want, great. But you don't get to call the shots for everybody."

David's desk phone emitted a long, low, and previously unfamiliar chime. An unlabeled plastic button at the bottom of the row was blinking; he reached by Oz and picked the handset up.

"I have merely one question," a voice said.

"Okay…" They were staring at him. David mouthed 'Howie'; Oz did not look surprised.

"What, my friend, is wrong with freedom?"

"Freedom. As in, freedom to vote?"

"In a way, but no politics. No, no, never politics." Howie's voice dropped. "We are talking, Dr. David, of human choice. Something that you have recently had experience with – experience on high."

Choice. Biggs and the cliff. And one very strange hallucination. David stared at the handset, then returned it to his ear. "I might not be the one actually prescribing the stuff, but the organization, the risk..."

"Risk is unavoidable," Howie said, "Except in that perfect, stable state: in death. And death is your enemy, is it not?"

"No – I mean, yes, but... dammit, how can patients really know the risk they take? Even an antibiotic, an aspirin – the list of side effects, of adverse consequences is almost too much to explain. And if a simple oral medication's that tough..."

"Our good Quinn is not devoid of conscience, despite his many charming affectations. He will see that the fine print is read, and read closely. What I am saying, my friend, is that life is in itself risk. In choosing one we do not choose another, but all of them must lead eventually to damage. As you well know, metabolism is decay."

"I know," David said, closing his eyes. "But later is better than sooner."

"Admittedly, yes. You proceed directly to the heart of the matter, as always. Minimize metabolism, as the Thinnas do with their diet. Or minimize the more egregious risks, that beastly smoking and the like. But all of them? Would you deny that change implies risk, that choice itself leads inevitably to risk; would you deny that in your own life?"

Biggs' hand, his own hand reaching for it, arms grinding into the ice-glazed stone. David looked from Oz to Junie, the arc of his past months. "No."

Oz heard the word and groaned, pulled in his wingtips and hung his head over them. Junie, however, studied David.

"Excellent," Howie said. "A wise man does not fear foolishness. Then our grand adventure will proceed?"

David met Junie's eyes again. "Yes."

Oz's head shot up, fingers smoothing his comb-over back in place.

"And Paula?" David asked.

"Ah. She may need to return, for private spiritual consultation. But not to the clinic, I agree – that would be foolishness indeed."

With that, Howie signed off, but David kept the silent handset to his ear and said, "Ms. Blanche makes her own deal." Meeting his oldest friend's instantly calculating gaze, he added, "But I won't stay unless you pay what she asks," and returned the receiver to its plastic cradle.

WHISPERS AND SHUFFLES could be heard from the hallway as David stepped to the door; Oz was huddling with Junie, pen to paper, as he swung it open.

"Group hug!" the Thinnas chorused; Nancy rolled her eyes but Quinn didn't seem to mind, even got David and the rest of them a good six inches off the ground in an ursine grapple.

After that, it was off to the waiting room to dispose of the many glossy HorTech marketing materials – vaguely titillating anatomic-transparency pamphlets, pheromone-impregnated tri-folds, holographic before-and-after condoms, and logo-bearing reading glasses – from every shelf, desktop, and ceramic toilet-tank cover on which Biggs and Paula had secreted them for display.

FIVE MINUTES LATER, as David discretely added two full teaspoons of sugar to a caustically bitter cup of medicinal tea and hoped the Thinnas wouldn't notice, Quinn, also discretely, grabbed the wastebasket where the publicity materials had landed.

Holding it close, he tip-toed towards his office, hoping to shield it with his bulk. Halfway along the corridor, however, he bumped into Junie on her way out of David's office, contract in hand. Oz followed her, looking poorer but not impoverished. As he squeezed by, she looked down at his stash and asked, "Mother Nature's way?"

He held the wastebasket closer. "Hormones are nature too, you know."

"They weren't so natural a few weeks ago. Or have you forgotten?"

"Give me a break – I was on my high horse."

She shook her head. "And now?"

"Now I'm being reasonable. The truly desperate are going to get it somewhere; this way I can take care of them, keep them out of trouble. A little muscle, a little hope, and – who knows? – the stuff could work. That'd be good, wouldn't it?"

Junie's gaze didn't shift.

"Shit." Quinn sagged against the wheat-grass wall, still holding the wastebasket. "Look – I'm a provider: I like to provide. Besides, pills are fun."

"Now I *really* respect you. And injections?"

"Even funner, according to some."

"Great." But she had to smile. Looking down the corridor, she could see that the morning's patients had begun to arrive. "Finish this later?"

"Lunch with Oz, for me. But they're talking about something after work."

"I'll be holding my breath, girl." Junie pinched his cheek, hard, nailing the same spot Nancy had. Then listened, amused, to his ear-blistering retreat.

THE UR-BAR, seven in the evening. The first stars were breaking out above, but to the west a lemon-yellow cloud floated over the Flatirons, opalescent in the sunset light.

Inside, there'd been another makeover, another struggle against the inexorable economic pull that seemed to suck every iteration of the bar toward the hidden graveyard in the basement. This week, the long dark space was graced by a glitterball, Bee Gees on the stereo, a fog machine – as if David ever needed to see fog again – and awful but iconic posters of big-haired actresses and posing eighties rock groups tacked at rec-room angles on the walls. But the scarred wood bar was the same, as well as the big booth at the back where he and Junie sat, waiting for the others to arrive.

Through the light-streaked gloom he saw a couple enter the bar. "Oh, no," he said, sinking low on the vinyl. "It's Sheyoni and Don."

"So? I thought you had to apologize to him for something."

"I told you that?"

"Early Saturday morning, ten thousand feet, a freezing rock-walled bedroom? Maybe you were asleep."

"But not dreaming," David muttered.

"What's that?"

"Nothing. In any case, you're right. And here they come."

"Uh-oh. I'll give you a minute." Junie got up and turned toward the bathroom.

"Wait—"

"You're divorced, David. New lives for all concerned. Trust me, she won't hurt you."

Trust you, David thought. And discovered that he did. Meanwhile, Don was sliding in across from him, Sheyoni still standing in the aisle.

"DON," David started. "Weren't you in the waiting room today? I was running by between meetings."

"I didn't see you," Don said, flatly.

"I know they had you scheduled for, um, well… Sorry I couldn't come over."

A pause, a slow exhalation, a level look. "Same here."

Don seemed even more upset than David had expected. Good thing he *hadn't* said hello. Still, David willed himself to sit up straight, look Don in the eye and say, "I owe you an apology."

"I'll say." Don's knuckles were stretched white, his furzy-haired forearms pumped to Popeye size – guess the stuff was *working* – as he kneaded a handful of bar napkins. Discarding the twisted wad, he pushed David's and Junie's beers along the narrow booth table, toward the wall and out of the way.

Wow. Don seemed really pissed – face red, temples throbbing, the whole deal. And with his blood pressure… it might be good to let emotions out, but you could blow an artery while you're doing it. Still, David figured it was best to get it over with, now. David clasped his hands before him, and said, "I'm sorry, Don, but I can't continue your injections."

"Big deal. I switched over to Quinn McIntyre. Women are better, anyway: it takes a woman, a *woman* doctor, to understand a man." A challenging glare across the Formica, interrupted only by a glance to Sheyoni, who nodded. Not that David had expected any help from her quarter.

In five years of practice, he'd never seen a terminated patient take it so hard. "Look," David said, "every doctor has a different approach—"

"A different *approach*?"

"—and I couldn't, in good conscience—"

"In good *conscience*?"

"In good conscience, of course... um... where was I?" How, he wondered, could he manage Don's disappointment if Don repeated everything he said?

Don's jaw worked, fingers tearing the napkins into ever-tinier shreds. "You think about that while I tell you where I was today."

"Okay," David said, agreeably.

"Shut up and listen."

"You don't have to be rude." Politeness, David felt, was an essential part of every doctor-patient relationship, terminated or not.

Don put his hands flat on the tabletop. "I was in the library. The *medical* library."

"Did some research at the hospital? Good. Then you probably know why I can't give you the hormone anymore."

"This... is... not... about... the... *injections*."

"Oh." David sat back. Don's reaction was completely off the charts. Was it the way he'd ridden him about his blood pressure? The flip-flop with closing the practice? Or maybe, maybe...

"The funny thing was," Don said, eyes drilling into David's, "The funny thing was, I couldn't find out anything about it."

"About... what?" David asked, remembering just why Don might be upset.

"IF P."

"I... F... P?" Remembering, and wishing very much that he was elsewhere.

"You know," Don said, his new deltoids, pecs and lats bunching beneath a soft hemp pullover.

"I do?"

"Oh, yeah," Don said quietly, leaning close and gesturing for David to come closer. Almost involuntarily, David did, as Don added, "It stands for..."

David was about to hazard a guess but Don beat him to it, spittle flying as he screamed, "INTRAPUSTULAR!"

Happily, David was able to get his shoulder up before Don's closed fist connected with the side of David's face.

It wasn't too bad, considering those bunched muscles; David let himself be thrown sideways and, in the interests of a peaceful resolution, dropped below the level of the booth's table, laying on the bench as Don crawled over the Formica, shaking out a stinging fifty-nine-year-old right hand.

David raised both of his in surrender, but Don wasn't interested in a truce, instead switching to his left, going with an open palm this time as he wildly hooted "FIDELO!", and delivered a resounding slap to one of his reclining victim's raised forearms.

David considered whacking him back, but Don was a patient, after all. Plus he knew he had it coming. Of course, Oz was the one who really had it coming – he'd started the whole thing – but that thought was soon extinguished by Sheyoni, leaning into view with a delighted and rather evil smile. Standing behind Don, she displayed a multi-carat engagement ring that flashed blindingly in a passing beam of glitterball light.

By the time David recovered from that, Don had made it fully over and was standing, if unsteadily, on the padded vinyl bench between David's sprawled legs. Eyes wide, David struggled to sit up as Don raised a hemp sneaker-clad foot, took aim on David's undefended crotch and triumphantly howled "—PENIA!"

Sheyoni, who'd heard Don's crazy story and had been thinking quite a bit about personal injury lawsuits, now came to her senses and grabbed Don's ankle, hoping to bring it harmlessly back to the seat. Instead, it sent her new beau crashing onto David – who, understandably unnerved and still impeded by the tabletop, watched Don's enraged face first grow rapidly larger and then, as that gnarly middle-aged body walloped onto him, slam into the padded vinyl beside his ear.

"It spelth IFP, you... you... muthamuker!" Don's voice was muffled, jammed into the lint-filled gutter between the bench's seat and back. The tip of his frizzy ponytail had been flung sideways into David's open mouth, and David sputtered it out – the combination of residual hemp shampoo and conditioner tasted terrible. It traced an itchy wet trail down his chin as Sheyoni dragged Don off him by both feet.

Don was struggling to get his arms up, with a clear design to go for David's throat, but was still trapped, as was David, by the bench's close confinement, and so could only rant, "IFP! Eye-fucking-Eff-Pee! But try to find it in a fucking textbook, or fucking online—"

His fury was more than impressive, especially to Sheyoni, even if it was vented, sequentially, into the rumpled folds of David's flannel shirt, the crotch of his jeans – which was really a little too personal – and finally the ancient vinyl as Don finished with, "—or in *any* fucking medical reference on the fucking planet!"

By the time the bartender had found his baseball bat and was heading their way behind the bar, Sheyoni had pulled Don to his feet. Nails digging into one hypertrophied biceps, she walked him in the opposite direction along the occupied barstools, the long row of interested but pointedly uninvolved occupants leaning forward to avoid his shouts and spittle. The bartender stopped midway, tracking the two with an appraising fisheye as they passed. Don, still twisted towards the back booth, hurtled a diminishing and increasingly repetitive series of curses.

Sheyoni – whose thoughts of lawsuits evaporated when she realized how David's lie, in the end, had completely sealed her deal with Don – pushed her fiancé into the street, but then paused and, with a wink, held up that ring again, its megawattage diamond still painfully refractile even through the artificial fog.

DAVID was looking blankly in the direction of the bar's glass door when Junie returned, slid in beside him, and asked, "IFP?"

He focused, then frowned. "You heard?"

"Overheard."

"You didn't come out," he said, as she reached in front of him to retrieve their miraculously unspilled beers.

"You're a big boy."

He nodded, drained his glass, and sat back against the seat.

Junie waited a beat, then asked, "So...?"

"You don't want to know."

A secret, Junie thought. Actually, she liked that.

After a moment's silence, David added, "What was it you said? About trusting you, and how she wouldn't hurt me?"

An answering smile. "Did *she* touch you?"

He considered. "No."

"Good. Keep it that way."

David looked at her, then at his empty glass and shook his head. She tried to hang an elegant dark arm over his shoulders but, even sitting, he was too tall. He slid down to make it work, then reached up across his chest to hold her fingers in his.

WAYNE watched the hoopla settle down, as the bartender returned to washing glasses, the bar's usual denizens re-attended their drinks, and a few of the more unusual ones headed toward the couple in the back. Jeremiah, meanwhile, had hardly seemed to notice – bar fights hadn't been news in their neck of the woods. No, his cowboy pal was lost in thought, dragging a broad and broke-nail fingertip through the wet rings on their booth's tabletop, until he frowned and said, "I'm thinking we should."

"Should what?" Wayne asked, staring at his friend's uncharacteristically unfinished beer.

"Santa Fe," Jeremiah said, pushing it over. "Remember?"

"Santa Fe. Really? I was starting to like this town. Weird, but no weirder than this place, and we keep coming back." Down below their feet – below the floor, below the stacks of varnished cowboy boots, the folded gingham vinyl tablecloths, dusty fern pots, panels of fake book spines and all the other cast-off props, and especially below the basement's reinforced concrete – a grin more skull-like than even Dr. Flint's cracked the red-gray alluvial silt that encased it.

"Weird's okay, but this is *different* weird. Just look." Jeremiah tilted his head towards the far booth, the odd crowd now gathered around it.

"I'm looking," Wayne said. "They're having fun; friends, or maybe they work together. All different types, mixing it up."

"That's what I mean."

"What's the matter with that? Some of them are even items."

"Who's an item?" Jeremiah turned full round, peering through the mirror-ball haze.

"Hey," Wayne laid his fingers on Jeremiah's forearm. "Don't be obvious."

"Maybe those skinny two," Jeremiah said, still peering. "I can see that. Though they should be home, not out drinking."

"They're still an item. Them and the ones that started it." Small and big and black and white, but they seemed to fit all right.

"If you say so." Jeremiah frowned.

"Plus the two squeezed in beside them." Couldn't Jer see anything?

"That Jezebel I pushed back on her stool the other night? The one with her hands all over that other *woman*?"

Wayne decided to let that one pass.

"Gals like that should have their own bar." Then looked at Wayne and said, "What?"

"You're unbelievable."

"Don't you talk to me like that, Wayne."

"I'm telling you, you're effing unbelievable."

"And *don't* you curse. You're as bad as that old guy, the one who made the scene." Jeremiah leaned forward on his elbows, western shirt cuffs stretching against their white-enameled snaps. "It's like, you know, out in the pastures. Not mixing the breeds. Your gay breeds, your straight breeds, what have you. It's... it's not *natural*. That's it – nature, nature's way: every kind of inclination has its own place."

"Their own bar to go to."

"You got it." Jeremiah nodded sagely.

"No, I don't got it. What I got is you're dead wrong. Mixing it up is good for people. Takes them out of their own heads, wakes them up a little. You could use some of that, you know."

"I could use a quiet evening at home."

"And you get that, we both do, get it when we need it. But we also need folks that are different, need to get knocked around a little, knock the corners off. You *need* to mix it up."

"Come on, Wayne."

"Don't act all hurt. Here – I don't want your beer. You finish it. And don't think everybody's after you. Ever since that darned cowboy romangedy..."

"*Ro-man-gedy?*"

"That's what the *Times* called it."

"It was one fine piece of cinema, and you better not start up against it."

"It was good, all right; can't argue with that. Made you cry, but worth it. Pretty rough going at the end, though."

Jeremiah studied his still-full beer. "You're dead right there, partner."

Wayne nodded, and then it hit him. "What if we made our *own* movie?"

Jeremiah looked up. "A Western?"

"Sure. But this time the good guys live, and everybody rides off happy. You know, into the sunset."

"I know they don't make that kind anymore."

"Why's that, you think?"

"Just the way folks are," Jeremiah said. "That's all it is, the way folks are. Want to get ridden hard, so beat up they forget what they been worrying about."

Wayne nodded. "Same as I said before. People need to get outside their own selves."

"Don't twist my words – we were talking about movies."

"Same deal; it's the *same darn* deal." Wayne reached under the table and grabbed Jeremiah's hand, grabbed it and held it so he wouldn't pull away. "We could write it together. The same, but different – different in a lot of ways. Like different kinds of folks going to a place like this, bumping up against each other and *not* getting into catfights."

"I'm telling you, nobody's going to go see some sweetheart movie. Not another one with only guys."

"Forget that. We don't have to go that way if we don't want to. Or we can, a little. You know, like I was saying: mix it up."

Jeremiah started to snap something back, but stopped himself, paused and squinted like he was looking through the wall and over the city, up the east side of the Divide, all the way past Lyons and even Laramie, up north to the windy plains behind the trailer he'd grown up in. "Maybe. It's not like you got to have a lot of gunplay, though that's fun. Just break their hearts a little. Remind them they're in there."

"See? You know what I'm talking about." Not letting Jer's grip go, Wayne looked deep, falling in, something that almost always worked. "You break their hearts and I'll mend them. With any luck they'll go home smarter."

"Wouldn't we have to head to... Hollywood?" Jeremiah looked worried.

"Maybe later... Naw, no way."

"Good," Jeremiah said, relieved. "From what I heard, Hollywood makes *this* look normal."

Behind him, sparks and the smell of ozone began to fill the rear of the room – the hard-looking gal giving the white-robed guy a shoulder rub as the rest of the crowded booth, acting kind of scared, leaned away. Wayne shrugged: it wasn't any stranger than your average branding party.

"Well... I guess," Jeremiah added, reluctance more for show than anything else.

"You guess the movie, or you guess staying?"

"I guess both."

"You mean it?" Wayne asked. "Cause I don't want to quit this place, not right now. Don't know why, but I can't. Just like I can't—"

Jeremiah started to pull away, eyes wide. "Don't say it, don't you dare—"

"—quit you."

"Aw, Wayne..."

23

THE MEANING OF DREAMS

- or -

Eterminal Cardiomegaly

A WINTER HAD PASSED, and then a spring and then a summer, but the seasons didn't matter in near-equatorial Phuket, where the monsoons hadn't hit, the blue bay stretched wide and placid, and lovely boys and girls – of age, of course; he always checked since Texas – strolled and smiled and sometimes lingered.

Quinn sighed and settled down into his hammock, one beefy forearm hooked over its woven edge and suspended in the air above the sand, fingertips tickled, ever so lightly, by the manicurial administrations of a lovely, doe-eyed specimen. Manicurial... or *woman*icurial? Not that every petty detail mattered. Still, he liked to think he maintained an eye for details, and strained to open one heavily-mascaraed lid. From deep within the weather-softened jute, he couldn't tell. Did it matter? Not to the mighty Quinn!

So far from home; so far from responsibility, the needy patients, the needy HorTech crew, the endless-if-paperless 'paperwork', the prayer-bonging cell phones... The real thing from the temple behind the swaying palms was much, much nicer: Bong... Bong... Bong... Even if, on closer listening, a large tropical insect seemed to be accompanying it: Bongzzzzz... Bongzzzzz... Bongzzzzz. An oddly familiar sound that, odder still, was apparently emanating from the sand beneath his hammock. Just about where he'd... left his macramé shoulder bag?

Holy Shiva's lingam, Batman!

Shooing his manicurist aside – a nicely sarong-filling lass, in fact, who gave an Asian *moue* of displeasure as Quinn's wet ruby nails headed for the sand – Quinn snatched at the bag, tumbled from the hammock and landed on his back, staring through knotted white string at a vibrating cell phone's green-glowing digits, a long international-looking series that ended with Nancy's mobile number.

Forget Shiva, Batman, and definitely forget the lingam – it was Kali, goddess of death, destroyer of fabulous vacations.

ON A FEATURELESS STREET of low office buildings in Burbank, Paula rolled her new and very expensive desk chair back, kicked off her new and very high heels, and swung her legs (encased, though not intentionally, in the same sheer smoke shade that Quinn favored) up to her new and very nice desktop. Just beyond her perfectly-turned ankles, two red lights blinked on the office landline – her new and very obsequious secretary, no doubt, telling her that Biggs was on hold, waiting. What did that French guy say? It's good to be king. Or partner. Or even... *boss*.

Maybe someday. For now, nearly equals, and it was good to be that. HGH was selling nicely, in Boulder and Omaha and points east, a business profit Biggs claimed the lion's share of. But Paula's future was secure – based on Biggs's slow dawning, in which he did the slow and Paula did the dawning, that women had more to spend than men did, and that they'd be happy to spend it on GuyLoreiLure.

THE VERY NEXT MORNING – early enough that his first patient was still being roomed, but not too early for the early-bird elderly – David called Dr. Flint. The voice that answered was even creakier than usual, though it might have been the speakerphones, David's voice bouncing off his closed French door while Flint's reverberated between, or so David imagined, the glass-fronted bookcases and low beams of an old professor's University Hill cottage.

"To what, may I ask, do I owe the honor of this intrusion?"

Crap. David could only come up with a particularly articulate, "Um..."

"My pathetic attempt at a joke, Dr. Black. Forgive me."

"Oh. Of course." But it was an intrusion, David knew, if a benign one. "I called to see, well... you didn't pick up your prescriptions this month."

"And you wondered...?"

David had the sense not to answer.

"Last month's pain meds were more than sufficient – for the rare patient, like myself, who prefers to stay awake. I'm really feeling rather fine. Better than ever, in fact."

David had his doubts, one being particularly worrisome. But if Flint planned an early exit, he'd hoard his prescriptions, not decline them. So David asked, "What's your secret, Dr. Flint?" – asked as both doctor and acolyte, both humoring a patient and ready to hear whatever the great man chose to pass along.

"Ah – my secret to long life and good health." A hacking cough, a gargling recovery, a panting pause, and then, "There are a few things."

"A list?" Maybe he *would* learn something.

"Calm yourself, Doctor. I'm not your girlfriend, with her 'Five-this' and 'Seven-that'."

David hadn't realized Flint was spending that much time with Junie, but only said, "I thought scientists loved lists."

"Not, shall we say, *mature* scientists – those who've learned how uncertain the world of theories can be. 'Five-this' can become 'Three-that', then nothing at all."

"But as you said, a few things have to matter – like diet, right?"

"Certainly. Not too much of any one thing, whether complex carbohydrate, fat – good fats, naturally – or protein. The data's also fair for a daily multi-vitamin, unless your patients are organic farmers. And yes," he sighed, "a supplement or two, tailored to individual risks and needs."

"And exercise, of course."

"Three hours a week, and not too hard, and fun."

"Fun?"

"If you want them to keep doing it. Exercise is supposed to reduce stress, not increase it. And don't forget medical care."

"I'm surprised to hear you say that."

"In moderation, once again. Even with prevention: lots of education, a scope or two, but no unnecessary body scans for lumps and bumps that don't need treatment. Which is not to say you shouldn't treat – blood pressure, cholesterol, diabetes – when a body needs it. We can talk all day about extending the *maximum* lifespan, but that's only for the few who'll make it past the century mark. The unsung glory is in getting the masses as close to that mark as possible."

"It all sounds, well… mundane."

"The basics are mundane by nature, Dr. Black. *Doing* them is the problem."

"Still… they're not exactly the way to live forever." Too late, he tried to bite the last word back; it wasn't one to use with a patient in Flint's condition.

"Forever?" Flint seemed entirely unoffended. "Forever is a dream-word, my young friend. Like infinity, eternity – the stuff of math and poetry, not of life. Live a hundred or a thousand years, *something* will take you down." A laugh, less bitter than resigned. "What matters is living; what matters is…"

"What?" David asked, leaning forward over his desk. Outside, the wind was building, buffeting the small square window above the exam table.

"A few *other* things. But don't listen to me; I'm just an old scientist, and they're too immaterial, attitudinal, relational. I'm not an expert when it comes to fairy dust."

David heard another fit of coughing, another recovery, another long and wheezing pause. "That's it," he said. "I'm coming over this afternoon."

"To wring those last puzzles out of me?"

"Please – you know why."

"Which is why I must decline. I know what I'm doing, doctor. You must not worry."

Worry. David had been wrestling with it since Flint began rolling back his meds a year ago. The truly surprising thing was how long Flint had lasted – as though there was one last important thing to do. Or maybe it was pure chance: like old soldiers said, you never hear the one that hits you.

Footsteps in the hall outside; his first patient should be ready. The wind shook the glass again, and David, even in the tightly sealed room, felt an errant chill – a chill that somehow threw him back to the Triad, to the reservoir, to that cloud-blown morning on the mountain, high above his life.

The wind would blow, then stop, and Flint might or might not be with them when it blew that hard again. A certain… uncertainty.

Something he could live with; something, he suspected, that was not that bad at all.

DON STOOD on the protruding lower balcony of his cliffside dream house, leaned carefully over the salt-resistant steel rail, and regarded the crashing waves below.

In... and out.

Smashing foam... then dark, encrusted rocks.

White... then black.

Life... then—

Stop it, he told himself, stop it now. There was absolutely no reason to go there. Absolutely none at all. His sixtieth hadn't been that bad – after all, between the supplements, the workouts, and the hair dye, he looked no more than forty. And felt no more than fifty – or, to be really, really honest, on the worst mornings, like this morning (rising with a groan, pre-vitamins and a full week out from his last injection in Boulder), fifty-three or four. Okay, okay: fifty-five.

But that was pretty good. A few weeks ago, Dr. Quinn, pinching Don's glutes to measure his body fat, told him he was only halfway there. Halfway back to youth, he'd said, with half a life to look forward to. One Hundred Twenty or Bust! Especially if he continued the doctor's hand-bottled formulation, tax-free if he paid cash right there in the exam room, a special discount Dr. Quinn liked to offer his best clients, as long as they wouldn't feel a need to mention it up front.

Maybe it was last night's birthday party. Totally romantic, servants sent home, guest list thrown away, leaving just the two more important players: Don, sharing his not-so-little chunk of Big Sur with Sheyoni... Sheyoni, with her radiating love, now unencumbered health, and elaborate indoor plans for the evening. Though a short nap, in retrospect, would have improved his performance even more. And what was with the sixty candles? Blowing them out would have sapped anyone's stamina. A good joke, though, the way they kept relighting themselves, burning lower and lower, the multicolored wax melting into the low-glycemic-index gluten-free hemp milk frosting.

All in all, he hadn't done so bad. His post-Yippiagra!™ headache had resolved, and the Pacific dawn was pretty, in a Nature kind of way. But then there were the waves. Big, then small, then small, then big again... kind of random. Which made him kind of... uncomfortable.

For some reason, Don thought of Sheyoni's favorite room, way off in the south wing of the ocean-bluff dwelling to his rear. The one she called the Family Room. He wasn't thinking of the thick-padded rug, the newest biggest photon plasma screen, or the amazing black leather massage reclining chair/bed, but the way the white-tiled walls kind of *gleamed* behind the Degas and the mood lighting – that, and the built-in drinks bar, especially the drinks bar, which was functional and convenient but sort of *too* functional, stainless steel and clinical-type faucets and those metal fittings on the wall, like the oxygen one, with its black rubber tube that could stretch to the recliner. Sheyoni said she wanted an Oxygen Lounge to recharge her metabolic batteries, and Don wanted her to have it, though after all the expense he wished she would use it, at least once.

Roll up the rug from the polished white linoleum floor, and you were left with something that looked very much like a hospital room. And maybe, subconsciously – although Don didn't give much credence to soft-headed notions like the subconscious – Sheyoni, in her infinite love and care, was thinking to the day, sixty years hence – Half a Lifetime! – when he might need it. Though it gave him the willies, and probably would until then.

White tiles, white linoleum... white foam, uprushing.

Black tubes, black bed... black rocks, the teeth of the sea.

That was it – that was why he'd thought of Sheyoni's favorite room. That and the way you couldn't know when the next slamming crest would come, or how deep the trough that followed. But you couldn't help trying, no matter how glum or pointless the pursuit. Don sagged down on his elbows, propped by the steel rail of the balcony, all that kept him from the drawing, sucking waves.

Wow. He needed to get back to Boulder, now. Back to business, to sales strategies and meetings, to supplements and injections and – although he was wasn't soft-headed enough to actually be aware of it – a metaphoric future held at bay. Just then, an entirely non-metaphoric presence materialized behind him, pushing him forward, pushing him toward the rail! He began to twist, but no, it was just Sheyoni, beneath baby-doll robe-and-nightie layers of chiffon, wrapping her warm arms around his waist, holding him still. While up against his back, those breasts, those wonderful spreading breasts – his last birthday gift to her, the deep-floating silicone not quite so warm or soft as flesh, but man, he had to be at least as proud of them as she was.

Which, he figured, as his pulse returned to normal, was what it's all about, right? Love, taking care of your partner. Like his taking care of her, giving her the breasts she needed. Or Sheyoni, who obviously wanted to take care of him.

A MURMUR OF JAZZ, accent lights shining down from the flocked black ceiling of the *Ur*-Bar's newest iteration, and Quinn and Howie, back at the long wood bar.

Quinn reviewed the empty shot glasses in front of him. Not enough. Not nearly enough. Of course he'd sped back from luscious Phuket to earnest Boulder, and of course he'd found that Nancy could not be appeased. It was entirely reasonable: if you'd loved me, she'd said, if you'd cherished me for who *I* am, you would have done the surgery. What she'd left out was who Quinn was – Thailand's temptations were simply too great. And a scalpel, no matter how skillful the green-scrub-wearing Thai artisan at its helm, was still an instrument of damage, from the sterile plastic handle to the shiny diamond blade. The whole sex-change thing seemed kind of sexist anyway, a capitulation to a world where penises, or lack thereof – Ouch! – defined everything. Why couldn't he be as feminine as he wanted, equipment be damned? As, after a veritable *opus delecti* of fabulous adventures, his equipment surely was.

The bartender was coming round again. Quinn pointed at the burly but not entirely unattractive young man, then at the semicircle of shot glasses. With considerably less reluctance than on Quinn's previous visits, the bartender shrugged, unscrewed the cap of a half-full liter of Diet Cola, and filled each to the brim. To Quinn's right, the corners of Howie's mouth raised ever so slightly, serenely if imperceptibly pleased.

Quinn, however, was still frowning as he studied the back booth in the bar's long mirror. Nancy was pressed up against her new distaff doppelganger, matched in age and close-cropped highlights and sturdy flannel, in low knowing laughter and the occasional piercing glance at Quinn's rayon-stretched backside. Like loves like, indeed. Still, the old Quinn, the famous Quinn, had always lectured that you needed to love yourself, best and first, and Nancy might have finally found a way. Plus her clone would do a way better job at those Thursday Book Club gender-issue discussions than Quinn, struggling and soprano, had ever been able to pull off.

The pair was partly hidden by the raptor spines and interwoven vine-like arms of the Thinnas, traitors to a man. Or woman. Which had been the problem. His loss of *their* affection was caused by nothing more than an innocent pinch – aimed at Adeline's behind (Flesh? Bone? He had to know!) but raising, it turned out, a nasty bruise on Thomas's. In quick retreat, Quinn had tried his reliable "Just keeping track of your body fat", but for once it hadn't worked. Two weeks, and not a sign of forgiveness.

At least Oz wasn't here. Like Nancy, the boss wasn't happy to learn that his employee's sex-reassignment therapy had not been surgical at all, but psychotherapeutic, as in a week of condom-clad role-playing with various good sports on a tropical beach. Worse, he'd said it was bound to lead to considerably more legal expense, as Quinn's alteration by the world's most prolific Dr. Snippy would have cinched any Boulder judge's sympathy, supported his claim of cross-sexual harassment by the Texas authorities, and greased re-licensure (not just in Colorado, but everywhere!) for life. But that dead cinch had come undone, and guess who'd get docked to pay the law firm's added hours? Quinn pondered another shot of Diet Cola, tilted his head and poured it down. Despite the ungodly profits he'd been generating for GBK Enterprises, he wouldn't be moving out of his garage-cum-cottage before spring.

A WHIRRING NOISE and a waist-high view: booths on the left, vinyl-topped oak stools looming on the right. Flint navigated between polywool fleece jackets, fake-fur vests, and vegan nylon ranger belts, eyes drooping as a bony finger worked the trackpad, shaking to a stop then swiveling to lurch forward again, weaving his way towards two familiar profiles. The wheelchair's autopilot, he knew, would have done a better job, but he wasn't ready to give up control quite yet.

WHAT, IN THE SMILING BUDDHA'S NAME, was that? Quinn looked over at Howie, whose stool had miraculously shifted a good two feet further down the bar. Between them, a pair of sharp crow eyes shone up from the shadows.

"Dr. Flint," Quinn said.

"Dr. Quinn," Flint croaked merrily, as his desiccated scalp gradually rose into the light. Once he had elevated to their level, the wheelchair's hydraulics shuddered to a halt, and its running lights assumed a blinking standby mode.

"Not Dr. Quinn, not anymore. Just 'Quinn'. Or Dr. McIntyre, if you must."

"Ah. I should have known. The immutable, rigidly consistent Dr. McIntyre. In thrall before the past, a willing victim to the force of history."

"More like the force of licensure."

Flint began to nod, then seemed to fall asleep, his head continuing its downward course... until he snapped upright, eyes wide. A flurry of skin flakes, accompanied by the last of his sparse hairs, floated gently, leaves in autumn, to the bar top. "Be that as it may," Flint said, unperturbed, "I still prefer 'Dr. Quinn'."

Quinn sucked in his cheeks and tossed his chestnut wig – surprisingly subtle, and purchased at the high point of Nancy's influence – back over his shoulders. Jane Seymour had nothing, absolutely *nothing* on him. "*Doctor* Quinn... Quinn Quinn, MD... Quinn Quinn, redux. You're right: I miss it."

"Right, not right – who cares? As of tonight, I'm retired."

"No more data juggling?" And hopefully, Quinn thought, no more midnight visits to pick though Quinn's charts.

"Not one more digit," Flint wheezed, then flipped up the wheelchair's control-studded armrest and pulled a packet of white papers from a hidden compartment. Tilting sideways to lever the packet up, he flopped it on the varnished wood. "My final publication."

Warily, Quinn touched the thick stack with a ruby sand-glazed fingernail, exerting just enough pressure to slide it partially around. *HGH: Prose and Cons.* "Looks dangerous."

"Innocent data, pure as driven snow. Every growth hormone patient, every clinic, ever. A lot of patients, but what drove the findings over the top – into statistical significance, that is – were the last one hundred... and twenty-six."

"The last hundred and twenty-six," Quinn said, carefully. Their new HGH clinic had had a *very* successful first year – treating, if he remembered correctly, exactly that many patients.

Flint winked laboriously. "All thanks to the primary prescriber at the cross-town branch of Boulder's finest longevity facility. A branch that, by its remarkable success, has become the newest economic feature on the fair face of our affluent, age-defying town. A final one hundred and twenty-six cases, all documented to the max."

"The max?" Quinn frowned. "By who?" Despite his natural eloquence, when it came to court-obtainable documents, Quinn had always favored one-line, carefully non-committal entries.

"Why, you, my dear doctor... as fleshed out by Ms. Blanche, who possesses a truly eerie gift to access electronic medical records – not only those from your clinic, but, as I said, those of every patient, far and wide."

"Sounds... illegal. Definitely illegal."

"Only until the releases were signed. The possibility of economic redress is a wonderful motivator. In this case, a class-action suit."

"Suit?" And class action, not malpractice: hundreds of millions, no limits at all. Quinn dragged the wig's curls close around his face. He could start working out, a whole different look. Canada, the frozen north, another new beginning.

"Sparing, of course, the outstanding medical staff who so carefully tracked its outcomes. And who, with an admirable lack of self-interest, composed this brave document." Flint's skeletal fingertips tapped the fine-printed lines below the title. Quinn fished cat's-eye reading glasses from the depths of his man-boob cleavage, held them to his eyes and leaned close. Three authors' names: Flint's, Junie's, and... his own. And below those names, a date.

He let the glasses drop. "This paper's already been submitted."

"Ah, yes. Submitted... and accepted. The online version should be available right about—" He consulted the watch that dangled loosely from his wrist. "—now!"

Quinn polished off another shot of Diet Cola, but its chemically-sweetened bitterness brought no relief.

QUINN PAGED THROUGH THE STUDY, counting the ways that Oz and Biggs were going to absolutely shit, which was why he wasn't going to tell them. Meanwhile, Flint was conferring with the bartender, pointing towards the top shelf behind the bar. A cobwebbed bottle was barely visible in the shadow-cloaked corner – a peeling white label, spidery inked script, the contents umbrous, nearly black. Neither Quinn nor Flint knew it, but the bottle had been the single intransigent feature through the *Ur*-Bar's many facile iterations, already decades-old when bottled, too expensive to sell and too expensive to discard, purposefully undusted and kept largely to lend the place, to the sharp of eye if not expansive of wallet, something beyond the vagaries of style.

The bartender hooked a short wooden stepladder from beneath the bar, climbed up and stretched toward the ceiling. Glancing over his shoulder, he asked, "You sure?"

Flint flashed his graveyard smile; the bartender gave an involuntary shiver and reached into darkness. After peeling away the bottle's cap of lead foil (designed to protect its contents, as is so often the case, from everything except itself), he pulled the cork. Across the scarred wood bar came the smell of autumn, of damp black soil beneath crushed leaves, and the distilled essence of amber light, all permeated with the nettle sting of life, persistent. Silence descended on the crowded room, as Quinn flushed in anticipation, Flint closed his eyes, and Howie pursed his narrow lips in thought.

The room's conversations resumed, even more animated than before – almost frantically so – and fully masking a stranger human song, one that emanated from somewhere below the floorboards. The faintest rumbling chorus of ancient groans, audible only to one (or three, in this case) with ears attuned to subsonics of a mortal hue.

The bartender, who had heard nothing, poured a viscous inch into an unadorned shot glass. Before pushing it across to Flint, he said, "That'll be—"

"Enough for me," Flint creaked, a carbon-black credit card appearing between two knobby digits. "But a double for each of my friends."

"Not for *her*," the bartender said, frowning at Quinn – who innocently batted his mascaraed eyes. "Not after last time. Or the time before."

The stepladder chose that moment to fall loudly on its side. As the bartender looked behind him and Howie gazed blandly up to the ceiling, Quinn snagged the bottle and, leaning back, held it fierce. The bartender turned back, not happy – Quinn had the sense not to bat his eyes again – then plucked Flint's card and, grumbling, walked down to the other patrons that sat along the noisy bar.

Quinn filled two more glasses, placed one in front of Howie, who ignored it, and raised his. "To life, and to the fight!"

"The fight and the *belief*," Flint said, as he slid his glass near the gray hairs sprouting from his nose, inhaled deeply, and turned a shade of purple only slightly less dark than the varnished wood beneath his sport coat's flayed elbows. Then recovered to add, "Believing in the things that work, and sometimes, up to a point, shy of the point of harm... believing in the things that don't."

"Like growth hormone, I suppose. In your study." Flint still hadn't raised his glass; Quinn sighed and put his down.

"*Our* study," Flint croaked. "Yes, like growth hormone – or caloric restriction." He patted the scaphoid space where his stomach should have been. "Who knows? It may have given this old husk an extra year or two. For the populace, however, starvation is unacceptable. Which means ineffective – which means passé. If something has been around awhile, but hasn't been adopted, you might as well write it off."

"Only the popular ideas survive? That's pretty Darwinian." Quinn eyed the elixir that lay limpid, beckoning and forlorn.

"Popular, proven, whatever. The freshness of a new idea lends it an undeniable excitement. The isolated research finding, say, that points us down a brand new path. We see the promise, not the cost, the unsustainable effort, the side effects. All the things that unfortunately reveal themselves with the passage of time. Yesterday's magic, my friend: dashed upon the rocks of experience, undermined by the follow-up studies, the Cochrane reviews and meta-analyses that belie its onetime promise."

"That would be depressing, if I agreed with you. But what about *tomorrow's* magic?"

"Collagen delinkage? De Gray's intracellular purges? Telomerase gene therapy? The lab coats are arraying their poisons, but for now, they're too dangerous by half. Cutting-edge modalities cut deep."

"No yesterday's magic, no tomorrow's magic, no magic at all." Or alcohol, apparently.

"On the contrary, my good Quinn. And you are good, you know. You possess both the fight and the belief, and are, despite your recent sartorial enthusiasms, the ideal representative for... Today's Magic."

"*Today's* Magic. Actually, I like the sound of that. Something a year or two out, people aren't dropping, unleashed cancer cells not popping up, new enough to still be fun. But wait – won't that be Yesterday's Magic, once we reach tomorrow?"

"Probably, though not always. Some ideas will make the cut." Flint ran his fingertips over the pile of printed pages again, the lightest graze, a last touch on a lover's cheek. "Think of it this way: you're free now. Free to pick the next big thing, pick and sell it, far and wide. Just do no harm... when you can."

Quinn forced his gaze from his untouched glass and looked to the study between them. "Safe isn't always easy."

Flint clapped him on the shoulder. Or tried to, a frail bird settling on Quinn's spaghetti-strapped bulk. "Just don't forget the basics, and, of course, the occasional virtuous beverage." He bent forward to his tiny glass and inhaled again – this time his flush was an incandescence from within, transilluminating the rice paper of his hollowed cheeks.

"Hold on there, cowboy." A physician's fingers went to Flint's scrawny wrist, while in the booth behind them, Wayne and Jeremiah looked up, searched the room, then returned to the latest edit of their screenplay.

"Not to worry, Doctor." Flint pulled his wrist away (Quinn let him, the pulse surprisingly steady) and finally raised his glass. "This fine electric vehicle will take me home and tuck me into bed. Forget the fight, forget the belief – let us drink to *passion*, to great loves and greater pleasures, sweet joy that burns our days and leaves but beauty in its wake."

"To passion? In that case, I surrender."

Flint's turkey neck hinged back and both drank deep. A veil descended, occluding light and sound, and time stretched out, a lifetime in an instant's dream. Quinn shook it off to find the *Ur*-Bar sparkling, for once authentic, fresh and new.

To his right, Flint gave a single cough, a moist and phlegmy bark. Quinn heard another sound beneath it: the shatter of crystal – Flint's drained glass – nearly buried in the happy-hour clamor. The old man's eyes had closed, his arm falling, as Quinn watched, onto a fat red wheelchair armrest button.

The machine immediately sprung to life, the seat hissing down as a stainless wand, topped by a flashing yellow light, simultaneously extended to just above their heads. Quinn grabbed for Flint's age-spotted wrist again, but the chair was already backing away, quick and spinning on four powered wheels to chart a sinuous path towards the *Ur*-Bar's door.

As Quinn's oversized pumps hit the floor, a white-robed arm reached round and pressed against his sternum. Howie, as if. Quinn pushed on, but that freckled, aquiline hand somehow stopped him, cast iron against his bulk. Just beyond the wooden bar, the wheelchair paused before the door, politely beeping. While Quinn struggled to rush forward, a patron opened the swinging glass, and Flint exited against a swirling flurry of snowflakes, heading in the general direction of his University Hill bungalow. As it trundled by the bar's sole window, the falling snow – the first of the year – transformed the wand's yellow light into a flashing golden snow globe, glowing once, then twice, then gone.

Quinn turned, angry, but found Howie facing the mirror, an empty glass between his empty hands, a tear tracing down his cheek. Quinn's anger disappeared – as always, with Howie, for no good reason. He regarded the cobwebbed bottle on the bar, thought better of it, and finished his remaining Diet Cola shots instead.

All around, the room continued its multi-channeled roar, a song of life and life only, as the sub-basement's inhabitants settled, sated, down again.

THE DECEMBER WIND blew brisk across the bay, whitecaps on the steely water between San Francisco and Angel Island. Late that morning, Junie and David had scattered Flint's ashes, as requested, on the parking lot that covered the rubble of his first Palo Alto laboratory. The wind had blown most of them to the waiting row of eucalyptus trees; He and Junie had dusted the fine gray powder off their clothes and driven, Junie fearless at their electric rental's wheel, up to and over the urban hills to the sailboat berths that lined Marina Boulevard, a stone's throw from the city itself.

"You sure she's big enough to cross an ocean?" David looked worried as he stood on the dock, windbreaker zipped tight to keep warm.

"Fifty-eight feet," Oz called from the cockpit. "Full nav, autopilot and instrumentation, with fuel to motor to Hawaii if we have to. And the finest captain in the business." He tugged his yachting cap snug on his brow, then bent to grasp a weather-chapped hand reaching up through the companionway.

Beatriz bounced into view – easily Oz's height, with dark hair to the level of her chin, brown eyes soulful but amused, a faint mustache she obviously couldn't care less about. She was wearing waterproof overalls but had otherwise stripped down to a t-shirt. The sight of her bare arms made David wrap his nylon jacket tighter, and Junie zipped the neck of her down coat – the only way, she'd said, she could manage the anti-Louisiana weather.

Beatriz looked up at them and asked, "What?"

Junie gave an involuntary shake. "Aren't you cold?"

"Just because I'm not a stick..." Shaking her head, Beatriz went forward, to squat by the mast and check yet another piece of pampered stainless-steel equipment. The hula-hoop hips that had driven Oz mad at college were still luxuriant, fully functional for wrestling forty tons of sailboat across the sea. She wasn't cold – she carried her own insulation, an evenly-distributed layer of adipose tissue that, for a reason David could not reveal, reassured him.

OZ'S AND BEATRIZ'S JOURNEY had actually begun much earlier – when Oz, who had luckily let go of his half-price pride and agreed to pay the mysterious internet Captain's day rate, flew out to their first, mutually surprising post-hula-hoop encounter, which immediately turned into a post-hula-hoop long weekend. It was followed by many others, interspersed with Beatriz's Denver trips to mend relationships with her estranged family, whose anti-hula sentiments she could finally forgive.

Through those months, David had watched his friend's bank vault heart unlock, while Junie figured Oz was almost turning human.

And now the big trip, away from this urban bay to Beatriz's warm islands, away and across the rolling blue-gray mystery she loved as much as the mysterious rolling dance that had lured her from Oz and family, from college dreams to painful life and now, alone no more, to sea-rocked dreams again.

Like all trips, though – like all escapes, like all adventures – it was more complicated than it seemed. Beginning late one November afternoon before their planned embarkment, when she'd paid an unexpected visit to David's consultation room, walked in and closed the door behind her.

"HE'S SO *BIG*," she'd started, "Almost purple when he's excited."

"Whoa," David said, and looked down at his desk.

"In *general*, I mean. Not—"

"Oh! Sorry." Whew. "You're worried because he's... heavier?"

Beatriz nodded.

"Same here."

"I'm no lightweight," she said, grabbing an inner tube of flesh. "But Oz..."

"I've been working on him for years. You know he's been trying, too."

"Do I. Those gourmet diets of his – all paté, all chocolate mousse, all steak tartare..." She made a face.

"And they all end up tasting terrible," David said. "Too much of a good thing. Then the next business deal comes along, and suddenly he's too busy to think about dieting. The more he makes, the bigger he gets."

"It'll just get worse?"

"He loves food, Beatriz."

"I do too. But I'm not gaining." She leaned forward in her chair, the front legs creaking. "Is it going to kill him?'

"Before the smoking? Maybe not. I'd like to see him quit *and* lose weight."

She frowned. "How much?"

David shrugged. "Twenty, thirty pounds would get him started. Might be enough to wean him off a few prescriptions, get him moving toward another fifty. He'll still feel like himself, just better. Forget 'ideal weight' – some studies even show moderately fat people live longer." He glanced at Beatriz. Oops. "I mean, overweight."

"Like I said, I could lose a little."

"Sure, but you don't have to, as long as you're healthy. Up to a point, and Oz is over that."

"Way over. Turning-purple-going-up-the-stairs over."

David sat back, shuffled some papers, then looked at Beatriz again. "Once, before you showed up, we were sailing – on the Reservoir, I mean."

Beatriz smiled, pityingly.

"We were joking about a guaranteed weight loss camp. I called it The Three Hour Cruise."

Now Beatriz looked confused.

"Reruns. From this old... forget it. The thing was, you'd drop your client on a desert island, leave some water and some vitamins, then take off. Oz said he'd be the first to sign up."

"A boat's an island in itself," she said, slowly.

David paused. "That trip you two are planning. How long?"

"All the way to Fuji? It could take months."

"Hmm," he said, and so did she, after which they sat in the quiet office, thinking.

"It's not just calories," David added. "He'll need some exercise, too."

"On a boat? I can only think of—"

She stopped herself and blushed. As did David, and then they sat and thought some more.

"YOU GOING TO LET US LEAVE, OR WHAT?" Oz sealed the collar of his

XXL survival shell and jammed his hands in its clammy pockets. He was hoping for open water by sunset, set the auto-tiller and retire to the cabin, see if they could celebrate a few big rolling waves. Followed by something tasty and revivifying – in a rare show of gastronomic trust, he'd left stocking the stores to Beatriz, who'd spent years cooking for that CEO she'd bought her vessel from.

David and Junie were still on the dock, saying their goodbyes to Beatriz. David looked down with a curiously mixed expression on a face that Oz had learned to read in boyhood. Envy, naturally, and naturally concern – he and Beatriz were crossing in the dead of winter – but also... guilt?

"Oh, *David...*" Oz crooned, heaving himself up the white fiberglass gangway.

"I'll let you say goodbye," Junie said, kissed Oz's balding crown and stepped away.

"Um..." David seemed unduly interested in the dock's splintered boards.

"Look at me." Oz reached to David's jacket, bunching the nylon in one stubby fist. "You *wanted* me to go on this trip, didn't you? Wanted a few months without Oz."

David smiled, if guiltily, and placed a hand, a friend's hand, on Oz's shoulder.

"Some changes at Forever?" Oz continued. "Sneak in another micro-raise for the staff? You are definitely up to something. And you know what?"

David shrugged, eyebrows up.

"I don't care," Oz said. "I guess you've learned, damn you, learned from the best. So go ahead, take your shot: manipulate *me*. I'm glad to see it, and glad to get away." He looked at Beatriz, untying the bow and stern lines and coiling them on deck. "Because I'll be living the good life, sailing with my sweetie on the blue, blue sea."

Surprising David and himself, Oz pulled him close and wrapped his arms around him. Then let go, stumbled back the bendy gangway to the deck, and turned away, toward the bow. "Get out of here, will you? I need to... I don't know... batten down some stuff."

ALMOST HOME, Beatriz thought, and kissed Oz on the cheek. Then cranked the gangway up, hopped to the wheelhouse and turned the key. Salt was in the air, cold and salt, the funk of fish and tide, everything she used to love around her. And still did, with one not-so-small addition.

The diesel coughed and sputtered and then caught, as Beatriz studied the narrow channel between the other boats, picking out the cleanest line to open water.

Oz gazed down at the instruments, really watching the black water that separated him from shore widen, watched the dock and David's oversize feet sliding away. By the time he'd composed himself, Junie and David had walked out to the end, shrinking with the distance, each raising a hand in farewell. With Beatriz's arm around him, Oz and she did the same.

JUNIE SAW OZ GO BELOW, then heard his voice come over the water, freakishly amplified by the boat's megaphone-like companionway, asking, "Honey, where'd you put the groceries? Are my smokes in these boxes?" Beatriz was busy raising sail; when she did not answer, Oz emerged to clamber – waddle, really – up to help her.

After the sheets had snapped and filled to carve a curving line of foam into the water, after the rental car's doors thumped shut in the moist air of the coast, after Junie and David tracked the increasingly distant triangle of white along the bay, then sped through the Presidio to catch a last sight of it from Land's End – and after they'd hustled down that walking path, stepped over the low barrier beside the histrionic 'Do Not Cross! Hikers Have Been Swept Away and Drowned!' sign, snuck around the bushes and found a safe spot two hundred feet above the waves – Junie turned her head and asked, "So what was with the boxes?"

"Boxes?" David sounded almost innocent.

"Nice try. You jumped about a foot when he asked her."

"Well..."

"Spill it." She settled back into his chest, his bent legs and long arms shielding her.

David umm'ed and ah'ed, then told her everything about Beatriz's visit, speaking close to her ear in the intermittent wind, his face glowing golden and hers burnt umber in the last of the sunset, the long soft glow that the mountains of his home – his and Junie's home, for now – denied those who lived in Boulder and along their eastern flanks.

"It was her idea?" Junie balanced the binoculars they'd brought on her knees.

"Fifty-fifty, I guess."

"Good. She can let him can blame you. But you still didn't tell me what's in the boxes." Junie located the boat, beating south towards the Channel Islands.

"Remember the Thinnas' early-retirement scheme?" David squinted into the fading light to find where her binoculars were sighting.

"Oh, no. The Nothing Bar?" The tiny boat was ripping through the swells, trailed by a straight line of white water.

"Vitamins, minerals, and six ounces of moist, chewy bamboo fiber. Everything you need to starve."

"But Oz *lives* to eat." The wake had become a comma, turning into the wind.

"I think he lives to live now. And I got Adeline to put some flavors in." The sail luffed, then filled again as the boat swung around, a rotund Oz-shaped spot gesticulating on the deck.

"Which one did he just discover – essence of kelp?" They were definitely headed back.

"I drew the line at seaweed," David said, distracted. "Chocolate, eggnog, that sort of thing. Plus a nicotine supplement in his, for the first few weeks."

"He's going to kill you."

"Maybe. He already tried with Paula, and that didn't work."

"So this is revenge?"

"Come on, Junie. This is what he said he wanted."

"Over a year ago. On a reservoir."

David shrugged. "He still said it."

"Like patients want what they say they want. Or what their doctors want for them."

"It's a good enough place to start. And what I really want... what I really want is for him to stay alive. Healthy and alive."

"Then you're in luck." She handed the binoculars over and he pressed his face against the rubber eyecups, peering though the lenses. Down below the last rays of the sun, in a wind-torn world that was only shades of gray and nightfall, the boat had turned on its axis again, heading once more toward the southern trades. "You want everybody to live forever," she added.

"Why not? You, this sun, this wind... why give any of it up? Of course I want everybody to live forever – for the same reasons I want to."

"You idiot."

"What?"

"You already do." She unzipped her jacket, undid a middle button of her shirt, and slid his hand in over her heart, her ribs, the curve of her breast. "You already live forever."

The wind surged again, whistling up the broken rocks beyond their feet. Same as on the reservoir that day, gusty and uncertain. Same as at the Triad, same as on the mountain, same as after that last call to Flint.

David started to pull his hand back, to zip her jacket and then his, but she held it still, her skin hot against his palm while his face grew colder, the heat stripping away. Just a gust, he knew, only a taste of what Oz and Beatriz were hammering into, their boat almost invisible with the distance, its sail a needle that yawed and then swung upright as the toylike hull cut through a rolling swell, one more in a line of swells that marched toward them from the Pacific. Just a gust, but the moan and shake of it took him down there, sailing into dark sea and random weather, rushing into an unseen rain-shadowed future. The boat might be Beatriz's, but the heavy weather was for all of them, no one could duck it, and the struggle, the life, was his.

Junie pressed his hand harder, pressed it down to the subterranean beat of her science-meets-voodoo heart. "You're alive in here, and you're alive in your own skin, right now, I can feel it. In this moment, and this moment just keeps rolling on and on."

David wasn't sure... no more than he'd been sure about closing his old practice, or walking out of the Forever Clinic, or the evening he'd walked back in. No more than Flint had been about his dream-words, eternity and infinity and especially forever, in the end. Even the Right Thing seemed dreamlike, immaterial, as changeable as life itself.

The thing was, being certain didn't seem to matter now. Instead, he wrapped his other arm around her and they looked out to sea again, there in the wind and falling dark and the now-vacant waves, all of it – *all* of it – forever changing, forever constant, forever alive.

With thanks to Michael Freedman, Meg Knox, Caitlin Hamilton, the crew and patrons of the Trident, the kind folks at the Boulder Historical Library, Peg Fletcher and BCH's Medical Library, and to faithful readers Jeb McIntyre, Steven Kasle, Patricia and Terrill Burnett, Amanda and Henry Vandeveer, as well as Susan Taylor Chehak, Stacy and Ravi Dykema, Otis Taylor, and the usual familial suspects, especially Sallie.

Please visit <u>howtoliveforever.com</u> for links to direct eBook downloads from Kindle, iBooks, Nook, and Smashwords, as well as complimentary short fiction and previous novels, including *The Mortalist.*

The author also welcomes comments at howtoliveforeverblog@gmail.com, particularly those that could be used to build a blog annotation of *How To Live Forever,* looking at both sides of the various medical, holistic, and longevity issues mentioned above.

www.ingramcontent.com/pod-product-compliance
Lightning Source LLC
Chambersburg PA
CBHW050906250626
47155CB00001B/121